THE DRAGON HAMMER
WULF'S SAGA
1

DISCARDED
from the Nashville Public Library

BOOKS by Tony Daniel

Wulf's Saga
The Dragon Hammer
The Amber Arrow (forthcoming)

Guardian of Night
Superluminal
Metaplanetary
The Robot's Twilight Companion
Earthling
Warpath

Star Trek Original Series
Devil's Bargain
Savage Trade

The General Series (with David Drake)
The Heretic
The Savior

For a complete list of Dean Ing books and to purchase all of these titles in e-book format, please go to www.baen.com.

THE DRAGON HAMMER

WULF'S SAGA

1

TONY DANIEL

BAEN

THE DRAGON HAMMER

This is a work of fiction. All the characters and events portrayed in this book are fictional, and any resemblance to real people or incidents is purely coincidental.

Copyright © 2016 by Tony Daniel

All rights reserved, including the right to reproduce this book or portions thereof in any form.

A Baen Books Original

Baen Publishing Enterprises
P.O. Box 1403
Riverdale, NY 10471
www.baen.com

ISBN: 978-1-4767-8155-6

Cover art by Daniel Dos Santos

Map by Randy Asplund

First printing, July 2016

Distributed by Simon & Schuster
1230 Avenue of the Americas
New York, NY 10020

Printed in the United States of America

10 9 8 7 6 5 4 3 2 1

For Cokie and Hans

THE DRAGON HAMMER

WULF'S SAGA

1

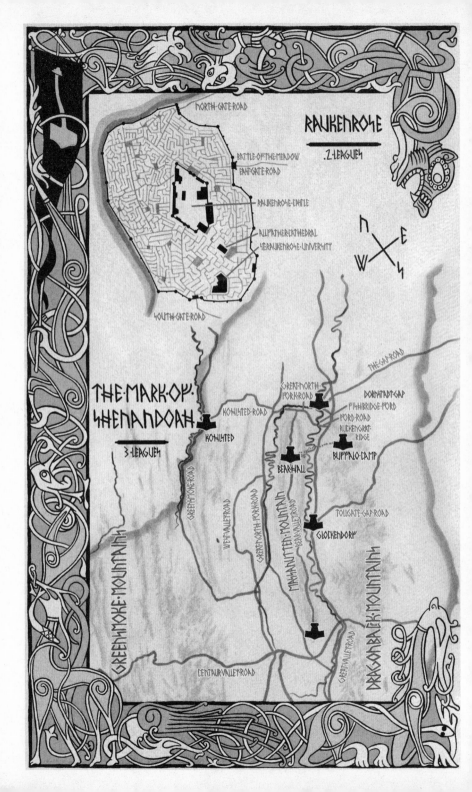

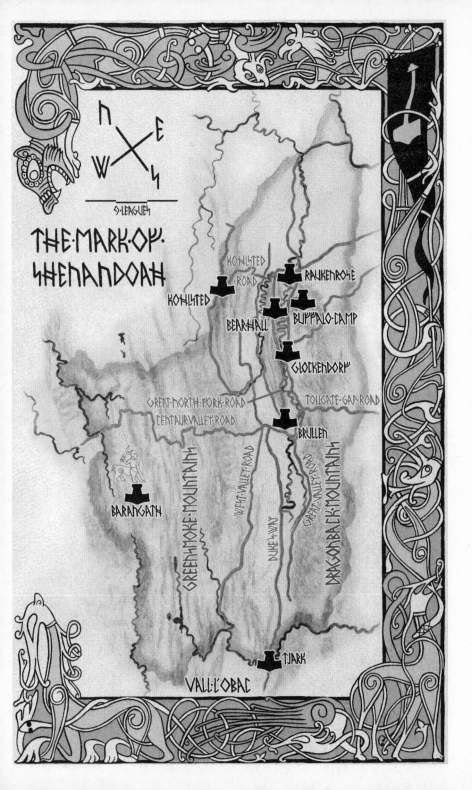

PART ONE

PART ONE

CHAPTER ONE:
THE CORPSE DOOR

Come to the tree.

The dragon was calling Wulf again tonight. Strongly. He felt like his skeleton might pull itself out of his body and walk away without the rest of him attached.

When the land-dragon called, he couldn't sleep. His mind felt like it was on fire, with thoughts flickering and flaming in all directions. It was as if the dragon was using Wulf's mind to think *its* thoughts.

He would look at something like a table or a chair, and in a sudden flash see it *backward and forward in time*. He'd see the cut pieces of wood that the furniture was made from lying in a pile. Another flash, and he'd see the chair, old and busted, its pegs popping out and its backrest broken, waiting in some dark corner to be used for firewood. And he saw it burning.

This kind of dream or vision could happen with people, too. He'd see them old. He'd see them as babies. He'd even see their dead, dry bones. That was when it really scared him.

But behind all these visions there was a much more powerful drive. It was the urge to *get to the tree.*

Not just any tree, but the tree from the nursery rhyme that he'd heard so long ago he couldn't remember not knowing it. The first memory he had was of his mother softly chanting the rhyme while she rocked him to sleep after he'd been crying. He couldn't even recall what he had been crying about, but he remembered his mother's voice singing the words.

The Olden Oak
Where dragon spoke
From in the bark
To old Duke Tjark

The Olden Oak was a huge tree in the square near Allfather Cathedral at the center of Raukenrose township.

Which meant it was *outside* of the castle that Wulf was *inside.*

Wulf knew he had to wait until after curfew, but the mixed-up thoughts churning in his head only grew more unsettled. Finally, it was time to go. He got out of his warm bed and used an ember from the fire to light a candle lantern. He got dressed by the lantern light, then armed himself with his favorite dagger. He opened his bedchamber door a crack. Now to get going.

This was not so easy to accomplish, though, because to follow the dragon-call he had to escape from his own castle. *Nobody* had any privacy in a castle. For one thing, there weren't hallways in the middle, just some passageways around the outside. Farther in, one room connected to another. Wulf had two brothers and two sisters, two foster sisters, and a foster brother, seven siblings in all. The fosters had rooms in the nearby castle towers, but his natural brothers and sisters had rooms that opened on the family great hall—a high-ceilinged chamber that at this time of night was filled with sleeping, snoring servants. Many of the servants were Tier, and they let out low growls and soft bleats when they dreamed.

The eating tables in the castle doubled as beds for the unmarried staff. Normally this was excellent, because a servant was just outside your door if you wanted a midnight snack or were cold and needed the fire in your fireplace built up. Not so good when you wanted to escape without anybody noticing.

As usual, the great hall smelled like fireplace smoke and just about every body and animal odor imaginable. The fire in the main hearth was banked, all the doors were closed, and there were no windows. Wulf's own servant, Grim, was asleep near Wulf's room.

Grim was not human. He was a faun: lower half goat, upper half man—except for the horns on his head. He was a Tier, a talking beast-person. Grim slept sitting up, his legs curled under him as a goat's would be, his back resting against the wall of the great hall next to Wulf's door.

Wolf's light flickered, and the faun opened his eyes. He looked at Wulf quizzically, stroking his wispy beard.

Wulf shook his head and whispered, "Going to the crapper."

Wulf had a chamber pot in his room where he could urinate at night, and where he theoretically could also do his other business, but he usually liked to go to the castle toilet instead. Grim knew this and wasn't surprised at Wulf's appearance in the middle of the night.

Still . . . The faun gave Wulf a sleepy look up and down. Wulf had belted his dagger under his thick cloak, which he had pulled around him for warmth, and he didn't think Grim noticed the knife. It was hard to tell *what* Grim noticed sometimes. He was famous among the castle servants for his absolute silence unless he was asked to speak.

Grim finally nodded, lowered his head, and closed his eyes. He was instantly asleep.

Okay. One obstacle down.

Wulf pushed the main entrance door open enough to slip out—it was well-oiled and didn't make any noise—then grabbed the big iron ring that served as a doorknob and pulled it shut behind him. Outside the great hall was an entrance chamber almost as large as the great hall itself. Its walls were hung with tapestries. A couple of servants, one a beaver man, the other human, slept on the wooden benches that lined the walls, but neither looked up when Wulf entered the chamber. Servants knew that if you wanted to get any sleep in a castle, you had to learn not to let every sound in the night wake you.

Off the other end of the entrance hall was a large stairway down to the castle doors. The doors were shut tight and bolted. No getting out that way without raising a ruckus. But to either side on the top of the stairs passageways led to right and left. These corridors circled the inner castle wall and led past several bays with arrow slits and holes for dropping boiling oil on any attackers who might make it this far inside the keep. Wulf took the hall to the right. The corridor was lined with tapestries—they were beautiful, but they were mostly there to keep the draft out. Along this walkway were the toilets. There were four of them, each at a spot where the passageway turned a corner.

Wulf went into one, so that he wouldn't technically have told a lie to Grim. Wulf liked Grim, and hated that he might get the servant in trouble.

The toilet was a board with a hole cut it in it. This was placed over an opening that led four stories below to the base of the inner keep, where the nightsoil was mucked out once a week. Wulf thought about actually using the toilet, but he didn't really have to. He'd gone before bed. Besides, he had to be on his way or things would get bad in a hurry. He'd tried to resist the dragon-call once, and had spent a day with a headache so awful it felt like somebody had taken an ax to his skull—and then beaten his entire body with the ax handle for good measure.

Wulf came out of the toilet and continued down the passage, heading for its very end, to a place people only went if they absolutely had to.

Wulf drew his cloak, made of fustian—coarse wool and rough cotton cloth—closer around his shoulders. His candle lantern squeaked as it swung on its handle. Under the cloak, his dagger rattled in its hard leather scabbard as he walked. Every little sound echoed.

"I sound like an army on the march," Wulf mumbled to himself.

To make things worse—way worse to Wulf—it shouldn't even be *him* who heard the dragon-call. It should be his oldest brother, Otto. Or even his other brother, Adelbert.

But not Wulfgang von Dunstig. Fourth child born to Duke Otto and Duchess Malwin von Dunstig. Third boy.

Not even spare to the heir. I'm not *supposed* to hear the dragon at all. Otto is, or even Adelbert. But not me.

He should only be able hear the call faintly.

So much for what he wanted. Again the call roared and burned through his mind and body. It socked him so hard, he stood for a moment trying to catch his breath.

Wulf glanced at the wall next to him. It glowed red and seemed to be mushy, as if it were made of some fiery, oozing liquid. The stones radiated heat, hotter than the hottest fire. Was he seeing the past or the future? Maybe this was the way rock formed? Then, just as he was thinking his skin would blister, the wall was solid stone again.

Wulf got his breathing under control then headed once again down the hallway.

Finally he saw the glint of crystal above him, shining in the lantern light. This was the rose quartz keystone at the highest part the arch. Carved into the smooth arch stones on either side of the quartz was a message.

THIS WAY TO HELHEIM

Helheim, the land of the dead. It was someone's joke from long ago. Maybe one of the former dukes. Maybe a stonemason playing a prank.

Standing here when it was after midnight, Wulf didn't think the joke was very funny.

He walked under the arch. The passage narrowed in stages, until at its end it was barely wide enough for two people to walk side by side.

It didn't need to be very wide. Nobody came this way unless they had to.

Everybody stayed away from what was at the end—the corpse door.

I would stay away, too, if I could, Wulf thought. This place is creepy.

The corpse door was an opening made for taking dead bodies outside to be buried. Most castles had one. Wulf wasn't sure why dead people weren't allowed to be hauled out the main door, but it never happened. When the corpse door wasn't being used, it stayed bricked up. The bricks were laid in, but *not* held in place with mortar.

That was key. It meant a single person could remove them and get out into the keep bailey.

Wulf sat down and put his lantern beside the opening. After a moment taking in the faint but cheery candlelight, he raised the globe and blew the candle out.

It was dark as pitch in the dead-end passageway.

Wulf tried not to let the darkness bother him. He pivoted on his butt and put his feet up against the stack of bricks filling the corpse-door opening.

This part was going to make a sound. There was no way to avoid it.

He pushed.

The bricks fell with a clatter on the flint pavement of the bailey courtyard.

He sat still a moment, calming himself. His breath was a mist in the dark hallway's end. There was only moonlight from outside to see by.

Wulf waited a few breaths to find out if the sound of the falling stones had gotten any of the servants' or guards' attention.

No footsteps. Nobody calling out in alarm.

He was probably okay. For the moment.

Wulf stuck his head through the corpse door and looked around. It was dark out there in the bailey courtyard—there was only a half moon shining in the sky tonight—but he didn't see anyone. The corpse door was set about knee-high in the wall. It was big enough to let through the body of a regular size grownup. A body went out, always feet first, with somebody on each side pushing and pulling.

A month ago, he'd seen the door used for Helga Svensson, a seven-year-old who had died of scarlet fever. Her blonde hair had been washed, combed, and plaited, but her face and hands were still splotched with the rash the fever made.

Seeing Helga Svensson taken out of the castle was what gave Wulf the idea of using the corpse door himself.

Wulf took off his dagger and held the scabbard in one hand to keep it from clattering against the stones. When his arms were clear on the other side, he carefully set the dagger and belt down on the outside flagstones, trying not to make a racket. Now it was time to get his own body through. He crawled through the opening headfirst—opposite of the way they took the dead bodies out. He pulled himself forward. Nothing happened. He wriggled. No movement.

Stuck.

Blood and bones, Wulf thought, this shouldn't be happening. Even a fat man could usually pass through the door.

Wulf felt with his hand and, with a sigh of relief, realized what had happened. His cloak had bunched up under him, and the rough stones were catching at its fiber.

If only I didn't have to wear coarse-weave tonight, Wulf thought, this would be so much easier.

But he did. He was about to get very dirty, and he didn't want to have to explain why his good linen shirt had gotten filthy. Also, he didn't want to be recognized, and the hood on the cloak could cover most of his face in shadows.

He planted his palms and elbows and humped the rest of the way through the corpse door. Wulf tumbled out onto the flagstones and quickly rose to a crouching position. Suddenly there was rustling behind him.

Wulf spun, his hand moving toward his dagger.

It wasn't there! Of course. He'd put it through first.

But then a questioning "meow" rang through the castle courtyard.

Great.

It was Grani, his sister Ulla's cat.

She meowed again. Grani was going to wake up the whole keep if she kept that up.

Had a servant accidentally left Ulla's door open?

Well, he could worry about that later when he—

Wulf turned to find the hilt of his own dagger poked into his face. Its round metal pommel, the part at the end of the handle, scraped against his nose. Startled, Wulf gasped and backed up against the bailey wall. A dark form standing in front of him chuckled.

"Figured I'd find you here," the form said in a low voice.

Chapter Two:
The Escape

The voice belonged to Rainer Stope, a boy who was a year older than Wulf. Rainer was a commoner, but he lived in the castle as Wulf's foster brother. Wulf's father had taken Rainer in to fulfill a bargain he'd made with Rainer's family. Wulf didn't know exactly what had happened, but he knew it involved Rainer's father lending a *lot* of money to the duke.

Rainer was not only Wulf's foster brother; he was Wulf's best friend.

"How'd you know I'd be here?"

"You kidding? You had that *look* all day," Rainer said.

"What look?" Wulf replied as he scooped up Grani, who had come through the corpse door and was rubbing his leg.

"Like you're about to vomit. Or like you have the flux."

"I guess I was pretty out of it." Wulf pushed Grani through the corpse-door opening, back into the castle. "Go find Ulla," he whispered to the cat.

Grani looked at him as if he were the dumbest rubbing post she'd ever seen. Then she turned and made her way back inside.

Rainer knelt beside Wulf. The two boys quickly bricked back up the corpse door.

"Blood and bones, why'd you have to scare me?" Wulf mumbled.

Rainer shrugged and smiled. He was not somebody who liked to explain things.

Wulf figured that Rainer had opened the wood shutters on his bedroom window and climbed down from the third story on the stone wall. Rainer had learned how to climb so well while capturing hawklings in his hometown of Kohlsted, a town deep in the mountains to the west of Raukenrose. It was surrounded by high granite cliffs where hawks loved to nest. Rainer usually visited home once a year in summer and stayed for a month. Wulf had returned home with Rainer a couple of times, and they'd gone climbing for hatchlings but hadn't found any.

Rainer had a broad face and a reddish complexion that seemed to be always rosy. There were rumors he had Skraeling blood, but Wulf knew Rainer was completely ignorant of his own ancestry. Rainer's hair was brownish black and curly. Rainer drew it back in a ponytail and bound it behind him to keep it from escaping in all directions.

Wulf's own features were nearly the opposite of Rainer's. His hair was blond and, except for the cowlick in front he couldn't seem to get rid of, straight. Despite the new sixteen-year-old muscles he hadn't quite gotten used to, he was lean and rangy. He figured he probably always would be. Rainer, on the other hand, appeared to be a seventeen-year-old mountain of strength. He was at least a hand and a half taller than Wulf. But being big didn't slow him down. Rainer could move with the speed of a raptor.

"Saw you checking Grer's charcoal chute today." Grer Smead was the castle smith. Although he was far beneath them in status, Wulf and Rainer thought of him as a friend. They'd spent the late afternoon in his shop, allegedly getting a shield rivet mended, but mostly just hanging out. Rainer clapped Wulf on the shoulder. "So let's go."

"*No*. You can't come," Wulf said. He tried to put a commanding tone into the statement, but this was hard to do while speaking barely over a whisper. "I've told you before, I forbid it."

Rainer shook his head and smiled a know-it-all smile. "Figured you didn't mean it." The moonlight glinted off his teeth.

Suddenly, boots clomped and chainmail clinked from across the bailey. A guard was crossing the courtyard. Rainer yanked Wulf down behind a stone column. The base of the column was carved in the shape of a coiled snake, and the snake's hissing face startled Wulf. He put his hand in over his mouth to hold in a gasp.

They sat still until the guard had passed and the sounds of his footsteps died away.

"It's Morast," whispered Rainer. "Going to the latrine."

"He'll be there half the night," Wulf replied. They both grinned and made sure not to laugh—at least too loudly. Captain Morast might be the toughest soldier on the guard, but he was famous for the moans and groans he let out when in the latrine and for the loudness of his gassy emissions.

They stood back up.

"If we get caught," said Wulf, "I'll be in trouble. But you'll get yourself kicked out of the castle for good."

Rainer shook his head. "You're in that dragon-spell thing that happens to you. You need somebody to watch your back."

"And that has to be you?"

"It does."

Rainer stood up and pulled Wulf with him.

"Curse it to cold hell, all right then," Wulf said. "Let's go." The truth was Wulf felt relieved. He really did like having somebody he could trust along with him. He'd gone to the tree both alone and with Rainer before, and having Rainer along definitely made him feel safer.

The two circled the bailey, moving quickly and hiding in shadows along the edge of the courtyard, each taking turns at the lead.

Rainer reached the shop first. He unsheathed his own dagger and poked it through the slit between the wooden door and its frame. He lifted up the latch on the inside of the door. It wasn't locked. You could pull a cord to raise the latch, but this would also set off a bell that was rigged to let the smith know someone had entered. Opening the door with the dagger kept the bell from clanging.

The two pushed the door open just wide enough to squeeze inside. They let their eyes adjust for a moment. The room was lit in faint red and orange by a bed of banked coals in the forge. A large set of bellows was nearby, its blowing end pointed at the forge fire.

Near to the forge was an oak barrel full of charcoal. And behind the barrel was the chute where the charcoal was delivered from outside. This chute would be their way out of the castle, and it was another reason that both of them— Wulf noticed that Rainer had dressed the same as he had—were wearing cloaks.

It took some twisting and turning, which Rainer, in spite of his greater size, was better at than Wulf, but eventually both of them worked their way through the narrow chute. They were now completely outside the castle—and also covered with charcoal dust. Wulf knew he would need to scrub his face like crazy before letting anyone see him in the morning.

Raukenrose Castle did not have a water moat, but it did have a barrier of iron-tipped wooden spikes pointing outward. This was called an abatis. The spikes were four elbs long and were set into the ground to point away from the castle. The abatis circled the entire castle like a crown, except for one opening at the main entrance, and was three layers thick. The stakes were set at a height to bayonet a charging man or horse. The points were checked for sharpness once a month, and one of Grer's duties was to forge replacement tips when they got too dull or rusty.

Fortunately, even though it was a good barrier against horses and men in armor, the stakes were not much of a problem to crawl under. Wulf and Rainer got down on their bellies and snaked beneath.

Finally, Wulf stood up.

I'm out of the keep. I'm free, he thought. The dragon would know he was on his way.

As if in answer, he felt some of the pressure ease on his mind, like a headache that suddenly stopped throbbing.

That's right, Wulf thought. Curse it, I'm coming.

Wulf turned and took a final look at the castle. It was impressive in the pale moonlight. Each of the stones of the castle wall was about the size of a man, and was made of granite from the Dragonback Mountains.

The wall stretched upward over a hundred-fifty hands. High above, cloth banners and flags popped in the chilly, early winter breeze. It was too dark to see them, but Wulf knew there were two sets with their staffs set in holes along the castle battlement. Every other one held a flag that would have the shape of a red war hammer stitched to a black background. The Dragon Hammer of Shenandoah. Wulf had a cape and a tabard with the same symbol on it. Next to each flag was a banner with the von Dunstig coat of arms on it. This was the buffalo *passant argent*, a silver buffalo with the right front leg raised as if stepping forward, stitched onto a green background. For six hundred years the humans, otherfolk, and Tier of Shenandoah had been ruled from this stronghold.

Raukenrose Castle. The place that had been Wulf's home for all his life.

Wulf shifted his gaze back down. He and Rainer stood for a moment adjusting themselves, straightening cloaks and daggers that had gotten crooked after the crawl under the barrier.

Suddenly, a grunting, bulllike bellow filled the air. It seemed to come from the castle.

"Did you hear that?" Wulf exclaimed.

"Hear what?" Rainer replied.

Wulf spun around as a dragon dream-vision surged into his mind.

Instead of the castle, there was a starlit hilltop. On that hilltop stood a huge buffalo looking up at the sky. It bellowed again. The eyes of the buffalo flashed, and moonlight glinted off its curled horns.

Then the vision faded away, and there was just a castle there. Wulf shook his head and turned back around. The dark streets of the sleeping town of Raukenrose lay ahead of them.

The buildings of the town were three, four, even five stories tall, each floor a little bigger than the one below. They *leaned*. At their tops, they were close enough to touch and sometimes did.

This made for *very* dark streets during the night.

Which was supposed to be all right, because it was long after curfew bell and no one was allowed to be out.

Yeah, right.

The kind of person who would ignore the curfew was usually the kind of person you did not want to meet on a dark street late at night.

Not all of them were human lawbreakers, either. There were also creatures who were bad news among the Tier and the otherfolk. Some of *those* had claws or teeth as long as daggers.

The two boys slipped into the shadows of the township.

CHAPTER THREE:
THE CHAPEL

Ravenelle Archambeault sat alone in the Chapel of the Dark Angel. She reclined on a padded pew reading a dark romance from a scroll. The scroll was thin, but long. Its parchment draped down over her red and black dress and almost touched the floor. The tale she was reading was in verse, and when she finished a stanza, she rolled the scroll up with one hand and with the other kept her spot. The truth was this particular romance, *The Red Rose Dies*, was one of her favorites, and she'd read it so often she practically had it memorized.

Ravenelle sat partly sideways on the pew, with one foot up on a prayer bench so that her dress and the scroll made a pretty curve flowing over her hip and leg down to the chapel's stone floor.

She took her mind from the poem and moved into the eyes of her bloodservant Madgel, who was also her lady's maid. Madgel had been sitting quietly nearby finishing up some sewing repairs, but Ravenelle had her stand up and walk in front of her so she could get the best view of herself through Madgel's eyes. The maid quickly set the sewing aside and did as her mistress commanded.

Ravenelle looked at herself through Madgel's eyes, then had the maid arrange her dress a bit more pleasingly to show just the toe of the silk shoe on the leg she'd crossed. The idea was to appear nonchalant but elegantly reading when Gunnar entered the chapel for his visit. Like Elania, the heroine of another favorite romance of Ravenelle's, *The Tower Falls*, always advised: it never hurts to make a pleasing impression when meeting a guest, especially if that guest is a prince. She had Madgel step to one side, and she looked at herself at the angle he would probably approach from the door.

Her hair was springing loose from its pins again. It was a raven-black tangle of tight curls and looked like a briar bush sitting on her head when she didn't brush it, and sometimes when she did. Her skin was brown from her Aegyptian ancestry, lightened by a Kalte grandmother thrown into the mix. This wouldn't have been unusual in her *real* country but stood out in Raukenrose, where everyone who wasn't a Tier or a tree was some variation on pale.

She tucked a curl behind a hairclip then moved back to Madgel's awareness and took another look at herself through her maid's eyes.

Yes, there, that will do. Thank you, Madgel, Ravenelle said. She didn't speak aloud but in the mind-speak of communion, so that Madgel heard her words as a voice within. *Take your things and go to my chambers. I'd like to be by myself when he comes.*

Yes, mistress, the maid replied. She gathered her sewing and left.

Ravenelle did care what her bloodservants thought, but she did not dip into Madgel's concerns over what her mistress was doing. She was afraid Madgel wouldn't be able to hide her worry that Ravenelle was making far too much of this appointment with Prince Gunnar, and feel sorry for her.

Ravenelle couldn't abide anybody, even a bloodservant, feeling sorry for her. She was a princess. She was going to be queen. She considered herself the last person someone should pity. But it *was* kind of ridiculous to be worried about the impression you might make on some barbarian princeling.

The train of thought made her uncomfortable, and she returned to *The Red Rose Dies*. She was near the end, where Zara, a noble maiden locked inside a cold, dark keep by her jealous father, loses all hope of rescue. She dies young, and her father buries her in a graveyard inside the keep, so that even dead, she can never leave.

This was the kind of bittersweet ending Ravenelle preferred in a romance. The final stanza always made her shudder.

Her knight is gone these hundred years.
Alone and pale she lies.
And where it reaches for her grave
The red rose dies.

The chapel—her chapel—was a pretty place. At least she thought so. And it was peaceful, usually. It was the one spot Ravenelle could go in Raukenrose Castle where she didn't feel constantly *irritated*.

She'd had the chapel decked out to look just like a mini version of the Chantry of the Dark Angel in the great cathedral of Montserrat. Well, as much like it as she could, given that she'd never actually been to the Chantry of the Dark Angel. She'd had to rely on taking secondhand recollections during communion when her mother made her yearly visit.

But she'd done everything in her power to get it right. There was the same white marble from the Sylacauga pits, the same ebony altar fixtures carved out of the hardest wood. It came from the true south beyond the equator. The wall hangings were thick and gorgeous drapes sewn from the deep red cotton-velvet and delicate black cotton lace that Vall l'Obac was famous for. Her communion cups were pure silver from Tenochtitlan, and the storage box where the celestis was kept was made of beaten gold.

Above the altar was the Dark Angel, chiseled out of a huge block of black obsidian from Mount Aetna, and completely life-size. Saint Ravenelle was the namesake saint of Ravenelle Archambeault. Her wings were extended in the V-shaped symbol of the Empty Hands of Talaia. Ravenelle loved reading here.

She was still reading when Prince Gunnar von Krehennest of Sandhaven entered from the transept. He closed—and *latched*—the door behind him. Ravenelle pretended to continue reading her book, but she watched him from the corner of her eyes as he walked toward her. His hard leather boot soles echoed on the flagstone floor.

"Princess, I've been looking forward to seeing you all day," Gunnar said.

"That's funny, I've been looking forward to you," Ravenelle replied.

"What are you reading?" Gunnar stood so he could gaze over her shoulder at the illumination on the page. It showed a red rose withering on a gravestone. "It appears sad."

"It's a story about a woman who was kept in prison by her father."

"Why do you read things like that, Princess? You should only fill yourself with happy thoughts."

"But it does make me happy," Ravenelle answered. "I may be a prisoner, but at least I am not her." She closed the book. "I'm allowed to love men other than my father, for instance." She gave him a sly smile. "Which is good, since I haven't seen him in five years."

"It has to be hard living here when your kingdom waits for you in the south."

"Oh, I manage," Ravenelle replied. "There are . . . benefits, even in dire situations. Not that I am in a particularly dire situation, since I *am* well treated, even if I am in most ways a captive. Anyway, you and I would've never met otherwise, and that's a benefit."

Gunnar smiled and put a hand gently on Ravenelle's shoulder.

"Put away your words, Princess," he said.

Ravenelle let the scroll drop gently to the floor of the chapel. "Would you like to commune, Prince Gunnar?"

"Very much," he replied. "I brought you something."

"Oh?"

The prince reached behind his neck and pulled a silver chain from beneath his black silk shirt. There was a small leather pouch attached to it by a jewelry bale. He took the chain off and held it out to show Ravenelle.

"I thought you might like your own supply of the new celestis," he said. "This will let us be together whenever we are nearby." He found the chain's clasp and undid its latch. He offered his other hand to help her stand up. "May I?"

Ravenelle stood and turned her back to Gunnar. He placed the chain around her neck. Then he brushed aside her hair and reattached the ends. The silver was still warm from his skin. Ravenelle opened the drawstring of the leather bag and reached a finger inside. She took a single black wafer from it. Ater-cake. She pulled the bag closed again. She pushed it under the neckline of her dress and between her breasts.

"Come to the altar," she said.

They took the two steps to the altar table. There Father Calceatus had obeyed Ravenelle's instructions and laid out the implements of her Talaia faith. There were silver pricking needles. There was a hemp string tourniquet with a steel twisting stick. Next to this was a silver bleeding chalice. And there were linen napkins to daub the wounds and clean up the implements afterwards.

Gunnar smiled and took her left hand in his. "May I, Princess?" he asked.

"Yes, you may," she answered. She pulled back the sleeve of her dress to reveal her arm up to the elbow. It wasn't really improper, but baring her skin to him like this sent a little thrill through her. He took the tourniquet and wrapped it around her arm just below the elbow. He gave it a couple of twists, compressing her veins tightly but not squeezing them shut. He was very good at this.

Then he took one of the needles and with a finger traced the vein in her arm from her wrist toward her elbow until he found where the blood was nearest her skin. With another smile, he pricked the needle in.

As always, there was the sudden coldness of the metal underneath her skin, but Ravenelle had long known how to control her shudders. Blood welled, then flowed freely.

Gunnar turned her arm over and squeezed a steady trickle into the silver chalice until it held several spoonfuls of Ravenelle's blood. He took the cleaning cloth and pressed it to the wound, holding it there until she clotted and the blood flow stopped.

"Now myself," he said. With a tourniquet and the other needle Gunnar repeated the pricking process on his own left arm. He squeezed his blood into the chalice with hers until it was a quarter full.

He held out his right hand and bowed. Ravenelle placed one of the ater wafers into his palm, and kept the other herself.

"You first, prince," she said, nodding toward the chalice.

Gunnar took the wafer between his thumb and forefinger and dipped it into the blood. He pushed it under so that it could absorb its full portion of the mixed blood, which it soaked up like a sponge.

"Princess," he said.

Ravenelle opened her mouth and Gunnar carefully placed the wafer on her tongue. She tasted the warm blood and the tang of the ater-cake wafer. The wafer was brittle. She pressed it against the top of her mouth and broke it, then chewed the pieces and swallowed them. She lifted up the chalice and took the ceremonial sip that allowed you to be sure the whole of the wafer went down and wasn't stuck in the throat.

She took her own wafer, dipped it, and put it in Gunnar's mouth. He seemed to swallow it whole with one gulp, then raised the chalice and drained the remainder of the blood from it. Ravenelle wiped out the blood cup with its special napkin then set it back on the altar table. Father Calceatus would come later and see that everything was put away correctly in the sacristy.

She and Gunnar went back to the cushioned front pew and sat down side by side. Ravenelle smelled the sandalwood scent he wore. Then the ater-cake began to have its effect. She closed her mind and traveled down the shining, silver-webbed tunnel that led into Gunnar's thoughts.

They were, for the most part, thoughts of the day. Seeing to a lame horse. Criticizing a silversmith who had done shoddy work when making a brooch he was planning to give to Ulla.

The prongs barely held the turquoise in, Gunnar thought. If Ulla were to jostle the brooch the wrong way—if she was out riding a horse, say—the stone would pop right out. Ulla would be embarrassed, he would be humiliated, and a very expensive stone would be lost in the mud of Shenandoah.

He'd give the man one more chance, and then, if there was no improvement, he'd have his personal secretary notify the Raukenrose Silversmith Guild that they had better reconsider this smith's master standing. If it came to that, he knew he'd be doing a favor to all the first families of the town.

Ravenelle experienced not only Gunnar's memory of the scene, but also his senses and feelings. The smoothness of the stone. The burnt-honey odor of the beeswax that the silversmith had used as a metal finish for his work. Gunnar's iron-willed determination to be and act like a prince in every circumstance.

He had to. His father would make his life miserable if he didn't. King Siggi had done that before, driving away Gunnar's unsuitable friends when he was a child, making one of Gunnar's tutors beat his charge when Gunnar had stolen an apple from a merchant stall. Then making Gunnar watch as the tutor's hand was chopped off for daring to strike a prince.

Oh dear, Ravenelle thought. She used the blood-bond thought-speech she'd learned years ago. It was *almost* like saying a word, then holding back at the last possible moment. Thought-speech took practice, and Ravenelle had already noticed that she was much better at it than Gunnar. That was to be expected. Gunnar was a Kalte prince, a barbarian.

He'd come to the castle to ask for Ulla von Dunstig's hand in marriage as part of an arranged alliance between Shenandoah and Sandhaven. She'd sensed that he was one of the holy host, but doubted herself. It had taken her several weeks to get up the courage to ask him to commune with her.

"You know I'm going to marry Lady Ulla?" he said aloud.

I most certainly do. That is why you are here.

"Yes, yes. But there is something . . . holding her back. I can't read her mind. Yet. That will come. But I can sense that something isn't right. I was hoping you could tell me what this thing might be."

How flattering that you would think of me for an explanation, she replied tartly.

"You do have a mean streak, Princess," Gunnar said, sitting up straighter and looking her in the eyes. "You live up to what the castle children call you."

The l'Obac Terror, and I'm not a bit sorry for it, she thought. *So there.*

"Well, my terror, what can you tell me about Ulla?"

A lot, Ravenelle thought. More than I'd ever let on to you. *I really don't know her all that well.*

"But she is your foster sister," said Gunnar. "I think you sell yourself short."

She and I aren't that close.

"Come on, Princess. I've seen that the von Dunstigs have made you part of their family."

Ravenelle took a deep breath. This wasn't going as planned. She would have to give him *something*, if only to get past him to unbolt the door.

Ulla and I like clothes and makeup. We like to pay attention to what we wear, for different reasons.

"Or the same reason," Gunnar replied. He smiled.

Might as well be pointing at himself, Ravenelle thought. But this thought she did not allow to be pre-verbalized and shared with Gunnar. She and Gunnar did connect. She couldn't deny her attraction.

But he's Ulla's.

Ulla won't care. She doesn't like him anyway.

But it could mess up a match, a carefully arranged alliance.

There was part of her that really liked the fact that the Prince of Sandhaven, the most popular man in Raukenrose, the man every girl in the castle was ready to faint over, liked to spend time with her, Ravenelle Archambeault.

She opened her eyes—she usually kept them closed during communion—and glanced at the prince.

His sea-green eyes were open, and he was gazing at her.

"I would like to kiss you, Princess."

Ravenelle almost guffawed. Good grief. It was like being in a romance.

"You are engaged to my sister."

"Foster sister."

"Yes, but I love . . . she's very important to me, all the same."

"I know," Gunnar said. He put a hand under her chin and tilted her lips toward his. He kissed her.

She knew it was wrong the moment their lips touched.

He's trying to get inside my head! He's trying to find out Ulla's secrets!

Ravenelle jerked away. Gunnar pulled her back to his embrace.

"Let me go!"

"Don't be a terror, little Princess."

"I mean it," Ravenelle said.

She called out to her bloodservants in thought-speech.

Help! Get in here, all of you!

We are coming, mistress!

She could hear them beating on the chapel door.

The door is locked, mistress!

Right. Gunnar had latched it behind himself when he'd come in.

Donato will break it in. Hold the man off until we can get there. This was the voice of Raphael, her faithful eldest bloodservant. He and Ravenelle shared thoughts like waves overlapping in the same pond.

All right, but hurry.

Ravenelle gathered her hand and slapped Gunnar across the face as hard as she could. He jolted back, holding his cheek. She had striped it bloody with her nails.

You're going to regret that, little Princess, Gunnar thought. *Now I want inside, and you're going to let me come in.*

With a mental thrust harder than any she'd ever experienced in all her years of taking communion, Gunnar forced himself inside her mind and forced her to think the thoughts *he* wanted her to think.

Thoughts about Ulla von Dunstig.

He is sifting through my memories! No. Nobody does that to me!

I am Ravenelle Archambeault.

I will be a queen of a nation much stronger than your petty kingdom. I am Roman. You do not mess with me!

Gunnar let out a grunt of surprise. And pain. His hands went to his temples.

"Princess, that *hurt*. How can you be that strong? He didn't warn me about—"

Then the door burst open and her bloodservants rushed in.

The tie with Gunnar was broken.

Gunnar stood. "We could have had something, Princess," he said. "We are both very alike, you know."

"I didn't want to have *sex* with you."

"Don't be an idiot, Ravenelle Archambeault, that's *all* you wanted." He turned toward her servants. "I'm leaving," he told them. "Your precious mistress is safe, you poor slaves."

He stalked past them and out the chapel door, leaving behind the lingering scent of sandalwood cologne and fresh blood.

Ravenelle wiped her face, and the palm of her hand came away red. She'd been crying and hadn't realized it. Here was another way she was not like anyone else in the castle. Another reason she would never fit in.

Like all true Roman aristocrats, Ravenelle cried blood tears.

Chapter Four:
The Tryst

Saeunn Amberstone held tightly to the hand of Ulla von Dunstig and pulled her hurriedly along. The two girls made their way down the underground passageway. This was a servant corridor that led from the castle at Raukenrose Castle to one of the kitchens that was a separate building. The passageway was pitch dark. It was lit by oil lamps during the day, but now the time was half past midnight.

Both girls could see nothing, but Saeunn had a sixth sense that Ulla did not possess. Like all of the Children of Starlight, she could sense the direction to her homeland, Amberstone Valley, from any spot on Earth. And she could always find her star in the sky at night. She just *knew* where she was. All elves did.

And sometimes her star also spoke to her.

Your land-dragon is stirring tonight, my child. The clutch is restless. Tonight we sing to calm them.

I hear you, my star, my soul.

Since she had been down this corridor several times before—with and without Ulla in tow—she also knew where to pull up short and stop walking.

Ulla, who truly had a terrible sense of direction even for a human, stumbled, but Saeunn caught the hem of her dress and steadied her.

They had gotten to the locked iron grate that covered the corridor at night. Saeunn put her hand out and touched the cool metal of the grate, then lowered her hand gradually until she felt the keyhole.

"All right, here it is," she said, guiding Ulla's hand to the spot. "Use the key."

After curfew the gate was locked and the key got hung in its place on the rack.

She'd been the one who had taken it. That was always her role. She could move a lot more silently and quickly than Ulla.

Stealing the key was also the least of the ways they were disobeying. If the duke and duchess found out—

No, *when* they find out, Saeunn thought. They are *definitely* going to find out. She didn't have to see the future to guess that much.

Ulla was breaking the rules big time.

Saeunn heard the voice of her star again. *You are restless as the dragon tonight, my child.*

I am happy, my star. Just a little overexcited.

Her star laughed a tinkling laugh like crystal ringing.

The humans interest you?

Yes, my star.

The girl you are helping?

Yes, she is untraditional.

And the other, the brother?

He's very intelligent. I do like him . . .

Take care not to become too attached, for you know—

Yes, I know. They die.

And we do not.

"Saeunn?" said Ulla. "Are you in there? You're doing that thing again, where you get all distracted and practically turn into a statue."

"Talking to my star," Saeunn answered. "We're done. Open the gate."

"Elves are really *strange* sometimes," Ulla said.

"It wasn't my idea to go rambling around in the dark, you know."

"Okay, okay."

Ulla slid the key into the keyhole with far too much racket. Saeunn figured Ulla's hands were trembling. There was the click of the lock opening. The gate was heavy, but well oiled. Ulla left the key in the lock. Saeunn would get it on her way back if all went well.

The girls pushed the gate open. It still squeaked enough as it swung on its hinges to worry them both.

Saeunn went first, and then Ulla tried to follow her through the gate opening, but banged into the bar on the side of the gate.

"Curse it," she whispered. "That's going to leave a bruise. I'll have to come up with some reason I got it. Thayer will *definitely* notice when she's dressing me tomorrow." Thayer was Ulla's personal maid. She was a bear woman, a Tier, a talking beast. You did not want to get on her bad side. "Well, we'd better start moving."

"Yes."

"Do you think anyone heard us?" Ulla asked in a whisper. "Can you listen?"

Saeunn's hearing was much better than Ulla's. They both knew it.

The girls stood still for a moment while Saeunn listened. She heard the usual castle noises—settling stones, mice scampering—but there were no footsteps. She did hear someone stumbling around in the castle beyond the entrance of the corridor, but then a toilet door in the castle creaked open and shut. Nothing to worry them down here.

"I think we're all right," Saeunn said.

Ulla squeezed Saeunn's hand, then leaned forward and bussed her cheek with her lips. "I love you, little sister. I would be lost without you," she whispered. "No matter what happens to me, you know that's true."

Ulla drew back, leaving the lingering scent of her perfume. It was exquisite, like everything else about Ulla. But what impressed Saeunn most was that none of her perfection seemed to have gone to her head. In fact, the von Dunstig children were certainly overindulged, but none of them were *really* spoiled. She'd met lots of other children of nobility elsewhere who were.

"Ready to go, big sister?" Saeunn whispered back.

Ulla smothered a giggle. "Oh, yes," she said.

Saeunn had not been lying to her star—even if that were possible. She *was* happy here in Shenandoah.

When she'd come, she'd expected to have to *endure* the place. She'd figured that Shenandoah was going to be a layover, a diplomatic stop she had to take for a few years. Her father wanted to explore an alliance between the elves of Amberstone and the Mark of Shenandoah.

The arrangement had been made with Duke Otto to foster Saeunn for ten years, which, she knew, would seem like a long time to a human but was practically a blink of an eye to a Child of Starlight.

People died. Elves did not.

Oh, elves might be killed by accident or in battle, and there were rare diseases that could kill them. But if she avoided any of these calamities, Saeunn would go on living for century after century.

Right now, though, she was very young for an elf. She was sixty-two years old. A teenager.

Although she'd been alive for decades, a lot of Saeunn's early life, especially the very first few years, had been spent in the star-trance. She'd lived within the thoughts of her star, and sang her star's part in the great song the stars sang to the dragons. Stars were not just friends to the elves. They weren't just family.

The stars *were* elves and the elves *were* stars. Like one of the saga singers had put it:

> *Light that splatters into matter,*
> *and to living bodies scatters.*
> *Souls of elves are starlight spatter,*
> *stars that come to Earth to dwell.*
> *Elves are stars and stars are elves.*

The souls of elves were made of starlight, and each elf shared that soul with a particular star in the night sky. Saeunn was her star made into a person upon the Earth.

She did not understand exactly how this worked, or why it should be. She'd asked her mother once, but her mother had smiled and replied, "Ask me again in a hundred years. Then you might be ready to understand the answer."

Saeunn might be over sixty years old, but because of the nature of elves, she had the mind, the personality, of a teenager. It took elves a *very* long time to mature into a grown-up.

Saeunn led Ulla the rest of the way down the corridor until they emerged into the outside kitchen, a single large room with four huge fire hearths for cooking. The dim glow of the half moon outside filtered through the kitchen's high-set windows. After the complete darkness of the corridor, there was moonlight.

Moonlight!

Saeunn was drawn to it like a cat to catnip. She stepped into a spot where the moon was shining through most brightly. To be touched by pure moonlight felt *good* to an elf, like a nice, long bath might to a human—only this feeling was a lot more intense.

"Uh, Saeunn." Ulla nudged her gently. "Moonlight's got you again."

Saeunn started. She blinked her eyes hard and shook her shoulders to bring herself out of the shallow trance.

"Sorry," she said too loudly, then continued in a whisper. "I'm back now."

"I swear you might stand there the rest of the night if I didn't say something."

"I might. You've seen me do it before."

Ulla nodded. "Okay, now for the scary part," she whispered. "Can you hear the bailey guard?"

Saeunn went to stand behind the kitchen's wooden door, closed her eyes, and listened closely for a moment.

The crunch of leather-soled boot on gravel. Clank of mailed shirt. Blowing of breath by a cold man trying to warm his cupped hands.

"Cold as a well-digger's butt," muttered a low voice.

It was Morast, who sounded like he gargled with gravel.

"He's near the middle of the courtyard," Saeunn said.

Ulla moved up beside Saeunn. She stared at the kitchen door as if she could see through it. "Is he moving toward us or away?"

Saeunn lifted a hand to tell her to wait. "Give me a moment."

The flap of the banners and flags upon the battlements. The yawn and sigh of the guard. Then the crunch of boots getting softer, farther away.

Saeunn turned to Ulla. "He's headed to the other side of the bailey with his back to us. Let's be very quiet and really quick."

Ulla nodded. The two girls worked together to open the kitchen door with as little noise as possible, and then only enough to let them to slip out.

They kept to the edge of the bailey and worked their way past the different trade stalls. When they passed a stable, Saeunn heard a horse start and stamp. She knew this horse.

"Soft now, Slep," she whispered toward the stable. "Everything's all right." Slep evidently heard her, because she settled back down.

Finally they arrived at their destination. Their hearts were racing, but neither girl was breathing hard. Despite her delicate looks, Ulla was in good condition. She spent a lot of time outdoors riding, walking, and climbing to spots where she could work on her paintings. She got plenty of exercise. Ulla did tend to tan, and so she had to keep herself well covered even in the hottest weather.

Saeunn glanced through the crack in the stall door of the smith's shop.

Yes, the bell ringer was tied off to the side. If it weren't, they might get a nasty surprise when the iron triangle tolled.

She quietly tugged on the string attached to the wooden latch on the inside and pushed the door open. Ulla slipped inside, and she followed.

"You're finally here," said a low male voice from the rear of the shop.

Ulla stepped into the light cast by the banked coals, her face beaming. "Told you I'd make it."

From the shadows stepped Grer Smead, Raukenrose Castle's chief smith.

He was a commoner. Ulla was a duke's daughter.

Humans and their rules. Saeunn shook her head.

This could be a major disaster in the making.

Or something amazing.

Or both.

Ulla stepped into Grer's arms.

Then they kissed. For a long, long time.

Saeunn stepped back toward the forge to give them more privacy. The heat from the glowing coals felt good against her back.

Finally Ulla turned her head from Grer and looked over

at her. "You should go to bed now, little sister," Ulla said. "Grer will take me back in."

Because he had to deal with woodcutters to get fuel for his forge, Grer got the best price. Wulf's mother, who knew a good deal when she saw it, had given him a contract to deliver a cord of wood for the castle fireplaces each morning.

He would trundle the wood in on a woodcart that would normally take two men to handle. Grer was incredibly strong from hammering metal all day. He would make several deliveries to different spots so that the staff could reach the wood more easily and get the castle fireplaces going. Castles were chilly in general, and now in the month of Gormanuder, a room could be downright freezing without a good fire to warm it.

To get Ulla back inside, she climbed into a burlap bag and Grer rolled her in on a cart full of wood. In fact, since one of the inside woodpiles was near her bedchamber, he was able to deliver Ulla right to her door.

"You don't want me to stand watch or something?"

Grer let out a low chuckle. "We'll be as quiet as mice," he said.

"And you have school tomorrow," Ulla said. "I've already kept you up way past your bed time."

This was true.

"Okay, sister. Good night. And good night, Grer Smead."

"Pleasant evening to you, Lady Saeunn," Grer replied. "Ulla and I . . . well, we thank you."

Saeunn looked at Ulla, whose face seemed aglow after the kiss. "I love my sister," she said. "So this makes me happy."

The night was chilly when she slipped out of the smith's shop. She got past the bailey guard once again, this time much more easily without Ulla, and made her way through the lightless kitchen corridor back toward the castle and her own bedchamber.

In the darkness of the corridor she spoke once again with

her star. *Ulla seems so happy and content, even though what she's doing is crazy. Do you think I will ever fall in love, my star, my soul?*

Again she heard her star's crystalline laughter. But this time her star did not reply.

Never mind, Saeunn thought. I already know the answer.

Yes, she would. And she knew whom she would fall in love with. She'd seen it in the moonlight on this and other nights.

Another disaster in the making.

Maybe it was just the moonlight affecting her, but it was funny how at the moment she really, truly didn't care. She was having too much fun.

Chapter Five:
The Olden Oak

Somebody was following them. Or some*thing*. Rainer was sure of it. He—or it—was being quiet, but Rainer heard the faintest clank of metal on metal. Maybe a sword in a scabbard. Maybe a knife getting drawn. And when he and Wulf stopped to figure out where they were and find their way, he heard footsteps. He'd have to be on guard. It was for sure Wulf would *not* be. He was deep in the trance he went into whenever, as he said, the dragon called him.

Rainer loosened the dagger in his belt scabbard.

Don't want it to get stuck when I need it, Rainer thought. Having a weapon you couldn't use was the same as not having that weapon at all. Speaking of weapons, what else could he do if they got attacked?

Rainer considered the options.

The cloak, if he could get it off in time. Whipping a piece of clothing at somebody you were fighting could be a very effective distraction. He'd done it before in practice rounds during afternoon training at the castle.

There were also loose cobblestones. You could pick one up and bash somebody's brains out.

Stay aware of whatever is around you and *use* it to your advantage.

Rainer could just hear Koterbaum, his arms instructor, lecturing on the subject—maybe after some boring match where both of the guys had been whacking around hopelessly. "A weapon doesn't have to *look* like a weapon," said Koterbaum. "Lose a fight in the yard and you walk away defeated. Lose a fight in battle and you don't walk away at all."

Koterbaum might be a dandy with that waxy moustache of his, and a suck-up to aristocrats, but Rainer still thought he was the best trainer he could ever have, and he felt lucky to be Koterbaum's student. In fact, he had to admit he practically worshipped the guy, at least as a teacher. Rainer had asked around and heard stories of some of the things Koterbaum had done in *real* war, like in the Little War when he had killed five guys who were surrounding him and trying to slaughter him. They story was Koterbaum walked away without a scratch. You had to respect that, and you were an idiot if you didn't listen when a man like that was talking about fighting.

Rainer and Wulf padded their way along narrow passages between buildings, feeling their way with the toes of their boots as much as moving by sight. Though the moon was up, not much of its light got through the cracks between the topmost floors of the buildings. They were taking darker streets on purpose, streets where the buildings leaned into one another and shut out the sky.

Most of Raukenrose's lanes were barely wide enough for an ox cart to pass, and definitely not wide enough for two carts to pass side by side. There were a few wide boulevards and several open squares, usually built around a central water supply, but the idea tonight was to *avoid* such places.

There was fog rising from the river. The fog made the air chilly and moist, and the cobblestones that lined the alleys were slippery. Everybody had emptied out his or her chamber pot from the upstairs windows before going to bed, and there was sewage slicking the street, some of it trampled down to a brown paste, some of it still in chunks. Even though the streets were usually washed down in the morning by the town guild's command, the air stank. Mixed-together urine, nightsoil, and dirty dishwater was a familiar smell in town.

You did get used to it. Sort of.

It was early winter, the first of Gormanuder, the month before Yule. The only people officially allowed out after curfew were members of the town guard and the nightsoil men.

In one or two windows along the lanes, candles burned as the tenants of the house took care of whatever chores they had that might be keeping them up late into the night. Rainer was grateful for these small lights, because they kept the alleyway from being completely dark. Whenever he had stray light from one of these candlelit windows, he took the time to look behind them. Nothing there.

But there *was*. He could sense it.

Finally they got to Allfather Square. It used to be the center of town long ago, but Raukenrose had built out in all directions in a crazy-quilt way. Now the square was in the southeast area of the town. Regen's Fountain was still a main water source for the township, though.

On the other side of the square was Allfather Cathedral, with its great central nave and tower topped by the Elder Bell. The cathedral was huge and beautiful—but unfinished. There were still years left of work to do on it. Cathedrals could take a century or more to build.

Saeunn would live to see it done, but Rainer figured none of his other friends would, and neither would he.

In the middle of the square was a big rock sticking out of the ground. It was about ten elbs high, as high as two men standing on one another's shoulders. The rock looked like a gigantic chunk of greenish quartz.

Wulf had claimed it actually *was* the upper barb of a dragon's back spine, and even that it was connected below to the Great Land-dragon of Shenandoah. Rainer wasn't sure *what* the rock was made of. He'd grown up in mining country, and he could see that it wasn't quartz. Too glassy. But it wasn't volcanic, either, like obsidian. It was tough as granite, and you could not chip pieces off with a hammer like you would have been able to do with quartz. If you could, the whole rock might have been taken as relics and souvenirs by now.

The Olden Oak grew partly around this large rock. The tree looked like it had sprouted in the ground on one side of the rock, but over the years it had wrapped itself around the green rock until it covered a lot of the surface of the rock— and covered it without the slightest gap between the wood and the rock. You could barely tell where rock ended and tree began.

The tree was allegedly planted by somebody named Thornfoot or Thornbush, something like that, one thousand years ago. It was supposed to have *already* been a thousand years old when it grew the Dragon Hammer.

> *Where dragon spoke*
> *From in the bark*
> *To old Duke Tjark*
> *Who made the choice*
> *To heed the voice*

A tree, but not this one, Rainer thought. He had a hard time believing an oak could get to be a thousand years old, much less two thousand.

Anyway, Wulf would know the history. He knew lore like that backward and forward. There wasn't a saga that Wulf hadn't read, either, and he could do long quotes from a bunch of them. And not just the easy parts, but stuff like the lists of dwarves or dragon names. Wulf also had a feeling for the rules and laws of the land like he was born knowing them. Which didn't mean he was mature enough to *really* get how people *actually* acted.

That's why I'm along, Rainer thought. I've got a year on him, and you can figure out a lot in a year, and not just the things the schoolmaster told you, either. Besides, he's my brother. I am *going* to protect him, no matter what he tells me to do.

Wulf wasn't a *bad* fighter—anybody that trained as much as they did would have a lot of basic ability with arms—but he was not going to be able to stand up to some dirty-fighting, experienced cutthroat in a dark alley.

I figure I can probably handle that for us both.

For whatever reason, Tretz had gifted him with super-quick speed and sharp senses. It was really hard for anyone to get the jump on Rainer.

Well, whether it was this tree or one of its ancestors, Duke Tjark was supposed to have broken off a war hammer that had *grown* from the trunk of the Olden Oak like it was some kind of branch. That had been over six hundred years ago. He'd used that war hammer to take on the evil shape shifters and the Snakeband Skraelings who had been terrorizing the valley. Tjark had done it, too. He had driven them out, and founded the Mark of Shenandoah.

Rainer thought it probably was a made-up story. After all, where was this great hammer? You didn't *misplace* something like that, and nobody had it.

The Olden Oak was real, though. It was right there in front of them.

In addition to the weird way it grew around the green

rock, it was also the biggest, most gnarled oak Rainer had ever seen. The canopy was huge, but the limbs had only a few clinging dead leaves by the time the month of Gormanuder came around. Right now, the Olden Oak looked like the skeleton of some gigantic beast against the starry sky, and the Moon seemed caught in its branches.

"Here's your magic tree," Rainer said.

"It's just a tree," Wulf said.

"Just a tree wrapped around a dragon that grew a hammer from its side."

"Or a hammer was stuck in the living tree by Sturmer himself," Wulf said. "That's what it says in one of the sagas."

He'll tell me which one, Rainer thought. He can't help himself.

"*Arinborn's*, in case you wondered."

Rainer did not believe in the divine beings. Or at least he didn't believe they should be worshipped. Wulf had once tried to tell him that it didn't really work like that, that the divine beings that he believed in wanted *devotion*, not worship, and there was supposed to be this big difference. Rainer hadn't seen it.

Any nature god was limited. There were things a god like that could not do.

There was only one true God.

And this God had sent a son named Tretz. Tretz was not a human, but a Tier. His kind were the strangest and rarest Tier of all, the mandrakes. Half-human, half-dragon. Mandragons.

Rainer touched his right arm. Underneath the cloak and his tunic sleeve he had the six-point star symbol, Tretz's aster, tattooed on his forearm. The castle contingent called it a butthole. Rainer didn't care. Most people knew what the tattoo meant.

Tretz had been yanked apart by six great chains attached to his legs, his neck, and his tail, each pulled tighter and tighter by huge ratchet wheels until he was torn into six pieces. And then he had miraculously reassembled, and come back to life even greater than before.

"All right, tell me. What happens in the saga?" Rainer asked, mostly to pull Wulf back to reality. His friend was lost in a trance, standing and staring at the Olden Oak.

"The saga? Oh, right." Wulf shook his head and rubbed his eyes. "Five hundred men tried to break the Dragon Hammer off," Wulf said.

"And your great-great-great-great-granddad was the one who did it, right?"

"Duke Tjark."

"Must be nice to have your relatives in the old stories."

Wulf nodded. "True. But Tjark broke it *off* of the tree. He didn't put it in," Wulf said. "Not like me."

"Better get tree stabbing, then," Rainer replied.

Wulf approached the tree. Rainer could tell that the dragon-call had him completely now. Wulf unsheathed his dagger and stepped up to the tree with it. To somebody else, it might have looked like Wulf was up to some prank, that he was about to carve his name into the tree, or maybe the name of a girl or something. People did that. The tree had a lot of scars.

Instead, Wulf drew his arm back and plunged the dagger into the oak, point first.

And in it went.

This amazed Rainer every time he saw, and he'd seen it more than a half-dozen times.

Not just the dagger tip, but the *whole blade* sank in, up to the hilt, like it was passing into butter. Wulf should *not* have been able to do this.

I couldn't do it, Rainer thought. No man nor even any of the bigger Tier was strong enough. Well, maybe a bear man. But it didn't seem like Wulf was straining in the least. No, he looked like somebody who was fitting a key into its lock.

It wasn't a miracle or the act of some god or divine being or whatever, though. Rainer was sure of that. No, it was magic. Magic wasn't a miracle. Their lore tutor, Master Tolas, had taught them that magic could be figured out. But Rainer had to admit he sure hadn't figured *this* magic out yet.

Wulf was gone, mentally. Connected to his dragon. Or to the land. He wasn't Wulfgang von Dunstig.

He was some kind of half-man, half-tree as far as Rainer could tell.

Out of it.

The shuffling again.

There in the township shadows. Somebody followed us. Rainer couldn't shake the certainty he felt about that.

Now I have to be totally on guard, Rainer thought. He pulled his own dagger clear of the scabbard and held it loosely in his right hand. He took a deep breath and looked carefully around.

Be aware of everything. Like your life depends on it.

The footsteps again, the very faint ones he'd heard before. Whoever it was had one of the lightest steps Rainer had ever heard.

You don't fool me, whoever you are. I know you're out there.

Suddenly, there was a soft whoosh and a thunk. Rainer spun to see that a black crossbow bolt had embedded itself in the Olden Oak barely a fingerbreadth from Wulf's head. The pale moonlight glinted off the shaft darkly.

The footsteps from across the square grew closer.

CHAPTER SIX:
THE LAND-DRAGON

Wulf gripped the dagger tightly. His other hand touched the rough bark of the Olden Oak and he leaned into it. But it was his dagger hand that truly made contact with the living insides of the tree. He felt *through* the steel, into the tree. Wulf's mind traveled into the rock, and then down. Down and out. Into the land-dragon Shenandoah.

Soon he was *everywhere.*

Shenandoah. The dragon we live on. Shenandoah meant the beautiful green valley, sixty leagues long. This was where most of the people lived. Wulf could sense them all. Villages. Farms lying under the moonlight, their wheat and corn bending in a soft breeze. Cotton and tobacco fields to the south, with grasshoppers and boll weevils chomping on them through the night, wheat and corn to the north. Sheep grazing on the upland slopes. The Shwartzwald Forest blanketing the peaks. Then climbing to Massanutten Mountain, the long flattop highland that ran down the middle of the Shenandoah Valley, and into the U-shaped depression indented in Massanutten's crest. This was Bear

Valley, where the Earl of Shwartzwald dwelled. He was a bear man, but the valley was filled with all kinds of Tier. Down again into the east Shenandoah Valley, where herds of eastern buffalo lived. Living with them were the buffalo people, talking animals who stood on two legs like men but had the heads of buffalos. They were herders of their lesser brothers and sisters. Most were asleep in the wigwams where they lived, but some guarded the herd at night from the purely animal wolves and bears. These guards sang low and booming songs to calm their herds and let them know all was well.

Across the western valley and into the deep forests of the Greensmoke Mountains. The centaurs lived there, half-human, half-horse. The centaurs had a lot of magic in their bones, and Wulf felt some of the centaurs sense *him* within the land-dragon right now.

Then back to the Shenandoah Valley and south, to Glockendorf, where the gnomes made their famous bells of iron and brass. The neatly kept little town, half on the surface and half in caves, was shut tight for the night. Gnomes didn't mess around when it came to security. They lived too close to the Roman colonies for that.

Running through it all, shaping the land with its waters, were the two forks of the Shenandoah River, a river that flowed south to north. Where the two forks joined and continued flowing north together was Raukenrose, ancient seat of the duke.

He could feel the township.

He could feel all the humans, otherfolk, and Tier, all at once, but each alone as a separate person also.

The Mark of Shenandoah. Wulf's country, his land. It was also the landholding of his father, the duke. Wulf's oldest brother, Otto—who was named after his father—would inherit rule of the mark after the duke was gone.

The true land-bond of Shenandoah belonged to Otto, not

to Wulf. That was what it *meant* to be the ruler or the future ruler of Shenandoah. The dragon chose you. It pulled you into its dreams.

He should not be doing this. He shouldn't be *able* to do this.

But Wulf didn't feel guilty, not really. It wasn't like he could do anything about the dragon-call. But he did feel afraid of what it might mean. If it ever came out that Wulf could hear the dragon, Otto would handle it. His brother was rock solid, totally committed to the mark no matter what. But there would be those who would say that if Otto weren't the chosen one, then the rule of the mark was up for grabs when Wulf's father died or when the disease that had already half wrecked his mind took its final toll.

That was why Wulf was sneaking out at night to visit the Olden Oak. That was why only his best friend knew his secret.

Wulf continued spreading out into his vision of the land. It wasn't like looking at a map, or even like being *in* a map. It was more like being the real thing, the land, part of it— like if something happened to Shenandoah, it would happen to him.

Third son. Not even spare to the heir. That's what the von Blaus and von Trausts and others of the castle boys taunted him with. But it was basically true.

Third son in a dragon-trance.

He had never been more confused in his life.

Third son, and the dragon-call and land-bond was coming to *him*? Most in the castle knew Duke Otto wasn't the man he used to be. It was a disease called morosis. His father was always grasping for words for this or that—things he knew very well before—and his sentences often trailed off into confusion. Many thought that it was high time for the duchess to let Otto, the eldest son, take the reins.

But Otto claimed that he did not yet hear the dragon-call,

so his father must stay in charge. When that time came, and not before, Otto would become regent.

The dragon-call should have come to his brother, Wulf thought. That was the way it always worked in the past. That was the way it was supposed to work now.

Rainer had asked him what land-bonding was like. He'd tried, but had not been able to put it into words for his friend, not really.

The land-bond was dangerous. You didn't *want* to come back, you wanted to dream forever the dragon-dream that was history, and the present, and even the future.

And there was the Dragon Hammer. He kept seeing it.

The war hammer that had been used by Duke Tjark to destroy the berserker horde and drive the shape-shifters and Snakeband Skraelings from the valley.

The hammer that had been lost, no one quite knew how.

After he'd been through the land, felt the night move over Shenandoah, he was pulled down. It wasn't violent. Only a small tug. But powerful.

The dragon wanted to show him the war hammer.

In the vision, he was staring down on the hammer's head. It seemed to be floating upright in a brassy, red cauldron.

Eight times the dragon had shown this to Wulf. This was the ninth. What was it for? What was he supposed to do?

He was out of his body, part of the walls, part of everything. Yet he could shift his attention and look around.

He moved closer.

Suddenly, the hammer swung back and forth, clattering against the walls of the cauldron, or whatever the containing chamber was. And even though the cauldron seemed to be made of shining fire itself, the hammer was not burned up. The curving wall held it in.

Bang! Clang! But the sound was wrong, like a trumpet note heard when you were deep underwater. The hammer looked as if it was stirring something inside the cauldron.

What am I supposed to do? I don't understand!

He moved closer still.

This time he *had* to try something different. Maybe he was wrong. Maybe he did, somehow, have arms and hands in the trance. Maybe somehow he could grab the hammer, hold it—

Wulf reached for the top of the Dragon Hammer.

He saw his right arm stretch out before his eyes. It grew longer and longer. Impossible. There was no way his arm was that long. But he strained.

And . . . managed to put his palm on the top of the hammer. For only an eyeblink.

A stab of cold like he had never felt before cut through his body. He jerked his hand away. It seemed to draw up inside him, to go back to normal length. His palm ached from the cold still.

He turned it over. There was a scar burned into his palm. Not just a scar. It was a deep stripe across his hand about the size of a knife hilt.

There was roaring in his ears. The clanging and banging had become one gigantic sound that shook him through and through.

Throbbing, roaring pressure. He was pushed up. Up, and out.

Above him, Wulf saw what looked like a huge set of roots. But instead of being anchored in the soil, they were anchored in the nighttime sky.

Then he realized what it was. The top of the Olden Oak. Its bare branches stretched up and spread out against the stars.

But he was seeing it from below, from underground. Underground, but rising fast. Getting closer.

The pressure pushed him out—

"Tretz's bones, Wulfgang!" came another voice, a human voice, from a long way off. "You have to get out of that tree!"

It was Rainer. He was tugging on Wulf's shoulder.

For a moment, Wulf was in two worlds. He was in the land-bond, trying to hold his thoughts together against the incredible pressure. Trying to hold on to the dragon-vision.

Rainer shook him.

"You have to come out!"

Wulf opened his eyes. He was lying on the ground and staring up at the Olden Oak's branches.

Rainer stepped over him, grabbed him under the shoulders, and yanked him up.

"I touched it! I think I almost had it."

"Not now," Rainer said, pulling Wulf all the way to his feet. There was a strain in his voice, and something else. It was shaking.

Rainer was scared.

Before Wulf could ask, his friend jerked Wulf around to face the south end of the square.

Across the square stood . . . something. Someone. It had the shape of a person. But its shape was barely visible in the night. Its skin wasn't just dark, but *black*.

Coal black.

The only reason it was visible at all was because it was rimmed by the half moon's faint light.

And then the smell reached them. The stench. It smelled like a dead thing. Wulf shuddered. He felt like he wanted to vomit. He glanced over and saw that Rainer was holding a hand to his nose and mouth. The smell was awful.

This was no man. It had no nose or mouth. Instead its face was pushed outward into a hooked beak. It cocked its head like a bird did and gazed at them with . . . they *were* eyes, but eyes with no whites in them. They were as inky black as the rest of it, just more liquid looking.

Blood and bones, what *was* it? Was it Tier, maybe some kind of vulture man?

Was there . . . there was a mention in the sagas. But he couldn't think of it, not now. He was too terrified.

The vulture-thing had something in its hands, which it let drop and swung back behind itself on a strap.

"Crossbow," Rainer said in a tense whisper. "Almost got you."

Then the thing spoke, if you could call it speaking. It was more like the screech of a rusty iron door opening, and it made Wulf cringe listening to it. But it was loud enough to hear from across the square.

"The hammer," the thing hissed. "Where?"

The thing reached to its side and drew a curved sword that was as black as the rest of the thing. Wulf recognized its design. It was a Roman falcata.

The blade glinted darkly in the moonlight.

The black thing walked toward them.

CHAPTER SEVEN:
THE DRAUGAR

Wulf spun around and grabbed at his dagger where it stuck in the tree. Tugged. No good.

Blood and bones, he thought. The dragon-vision is gone. Can't pull it out.

Maybe that wasn't true. He didn't know for sure. He gave the dagger the hardest tug he could.

It didn't budge.

Yep, it was stuck there.

He turned back around. Rainer had drawn his blade and had moved between Wulf and the dark being. Rainer was trembling.

"What *are* you?" Wulf called to it. His own voice was shaking.

The dark being did not reply. It didn't break its steady stride. And there was something in the way it quivered as it moved, like it didn't have bones.

Rainer got into a fighting stance with his dagger. It wasn't a sword posture, but more like a ready position for boxing. Made sense. Rainer studied fighting the way Wulf studied the sagas.

He couldn't let Rainer face this thing alone. Wulf started to move up beside Rainer, but Rainer glanced back, saw what Wulf was up to, and shook his head.

"You've got no blade," he growled.

"I've got my hands," Wulf said. "And, blood and bones, I have my teeth if I have to use them." He went to stand beside Rainer.

At the sight of the two boys standing side by side, the thing stopped. It was five long paces away. It was as tall as a very tall man. The smell it put out was incredibly intense.

In the country, Wulf had once passed a dead horse that had been crawling with maggots. This smell was way, way worse.

The thing looked at Rainer and then to Wulf with its half-vulture, half-man head.

The grinding whisper-voice came out of it again. This close, it was a sound that made you cringe, like the sound of fingernails on slate.

"Where is Tjark's hammer?" it screeched. "Thou know'st."

Suddenly Wulf wanted badly to answer. He felt compelled. The black thing had the right because it had the power. Who was he to keep it from what it wanted?

He was nobody. He was filled with the complete certainty that if he didn't tell, the thing would tear him apart.

The only trouble was that he *didn't* know. He didn't know if any of that part of the dragon vision was real or what it meant.

Wulf shook his head. "No idea," he said.

"Thou know'st," it insisted. "Boy heir."

"I'm not," Wulf replied, his voice shaking only a little. "You've got the wrong guy."

Quickly, faster than a man ought to be able to move, the black thing jumped toward Wulf. It reached for him with its free hand.

He stared at the gaping beak with its tearing, hooked point.

"Thou know'st."

Wulf drew his hands back and got ready.

I'm going down swinging.

Somehow, Rainer was quicker than the dark thing. He charged toward the thing and met it head on. But Rainer had too much momentum. The dark thing stepped to the side, and Rainer stumbled past it—

There was nothing between the dark thing and Wulf now.

The beak. And now arms reached out, black arms, fingers not fully formed but sharpening to points, like spears. Talons.

Wulf faked to his left, then threw a punch with his right as hard as he could.

Nothing but air. The black thing was too quick. It had ducked.

Claw hands grabbed Wulf by the neck. The tips of claw fingers dug into his skin.

Then the thing lifted him up, completely off his feet, and held him dangling by his neck. It turned the edge of its sword against Wulf's throat. Wulf grabbed at the thing's hands and shook himself, trying to get free, but it was no use. The thing's grip tightened.

"Thou know'st. Tell me." The thing was in Wulf's face. Its beak was a finger length from his eyes.

The talons squeezed his neck harder. The blade cut deeper.

Rainer appeared again over the dark thing's shoulder. He had found something to grab hold of. The thing's cloak. It was black, but it seemed real enough. Rainer clung to the fabric and pulled himself up onto the thing's back and, with a yell of determination, drew his dagger across the black thing's throat.

The sword moved away from Wulf's throat. Wulf watched as a gash opened up in the thing's neck from the dagger stroke. It oozed black fluid, too thick and syrupy to be blood. Then the gash closed up almost as fast as it had been formed.

Wulf twisted and kicked at the thing's chest. The thing's hold on him weakened for a moment and Wulf struggled free. He stumbled back, in too much shock to do anything but watch.

Rainer stabbed his dagger into the thing's right arm. The arm went limp, and the thing dropped its falcata. But this wound sealed again, and the black thing reached for Rainer with taloned hands. Rainer scrambled around on its back, using the thing's own head to dodge.

Wulf lowered his shoulder and charged.

Duck down low. Slam into the midriff.

He felt the boneless, syrup-like softness of it. But his charge caused the thing to stumble back.

This was what Rainer needed. Rainer dropped his dagger, which obviously wasn't working. He grabbed a handful of bolts from the crossbow quiver hanging from the thing's belt. With one in his right hand, he stabbed again, this time into the side of the thing's head.

The crossbow bolt slid in.

If the dark thing had a brain, the bolt had sliced a wide gash deep into it. Rainer took another bolt and stabbed again. He left that bolt in as well and stabbed with the third.

There were three black arrows pushed all the way through the thing's skull. Black ooze flowed. Yet still it would not die.

With a big jerk of its body, the dark thing went completely rigid. This sudden movement caught Rainer off guard, and he was thrown from the thing's back. He landed in the dirt near the green rock's edge. Wulf straightened up from his charge.

He was face-to-face with the dark thing once again.

There were three crossbow bolts sticking out of its head, one with its tip coming out of the thing's right eye.

The thing opened its mouth again, and a black tongue shot out.

It hissed, the black tongue twitching like a snake.

The hiss did not stop, and the horrible smell of the thing's expelled breath was all around him.

Stinging eyes. Burning skin. Wulf put a hand over his face and nose to keep from breathing any more of the rotten air.

Then Rainer was on his feet again, behind the thing. He had picked up the black falcata. He slashed into the thing's side, crying out "Tretz" as he did so.

Like some mushroom fungus full of spoors, the thing exploded. Then—

Poof!

It turned into a cloud of dust. No skin. No gore. No pieces anywhere. And the sword disappeared from Rainer's hands.

Only the stench remained.

Wulf stared ahead, shaking like a leaf in the wind. He stood that way until he heard Rainer groan. His friend had been thrown several paces away by the explosion.

Snap out of it. Rainer needs help.

He ran quickly to Rainer.

"You all right?"

Rainer shook his head to clear it. Wulf lent him a hand as he pulled himself up.

He rubbed his wrist.

"Ouch," Rainer said. "Like a hornet sting."

But the wrist seemed to move in all the right directions.

Rainer started walking in a semicircle through the dirt of the square. Wulf didn't understand what he was doing until Rainer stooped and picked up the dagger he had dropped. He cleaned it against his cloak, looked it over again, then slid it back into its scabbard.

From out of nowhere, the answer came to Wulf—what he'd put out of his mind before so he could concentrate on surviving.

"*Henli's Saga*," Wulf said.

"Huh?"

"That was a draugar."

"A what?"

"Thousands of years ago. Four elves sold their souls to evil," said Wulf.

"How does anybody know that?"

"They've been seen since."

He turned and looked at the spot where the dark thing had disappeared. There was nothing. He checked the ground. No sign of a body or even of a deflated skin sack or anything like that.

Wulf looked around. There was candlelight behind a few windows. The noise had awakened the townspeople who lived around the square. Somebody would be out; someone would be sent to get the town guard if he hadn't been already.

The night could end in a completely stupid way, with him having to make a lot of explanations. He and Rainer needed to go, and fast.

"Let's get out of here," Rainer said.

"Yeah, we should." Wulf turned dejectedly back to his dagger, still stuck in the oak. "I can't pull it out when I'm not in the dragon-vision, and I'm pretty sure that's done for tonight."

Rainer, too, gave the dagger a giant tug, then let go and stumbled back.

"Well, I sure as cold hell can't, either." He panted from the effort.

They had to go.

"We are so in the crap-hole," Wulf said, shaking his head glumly.

Rainer put a hand on Wulf's shoulder.

He pulled Wulf along, and the two soon lost themselves within the maze of the town streets.

CHAPTER EIGHT:
THE TRUTH

The night wasn't over yet for Wulf, although he wished more than anything that it could be. There was still the abatis to crawl under. He and Rainer slunk through the dirt and finally stood up near the castle wall.

Then, of course, there was the charcoal chute to deal with. He was already beginning to feel sore. The last thing he wanted to do was twist his way through that narrow opening. But there wasn't any other way into the castle apart from walking up to the front gate and banging on it to be let in.

So. Deal with it.

He pulled back the metal flap that covered the opening on the outside. From this side, it was just a bit too high for him to comfortably climb through.

"Give me a leg up, will you?" he asked Rainer.

Rainer laced his fingers together and made a step for Wulf.

He twisted his shoulders to squeeze through the narrow opening. That was usually the hardest part.

Then, bending his way through, Wulf heard a sound.

Great. There was somebody here.

It was a gasp. Somebody was frightened. Or surprised.

Wulf was still for a moment. Had he been seen?

Then he heard it again. A woman.

He quickly pulled himself back out and whispered to Rainer to be as quiet as possible when he came through. Then Wulf twisted his way back in, trying as best he could to follow his own advice and not make a sound.

He heard it again. A gasp and a quick breath. He pulled himself out of the chute and peeked over the charcoal barrel.

In the wan glow of the coals, Wulf saw something horrible.

His sister.

Ulla.

A man in the shadows had his hands around Ulla's throat!

Wulf jumped forward in a fury. He slammed into the man, pulling him away from his sister. Then he used the weight of his charge to take the man down to the shop floor. Wulf reached for his dagger to put to the man's throat and end his sorry life.

And found the empty spot at his waist. No dagger.

Blood and bones! Have to choke him instead.

He went for the man's throat with his hands. To his surprise, the other did not resist. In fact, he gazed serenely up at Wulf as Wulf wrapped his fingers around the other's throat. Then Wulf's grip slackened.

"Grer?"

"Hello, m'lord," the other croaked.

It was Grer. The castle smith. His friend.

"Blood and bones! What are you doing, little brother?" said his sister in a hoarse whisper. "Get off him. Get off *now!*"

"But, Ulla, I—"

Grer didn't say anything. He blinked up at Wulf with an

expression that seemed like it might be the beginning of a smile.

Is he going to *laugh* at me while I choke the life out him?

"Get off, curse it," said Ulla, tugging at Wulf. After a moment, Wulf let her pull him away. He sat on the floor next to Grer, felt something in his eyes. He realized he was crying. He wasn't sure why. It had been quite a night.

Grer slowly sat up, as if to test out his body to be sure it still operated after the choking session.

"Bones and blood," said a voice behind them all. Rainer emerged from the charcoal chute. "Imagine finding you two here." But Rainer did not seem very surprised at all.

"What . . . what the cold hell is going on?" Wulf asked, fighting down another sob.

"Settle yourself, brother, and I'll tell you," Ulla replied.

He had liked Grer, he really had. But for Grer to put his hands on his sister like that . . .

"I'll have to kill him," Wulf muttered. "I'm going to."

"Wulf, shut up," Ulla said, more loudly this time. "Let me speak."

Ulla was usually full of happiness and light. When she sounded this stern, she had something important to say. Wulf forced himself to be silent. He waited.

Ulla started to speak, then hesitated. She looked irritated, mad at having to figure out how to put into words something she didn't want to say at all.

Meanwhile, Rainer came over and helped Wulf to his feet. Wulf felt weak. He was glad of the aid.

Ulla. With a man she isn't supposed to be with, he thought. *Really* isn't. What will Father do? Sturmer knew, what with the state his father's mind was in these days. He might send Ulla away. No, he can't send her away! I don't want that!

Wulf loved his sister. The thought of losing her was too sad to even think about.

Grer, too, rose to his feet.

"I don't like standing around like this—like we just got caught at something," Ulla said.

"You did," mumbled Wulf.

"Can we sit?" Ulla said. She sniffed the air. "What is that horrible smell?"

Wulf was bewildered for a moment, then realized what his sister was talking about.

Me. And Rainer.

"Uh, we might have stumbled into a dead mule in the dark," he said. "You don't want to know any more than that."

"No, I really don't." Ulla looked around, then went to the shop anvil. She leaned against it. "Please, just sit, Wulf."

"No." Instead, he stalked to the banked coals of the forge and warmed his hands over them, his back partially turned toward his sister.

Grer got up and went to join Ulla by the anvil. He was a tall, rangy man. Wulf noticed Grer's hand touching his sister's arm. Even that sight made him mad.

Rainer, meanwhile, found a stump to sit on. He did not look at Ulla and Grer, but gazed at his fingernails.

"I'm sorry to surprise you this way, Wulf," Ulla began.

"Surprise me?" Wulf said with a snort. "Amaze me is more like it. You know what the alliance with Sandhaven means."

"Yes," Ulla said. "Other things matter, too."

"Other things? Sandhaven has been demanding insane toll taxes. They're threatening to cut us off. They control our access to the *sea*, Ulla. What other things?"

Ulla's forlorn look returned. "Little brother, you are apparently the last to know," she continued, "except for Father, of course. Mother—well, I think she suspects."

"Suspects what?"

"Grer and I. We're in love."

"Love? *Love!*" Wulf turned imploringly toward his sister. "But Ulla, he's . . . he's *the smith.*"

Ulla sighed. "You have a firm grasp of the obvious, Wulf."

"You *can't* be in love with him. That's not what we do. Marriage isn't like that for people like us."

Grer snorted. "People like *us*? Listen at the young lord. And haven't I seen you mooning after a certain elf more than a little?"

"You leave her out of it," Wulf said. "She's older than you."

"Be that as it may, m'lord Wulf, I'm as much of a *person* as you are," said Grer. "I think you know that. I hope you do, or I've fully mistook you." The tension went out of the smith, and Grer shook his head sadly. "Anyhow, if you doubt I'm a person, rip me open and see for yourself. At this point, I might even welcome it."

"What do you think we were doing when you poked out of . . . wherever it was you came from?" said Ulla.

"Aye, the charcoal chute," Grer put in. "I should've known there would be trouble when I left it unlatched at curfew. But I thought your brother'd be gallivanting about the town. He's done that before and not been back till dawn. We'd be gone."

Grer stepped over to the chute and moved a large hook through an iron ring to latch the charcoal chute shut. The hook was so large and heavy that it would have been difficult for both Wulf and Rainer together to lift it, but Grer did it one-handed. He turned back to find an annoyed Ulla staring him down.

"You gave him a way to *sneak out* of the castle!" she said. "Grer, I'm surprised at you."

"If I didn't, he'd find another way to do it," Grer replied evenly, and returned to her side. "And it might be a shade more dangerous way, at that. The sewer below the floor might work, for instance. You want to see Lord Wulf crawling through *that*?"

"He smells like that's exactly what he did."

Grer smiled. "Aw, I could see the pining mood was upon the boy and there was no fighting it for him. Way I figure, he's found some speakeasy pub in town that'll let him drown his sorrows over the Lady Saeunn."

"Shut up," Wulf mumbled.

"Still, what if something had happened?"

"Something *did* happen," Wulf said. "I came back here and found him *groping* you."

Ulla laughed. "It was more like *me* groping *him*, little brother. And him trying his best to fend me off."

"I've told you before, Ulla, we mustn't go further if we're to have even a thin reed's worth of a chance together," Grer said earnestly.

"But you *don't*," said Wulf. He turned from the forge coals to face them head-on. "You'll *never* be together."

Grer shook his head. "Never's a long time, lad. I'll bet the iron thinks it will *never* come out of the ore, but one day it does and I beat it into a sword."

Wulf turned to his sister.

"What about Prince Gunnar?" he asked. "The man came from Krehennest to propose to you, Ulla. They'll drop the tolls if you two get married. Plus, they have to help us hold the balance with the Romans or they'll try to take the north again."

"Listen to you, a politician already," said Ulla. "Even more than Otto, and that's saying something."

"Just like *you* when you're thinking straight," Wulf put in. "You're a von Dunstig."

"So I believed," Ulla said, and gazed up at Grer with a smile. "But things happen."

"Things? Like losing half the mark's trade?"

Ulla sighed, turned her gaze back to Wulf. "Gunnar is a problem," Ulla said. "I don't think anyone ever said no to him before."

"So *you're* planning to be the first?"

"What do you expect, Wulf?" said his sister. "He's a brute. Those indentureds in Krehennest—I can't bear it. And you know what they did to the Tier. Massacres, Wulf. Extermination."

"The Tier and otherfolk are welcome in Shenandoah. What else can we do? We need Sandhaven as an ally."

Ulla shook her head. "Yes. But the truth is that the thought of Gunnar's hands on me makes me shudder."

It was too much to take in at once. His sister did not just have no feelings for Prince Gunnar, she totally *hated* him.

And she was in love with a tradesman.

A baker or a brewer? Nope. A soot-covered smith.

The smith and the duchess. It sounded like one of Ravenelle's romance stories.

Wulf held out his arms to Ulla, begging, hoping, for an answer. "Ulla! What are we going to do?"

"I don't know," she said. She crossed her arms.

"*That's* why Grani was out," he said. "You let her out when you came here."

"The little vixen slipped between my legs when I was . . . making my way out the maid's door."

"The maid's door? Do you mean to tell me the *servants* are in on this, too?"

"No. I can't tell you any more without betraying someone," Ulla replied unhappily. "But I have to see Grer *somehow.*"

Grer unfolded Ulla's crossed arms and took her hand. The gesture upset Wulf more than any of the words that had passed between the two.

It was tender. It was caring.

It was totally wrong for a smith to lay his hands on a high-born lady.

"It's just . . . I . . ."

Ulla shushed him. "And where did *you* go, anyway?" she asked.

Wulf looked at Rainer, miserable.

"It's my fault, Lady Ulla," Rainer said, looking up. "Some boys from town were pushing us around today. They said they could beat us anytime anywhere, and we went out to meet them."

"That right?" said Grer. He had a skeptical look on his face. "And is that where Lord Wulf and you have gone on your nights out for the last few weeks, Mr. Stope?"

Rainer gulped, caught out in the lie. "All I can say is that we got into a scuffle in Allfather Square. Wulf kind of, well, rammed his dagger into the old tree there, too. It got stuck tight."

"Oh dear. Are daggers really so easy to tell apart?" Ulla said, striking at the most immediate part of the problem, as she always did. "They all look alike to me."

"That was one of mine, if it's the blade I'm thinking of," Grer said.

"It is," said Wulf.

"People will know it belongs to a rich man," Grer mused. "Maybe it's beat up too much to see my maker's mark . . ."

Rainer shrugged. "Yeah. Maybe."

"Oh," Ulla replied. "That's not good."

"There weren't any other boys," Wulf suddenly said. He hated that he'd caused Rainer to lie. He also hated the actual truth, but he had to tell it—at least part of it—if for no other reason than Grer had already guessed something was wrong with their story. "It was just me and Rainer. No one else. I was answering a dragon-call. Ulla knows what that is, even if you don't, Grer."

"That's not possible," Ulla said.

"Like it's not possible you are in love with a smith?"

Ulla's surprised expression became thoughtful.

"This is *good* news, really. Otto and I have worried . . . We thought the dragon-call might have passed out of the family. He has been waiting for it to happen, and it just hasn't."

"It will," Wulf said. "I know it will. This thing happening to me has got to be some kind of . . . mistake."

"All right, Wulf," Ulla said with a calmer voice. "Tell me the rest."

"The Olden Oak is a gateway," Wulf continued. "I was *in* the dragon-dream, Ulla. You know that's not supposed to happen. I saw . . . was shown the Dragon Hammer. And then we had a fight with a draugar and it's all messed up and I don't know what to do . . ."

His voice trailed off. Everybody was quiet for a moment.

Ulla finally broke the silence. "I don't understand the rest, but I do know about the dragon-bond. That *is* going to be a problem," she said. "More than any lost dagger." She touched her hand to her chin, considering.

"No, it's not," said Wulf. "I'm not going to let it. There is no reason anybody needs to know."

His sister smiled. It was a sad and knowing expression. "Yes, of course you won't," she said. She reached out and put both hands on Grer's now. "So—we each have our secret. You will keep mine and I will keep yours, little brother."

"Who would I tell?" said Wulf. "Seems like everybody but Father and Prince Gunnar knows about you and Grer anyway."

"A draugar?" Grer said, rubbing his chin. "Are you sure?"

"Wulf is sure," Rainer replied. "He read about them in . . . what was it?"

"*Henli's Saga*," Wulf muttered.

"And you came back alive?"

"Rainer killed it," Wulf said.

"Rainer killed a *draugar*?" Grer asked.

"I didn't," Rainer said. "It just kind of disappeared."

"After you stabbed it with its own arrows and sword," Wulf put in.

Grer looked at Rainer, who nodded and shrugged, as if he did that kind of thing all the time.

"This is very interesting." Grer shook his head. "I want to hear a *lot* more about this, boys. Tomorrow."

Rainer stirred. "Lady Ulla, I should get your brother and myself to bed now," he said.

"Yes. How will you get into the castle?"

"Wulf's got a secret way," Rainer answered with the slightest grin. "And I've got climbing to do."

"I know you think you can climb anything, Rainer, but you must be very careful," Ulla said.

"I promise."

"And both of you take a bath," Ulla said.

Rainer rose and made a small bow toward her. "M'lady."

Suddenly, the charcoal chute clattered as if someone were shaking it. The great hook rattled in its latching ring, but did not come out.

"What the cold hell was that?" Grer said. "I must've pulled it shut unevenly or something."

"Maybe," Wulf murmured. He stared at the chute, dreading to see it rattle again. But nothing happened.

Rainer touched his shoulder and broke him out of his trance. "Come on, it was the wind," he said. "You need sleep. So do I."

Wulf allowed himself to be turned away from the charcoal chute. But as he left the smith's shop, he could swear he heard the faintest whisper from nowhere, from everywhere.

"Thou know'st," said the whisper.

No one else seemed to notice but him. So maybe it was his imagination.

Maybe.

Chapter Nine:
The Trance

Saeunn stood by the window of her bedchamber staring up into the sky. It was still dark, but there was the faintest trace of dawn on the eastern horizon. The window was open and a chilly wind was blowing. Her white cotton curtains billowed around her. Her blonde hair was loosened from her braids. It whipped about. Saeunn didn't pay it any mind.

Ulla had been right. She had only meant to glance out and say good night to the moon. Instead, she'd gotten awestruck by the moonlight, and by the stars twinkling.

Saeunn shivered. She'd stood in the same spot for hours feeling the delicate weight of moonbeams on her skin. She had been listening to the stars sing the Dragon Song.

Tonight there was unrest. The dragons were having troubled dreams, and the song was not calming them very well. The stars did not seem to know *why* this was happening. Or if they did, it was something they could not say to her because she was so young. But she did catch one part of the song. It was the part that had frightened her since she was a very young elfling.

Hidden in the dragon clutch an ancient evil spirit lurks.
Made of emptiness, it stays wherever dragon life is slain.
It would steal the dragon thunder,
*   it would kill them as they slumber.*

Frustrating not to understand why they sang this.

But then there was the calm moon, splashing her light to the Earth.

Planets, comets, Sun and Moon,
*   keep the dragons' world in tune.*

Standing in the shower of moonlight, Saeunn thought about her future.

There was the Plan. The hundred-year plan that every elf child of Amberstone was supposed to follow. Visit the other elf-kin in the Old Countries. Learn their skills. Healing. Mind-speaking. Spend days, even years, talking with your star. Listen to the Dragon Song and try and try to understand how it holds the world together. Then, when you are ready, truly ready, return home and stare into the giant eye of your dragon, the Drake of Amberstone.

You were supposed to find your purpose in life there.

So far, she had followed the Plan exactly. She'd spent years learning healing in the Old Countries. She'd lived with the Smoke Elves and studied their mind-speak and tree-talk. Now she was in the Mark of Shenandoah on a diplomatic mission. Her family had trusted her to carry it out.

She wanted to. She liked doing things well. She wasn't particularly proud of that fact, because most things came naturally to her and you couldn't really be proud of just *having* a talent. She did feel like she was doing a good thing when she was using the talents that the stars gave her in the best way she could.

And so far she had done what she was supposed to here in Raukenrose. She'd been a true elfling when she'd first come. She'd had the appearance of a human child of perhaps six. The following years had been time for inner growth as well as outer—the elven version of puberty. Using the healing skills and bodily understanding she'd picked up from the Old Country elves, over the past ten years she had let herself mature into a teenager in appearance to match her changing personality.

She'd also studied the ways of men. She'd learned how human children behaved, and what humans thought of elves. She'd gotten to know the country and the people very well.

Why was she feeling uneasy tonight?

Her window faced southwest, and this morning the moon was setting to the south, so that Saeunn had a full view of it. Saeunn closed her eyes and felt the last moonbeams reach her before it sank under the horizon. As soon as the half moon disappeared, its spell on her was broken.

Saeunn sighed. She would sleep now. She didn't absolutely have to, because being in a moon trance was almost as good as sleep. But she had a full day ahead of her.

Soon it would be time for her to leave Raukenrose. She did want to get back to Amberstone Valley, her birthplace. It was a place where parts of the living, dreaming dragon stuck out through the surface of the Earth. In Amberstone Valley, the ground itself churned with dragon heat. Muddy fountains there seethed with sulfurous dragon breath. Boiling water touched by dragon fire erupted in geysers into the sky. Even the river that formed the valley steamed.

In Amberstone Valley, you could gaze into the half-open eye of a dreaming dragon.

Dragons sang the Earth alive,
and all that breathes beneath the skies.

Every soul born slave or queen
  comes from the stuff of dragon dreams.

At the same time, she didn't want to leave Shenandoah.

She had friends here—good friends, for the first time in her life. She cared deeply about her Raukenrose family. She had brothers and sisters of her own, but they were much older. Her nearest sister, Bealle, was one hundred fifty years Saeunn's senior. She loved Bealle, but the two of them didn't really have very much in common other than being related.

But the von Dunstigs were human, and they would all be dead in a hundred years. She would live on. Her parents had warned her to stay away from emotional ties with humans.

Some elves were really good at that kind of detachment. She wasn't.

The more she came to understand humans and . . . well, whatever Ravenelle was, with her body given over to the Roman mold . . . the more she *liked* how hot these mortals' feelings could be. Each of them was like a raging fire inside.

Elves might have starlight for souls, but the souls of men were bits of the soul of a dragon.

She was as drawn to that inner fire as much as she was to the moonlight.

Especially Wulf.

The future was always leaking into the present for elves. When she got back to Amberstone she could ask the elders why her feelings had developed so strongly for humans. That was what the elder elves were for. Advice. Understanding. Peace.

When she got back to Amberstone, she would have a lot to ask the elders.

If I get back to Amberstone, she thought.

She shivered.

Why is it so cold in here?

As if in answer, a line from an ancient elven verse Saeunn knew suddenly flowed into her mind.

Karltundelkan nalith Ebereth Serian.

It was a piece of the old tale of the elf maiden who had given away her star to raise her lover from the dead. There was an Old High Kaltish translation of the phrase that Saeunn knew.

Then darkly fell Amberly Reizend.

She shivered again.

My star? Were you singing to me?

Yes, my child, my own.

Amberly Reizend was an elf woman who had done what many considered to be impossible. She had transferred her star—which was an elf's soul—to her lover, who had succumbed to one of the few diseases that could kill an elf. Then she died.

The swan at the dawn
With its heartbroken call
Is the echo of Amberly Reizend

The dim moonlight seemed to pool in swirls of light and darkness before her eyes. Saeunn could see it now: turmoil gathering in her future. But she couldn't see past it.

My star, my own, why do you sing this song?

Her star didn't reply for a very long time. Finally she spoke. Her only words were the same lines from the verse, in Saelith, the language of the elves.

Karltundelkan nalith Ebereth Serian.

As suddenly as it had begun, Saeunn's shivering stopped. The Sun, still below the eastern horizon, brightened the sky. But the words from the poem echoed in Saeunn's mind. Was it a warning, a prophesy? Or just a pretty song? *Then darkly fell Amberly Reizend.*

PART TWO

PART TWO

CHAPTER TEN:
THE MASTER

Wulf woke up lying on the floor of his bedchamber wrapped in a blanket. Getting to sleep had not been a problem last night after his return. He'd been completely exhausted. He'd stripped off the fustian cloak and thrown it in a bundle in a corner. The dead smell had still lingered, so he'd tossed the rest of his clothes in the pile, too. Then, not wanting to ruin his down mattress by the stink he still carried on his skin, he'd stripped off a blanket, wrapped himself up in that, and fallen asleep on a bearskin rug near the fireplace.

He'd dropped off instantly. But when he opened his eyes to the morning light, it all came back to him full force. The land-bond where there should have been only the slightest feeling. His sister's being with, of all people, his friend Grer, the smith.

The draugar attack.

It mixed in his head like some horrible pudding until he groaned trying to keep it straight.

First things first. He needed to get the stink of the dark thing completely off him. Tomorrow was the usual bath day for the week, so there would be no tubs ready. It would have to be a cat bath or nothing.

As if in answer to his desire, Grim came in with a half-barrel urn of hot water for Wulf's washing bowl. The faun was really strong, even though he didn't look that muscular at first glance. Wulf figured that it was in the way Grim used his backward shaped legs to lift. It gave him perfect balance, and he could keep the weight on his haunches and not on his arms that way. The servant set the filled washbasin down on the rug beside Wulf. As usual, Grim didn't utter a word.

Wulf looked around. His clothes from the night before were gone, probably taken away by Grim while he still slept. Grim had lit the fire as well. When Wulf peeled himself from the blanket, his room was warm.

Grim went to stand silently beside the door. Wulf sat up cross-legged on the bearskin rug. He soaped up and bathed with a sponge of dry peat moss, trying to keep the run-off in the washbowl, but not caring if he slopped water all over the floor in the process. He needed to get *clean*.

He asked for more water from Grim, and dunked his head entirely before scrubbing down and rinsing once again.

Wulf wrapped himself in a newly washed blanket and went to change into the clothes that Grim had laid out for him on the bed.

Before Wulf changed, he pulled the blanket around his shoulders. He took a long drink from a cup of the coffee Grim had set on the side table. Perfect. Grim had also brought in a glass of blackberry juice, and Wulf downed it. He hadn't realized how thirsty he was. He got dressed in light gray pants and a white linen shirt. Over this he wore a green and gray wool surcoat, which was a sleeveless vest that fell about to the middle of his calves.

When he was done, he stood straight and let Grim tidy up his rumpled appearance. The faun brought the surcoat front together and tied on Wulf's belt. Wulf's hair was beginning to dry, and the faun brought him a whalebone comb to run through it.

Grim opened the window shutters. Through the glass, Wulf could see that it was well past sunrise. The bell in Allfather Cathedral must have rung the morning bell tolls, dammern and melken. They had hadn't woken him up. Today was Sturmersday, which meant he'd missed going out with his father. His father went either hunting or falconing on Sturmersdays, but early. Today it was falconing. He'd be out with the birds till noon. Wulf had a standing invitation to skip morning lessons and come along. Wulf's father, Duke Otto, believed that bringing his children on hunts was as important as anything the lore masters had to teach them.

I could have gotten out of morning lessons, Wulf thought. Curse it to blood and bones.

Now he would have to explain his absence to the tutor.

He was starving. Grim came to the rescue again with breakfast on a large platter, which he put on Wulf's desk. Wulf sat down at his chair to eat, while Grim knelt and pulled on Wulf's wool socks and boots. Breakfast was two eggs over easy, their yolks running as Wulf liked them. There was fresh-baked bread to sop with, along with three links of buffalo sausage and a bowl of grits. Wulf shoved all of it down, barely taking time to chew. He drank two more cups of coffee to top it off.

Wulf felt like a new man when he was done—that is, until he saw his reflection in the looking glass inside his wardrobe door. His eyes had dark circles under them. There were a couple of patches of charcoal dust left on his forehead. Grim, standing nearby, handed Wulf a damp cloth without having to be asked, and Wulf rubbed the smudges off.

Rainer raised his eyebrow in greeting when Wulf came into the classroom. First things first. Wulf excused himself to the tutor, Master Albrec Tolas. Tolas scowled at him, then nodded his acceptance of the apology. Wulf took a seat in a corner chair.

Albrec Tolas was a gnome. He was barely taller than a seven- or eight-year-old human. But he was not a child. He had the round features of his people, but you would never think of Tolas as chubby or slow. He kept himself fit with lots of exercise. Despite the reputation of gnomes for being pleasant, easygoing creatures, Tolas was downright ruthless as a teacher. In his classroom you learned—or else.

Wulf had found out about what that meant when Tolas, recognizing Wulf's gift for memorizing the sagas, had set him to work on the king of them all, *Andul's Saga*. It was Wulf's favorite. What Wulf liked most about the story was that it didn't have much magic in it. It *did* have lots of battles, sword fighting, poisoning, and drinking from skulls.

But there in *Andul's Saga,* near the very beginning, and for no reason Wulf could figure out, was a weird list of names. The skald, the teller of the saga, was supposed to recite these to get things going. This list was known as the "Roll Call of the Dwarves." Nobody was sure why it was there. But, for nearly a thousand years, the Roll Call had been stubbornly passed from storyteller to storyteller, memorized and re-memorized.

Wulf had figured he could skip the dwarves. Nope. After class one day, he'd gotten instructions to meet the tutor in the castle library afterward. Wulf remembered that his stomach had been grumbling—and he was going to miss midday meal.

The gnome was also the castle librarian. The library was filled with rune-covered scrolls in bins. On shelves were vellum codexes, and a few books made with papyrus pages. This was Tolas's office while at the castle. And this was where Wulf began to learn the Roll Call of the Dwarves.

Wulf and Tolas had sat down at an old oak table in the library. Tolas had Wulf spread his right hand out on the table. Tolas asked for Wulf's dagger—it was the same dagger that was now stuck in the oak tree at Allfather Square—and Wulf handed it over.

The gnome had then played mumblety-peg with Wulf's *fingers*. He started poking through the space between the fingers with the dagger point, going back and forth, back and forth, as fast as Wulf could call off the names of the dwarves. He'd stab into the wooden table between one of Wulf's fingers and then the next as Wulf called off the list he was supposed to have memorized from *Andul's*. When Wulf missed one or got one out of order, Tolas missed, too. He delivered a small but painful prick to the skin of a finger. It wasn't long before Wulf's fingers had little blood roses all over them.

Wulf had threatened to tell his father. Tolas had taken a puff from his pipe, then sat back and dared him to. This had shut Wulf up on the matter. Tolas had probably known it would. Wulf hated to ever appear to be whining around Duke Otto. He spread his hand back out on the table.

"So you want to continue, von Dunstig?" said Tolas. "Or should we just cut your fingers off now because you'll never get it?"

"I'll get it. Go on," Wulf had demanded. "The first one is Lori!"

"Good," the gnome said, and stabbed down expertly and powerfully between Wulf's thumb and forefinger. "Next?"

"Swert."

Pop, went the dagger between forefinger and long finger.

"Nim," Wulf said. "Slanhanker."

Pop. Pop.

"Fremdeb, Kor," Wulf said, even faster. Tolas did not miss a beat. The gnome was really *good* at this. "Those are the Five Hewers, masters of copper and bronze."

"Yes, now give me the shapers of arrow and spear."

"Gelbert, Knitbert, Shem, Sothi—"

Pop, pop, pop, pop went the dagger into the wood of the table.

"And . . . and, and, and . . ." Wulf tried to remember. The dagger hovered over his pinkie.

Egbert, Ilbert, Ulbert . . . no, no, no . . . something "bert" . . .

The dagger began to descend.

Not fair! I didn't get it wrong yet! I didn't get it . . .

The dwarf's name came to him.

"Unbert!"

Pop. The dagger struck precisely to the outside of his pinkie, missing it by a hair's breadth.

That had been two years ago. By now the Roll Call of the Dwarves was second nature to him, and Wulf was working on part three of *Andul's*. What was more, he used Tolas's knife trick on *himself* when he was having trouble with one of the saga lists.

Now Wulf sat through the lore lesson, which had something to do with famous northern cathedrals dedicated to both Sturmer and Regen. Normally this would have interested Wulf. There weren't many cathedrals for two divine beings at the same time. But today he was having trouble concentrating. Then thankfully he heard the midday bell ring from the cathedral. Wulf stood and begun to file out. When he was almost out the door, Tolas called him by name.

"Lord Wulfgang, stay a moment please." Tolas called him "Lord Wulfgang" when the cousins were around, "von Dunstig" when he was the only family member present.

Tolas said nothing else until the others had left. Wulf heard the boys' chatter ringing off the stone walls of the castle hall as they made their way toward the midday meal and a rest period before afternoon fight practice.

"Sir?" Wulf finally said.

The gnome hopped down from his box and went over to gather up several of the scrolls and *Masshoff's Codex of*

Cathedrals he'd taught from. Tolas always reshelved these materials carefully in the castle library after class. During class, though, he used them as if they were common and familiar objects.

"You look terrible, von Dunstig," said the gnome. "Are you sick?"

Wulf shook his head. "No, sir. I don't think so."

"How is the third section of *Andul's* coming?"

"Fine, sir," Wulf said.

"No doubt you were working on *Andul's*, and that's why you were late to my class."

Wulf felt his face blush. Tolas could always catch him off guard. Sometimes he wondered if gnomes could read thoughts. "No, sir. I overslept."

"I see." Tolas rolled a scroll neatly and loosely. He'd taught Wulf never to roll them too tightly, since that was bad for the sheepskin. He tied a leather strip around it to hold it in place.

Tolas was the size of a child, but you ignored him at your own peril. He was very good and very quick at whacking with a stick, for one thing. Koterbaum, the marshal of weapons, had asked *Tolas* for lessons in fighting with singlestick. The two practiced once a week together.

The gnome and the human weapons master were on friendly terms, even though both were about as opposite as could be in personality. Koterbaum was a good instructor, but he also wanted the boys he worked with to like him. Tolas didn't care whether his students liked him or hated his guts.

The gnome had on a gold and gray University of Raukenrose robe. He wore a purple shoulder covering. He also had on a striped black, white, and red sash under the shoulder covering that went down to his waist. All of these things meant that Tolas held a high position at the university. One of the university's highest ranked scholars was always given the honorary appointment as castle tutor. This person usually sent a student aide to do the actual teaching. Not Tolas. He took his appointment seriously and taught at the castle in the morning. In the afternoon and evening he was back at the university, where he was docent of law and lore, and a master of the library.

Tolas's feet stuck out from under the folds of the robe, and, like all his folk, they were covered with a mat of curly hair down to the tips of the toes. Bound to the sole of his foot was a strip of flat leather that was as thin as a piece of scroll parchment. This was as much of a shoe as the tutor wore. Wulf had heard Tolas more than once muttering about the "dictatorship of boots, imprisoning the toes."

Tolas set down the scroll he was rolling up and reached inside the front of his robe. From one of the many pockets in his robe he pulled out a clay pipe with a long stem. From another pocket, he took a tobacco pouch and a clump of dried willow sticks. He picked out one of these wands and handed it to Wulf. "Do me a favor, von Dunstig, and light this for me in the fire."

Wulf took the long stick to the fire and got a good coal burning on the end. When he returned, Tolas had loaded his pipe with tobacco and put the pouch away. Tolas accepted the burning stick, put it to the tobacco wad, and took a long drag on the stem of the pipe. He breathed out a couple of huge clouds of smoke until the tobacco was all the way lit in the bowl. After that, he took a long first puff, blew out the burning end of the stick, and pulled the pipe from his mouth. He handed the stick back to Wulf, who took it over and tossed it in the fire. He went back to stand in front of Tolas.

"A curious thing that may interest you, von Dunstig . . . I was walking over from my quarters at Ironkloppel this morning," said the gnome. "Now, as you may or may not know, the quickest path between here and there is through Allfather Square."

Uh oh.

"Now usually I enjoy my walk through the square. The oak is magnificent, a marvel of its kind. It is Eastern white oak, by the way. I estimate its age to be around four hundred years. Not the original Olden Oak, of course, but a remarkable tree nonetheless. Usually it is just myself and the oak tree in communion. But not this morning."

Tolas took another drag on his pipe, and breathed out. They both watched the trail of smoke as it rose.

"There was a crowd gathered around the oak this morning," he continued. "Naturally, I wanted to see what the excitement was about so I made my way through the crowd—nearly got stepped on a couple of times, let me tell you. I'm sure it was an accident." Tolas took his pipe from his mouth and frowned at the stem. "At least, pretty sure," he added darkly.

"What was it all about, Master Tolas?" Wulf asked.

"I'm coming to that," said the gnome. He carefully took the pipestem in his fingers and expertly broke off a section of the clay. This gave him a new mouthpiece. He did this whenever the taste of the pipestem got sour. He handed the used bit of pipestem to Wulf. "Take care of this on your way out, please, von Dunstig."

"Yes, Master Tolas."

Tolas pulled in and puffed out another cloud of smoke. He smiled. Evidently the stem now tasted better to him.

"As I was saying, I finally got to the front of the gathering—there were perhaps fifty people there, all told—and had a look at my friend the tree. And what do you think I saw?"

Tolas gazed up at Wulf as if he expected him to know the answer. And, since he *did*, Wulf almost blurted it out. But he managed to keep from doing that and answered, "I don't know, sir. What was it?"

"Someone had plunged a *dagger* into the Olden Oak."

"A dagger, sir?"

"That's right. And not just a little way in. All the way to the hilt."

"That would be . . . well, almost impossible to do, sir."

Tolas nodded. "And yet *not* impossible, because I saw it with my own eyes. Several of the older town boys were trying to pull it out, but no one had any luck with that. I suppose someone may eventually chisel it out, which will be bad for the tree, but probably not fatal. I guess my old friend the tree has seen worse." Tolas took a puff. "Much worse," he added.

"I'd hate to see the tree harmed, sir," said Wulf. "Will that be all, sir?"

Tolas nodded. "I recommend you get some rest directly after your afternoon practice," he said. "You look terrible, like you're coming down with something."

Wulf nodded. "Yes, sir. I'll do that." Then he remembered. "But Rainer has a match, and I'm going to be his second."

"Not the best day for it, perhaps. Mr. Stope didn't look so well, either."

Wulf shrugged. "You know Rainer. He won't back out."

Tolas nodded. Wulf turned to go and had taken a step when Tolas called him up short.

"Oh, von Dunstig?"

"Sir?"

"Speaking of daggers, where is *yours*?" Tolas pointed his pipestem toward Wulf's belt. "You usually wear it attached to a dirk frog strap there on your belt, do you not?"

"I do, sir," Wulf answered. Now he really was flushed, and about to break out into a sweat—he could feel it coming on. He scratched his chin nervously. "I must have forgotten to bring it this morning. I overslept and was in a big hurry to get here."

Tolas nodded. "And your servant didn't remind you?" he said. "Very unusual, because your man—I should say your faun—is quite competent, I hear."

"Yes, sir. Grim's the best, sir."

Tolas eyed him for a moment.

Here it comes, Wulf thought.

But then the gnome shook his head and went back to rolling a scroll. "Good day, von Dunstig."

"Good day, Master Tolas."

Finally he was out the door and away. Rainer met him in the hall.

"What did he want?"

"He says he saw a big crowd around the Olden Oak this morning," Wulf answered. "They were looking at the dagger."

"Great," said Rainer. "So much for nobody noticing it." Rainer sniffed the air. "Did you manage to take a bath?"

"Yeah. You?"

"In the horse trough by the stables," he replied.

"I'd hate to be the horse that had to drink *that* water," Wulf said.

Rainer nodded his head. "What about the draugar last night?"

Wulf frowned. "I think you killed it." He wished he sounded more convincing than he did.

"Wulf, that's the weirdest thing I've ever seen."

They turned and made their way toward the dining hall where the castle children were usually served a midday meal.

"I can't think straight right now," Wulf said. "The draugar, and Grer, and the rest. I don't know."

Rainer slapped Wulf on the shoulder and grinned. "We'll figure it out. Right now, I'm going to play a round of Hang the Fool." This was Rainer's favorite card game. "The l'Obac Terror thinks she can beat me again, but I'm going to crush her and break her spirit."

"Uh-huh."

The l'Obac Terror was Ravenelle Archambeault. Like Rainer, she was a castle fosterling, but under very different conditions. Ravenelle was a war hostage. Her staying in Raukenrose was a pledge of truce from Vall l'Obac, the country that was on the border of Shenandoah to the south.

Ravenelle was not happy to be in the castle. She was not happy to be in Raukenrose or Shenandoah. She could be very mean about it, too. But at the same time, Wulf couldn't help liking her. She had an incredible imagination. Plus, they were drawn together because they were both readers. Ravenelle's rooms were filled with actual books, sent up from the Roman colony by her very rich family. They were all written in Tiberian. Ravenelle read it fluently. Wulf could read it, but only slowly and with a dictionary nearby.

Most of Ravenelle's books were popular in the south. He'd read a few. Ravenelle called them "heartbreaking tales of ardor and terror." They usually involved a misunderstood heroine, often a governess or disregarded princess, and some kind of brooding hero. He was always royalty, but had fallen on hard times. They took place in crumbling old manor houses overgrown with roses and castles full of ghosts. The books frequently ended with both lovers dying in some weird but fitting way.

He remembered one of them where the governess was rushing to meet her lover after receiving an urgent message from him. She believed he had finally overcome his father's objection to their marriage. She pushed the horse hitched to her one-horse carriage too hard, and when the carriage bounced, her long hair had gotten tangled in a wagon wheel. This broke her neck. Her lover, on the other had, had found out just what his father's opposition had been about. The governess was actually the hero's half-sister. When he found out his lover—and sister, yuck!—was dead, he had died of shock and a shattered heart.

Wulf knew Ravenelle wanted to be *in* one of those stories and half the time imagined she was.

He sighed. "Maybe I'll go take a nap. There's nothing like Ravenelle to make a day even more complicated."

"Yeah, on second thought, let's avoid her," Rainer said. Wulf knew Rainer would never do this. Ravenelle was their friend, despite her mean temper. The odd ones in the group of castle children tended to stick together. "She's the only one around here who can play me a decent game of cards, though." He nudged Wulf. "Come on," he said. "You know *she'll* be there. She and Ravenelle are tight as barrels these days."

Saeunn would be there. Saeunn Amberstone.

The truth was that Wulf was in love with her. Rainer knew it. Wulf knew it.

And the hard and painful certainty was that all Saeunn would ever feel for Wulf—no, *could* ever feel—was pity.

Maybe he was stuck inside one of Ravenelle's romances himself.

Chapter Eleven:
The Match

Hang the Fool was a card game with lots of strategy and bluffing. That was why Rainer liked it. It also had cutthroat action. You had to make quick decisions. You had to either keep a card or throw it down in a rush before the other player could take the trick. Wulf figured this was why Ravenelle was good at it.

You bid on how many tricks you thought you'd win and whether you could "hang the fool" and take all the discards. When you played with two people, the idea was to build up a valuable middle tower of cards between both players until somebody went on the attack to claim them all. Then the game turned into all-out card war.

They set up a card table in a corner of the dining hall after the midday meal was served. The table was below a window of red and blue stained glass. It was also in Wulf's favorite spot near the huge fireplace. Logs the size of tree trunks burned in the fire on cold autumn days.

Rainer was right. She was here.

Saeunn sat nearby. She didn't join the game, but put on a

puppet show with a woman's stocking that had holes in the toe for Wulf's other sister, the youngest von Dunstig, Anya, who was eight. Saeunn had two fingers stuck out through the holes and was pretending they were the antlers of a deer that kept getting caught on things. Anya thought this was very funny.

Wulf quickly lost interest in the flow of the Hang the Fool game between Rainer and Ravenelle. He pretended to laugh with Anya at Saeunn's puppet drama, but really he was taking the chance to gaze at Saeunn herself.

Saeunn was a castle fosterling, like Rainer and Ravenelle. Her presence was a sign of the alliance between Duke Otto and Saeunn's folk, the elves of Amberstone Valley. "Elf" was the Kaltish word for Saeunn's people. It was not one they used themselves. They called themselves "Saelith," which meant "star-born." Wulf had learned a little of Saeunn's language—mainly so he could have her as a tutor.

Under her long, unbound blonde hair, Saeunn's ears were pointed, and her eyes were slightly slanted. They were ice blue. She looked about sixteen or seventeen. She was the most beautiful thing that Wulf had ever seen. The problem was, she *looked* like a teenager, and, for an elf, she was still considered a teenager. But Saeunn was actually sixty-two years old.

"Full tower!" Rainer said after examining two new cards he had picked up. "I'm coming for you!"

Wulf tore his gaze from Saeunn and returned his attention to the game.

Rainer played a castle and a moat, two of the cards in the game deck.

"Really? You *meant* to do that?" asked Ravenelle.

"Sure did," Rainer replied with a grin—a grin that quickly fell into a frown as Ravenelle played card after card on top of his two, literally crushing his hand under hers with better cards. He groaned as Ravenelle scooped up the tower and added it to her pile of already-won tricks.

"You thought you could beat me?" she asked him.

"I have before, m'lady," Rainer replied moodily.

"You've only got a year left to come out ahead, Stope," she said, tapping her growing set of tricks. "Better start winning." Ravenelle liked to use Rainer's last name. It was maybe a ploy to remind him of his commoner origin, Wulf figured. He couldn't help thinking that Rainer enjoyed that she called him that, though. The two had an odd relationship. They were friends who were destined to become enemies one day.

Ravenelle Archambeault lived in the mark as a kind of royal prisoner. Twelve years ago, the army of Shenandoah had defeated Vall l'Obac at the Battle of Montserrat.

This ended the Little War. It was called "little" because the allies of Shenandoah and the Holy Roman Empire, to which Vall l'Obac belonged, had stayed out of the fighting.

Wulf had barely been born at the time of the Vall l'Obac surrender. Part of the peace treaty was an agreement that the daughter of Queen Valentine and Crown Prince Piet would be raised in Raukenrose. She would not be allowed to return to Vall l'Obac until she turned seventeen, although her mother, father, and other family members were allowed to visit once a year.

That daughter was Ravenelle.

Ravenelle constantly reminded everyone that she was not in Raukenrose of her own free will. She would be moving back home to Montserrat the moment she turned seventeen. Ravenelle considered herself Roman, not Kalte like Wulf, Rainer, and everyone else in Shenandoah. Her religion was Talaia. She got one whole day to herself a week for ceremonies with her priest. Ravenelle owned slaves, and she was allowed to keep three of them in Raukenrose, even though slavery was outlawed in the mark. She called them bloodservants.

Ravenelle was *also* a von Dunstig. Her grandmother, Crown Prince Piet's mother, was Wulf's great-aunt Sybille von Dunstig, who had married into the Vall l'Obac Archambeaults. This made Ravenelle and Wulf third cousins.

It was complicated.

Ravenelle's hair was a tangle of coal black curls that she held in place with at least a dozen hairpins and, usually, a scarf of crimson or black. Her eyes were brown, and her skin was brown from her Affric ancestry. She dressed like a woman of the south as well. Today she was wearing a red silk dress with a black brocade of lace over it. What was more, the dress was held together in the back not with clasps or brooches like Kalte girls and women used but with something almost entirely missing on Kalteland clothing.

Buttons.

"Are you watching the match?" Rainer asked her. "It's Hlafnest again. I'm on ax and he's got sword."

Ravenelle smiled wickedly, and looked over at Saeunn. "We women might happen to look out from the balcony during the boys' afternoon exercises if we take a notion."

Rainer gathered up the cards to put away. Wulf knew Rainer liked for Ravenelle to watch him fight, especially on days he lost to her in a Hang the Fool game.

"It will be interesting to see Hlafnest von Blau cut to pieces. One less knight of the mark to trouble with."

"I won't be cutting him to pieces," said Rainer. "I thought I'd just knock him on his butt a few times." Rainer shrugged. "Hlafnest is good. He'll give me a fight."

"Of course we'll watch," Saeunn replied quietly. "The other girls have been talking about the match all week." Saeunn wriggled her fingers, and Anya giggled. "I hear that there have even been bets placed. Many silver thalers will be changing hands today."

"Really?" said Rainer. "And did you bet on someone, m'lady?"

"No," Saeunn replied. "But it was interesting to see

who did." Saeunn glanced over at Ravenelle. "Wasn't it, Ravenelle?"

"They're all betting against you, Stope," Ravenelle said.

"That's stupid," Wulf put in. "Everybody knows how good Rainer is with an ax."

"I guess they really believe highborn blood will win in the end. But that's rather irrelevant considering it is *Kalte* highborn blood," Ravenelle replied. "I imagine the girls also believe Koterbaum will fix the match for Hlafnest von Blau."

"He won't," Wulf said. "Koterbaum's a suck-up, but he's fair."

She turned to Wulf and smiled sweetly. "Yes. So I placed a thousand thaler wager on Stope, of course."

"A *thousand*?" Wulf said. That was a lot of silver.

"Truthfully, I don't much care whether Stope wins or gets his brains bashed out."

Wulf knew she did care. She was lying to get a rise out of Rainer. This was practically impossible, though. Rainer knew Ravenelle's ways too well.

"It's the principle of the thing. I never bet on Kalte nobility," Ravenelle continued. She gave Wulf an evil smile. "I'm very much afraid that sooner or later, you're all going to be losers."

Wulf was exhausted by the end of afternoon practice. The sun was blazing. Even though it was late fall, there was no way to stay cool when you were dressed in two stone of armor and had an iron bucket on your head.

He'd taken far more whacks than he'd given today. This nine weeks was short sword for him, so at least he hadn't had to pull around a wooden mockup of a long sword. In two weeks, the schedule would swing around to hammer and ax. Rainer, being a year older, was in with the older boys working on broadsword.

He's going to be pretty tired, Wulf thought. And then he still has to fight his match.

Wulf's small shield, his buckler, felt like a lead weight on his arm. He made his way to get a drink of water and then got back to practice.

Forms and charges came first. This meant whacking on a partner using a set of moves both you and he already knew. The charges you made on a battering pole. On his first charge, Wulf missed the pole entirely. This was only the latest of the mistakes he'd been making all afternoon.

"You're only good for sparring fodder, today, m'lord," Koterbaum told him. "Go mix it up with the ten and elevens for half pikes, why don't you."

Wulf nodded and headed over to the other side of the yard to tutor the younger boys.

This change didn't get Wulf out of the final exercise of the day, maneuvers. He trailed behind as the gang of boys climbed walls, walked logs, and crawled on their bellies under a small section of abatis. From bell to bell, practice took a three-watch. After that were the matches, which lasted till dinner bell.

Koterbaum could assign match partners, but usually the older boys called each other out. Sometimes this was because they had a score to settle. Hlafnest and Rainer didn't have any particular gripe. Hlafnest just didn't like that a commoner such as Rainer was allowed to act above his station. He'd called Rainer out a week ago over kicking dust onto his boots. Something like that. Wulf couldn't remember the supposed offence.

Rainer, who never backed down, accepted. So today Hlafnest von Blau and Rainer Stope were the main attraction.

The fights were held in the castle bailey, and took up a good portion of the center. This was the same bailey that Wulf and Rainer had carefully skirted around the night before. The match area was marked with a circle of white lime. Stepping or falling over the lime meant you lost a point. Getting knocked down and dominated meant you lost a point. Three points against you and you lost the match.

In matches, the weapons were real. Blunted, but real. You fought in armor.

One of the younger boys served as squire and helped Rainer arm up in a corner of the bailey yard. Rainer had for torso protection his favorite hauberk underneath. This chainmail shirt was made with the six-hand ring weave he preferred. The mail shirt was belted and hung down over his thigh. On top of the hauberk, he wore a cuirass, a plate armor breast and back plate. He wore steel cuisses on his thighs. Greaves were attached to his shins, and these came down to cover the upper part of his armored shoes. The shoes were steel plate sewn onto leather. Steel brassarts covered his upper arms, vambraces covered his lower arms. On both hands, he wore gauntlets covered with mail sewed onto leather. These came most of the way up his forearms for protection there.

With the squire's help, he put on a wool arming cap. He pulled up his hauberk cowl over the cap. Finally, over both of these, he wore a helmet of battered iron. The helmet was not a full steel casing with a bevor over his face. Rainer hated fighting when he could barely see. The helm came with a face protector called a grima hinged onto the front of the helm that covered eyes, nose, and upper cheekbones.

You were supposed to avoid blows to the head in match combat. Wulf knew that was easier said than done, even when you were trying.

Rainer's buckler was oak. Rainer had no family crest. Instead, there was a red crow in profile painted on it. This was the symbol of Kohlsted, the township Rainer came from.

Wulf had on a mail shirt, and had a helm and scabbarded sword nearby as well. On the off chance Rainer had to bow out of the match, Wulf might have to fight. Rainer always chose Wulf as his second.

There was a short ritual before the match with each of the fighters' seconds meeting in the center of the limed circle to go over the ground rules with Marshal Koterbaum. Wulf plopped on his helmet indifferently and went forward to listen to Koterbaum lay out the basics yet again.

"No eye stabbing. No neck hewing. No stepping on feet."

Wulf still felt a bit woozy from the day's exercise, and at first didn't notice Hlafnest's second approach. Then a shadow fell over Wulf's face. It was a man nearly two hands taller than Wulf, and much broader in the shoulders. He was dressed in full armor, not in mail only, as Wulf was.

Wulf did not recognize the man until he reached the center of the combat circle and took off his helm. The man smiled.

It was Prince Gunnar of Sandhaven.

"You're . . ." Prince Gunnar considered Wulf with a quizzical expression. "One of the von Dunstigs, aren't you?"

"I am, Prince Gunnar," Wulf replied. He did not volunteer his name to the prince, but Gunnar didn't seem to care.

"Well then. Your servant," the prince said, and bowed.

"And yours." Wulf returned the gesture. "Seconds don't usually come in full armor," he said.

"They do in Krehennest," Gunnar grunted. "Among men."

They both bowed to Marshal Koterbaum, who looked very nervous.

"Your Excellency, if I had known you wanted to attend a match, I could have arranged a much more comfortable viewing spot for you," Koterbaum stammered.

"This will be perfectly fine."

"But generally here in Raukenrose, in the castle, I mean, the warriors, the adult warriors, do not participate. This is meant to be a training method for boys." Koterbaum wrung his hands together and looked at Gunnar imploringly. "And you, m'lord, while welcome at any time, of course, you, I mean to say, are *already trained.*"

Gunnar laughed, and slapped Koterbaum on the shoulder. "I'm merely serving as von Blau's second, Marshal," he said. "I believe the rules allow for this."

Koterbaum nodded. "They do, Your Excellency. But Prince Gunnar, this sort of thing seems, well to be, well—"

"Beneath me?" Gunnar said with a dry smile.

"Not precisely what I was trying to say," Koterbaum answered. "But you understand what I mean, I think?" He pushed out his final words in a squeak.

"I do," Gunnar replied. "Marshal . . . what is your name?"

"Koterbaum, Your Excellency."

"I'll remember that," said Gunnar.

Koterbaum began to visibly shake. Wulf had never seen the arms master react like this before to . . . anything.

Koterbaum was afraid.

Not of Gunnar's presence. Koterbaum wasn't afraid of anyone in combat.

He's afraid of what Gunnar might do to his life. What the prince could do to his family.

The man was going to be King of Sandhaven one day, which included the Chesapeake Bay. He would have spies at his disposal. Assassins. He would have trade connections that could ruin the entire Koterbaum clan.

You didn't want to get on the wrong side of him.

"Proceed with your instructions, arms master."

Gunnar put his helmet back on. Wulf did the same.

Shaking his head, Koterbaum quickly called for the match to start, and both seconds returned to their sides. Wulf stood next to Rainer and turned to look across the circle at Hlafnest and Gunnar, also standing abreast.

"What was that about?" Rainer asked him in a low voice.

"I have no idea," Wulf replied. "I don't like this, Rainer. Why don't we concede the match and get the cold hell out of here?"

Rainer considered for a moment, then shook his head. "No, let's see it through. I'm curious."

"You know this fight is meaningless."

Rainer smiled to the crowd and spoke through his teeth to Wulf. "Not exactly true. He challenged me—which was really a challenge to *you*, because he knows we're friends. I can't have that."

"My honor will be fine. We'll take the von Blaus on later like we always do."

"No," Rainer said. "After last night, I want to fight something that clangs when I hit it."

Rainer set his chin, and Wulf saw any further argument was useless. "All right," he said. "Keep your left side up and use that buckler as a weapon and not just a shield."

"Yes sir, Marshal, sir," muttered Rainer.

Koterbaum called the combatants to en garde, and Rainer entered the ring.

Wulf looked up at the castle's main balcony. There were the girls of the castle cohort. Their colorful linens and silks set them apart from the gray walls. It didn't take Wulf long to pick out Saeunn. Her blonde hair, always unbound, shone in the afternoon sun.

She looked concerned.

Does she think something is wrong? I'm sure not liking this at all. What is Gunnar doing here?

He glanced up at Saeunn again, then turned his attention back to the fight.

After a moment's hesitation, Hlafnest let out a roar and charged Rainer. It was almost too easy. Rainer ducked his sword, then, his reflexes as fast as ever, spun around and caught Hlafnest between the legs with the two sides of his outstretched battle-ax. Hlafnest went down in a clatter of mail and plate armor. Rainer was on Hlafnest's back instantly and drove the end of his ax handle between Hlafnest's shoulder blades. The other let out a grunt.

If this had been actual combat, Rainer would have aimed for the unprotected back of the neck. All would have been over for Hlafnest von Blau forever.

Rainer took the point. He climbed off his opponent. Hlafnest waited a while to catch his breath, and stood up. He walked shakily back to his side of the ring.

Koterbaum glanced at Rainer with an imploring look, and Wulf had to smile.

"Marshal wants you to go easy on him, seems like," Wulf said to Rainer. "Don't you do it."

"I won't," Rainer said. He turned back to face the ring. Koterbaum called en garde. Hlafnest took a step into the ring—and then something odd happened. He went down on a knee, and one of his greaves—the armor that covered his shins—fell off. He picked it up and looked at the hasp.

After a moment, he called out to Koterbaum. "Marshal!" Koterbaum approached. So did Prince Gunnar. Hlafnest showed Koterbaum the greave. Gunnar looked it over.

"What the cold hell are they up to?" asked Wulf.

Rainer chuckled. "He's broken it," he said in a low voice. "He'll want a draw."

"Well, give it to him," Wulf said.

Rainer reluctantly nodded. "Yes, all right."

Koterbaum and Prince Gunnar stood up and crossed the ring to Rainer and Wulf. The crowd around the ring had been getting noisy. Now it turned quiet.

"Most unfortunate," Koterbaum said. "The greave cannot be mended in the time we have available, and no other will suit the purpose, his lordship claims."

"I understand," Rainer said. Wulf saw him suppressing a smile. "I am willing to offer Hlafnest a match draw if he wants."

"Sir von Blau to you, commoner," Gunnar said with a pointed glare at Rainer.

Rainer returned his gaze steadily for a moment. He nodded. "As you say, Your *Excellency*," he replied. "*Sir* von Blau gets a draw."

"Yes, well," said Koterbaum. He was wringing his hands again. Not a good sign, thought Wulf. "You see, Prince Gunnar is the second, and he has requested . . . I should say, he *wishes*, to continue the match."

"What?" Wulf said. "Hlafnest is supposed to fight without a shin cover?"

"Not at all," said Koterbaum. "No, I should say that Prince Gunnar wishes to step in and finish *for* his lordship."

"Finish?" said Wulf. "What does that mean?"

Gunnar reached over and gave Rainer a slap on the shoulder. "Come, boy. It will be fun. How often does a commoner like you get to take on a real prince?"

Rainer didn't flinch. He met Gunnar's gaze, and the two locked eyes. "I have a real duke's son for a friend, and I serve a noble house," he said. "I don't need to beat up princes to prove myself."

Gunnar frowned. "Impertinent," he said as if to himself. "This will be fun."

"I do not wish it," Wulf found himself saying.

Gunnar turned toward him. "And *you* are . . . *which* von Dunstig?"

"I am Wulfgang," he replied.

"The third son. Of course. Ulla's little brother."

"I have that honor."

"And it is an honor to be the brother of Ulla," Gunnar said. "I intend to see that it remains an honor."

"What are you talking about?"

"I think you know," Gunnar said.

"I have no idea what you mean."

Gunnar considered Wulf a moment. "More's the pity,

then," he finally said. "But we will finish this, the commoner and I. Here. Now."

"No," Wulf said.

But then Rainer stepped between him and Gunnar, facing Gunnar. "Yes," he said. "Let's do that, Prince."

CHAPTER TWELVE:
THE PRINCE

Without giving a hint of his intention, Rainer suddenly charged Gunnar. With his battle-ax held crossways in two hands, he rammed into the prince's chest and knocked the other backward. Gunnar, completely taken by surprise, stumbled back. Rainer pushed him again, and the prince tripped backward, falling onto his butt.

Rainer turned the battle-ax and pointed its tip at Gunnar's face as the prince looked up, furious.

"Don't you *ever* speak ill of Lady Ulla again," Rainer said in a low, clear voice. "Do you hear me?"

"Think what you do, boy," said Gunnar.

"Swear it," Rainer shouted, poking the battleax closer.

Gunnar looked down at the point, as if this were a sight he had never expected to see for his entire life. After a moment, he laughed. He laughed loud enough for everyone to hear.

Wulf thought it the most faked sound he'd ever heard.

"I swear it because I have never done anything *but* uphold her good name," he said. Then, speaking louder, he called out. "I wish only the best for Lady Ulla, as all know who know me." After a moment, Rainer backed the ax head away. Gunnar took the chance to brush it aside. He quickly scuttled out from under it and regained his footing.

He cast a look of hate at Rainer and said in a low voice, "You are going to wish you hadn't done that, boy."

Rainer said nothing. Koterbaum, who seemed to have been frozen in place, suddenly moved. "Well, now that we're friends, why don't we—"

"Why don't we get on with the match," Gunnar said. "Why don't you get out of the way and let us do so, Marshal." Neither was a question.

"Yes, I suppose we could—"

Gunnar smiled at Rainer and raised his sword. "En garde," he said.

Rainer raised his ax, and Koterbaum slowly backed away.

Rainer gave Wulf a quick glance. "Out of the ring, Wulfgang," he growled. "Please."

Wulf hesitantly stepped out.

That was when Gunnar charged. Rainer raised his buckler just in time to take the blow, and wood splinters shot in all directions. Gunnar yanked the sword free, pulling Rainer part of the way toward him in the process. Rainer stumbled to the side and scuttled away from another blow aimed at his head.

That shouldn't happen, Wulf thought. How does a buckler splinter like that?

There was only one way it *could* happen.

Gunnar was using a sharpened sword.

Rainer quickly regained his footing and stood facing Gunnar. He was breathing hard. The prince moved in. Rainer drew him back, retreating slowly around the circle, while Gunnar probed with his sword tip, attempting to find a way through Rainer's defense.

He's good, Wulf thought. As good as Rainer. And bigger.

Fast as a cat, Rainer attempted another charge with his

ax, but this time Gunnar was waiting. He turned it aside deftly, then brought his sword around to take a slice at the back of Rainer's legs. A red line opened up across the back of Rainer's thighs where the cuisse didn't meet. Rainer spun about, blood dripping from his legs. Now Gunnar charged. Since he was without shield, he led with the point of his sword.

Rainer didn't even try to get out of the way, and Wulf gasped. Gunnar was going to run him through.

But at the last moment, Rainer crouched under the path of the sword. Gunnar tried to correct, but too late. He missed, and his momentum brought his legs into the crouching Rainer full tilt. The prince went into a roll, his sword flying away as he fell. He recovered his feet quickly, but now Rainer was standing as well.

And Rainer had his battle-ax.

Hack him to pieces, Rainer! Wulf thought wildly. Off with his crap-filled head!

But Rainer didn't do that. Instead he lifted his ax in two hands and—threw it to the side. He stood facing Gunnar weaponless.

"No, Rainer!" Wulf shouted. "He's trying to kill you!"

The prince smiled, though he was breathing too hard to let out a laugh.

The two charged. They met in a clash and clang of armor near the center of the match ring.

Rainer, despite his great ability, was only seventeen years old. Gunnar was twenty-seven and experienced at Viking raids. He also had at least a stone in weight on Rainer.

Rainer tumbled over backward with Gunnar on top of him. In the jumble that followed, Gunnar managed to get his legs around Rainer. He sat up, straddling Rainer's chest.

Gunnar put two gauntleted hands together and pounded down on Rainer's face. His blow caught the facemask, the grima of the helmet, and broke it away. The next blow broke

Rainer's nose. Rainer let out a shout of agony and twisted his head away. He tried to raise his hands to defend himself, but Gunnar batted them away. He brought an elbow against Rainer's temple.

This knocked Rainer unconscious. His head rolled to the side. Gunnar raised his hands to deliver another blow—

And Wulf was on him, hitting, biting, screaming at the top of his lungs, not caring how he stopped the prince. He caught a finger in his mouth and bit down. Gunnar jerked his hand out of Wulf's mouth with a cry of pain, and Wulf felt skin strip away.

Good.

He spat it out in a bloody wad.

Then Wulf felt as if he'd run into a stone wall full tilt. His body shook. Gunnar had struck him, hard.　Another blow to the head.

Wulf fell to the ground. He slowly rose to his knees. There was something dark in the sand. A form shaped like a person, almost like the dark thing from the night before. Could it be?

"Thou know'st," came the nasty whisper again.

Wulf shook his head to clear it.

He reached out for the dark thing. His hand passed through it. His fingers touched only flint flagstones.

Gunnar's shadow, he thought. I'm looking at Gunnar's shadow on the ground.

"That will be enough," someone said. The voice was commanding. He recognized it. Yes. He knew that voice. "Back off, sir, or I will make you back away."

Wulf turned his head in the direction of the sound. There, standing a few paces away, stood Master Tolas. He had his walking stick.

"Beg pardon," said another voice. "Are you speaking to *me*?" Accented. Not from these parts.　Chesapeake accent. Oh. Gunnar. That was the name.

And then it all came flooding back to Wulf, along with a pounding ache in his head. He blinked, rose to one knee.

"I am speaking," said Tolas. "The question is: Are *you* listening?"

Gunnar shook his head in disbelief. "Who are you? *What* are you?"

"I am a gnome," Tolas said. "More importantly to you, I am Master Albrec Tolas, librarian and tutor to House von Dunstig. And these boys are my *students.*"

Tolas took a step toward Gunnar and pointed his staff at the man. "If you will not back away, I am afraid you leave me no choice."

"No choice to do *what*?" asked Gunnar in amazement.

Albrec raised his stick. He scowled at the gathered boys who were clumped around the circle.

"Listen to me, you men of Shenandoah," he said in a loud voice. "Do you think that line on the ground is something you cannot cross? Do you have any idea what 'duty' means?"

He pointed the stick at the chalk. Then he found a face in the group, Wulf's cousin who was sixteen. "You, Atli von Dunstig," he said. He turned to another of the boys, the son of his father's thane Rokvi, who headed the tax collection service. "You, Vinnil Rokvison." Tolas's gazed passed around all the boys. "Kilmund, Beimi, Endil Haraldson." His gazed lighted on Hlafnest. "And especially you, Hlafnest von Blau. The rest of you, all of you—Wulfgang von Dunstig is the son of your *lord,* your *duke.*"

Tolas pointed his walking stick at Gunnar. "Who is *this* person to you? What do you owe him?" Tolas brought his stick down hard against the flagstones of the courtyard. "Nothing! He is nothing. You owe him nothing."

Gunnar straightened. "Now, just a minute, gnome—"

Tolas cut him off, continued addressing the crowd. "Are you going to call yourself maggots for the rest of your lives? Are you? Do your duty! Defend Lord Wulf!"

For a moment, there was stillness. Then the assembled boys moved as if mesmerized.

They moved toward Gunnar.

Gunnar looked at them a moment, then began frantically searching for his dropped sword. One of the younger boys, Harek, had already picked it up. He showed it to Gunnar with a sly smile. The prince tried for it, but Harek threw it away, behind the advancing boys.

"Stand back!" Gunnar said. He was holding the finger Wulf had stripped. Blood was dripping from his hands. "I command you to stand back!"

The boys did not obey. They moved forward, slowly closing in.

"Shenandoah scum!" Gunnar picked out a part of the encirclement and stalked toward it. The boys did not move.

"If you hurt those boys, you will pay a very high price," Tolas called out after him. "Consider, Prince."

Gunnar pulled up short just before he would've bowled over Audmund Ingvisson.

Audmund was only eleven. He was normally a timid little guy, but now he stood his ground bravely. Wulf was proud of him.

"Let me through," Gunnar shouted into the boy's face. Audmund didn't move. Several of the larger boys came up behind the prince. Before he could do anything about it, arms were on him. These were the seventeen and eighteen-year-olds. Two of Wulf's cousins Thrym and Skalli von Dunstig, who were even bigger than the prince. Plus, they were muscled from ten years in Koterbaum's practice yard. Gunnar tried to shake them off. They held him firm, and others joined them.

"Let me go!" the prince shouted. He tried to twist away, but couldn't break their grip. Then, as a group, they frog-marched Gunnar toward the courtyard exit that led to the castle gate. When they got to the stone columns of the exit, they pushed him forward. Gunnar stumbled into the path beyond. Wulf could not see what happened next, but heard shouting that had to be Gunnar. Wulf couldn't make out the words from this distance, but it sounded like the prince was cursing them all. After that, Gunnar must've either gone to the guards for protection or left the castle completely. The group of boys, so unified moments ago, turned around and milled back into the bailey courtyard in groups of three or four. Gunnar did not follow them.

Tolas meanwhile hurried over and knelt beside Rainer. Wulf pulled himself to his feet and went to join him. "That one will be back, and with reinforcements. We have to get Mr. Stope to help quickly."

"Should we send for the doctor?" Wulf mumbled. "I can—"

"The doctors be cursed," Tolas answered with a dark laugh. He thought for a moment. "Our young elf," he said. "She has training from her folk over the sea. They are known to be effective healers."

"Saeunn?"

"Yes. Let us take him to quarters." Tolas stood up, looked around, and called out. "Koterbaum, you fool! Get over here!"

The arms marshal stumbled toward them as if commanded by a lord.

"Get help to carry the boy inside," Tolas said. "Two or three of the older lads should do it. Make that useless Hlafnest von Blau one of them, too."

Koterbaum stood there, doing nothing. Tolas took the staff and whacked the marshal across the shins.

"Blood and bones!" yelled Koterbaum. "Curse it all!" But suddenly complete awareness seemed to flood back into him. "Yes, of course, Albrec. You're right. I'll do it now."

Koterbaum called out a couple of names to bring help. He turned back to Tolas and shook his head. "They wouldn't have done that for me, Albrec, ganged up on him like that."

Tolas considered his staff. "Possibly not," he said. "But there are always other options. You of all people should know that."

Wulf didn't listen to them anymore. He turned to his friend, cupped Rainer's head in his arms. "Wake up, Rainer," he said. "You can wake up now."

But Rainer did not wake up. His head dropped to the side as three of the older boys, including Hlafnest von Blau, raised his friend and carried him into the castle. Wulf stumbled behind in a fog of worry and regret.

Chapter Thirteen:
The Touch

Wulf called for Grim when they got inside the castle. The boys, with Wulf in the lead and Tolas chugging after them, brought Rainer up the spiral staircase that led to the third floor and Rainer's bedchamber. There they laid him on his own bed. Wulf told them all to go.

Hlafnest was the last to leave. He turned to Wulf. There was a look of shock and sadness still on his face. "I'm sorry, Wulf. I let him push me to it," he said. "I didn't think anything like this would ever happen."

Wulf nodded. "I understand," he replied. "Now get the cold hell out of my sight."

As Hlafnest left, Saeunn and Ravenelle entered the bedchamber, almost running into him. Ravenelle glared bloody murder at Hlafnest as he passed. Behind them, Grim arrived with two other servants and Fedder, the castle arms keeper, who was a Tier, a badger man.

Badgers were one of the Tier who looked very similar to humans. Only the shape of his face and his black, wet nose showed what he was.

With Wulf's help, he removed the armor from Rainer while Rainer lay motionless on his bed. Fedder had been Koterbaum's assistant and equipment handler for years. He worked off Rainer's mail shirt, moving Rainer's body the least amount that needed to be done to get the shirt over Rainer's head.

"Did this quite a few times in the Little War," the arms keeper said. "It's never easy on a body, but has to be done or you might not spot all the wounds."

The two left, and Tolas was about to speak to Wulf when he noticed something over Wulf's shoulder and made a deep bow.

Wulf turned to see his mother, Duchess Malwin.

She stepped inside and hugged Wulf. "My child," she said. He was surrounded by the familiar clean scent of her fresh linen and silk dress. "What's happened to you?"

"I'm all right, Mother," Wulf said. "Just a little banged up in a match. It's Rainer we're worried about."

Duchess Malwin reluctantly let Wulf go. She stepped over to the bed and gazed at Rainer for a moment. Then she sat down beside him.

"Oh, my dear one," she said. She touched his forehead gently. Then she pulled up an eyelid and saw that he did not respond. "He's completely insensible, I take it," she said. She looked to Saeunn. "Can you help him?"

"I think so, my lady," Saeunn replied softly.

The duchess stood up, held a silken handkerchief under her chin, and took a long look at Rainer lying there in his quilted arming shirt. There were several deep bruises and patches of blood on the cloth from wounds underneath.

"I swore to his mother to take care of him," she murmured. "And we do love him." She turned to Saeunn. "I'll leave maids for errands, and call for the physician, but until then, do what you can, Saeunn."

"Yes, m'lady," Saeunn answered.

Wulf's mother shook her head. "I have inquiries to make into this matter. I'll be in my chamber. Send word if you need anything, anything at all." She started to leave, then turned once more to Wulf. "Are you sure you're all right?"

"A headache and some bumps and bruises, Mother," he said. "The boys in the yard, they came to my rescue, believe it or not."

"As well they should," the duchess replied. "I want to hear the whole story of this. But first, let's make sure Rainer is all right."

"Yes, Mother."

The duchess left. Her trusted lady's maid, Kinvis, who had been outside in the hallway, followed her, but three other maids remained in the hall, awaiting instructions. Wulf ducked his head out into the hall and saw Grim standing by for orders.

"Keep visitors out," he told the servant, then closed the door.

Now with Tolas and the three fosters in the room, Wulf noticed how small Rainer's bedroom really was. It was maybe a quarter the size of his own. There was a desk and chair, a wardrobe, and two chairs for sitting by the fireplace. One of the chairs was pushed toward the fire. It had a pair of boots resting on it. Wulf recognized these as Rainer's hobnail boots he'd worn the night before. He'd left them to dry and worn another pair today.

Wulf took the empty chair and moved it over to the side of the bed for Saeunn to sit down. She gave him a worried smile. Then she sat and looked at Rainer for a moment, like she was sizing up a problem to solve during one of Tolas's lessons.

Wulf meanwhile took the hobnail boots from the other chair and set the chair at the foot of the bed for Ravenelle. At first she didn't take it but pushed the chair to the side and remained standing, staring down at Rainer.

"This is my fault," she said in a low voice. Wulf stepped up beside her, touched her arm. She looked up at him. "I'm sorry," she said.

"*You* didn't do anything, Ravenelle," Wulf answered softly.

But red tears were forming in her eyes. "You don't know," she said fiercely. Then she shook her head furiously and turned her gaze back to the bed, saying no more. Wulf took her arm and guided her into the chair, which she let him do this time. He went to stand beside Tolas on the other side of the bed.

Rainer was more battered than he'd ever seen anybody. Wulf looked across the bed to Saeunn. The last light of the day streamed through the single window of the room and struck her face with a golden glow.

"She will help," said Tolas.

Saeunn got to work. She expertly examined Rainer's body, finding bruises, following them to the worst point of injury and probing deeper, looking for, Wulf supposed, broken bones, damaged organs, things like that. People were like animals on the inside. He knew that was true. But it really hit home when the person was someone you knew and they were not moving except to breathe.

Is he going to die? Is he already on the way?

Saeunn looked up at Wulf. "I've called him back," she said. "It did not take a large effort. He's strong. He's here with us again, fighting to wake up." She passed a hand over Rainer's eyes and he lost tension in his face and seemed to rest easier. "Sleep a little longer," she said. Then Saeunn quickly moved her hands together, placed fingers on either side of his split and broken nose—and, with a quick twist, reset it. "There."

She daubed away a spray of blood she'd released and handed the handkerchief to Wulf. "Give that that to your manservant and tell him to burn it. And while you're out there, have one of the maids bring me warm honey and fennel in a compress. Tell her to ask Betani, the cook's assistant, for these things. She knows her herbs. This will help the cuts on his legs."

Wulf had totally forgotten about the gashes Gunnar had slashed across the back of Rainer's thighs.

Wulf rose and took the bloody rag away. He found Grim and gave the maids Saeunn's instructions. When he returned, Saeunn was speaking to Tolas.

"—bleeding under the skull is what worries me. I've stopped it, I think, but he has to rest for two or three days until he heals enough to keep the vessels from starting to bleed again." She looked to Wulf and Ravenelle. "That means we've *got* to make him rest."

"That'll be a challenge," said Ravenelle. She blurted out a short, nervous laugh, but the worried expression stayed on her face.

"He may want to get up and finish what he started," Wulf said.

"Then he's a fool," Tolas said. "And so are you if that's what you're thinking of doing." The gnome tugged at his chin, which was beardless but pudgy enough to let him get hold of a flap of skin. "That prince has gotten into his head a dislike of this boy for some reason. It would be a good idea to find out why."

"It was me," said Ravenelle. "He got the idea from me." She looked like she wanted to say more, but bit her lip instead.

"What do you mean, Princess Ravenelle?" said Tolas.

"I—I can't tell you."

Tolas looked at her curiously. "I can only think you are you talking about Talaia communion."

Ravenelle looked up, startled. "How did you know that?"

"I have heard that the Kingdom of Krehennest has established a regular trade in slaves and sugar with the south," Tolas said. "With such close relations between countries, it stands to reason the Talaian faith has spread north. Perhaps the Krehennest royal family has converted?"

"But that can't be the truth," Wulf put in. "Gunnar is a Kalteman."

"Yes, that's exactly what happened," Ravenelle replied, ignoring Wulf's comment. "He told me so himself. The first time he and I . . . when he tried to commune with me."

"So you two talk—inside your heads? Or is it something worse?" Wulf asked. He couldn't believe she would do something to purposely harm Rainer.

"The communion is not like talking," Ravenelle replied. "It's more like when you finally understand something you've been trying to figure out. The meaning just comes to you."

"What happened?" Tolas asked.

"He wanted to know about Ulla. I wouldn't tell him anything. But he was strong. And he kept trying, kept pushing at me."

"I still don't get how it's your fault, then," Wulf said.

Ravenelle frowned. "He had to have gotten something, some thought, from me. How else would he have known Ulla is in love with a commoner?"

"She's not—how do *you* know that?"

"Come on, Wulf. It's not exactly big news around the castle. Everyone knows."

"But *Rainer* isn't the one after Ulla," Wulf continued, "It's someone else, it's—" He almost finished the thought, but did not. He would keep Ulla's secret.

"Perhaps the princess's explanation makes some sense, however," Tolas put in. "If Prince Gunnar learned from her that a commoner was after his bride, the prince may have decided to take out his rival."

"Stope's the only commoner any nobleman could believe would have the nerve to go after Ulla," Ravenelle said. "Anyway, Stope gets tangled up in my thoughts a lot."

"What does that mean?" Wulf asked.

Saeunn smiled the slightest smile and removed her hands from Rainer's head. "Once we get the dressings applied, I think he'll be all right," she said softly. "We should get word to the duchess."

Wulf barely heard her. He'd just realized something else that shocked him.

"Are you in love with Rainer?" he asked Ravenelle. "Is that it?"

Last night is enough to deal with, he thought. Is everything going to turn upside down now?

Ravenelle was crying. Little droplets of blood ran down her cheeks. She swiped fiercely at her tears with her sleeve.

"I hate this place," she said. "I hate everything." She stood up. "When I get out of here, I'm never coming back." She ran to the door and flung it open, then slammed it shut behind her as she left.

Nobody spoke for a moment. Wulf turned to the others.

"I don't believe it," he said. "Talaia is mumbo-jumbo, not real."

"It's real," Saeunn said. "And more evil than Ravenelle can possibly imagine." She touched a single finger to Rainer's forehead. "He'll sleep until tomorrow night."

"Why don't you have your man stay outside on watch," Tolas said to Wulf. "He seems very competent."

"Yes, I'll tell him," Wulf said.

"You've been through a lot. You must get yourself looked after," said Tolas, touching Wulf's arm gently. "I have my duties at the university, or I would see to it."

"Look, Master Tolas, I want to stay," Wulf said. "The doctor will come here anyway. I'll sit by the fire."

"Very well," Tolas said. He walked to the door, then turned and considered the three who remained in the room.

"It seems I did not wholly fail with you three," he said. He seemed like he was about to add something more, but then bowed slightly and went out.

Wulf sighed. He slumped down into the chair he'd pulled up for Ravenelle.

"I'll stay with you," said Saeunn. "There is more mending to do for Rainer." She looked at Wulf with her usual calm and serene expression. "And for you, Wulf."

"Tolas," he said. "Who would have thought he'd be so awesome—you know, today when we needed him."

"He's one of a kind."

"And do you *really* think it's real, Talaia mind reading? Red-cake and the holy host and all that?"

"Yes, I do."

"Okay," he said, and yawned. "But you're friends with Ravenelle."

"Yes, she's my friend."

"Are you *my* friend?"

"Yes, Wulf."

"Just friends?"

Saeunn cocked her head and looked at him with the slightest of smiles. "Don't ask me that, Wulf."

So. Now he knew where he stood with her. At least that was settled. Just friends it was, and would be. But he still felt like he wanted to tell Saeunn his doubts, his worries. He felt like he could tell her anything.

"I fought a draugar last night."

Saeunn nodded. "I'm worried," she said, "There are three of them, you know. The draug are terrible beings."

"Yeah. And they stink."

Saeunn didn't answer. She moved her chair toward him and reached out and touched his arm. Wulf jerked up, suddenly alert, but then he felt a calm trickle over him. There was a sound in his ears like a mountain stream falling over rocks.

"Rest for a while," Saeunn said. "Your servant outside will take care of anything that needs tending to."

"All right," Wulf said. "I guess that would be okay. To rest, I mean."

"You need to heal, too," she said.

Wulf wanted to reply, but he was so tired, so ready to let it all go for a while. Saeunn was here. She was staying. That was a good enough reason to remain just where he was.

And when he had almost dropped off, when he was more asleep than not, and there was no climbing back to wakefulness, not for a good long while, Saeunn leaned closer.

"Ravenelle and Rainer," Wulf muttered. "Didn't see that one coming either. They're doomed."

"They're not the only ones," Saeunn whispered. But Wulf was already asleep.

Saeunn quietly stood and went to stand by the window and gaze up at the sky, which was now dark enough for the stars to appear for the evening.

Her star.

What does it mean, my star, my own? Can one of the draug really be here in Raukenrose?

It's a time of turmoil, my child my own. Do you doubt what the young men saw?

No.

Then a terrible shadow is falling.

Which draugar is it? It can't be all three, can it?

I do not think so. Geizul is in Rome. Gauss works in the south. This is probably Wuten.

Who can stand against a draugar?

Yet someone has.

They said they killed it . . . him.

They have forced him to change forms. He won't like that.

We can't stand against something like this. We need help.

Her star did not answer for a while. She twinkled in consideration.

There is one who might aid you. He was once a draugar. He may know what to do.

Eifer? The Gray Company? But I thought that was just a story.

It is just a story. That happens to be true.

Can he help?

His ways are strange. We will ask. The star's voice softened. *But you have enough worries for now, my child, my own. Tend to your wounded. Look after your heart.*

I will do what I can, my star, my own. My heart . . . seems to have its own will.

Gentle, sparkling laughter. *Tend it like a garden and you will find your answers, my child, my own. And remember, I love you.*

And I love you.

Rest, my child. We are being useful and we are together with people who care about us. That is enough for today. Rest.

Wulf woke near dawn. A single candle burned on the bedside table. Saeunn was still there, and still awake.

"How is he?"

"Better."

Wulf sat up in his chair and looked at Rainer. Sometime in the night, Saeunn or someone had put on ointment and several bandages. His legs stuck out from beneath the covers. They were wrapped around the knees with strips of cloth that must've held in the honey and fennel mixture Saeunn had ordered.

He turned and looked at the window. The faintest of gray morning light shone through the chinks between the boards in the closed shutters.

"What time is it?" said another voice in the room. Wulf and Saeunn were both startled. They turned to see Rainer, his eyes open, sitting up in bed. "What are you two doing, anyway?"

Wulf followed his gaze and saw that he was looking at Saeunn's and Wulf's hands, holding on to one another. Saeunn smiled and gently withdrew her own.

"Waiting for sunrise," she said.

Rainer nodded. He winced and put a hand to his head. "I didn't win, I guess?"

"It was pretty much a draw," Wulf said.

Rainer let out a ragged breath, but followed it with a smile. "That prince is going to wish he'd killed me," he said.

PART THREE

PART THREE

CHAPTER FOURTEEN:
THE ADHERENTS

Out with the gnome! Out with his unclean ways! Gnomes lie. They steal. Their smiles are evil, and their hands are dirty from counting their hoard of filthy coins. This one is the worst. He's clever. He's dangerous.

He's my friend.

He must go! Go, go, go! The gnome must go!

The constant chatter was what got to him. The voices. The repetition of the same idea using slightly different words. Yes, that was it. The never-ever-ending stream of words, words, words.

He had once loved words. That was what had set him apart.

That was what he and Albrec Tolas shared, and what had made them good friends over the years.

He's the enemy. He wants to kill us. He wants to kill you.

No.

Gnomes drip with hate. He hates you!

But even the cluster of voices in his head couldn't convince Master Docent Lars Bauch that Albrec Tolas hated *him* in particular. He and Albrec had shared too many beers for him to think such a thing. They had shared too many late evening conversations, gentle jokes about students and their jobs at the university—not to mention many, many pipes of good tobacco.

The chatter shouldn't bother him. He was part of the Adherents now. He should welcome the voices. He'd chosen freely to join. Nobody had forced him. He was part of them, and they were part of him.

So why did his head feel like it was about to split open from all the jabbering?

He admitted the failure was his own. But couldn't they, just once in a while, *shut up?*

Your doubts are the problem, not us. Trust us! Trust us! We know. We know all about filthy gnomes!

Bauch missed being alone. He hadn't been truly alone for the past year and a half. He had loved his visits to the university library before he'd joined the Adherents. His gold and gray robe, showing that he was a full university scholar, allowed him to wander to his heart's content in the restricted section in the library where the scrolls and codexes were shelved. Sometimes he would just stand in the library and take in the smell of ink and sheepskin. As a boy growing up the second son of a country squire, and a very sickly boy, he'd spent many days in his father's small library while everyone else played outside. He felt safe there. He'd dreamed of living in a roomful of books once he was grown.

That was another thing he shared with Albrec. They both were, at heart, librarians first and foremost. They would talk about new scrolls added to the university collection, wonderful scraps of poetry scratched down hundreds of years ago by some mostly illiterate, genius skald, or codexes filled with ancient scholarship—things they'd come across all the time in the library's vast collection. They could even spend a whole evening discussing simple things like the storage and care of manuscripts.

He was going to miss Albrec.

Sentimentality! You have your position to think of.

Yes, he had his position to think of. He'd done it, what he set out to do as a boy. He didn't literally *live* in a library, but he had a two-room apartment attached to Klugheit College, one of the nine colleges and three women's halls that made up Raukenrose University.

Putting up with the chatter of the Adherents was worth it. He was a soldier—well, a mental soldier—in the cause of reason. His task was to bring rational philosophy to the superstitious, heathenish mark. He had always hated the divine beings. What had they ever done for him? Had they cured him of his constant cough and weak, spindly legs? No. Because they couldn't. Regen, Sturmer, the Allfather. What nonsense!

He wished he could make Albrec see the beautiful simplicity at the heart of the Roman belief system called Talaia. It was a philosophy that had built an empire and created a high culture that put the ugly and simplistic ways of the northern heathens to shame. When he had gained his first position as docent of Klugheit, he had taken it as his greatest responsibility to break his students of the misguided ideas they'd gotten from their parents and families. He would expand their minds. And he had. For the past twenty-three years Bauch had risen through the ranks of the university system to become master docent of history and lore. His introductory class was part of the required curriculum, and he didn't have to drum up students anymore like most of the other docents.

His teaching fees had gone up as well. He liked to tell students that he *chose* to live at Klugheit Chambers near them when he could really afford a much grander place— which was very true.

But there was always failure lurking in the back of Bauch's mind. Every term he chiseled away trying to break his students of their heathen delusions, and every term he succeeded with a few. But then those would move on to other classes or graduate, and he was once again faced with a bunch of students made ignorant by their upbringing and their parents.

Maybe that was the real reason he had started taking the red-cake. It was the sheer boredom and grind of teaching the same material over and over again. All of the students had started to look alike and sound alike. It felt as if he was getting nowhere against the heathenism and ignorance that surrounded him.

He knew that the Adherents were taking over Klugheit College, and he'd resisted it at first. Secret societies seemed so silly. But one day he had tried the celestis, and after that everything changed. Then the new celestis, the blackened ater-cake, came along, and everything changed again.

The Adherents. It was really only a community of like-minded scholars. Yes, they did occasionally exchange wafers dipped in one another's blood. But the blood was collected in tiny glasses. It was Roman and civilized.

Each docent of the Adherents had one thing in common. He or she thought it was only a matter of time until Talaia philosophy swept the north.

No more divine beings. No more teaching the laws of revenge killing and lore of animal sacrifice. No more heathen ugliness. No more silly superstition.

Some called this treason. Some might agree that it was treason and welcome it. For Bauch, there was nothing treasonous in freeing people from illusions that chained their minds. And for those who clung to the old ways—

There are casualties. Regrettable causalities. There have to be. All revolutions have them.

Like today.

Albrec Tolas was Bauch's friend. They had both come in at the same time and, although he was not fond of gnomes, they had hit it off. They both had an interest in Harrald Harraldsson the Younger and his sagas first written down seven hundred years ago. Bauch believed "Harraldsson" was secretly a nobleman, probably Sir Gustav von Kinder, and Harrald Harraldsson was a name he used to hide his identity. Albrec insisted that Harraldsson was a commoner, just like Harraldsson claimed to be, and that he had performed his tales for money in the taverns. Though they never could agree on Harraldsson, they'd become friends.

Now every Regensday evening after classes they had a standing appointment to drink a mug of beer at the Wiesel and Frosh Pub near Ironkloppel College, where Albrec was a master docent. They'd come to know each other pretty well. Bauch had told Albrec about his dictator of a father. Albrec had confided that he felt very alone here in the north. Ironkloppel was a college that welcomed gnomes both as students and as docents, but outside of the halls of the college there weren't a lot of gnomes in Raukenrose.

Yule had come and gone. Now in the coldest month, Wintervoll, he was going to destroy his friend's life.

They found their usual table. After taking off their winter cloaks and draping them over the stools for padding, they called for fresh pipestems and firebrands. When the pipestems arrived, they'd broken off the used ends, packed their pipes with tobacco taken from the leather pouches produced from their university robes, and now both lit up the first smoke of the evening. Albrec smoked the strong perique that gnomes liked so much. Bauch stuck with the more common orinoco.

Tell him. Get it over with. Do it!

All right.

"Albrec, there's no easy way to say this."

The gnome had been contentedly watching the smoke rising from his pipe. Now he turned and faced Bauch.

Beady eyes. Gnomes had such devious, beady eyes.

"What is it, Lars?" Albrec said, gently but firmly.

"I . . ." Bauch faltered and put his pipestem in his mouth and pulled a cloud of smoke into his mouth.

"Come, out with it."

Bauch blew the smoke from his mouth and lowered his pipe.

"Very well. The faculty guild has voted, and they've decided to . . . I hate to even say this . . . take back your scholarship privileges at the university library. And you know that without scholarship privileges—"

"I'm not a university scholar anymore. I can't wear the gold and gray," Albrec said with a sigh.

"You act as if you expected this."

"I suspected something. Not exactly this. And I never thought *you* would be its messenger, but I suppose I shouldn't be surprised."

"I'm sorry, Albrec."

"To be sure," the gnome said. He puffed a moment on his pipe, considering. "I can't go back to being just a master docent at Ironkloppel, of course. The guild knows that I gave up being master when I became a university scholar, and now Raffen Mohaut has that spot. They are throwing me out of the university."

The life seemed to go out of the gnome's muscles temporarily, and he lost his balance on the stool on which he sat. He tottered for a moment before he caught himself. Then he straightened himself again. Albrec *never* lost his balance. He never even slumped as far as Bauch could recollect.

"He carried through with it," the gnome muttered to himself. "He doesn't make idle threats. I'll give him that."

"He? Who are you talking about?"

"Gunnar von Krehennest of Sandhaven."

"The prince that's marrying the duke's daughter?"

"He vowed vengeance on me two months ago. It looks like he has kept his vow. Or someone close to him has."

"I can't say one way or the other. You know I am sworn to secrecy when it comes to guild business."

"That has never stopped you from blabbing before, Lars," the gnome said. There was a sad smile on his face that let Bauch know he wasn't angry. "But I understand."

Make him think it was only that! He must not find out what is really happening. He must never suspect about the soldiers.

"All right, yes. The Krehennests are huge benefactors to the school. They practically paid for Brent College. The Sandhaven scandal you involved yourself in was the final straw, Albrec," Bauch said. "You know your opposition to new methods has caused a lot of grumbling among—"

"My *what*?" the gnome broke in with laughter. "Opposition to new methods? That's got to be a joke! I helped Ute Geldennov establish the investigative magic department at Herbstern Hall. I proved the Doren werewolf manuscript was authentic lore."

"No one denies your credentials, Albrec. They are impressive."

"Not as impressive as having the correct political opinion. And the fact that I am against the insanity of this . . . dunces' society of traitors you call the Adherents that seems to have taken over half the colleges pretty much sealed my doom, didn't it?"

"Now, Albrec, don't get upset. Traitors? Not at all! It's the rational method the Adherents want to adopt, not the Romanish religion with its dragon slaying and blood-dipping. If you strip their idea of its religious frills, it is a powerful tool for mental development and rational thinking."

"The composition of the Talaia cake substance is not understood. But we do know that it has to be dipped in blood for it to work. Human blood."

"But the blood is nothing, just for show and to impress the ignorant," said Bauch. "We could reduce it to parts, discover where its true power lies."

"It is very irresponsible to encourage students to experiment with it—and to take it yourself . . . you are playing with fire, Lars."

"But the advantages, Albrec! To be able to push knowledge directly into a student's mind. Imagine how it might be used in society as well. The projects for the betterment of humankind!"

"I am not humankind."

"Oh, you know what I mean. That second town aqueduct, for instance, the one that the castle engineers have been trying to construct for the last three years and never get anywhere on. With collective action it might be done in a month. In a week, even!"

"The Tiberians use the celestis to keep millions in slavery down south. There is plenty of collective thought and collective action there," Tolas said quietly. "This doesn't bother you?"

"*We* are different."

We are better! Better! Don't listen to him! Stay the course!

"The Adherents won't use it that way. Albrec, we are at the dawn of a new age. The old ways no longer apply."

Albrec took another long draw on his pipe. He shook his head sadly. "You were a good friend, Lars. Knowing I had our Regensday mug to look forward to really helped make up for my isolation here."

"I still am a friend to you, Albrec. If you would change your old-fashioned ways, all could yet be well. I can get . . . I have some of the new celestis. We call it ater-cake. Try it. You'll see things differently."

"Thank you for the offer, but I am afraid I have to decline. There are a great many areas in scholarship and life where there are no easy answers. The Talaia way is not one of them. I will not be a part of anything that creates millions of slaves, including gnome slaves. I will keep my own mind and my own thoughts, thank you very much."

"There it is. That's where your true loyalty lies. The gnomes." Bauch shuddered at the thought. "You are very much the exception, my friend, but gnomes are filthy things, lending money at high interest, ruining gentlemen whose boots they are not fit to clean."

"I'm sorry to hear you say that," Albrec replied in a flat, strained voice. "The Lars Bauch I once knew never would have let words like that pass his lips. Or even have thought such hateful things."

Albrec set down his pipe and reached over and picked up his beer. The mug was two thirds full, but he drained it in one long gulp.

"I'm going to miss you, Lars. But I'm going to miss the library most of all. It is . . . a remarkable place."

Was there a tear in those beady, gnome eyes?

Sorry for himself. Gnomes steal books and sell them for money! Ask him how many books he's stolen.

Bauch knew this was nonsense, but you couldn't tell the voices anything. They were the ones who did the telling. At least he could keep a dignified silence.

"Tell the guildmaster that I'll leave my robes and my key to the colleges in my apartment." Albrec shook his head grimly. "Good-bye, Lars."

The hammer! Ask him about the Dragon Hammer before he goes!

"Albrec, there's something else."

The gnome rubbed his forehead as if he had a headache. "Yes?"

"There are rumors. Hints. That your kind, that gnomes

have . . . stolen the Dragon Hammer of Shenandoah. The guild would like to know if these are true."

"You mean the *Adherents* would like to know?" Tolas said. "Has the celestis driven you completely crazy, Lars? Do you really want to toy with a mighty relic like that?"

"We would like to prove that its power is actually the power of planting nonsense in men's minds. If the hammer were to reappear and the forces of reason destroyed it . . . this would be a symbol that rationality has won out over superstition."

"You think the people would see it that way?"

"'When the Hammer returns the King of Dragons will rise?'" Bauch laughed.

"It's from our old friend Harrald Harraldsson, Lars. A skald who once meant a great deal to both of us."

"Yes, yes. But come on, Albrec! They are just poetic words. You can't think they are . . ."

Albrec smiled sadly. "True?"

No more! Do not hint at the plan! The gnomes must not know! Gnomes are devious!

Albrec lowered his hand and looked Bauch straight in the eyes. "Lars, if I did know where the Dragon Hammer was, which I don't, I promise you I would die before I told you and your clueless faction."

Albrec slid down from his stool and pulled his winter cloak tightly around himself until it completely hid his university robes. He looked up at Bauch for a final time.

"I do want to warn you of one thing."

"What is that?"

"Be careful what you wish for, my old friend. You may get it in full measure."

And with that, Albrec Tolas flipped the hood of his cloak over his head and left the Wiesel and Frosh for the last time.

Gnomes look so innocent and childlike with their hoods, but underneath they are scheming, scheming, scheming!

Bauch watched Albrec go. He wanted to feel the sadness he knew was inside him somewhere.

No time, no time for that!

The voices were right. There was so much to do. Now that the Adherents had taken over Klugheit College, it was easy to find rooms in which to hide the troops that were being steadily smuggled in to Raukenrose. There must be over a hundred soldiers hidden away in Klugheit. Space was needed for them in the library basement.

Albrec had to go. He would have discovered the soldiers. He knew the library too well.

The revolution truly was coming. It might start with blood, but it would end in the light of pure reason.

At least that's what the chattering voices in his head, the other docents he was mentally connected to—the voices he could not shut up, dam up, or turn off—told Bauch over and over and over again. Sometimes he thought he just wouldn't be able to take it anymore.

He reached into a pocket, popped a wafer of ater-cake into his mouth, and swallowed it without chewing. He chased it with the last of his beer. Since the chattering could not be stopped, at least he could turn *himself* off for a while and disappear into the Adherents.

Don't worry, said the voices, *we will never stop talking, but one day you'll see the light of true reason, and you won't feel bothered anymore. Soon everything is going to be fine. Completely fine. Don't worry. Let us do the thinking.*

So that is exactly what Master Docent Lars Bauch did. And they were right. Soon the ater-cake kicked in. The Adherents took total control of his wayward thoughts—and everything was completely fine. He wasn't alone anymore. He *was* the chattering, and the chattering was him.

CHAPTER FIFTEEN:
THE INGOT

As abruptly as it had come, the yearning seemed to go away. The next day, and the next, Wulf felt no desire to return to the Olden Oak and enter back into the land-bond. A week passed. Then a month. Two months. Maybe it went away because he didn't have the dagger anymore, but he knew there was nothing magical about the knife. This wasn't the first time he'd heard the dragon-call. Several times, when he was younger, he'd entered the land-bond just by touching something old and connected to Shenandoah. Maybe it was because the Olden Oak had part of *him* by holding on to the knife. But whatever the reason, Wulf felt relieved not to have the impossible-to-stop urge to sneak out, hide what he was doing, and get to the tree.

Even though Saeunn believed there wasn't going to be any permanent damage, Rainer had been hurt pretty badly, and he lay in bed for more than a week. When Wulf got to class the next day, and every day thereafter, something odd had happened. The other students, even the older ones, began to show him respect like they never had before. Tolas calling them together at the match had changed the way they thought of themselves. He decided this was the first time they'd defended something worthwhile. It wasn't him, it was his family name, but that was all right with Wulf.

As for Tolas, what had been respect, or fear from his students, turned into near worship. It was as if every boy in the class expected the gnome to throw down his scroll or his map and lead them into battle. Tolas, for his part, acted as if nothing had happened.

So it was a complete surprise when Tolas announced that he was leaving his position, and Raukenrose itself, for good.

"I regret to inform you that I shall no longer be either the Raukenrose castle librarian or your tutor after the end of this week. I believe each of you has some measure of promise within, however meager, and I shall regret not having the chance to bring it out in you. You'll have to make do, and that thought saddens and somewhat frightens me."

Everyone wanted more details, but the gnome refused to say another word.

"But what about your university classes?" Wulf asked the tutor. The gnome sadly shook his head, and said nothing in reply.

Wulf was sure Prince Gunnar was behind this, but how?

Rainer continued to improve slowly. Ravenelle ignored her studies and spent most of the days playing Hang the Fool with him in his room. She even sent her bloodservants away when Rainer said that they made him uncomfortable.

"Can't stand those eyes of theirs—the way they look at you like puppy dogs, or cows," he said. "It's unnatural."

"That devotion is *real*," Ravenelle said. "They don't want to be anything else, and you can't change that."

"Well, I don't have to deal with them, do I?"

Ravenelle had gruffly agreed that he didn't.

A month passed.

And then Duke Otto called a feast in one week to announce the engagement of Prince Gunnar, heir of Krehennest, to Lady Ulla von Dunstig of Shenandoah.

The castle smith shop usually closed up in late afternoon after the cathedral rang dammerlight bell, but Grer had stayed after the apprentices were let off to go to Regensday market in the village. He'd mentioned he wanted Wulf to help out with forging a replacement dagger. Wulf had eagerly accepted. For some reason it always felt better to have weapons he'd seen made, or even helped in forging. Usually this meant he got to make a hammer strike or two, and then the real smith finished the work. This time Grer offered him the chance to be in on the making of his new dagger from the very start.

He separated out the iron ore from a metal bin set on a big oak table, while Grer gazed over his shoulder and pointed out the best pieces. Rainer looked on from a corner of the shop where he was leaning against a wall for support.

"Why don't you pick the chunks out yourself?" Wulf asked Grer. "You're telling me exactly which ones you want me to choose, after all."

"I'm just making suggestions. You can throw one back if you don't like the look of it," Grer replied.

Wulf smiled crookedly at Grer. He picked up a random bit of rock and tossed it back into the bin on the table in front of him.

Grer sighed, and shrugged. "Of course, that *might* be top-grade ore you just threw away there, young master," he muttered.

After a moment, Wulf reached back over and grabbed the chunk again, putting it back in the pile they were using. They kept doing this until there were enough ore chunks to fit into a small grain sack. It weighed a half stone or so. The ore didn't feel at all like iron. It felt like a bunch of rocks. He wondered if they had gotten together enough to make a nail, much less a new dagger.

Grer didn't seem concerned. He took the ore and put it in what looked like a clay brick with a hollow inside. When this was full, he sprinkled in some charcoal, and then covered it with a clay top. He called this ore container a crucible.

"The crucible's not clay exactly," Grer said. "Special blend I make and fire myself. Tough stuff. Won't crack in a furnace."

The furnace was a chimney stack in one corner of the smith's shop. Above was a hole in the roof for the smoke. The furnace was about Wulf's height. His arms would just fit around the chimney upright. It was made of three parts, each one a hollow piece that could stack on top of the other. Grer started out on the bottom with a layer of charcoal on a wire grate. The grate was to hold the charcoal up and let air come in, where there was going to be an opening, and shoot up the chimney.

He put the crucible full of ore on top of this. Then he covered the crucible with more charcoal. He put two more chimney-flue pieces on top of the bottom piece, then began to seal them up with wet mortar to keep smoke from leaking out the cracks. Grer worked steadily and seemed in a contented mood. After a while, Wulf couldn't stand it and asked him the question he'd been dying to find out about.

"So, have you heard about the marriage?"

Grer looked up from his mortar work. "The marriage?"

"My sister. Ulla. To that pig."

Grer nodded. "They don't tell us much down here in the bailey, but yes, I did pick up a rumor or two."

"Come on, Grer," Wulf said. "I thought you would be going crazy over it."

"Have to accept reality, m'lord," Grer replied. He looked up at Wulf. "We all do."

"What about smiths?" said Rainer from his corner.

"I'm talking about reality, Mr. Stope," Grer replied. "We smiths deal with it every day. You forget what you're doing and you'll lose a hand, or your eye, or your life—like that!" Grer snapped his fingers, flinging wet mortar in all directions when he did it.

Finally the furnace chimney was done, and it was time to light the fire. Grer gave this job to Wulf, who took a shovelful of hot coal from the forge and placed it on the bottom of the furnace stack, beneath the wire grate that held the first of the charcoal. Grer lugged one of the big forge bellows over to the furnace and had Wulf pump a stream of air onto the hot coals. Rainer wanted to help, but after a couple of pulls on the bellows handle he felt light-headed and had to watch.

Wulf pumped and pumped on the bellows. The charcoal layer under the crucible caught. Smoke began to pour out of the top of the furnace and drift toward the hole in the ceiling. Some didn't make it, and the smith shop got thick with drifting smoke.

Wulf felt angry, and it made him pump harder. He was mad at Grer for giving up on Ulla, even though Wulf himself had been the one telling the smith that he had to.

But I didn't know Gunnar then, Wulf thought. Ulla might have seen things too simply, but she had been right in her heart. I should have trusted her.

Pump. Raise the bellows handle. Pump again. And again.

The fire on the bottom of the furnace stack grew hotter.

Then Grer told Wulf to put another shovelful of coals down the top of the furnace chimney. Wulf did this, then returned to pumping the bellows. Soon all the charcoal was lit in the chimney and smoke was pouring out. Wulf could feel the intense heat of the furnace even through the thick walls of the ceramic chimneypieces. Sparks shot out of the top every time he pumped the bellows.

Finally, when he thought his arms couldn't take it anymore, Grer told him he could stop. Grer handed Wulf a dipper of water from the shop drinking-water barrel, and Wulf downed it thirstily.

They waited as the charcoal burned. Wulf was too tired to strike up any conversation. He watched the sparks fly from the top of the furnace.

Finally, Grer judged it was time. Wearing thick leather gloves and a leather shirt and leggings, he broke apart the furnace chimney with a few knocks of his hammer. He carefully set the pieces of the flue aside for later use. A big pile of ashes flowed out. In the center of these was the crucible, now blackened from the intense fire. The clay itself, or whatever the material was, glowed red hot in the faint light of the shop.

Grer knocked off the top of the crucible, looked down in it, and smiled.

"Well, come have a look," he said, motioning for Wulf and Rainer to step over. They gathered around and gazed down into the crucible. "We've got good steel ingot here," Grer said. "Fine steel. It'll be a pleasure to work it."

The steel didn't seem like much. It was spongy looking, and still had rocky pieces in it. Grer told them that this would all come out in the heating and reheating during forging.

"That's what all the beating and clanging is *for*," he said. "To knock out the impurities, and to find the shape of the blade."

It was hard to believe there was enough metal here to make a blade. The ingot was about the size of large marble, or a stone you might use for throwing in a sling. After it cooled, it would easily fit into the palm of Wulf's hand. Grer picked the ingot up with a pair of tongs.

The smith noticed Wulf's and Rainer's dubious expressions. "Plenty there to make a dagger," he said, clapping Wulf on the shoulder. "I'll get started tonight. Maybe two days of work, and then you boys can come for the final quench." He winked at them. "Then it'll either shatter into pieces or be the finest blade you've ever seen."

Wulf put out an arm to help Rainer on the walk back to his quarters. They turned for the door. There was a loud clang. They turned as Grer brought down his hammer and made a second strike on the steel ingot. The smith looked up at them and grinned. His white teeth gleamed in his sooty face.

"Remember, two days," he said, and went back to work.

Why the cold hell is he so happy? Wulf thought.

And then the truth dawned on him.

In two days, Grer and Ulla were going to run away together.

They want to say good-bye. To me.

CHAPTER SIXTEEN:
THE QUENCH

The next night was the first complete family meal since Rainer had gotten hurt.

The table was made of two wide planks, at least three paces long. They had been made from a fir tree that was supposed to be over two thousand years old. It had been lugged over the Greensmoke Mountain passes in Wulf's great-grandfather's time. It was made into a feast table for the marriage of Wulf's grandparents Sturm von Dunstig and Anya Blaurfleuse. Wulf had no doubt that his father meant to use it again as the main table for Ulla and Gunnar's wedding feast.

Family meals included the fosterlings, so Rainer, Saeunn, and Ravenelle were there. Also the castle officers who were considered gentry. Koterbaum had a place, as did Duke Otto's chief advisor, Count Volsung, and, on a special chair with a raised seat, Master Tolas. And, of course, all royal guests were invited to join the meal each evening. This meant Prince Gunnar von Krehennest was there.

Wulf spent the first part of the meal glancing over at Gunnar, who sat near to Ulla, and wishing he could kill the man. If Gunnar noticed Wulf's glower, he didn't show it. He and Duke Otto had a friendly argument over the dock tax at Krehennest.

When Gunnar gestured with his hands, Wulf noticed the linen bandage on a right fingertip.

From my bite, Wulf thought. I hope he gets the green rot and dies.

But that was unlikely this many days after the wound had been made.

The only indication of tension came when Gunnar looked down to Tolas, who sat near the bottom of table away from the duke. "I heard you will be leaving Raukenrose soon, Master Gnome," he said. "Is that so?" He gave a small chuckle, as if amused to be speaking to a gnome at all.

"It is, Prince Gunnar," Tolas answered evenly. "I will depart just after the upcoming feast. I have been the dear lady Ulla's tutor since I looked down at her and she looked up at me, and the duke has graciously asked me to remain so that I can see her pass into her womanhood."

Ulla blushed, but said nothing.

"Wish you would stay on for good," Duke Otto said through a bite of roast buffalo he held up, speared on a knife. "You're always welcome in the castle."

"I've lost my position in the university library and on the faculty," Tolas said. "I would be doing the castle a disservice if I remained. The castle tutor has been part of the university faculty for over two hundred years."

Duke Otto nodded. "True, true, and I won't tell you gold and grays your business," he said. "It's a shame. A cursed shame."

Wulf heard a sniff next to him. Anya sat beside Wulf. She was almost in tears. Wulf reached out and took her hand. She squeezed his tightly.

"Where will you go, Master Tolas?" Wulf's mother asked.

"Home to Glockendorf, m'lady," Tolas answered. "I'll see

my family then travel for a bit. I have a friend among the Greensmoke centaurs I'd like to visit. Remarkable scholar. We write, but I haven't seen him since we were at college together. Then perhaps to Bear Hall. The earl has a magnificent library, and he's given me a standing invitation to visit it. He's got a scrap of a poem called 'The Conjuring of the Were-beasts' that I've wanted to examine in person since the moment I heard of it."

"My old friend Earl Keiler!" shouted the duke, spewing bits of food back onto his plate and into his beard. He didn't seem to notice, but Duchess Malwin took a napkin and wiped the particles away.

Wulf noticed that Ravenelle tensed up when Keiler was mentioned. Ravenelle had been afraid of bear people since she was a little girl. It was so bad that it sometimes even gave her nightmares. Keiler in particular frightened her whenever he visited the castle.

Tolas waited until the duchess had finished cleaning the duke's beard of crumbs, then answered. "Yes, Your Excellency. I was under Earl Keiler's command in the Little War, you know."

"Indeed? And him a bear man?"

"Yes, Your Excellency. We got along quite well. I was one of his aides, as a matter of fact. A sort of secretary to the earl."

"Extraordinary."

Father used to remember Tolas from the war, Wulf thought. Earl Keiler had been the commander of the army, and the duke was constantly in his headquarters during the fighting.

Another memory his father's disease had wiped away.

Ulla suddenly broke her evening of silence. She seemed on the verge of tears. "But how will you make a living after that, Master Tolas? I'm worried about you."

"It will be all right, m'lady. I thought I might go into the family trade."

"And what is that?" asked Gunnar with a chuckle. "Doll houses?"

Tolas smiled slightly, and bowed toward the prince. "Not quite, Prince," he replied. "Bells."

"As in ring-a-ting-ting? Little bells?"

Tolas shrugged. "Little bells, big bells. Any sort you might imagine. Members of the Tolas clan are the best bell-smiths and belltower refurbishers in all of Shenandoah. It is how my siblings and most of my relatives make a living."

"Honest work," said Duke Otto. "May you prosper, Master Tolas."

"Thank you, Your Excellency," Tolas said, and returned to his meal.

The duke set down his knife and looked to his left at Gunnar. "You don't have gnomes in Krehennest, do you, Prince?"

This was one of the moments when Duke Otto's increasing confusion of mind showed. He knew his history. If he were in his right mind, he would never have brought the subject up with Tolas at the table.

"No," said Gunnar. "We got rid of them some time ago." Gunnar made a slight head bow toward Tolas. "No offense."

Tolas did not reply, and he did not return the bow.

Duke Otto picked up his knife and took another bite of the meat. He chewed a moment, then spoke. "You best have killed every last one of them, Prince," he said. "I'd hate to have gnomes for my enemy. Nasty fighters."

"I'll keep that in mind, Duke," Gunnar said. The prince tried to suppress a smirk, thinking he was in on a joke with the duke, but Wulf saw that his father was serious.

As usual, Wulf's brother Adelbert wanted to talk about sailing and the sea with Gunnar.

"I've had more news on the new headmaster at Halbinsel," said Adelbert to Gunnar.

Gunnar sighed. "Have you, Lord Adelbert?"

"Yes, an expansion."

Adelbert had attended Halbinsel Academy, the nautical university in Krehennest. Adelbert had been crazy for the sea since he was a child playing with toy boats. The duke and duchess had sent him to Halbinsel, and he'd graduated two years ago. Adelbert had done a lot of traveling around the Chesapeake Bay, but he had never been out in the Mesantic Ocean. Now that he was back inland, he was afraid he never would.

"Wolfram has done lots of viking to the south," Adelbert said. "Is it true he's planning on adding a school for marines to Halbinsel?"

Gunnar looked bored with the question. "I'm told he plans to make major changes, but I'm afraid I don't know much more than that," the prince replied. "My interest is more to the west." He winked at Ulla.

Wulf gritted his teeth in anger.

"But there's already a land-sea school at Messer's Cape," said Adelbert, too interested in the topic to notice Gunnar's attitude. "Wolfram isn't going to close it down, is he?"

"Really, Lord Adelbert, I have no idea," Gunnar said. "The future of Sandhaven is in cotton, tobacco, and selling slaves for the Romans. It isn't in dangerous sea journeys."

"But you need ships to carry the cotton and tobacco you sell," Adelbert said. Diplomatic of him to leave out the slave trade, Wulf thought. "And you have to have a navy to protect your ships from those Romans when they decide to take what you've got instead of paying for it. The raids go both ways."

"The combination of the interests of Sandhaven and Shenandoah will create a great land power. The sea trade is too risky to build an empire on."

"An empire?" said the duke, turning toward Gunnar. "What empire?"

"In a manner of speaking," Gunnar replied with a smile.

"But the tie between Ulla and myself will go a long way toward uniting our countries."

"That's certainly the hope," the duke replied. "No more strife. You'll cut those huge port tariffs on Shenandoah goods and stop impressing our rivermen into your navy."

"From what I'm told, it's hard for the press gangs to tell a man of the mark from a Sandhavener. And they all claim to be from somewhere else, of course."

Surprise. Not. Nobody wants to be forced into years of service on a ship that's a thousand leagues from home, thought Wulf.

"I disagree. The accent is pretty prominent," Adelbert said. "Everybody at Halbinsel could tell I was a foreigner."

"Look, I have no opinion on the squabbles of a few sailors. I'm a landlubber and always will be," said Gunnar. He shrugged. "I don't even know how to swim."

Adelbert looked shocked. "But you're going to be king of a seagoing nation, Prince. You really should learn how."

"I understand most sailors don't know how to do it."

"True, but most officers do. You should learn."

"Yes, my father says so, too," Gunnar replied. "One of these days. I've got time."

"I'd be happy to give you some lessons."

"I'll keep that in mind."

Maybe we can drown him, Wulf thought. If we can find a way to dump him in the Shenandoah . . .

Being around Gunnar made him furious, but he knew he couldn't let the feeling take over. He turned his attention to other people at the table.

Wulf's other brother, Otto, was in a deep talk with Count Volsung about building plans for the great West Road, a corduroy trail made from split logs. Its purpose was to connect Shenandoah with the Monongahela River and points west. The duke had started building it just before the Little War.

After the meal there was a story. His father had called in a skald to tell the tale of *Kraki's Saga*. This was the one about Kraki and his twelve warrior brothers. All of them were were-creatures. These were supposed to be the first Kaltemen to cross the Mesantic. They fought and killed many Skraelings, the elder race of men that was already in Freiland. But every time they fought, they had to turn into beasts—into bears, and wolves, and even hawks and ravens. Then, after one huge and long battle, they forgot how to turn back into people. *Kraki's* was not one of Wulf's favorite sagas. It had been written down only a hundred years before, many centuries after Kraki met his doom. Still, Wulf knew the saga pretty well. His favorite part was the bleak final few lines. He had memorized those lines years ago and now mouthed them along with the skald.

> *They disappeared into the west.*
> *They fathered the bear and the wolf tribes.*
> *They roam the great mountains.*
> *They can suffer, but they cannot die.*
> *One day they will learn to be men again.*
> *When that day comes, they will know death*
> *And be glad in their hearts.*

Then it was time to settle in. Curfew would ring soon, and the fires must be banked, food stored away, and the castle secured.

Wulf got up to go, but found an arm draped around his shoulder. It belonged to Prince Gunnar. He was wearing a linen shirt covered with a beaverskin cape, and the metal pin that attached it scraped against Wulf's ear. Gunnar gave Wulf a quick squeeze, then let him go.

"So, Lord Wulf, no hard feelings?"

Wulf shook his head and looked up at the prince. "I think that one day I'll kill you," he said.

Gunnar stood back and stared at Wulf in amazement for a moment, then laughed. "Very well, boy," he said. "At least we know where we stand." He leaned over again and spoke into Wulf's ear in a low voice. "I'll remember your attitude when I take your sister home with me."

Ravenelle stepped up beside him as the prince stalked away. "Good thinking, von Dunstig. Push him into being horrible to your sister."

"It's really hard not to bash his teeth in," Wulf said, staring after Gunnar.

"Yeah," Ravenelle replied. "But actually doing it—that's the hard part."

"At least he didn't sneak into my head and steal my thoughts," Wulf said. Ravenelle scowled and punched him hard in the shoulder.

"Sorry," Wulf said. "I didn't mean it. Not like that."

"You're right," Ravenelle replied. "He should pay."

Heat, beat. Heat, beat.

Repeat.

The making of the new dagger seemed to go on endlessly as Grer shaped the blade on his anvil. This was the final stage, Wulf knew. Grer had been at it for more than three night watches, a length of time that stretched from the evening before into early this morning. It could take up to half a day to shape a blade, and even longer to hone and polish it after it was quenched and ready to take an edge.

The hammer strikes were not hard, not any longer. Grer held the dagger by its metal tang—the part of the dagger that would have a handle wrapped around it—and worked the blade one more time with small, precise taps of his hammer.

It was looking to be a thing of beauty. Of course, it wouldn't take on its finished form until polishing. And there was always the chance that in the quench after the final big heating, the steel would shatter. Grer used a quenching liquid made from whale oil imported from Nantuket. This oil was flammable, and when he withdrew a piece from the quenching barrel, the oil on its surface was on fire. Seeing a flaming sword or dagger was something nobody forgot. Grer usually put the flame out by thrusting the weapon into a bin of sand. Sometimes, though, he let the oil burn out on its own, especially when Wulf, Rainer, or the other boys were watching.

"Once more into the fire and then we're done," Grer said. Wulf's and Rainer's ears were still ringing from the clang of steel on steel, and neither of them heard the creak of the shop door opening, or the jingle of the iron triangle announcing that somebody was coming in.

Ravenelle stepped through the door and looked around to see who might be in the smith's shop. She spotted Wulf and Rainer and nodded with a sly smile. Next through the door was Saeunn. Ulla was behind her.

When Ulla spotted Grer, a smile spread over her face. It was a smile Wulf had thought he might never see again on his sister's face after their horrible dinner two nights ago.

Grer put down his hammer on the anvil. The two came together and embraced.

"They haven't seen each other for over a week," Ravenelle said to Wulf.

"They haven't?" He'd figured they'd continued sneaking out each night to meet. "But how did this get arranged, then?"

"How did *what* get arranged?" Ravenelle asked.

"The elopement, of course."

"What elopement are you talking about, von Dunstig?" Ravenelle said. She sounded totally innocent of any knowledge of such a thing.

"You mean—I thought for sure they were going to go off together. I thought—" Had he just been imagining it? Was the idea that Grer and Ulla would be married a delusion he'd made up in his own mind because he hated the alternative so much?

Ravenelle punched him in the arm. "Of course they're running away together," Ravenelle said. "It's incredibly romantic."

Ulla and Grer kissed. Wulf felt a huge sense of relief inside.

Ulla is going to be happy.

Then there was a low whistle, a human whistle, nearby.

"Well, well," said a voice from the smith shop doorway. "What a little pack of Shenandoah weasels we have here."

It was Prince Gunnar. Beside him was Hlafnest von Blau. With a dark smile and a shake of his head, Gunnar entered the shop. Hlafnest followed and closed the door behind them. "Latch it," Gunnar said to Hlafnest. "Nobody's getting away this time."

"You must stop this, Gunnar," Ulla said. "You can't have me. You have to see that."

"Oh, I'll *never* have you. It's the other I'll take now," Gunnar said. He turned and caught Wulf in his gaze. "What's the little one's name? Anya?"

Wulf felt a hot rush of anger boil up. "Leave Anya alone," he growled. "She's eight years old."

"And yet your father *will* offer her to me, and gratefully, after he finds out about this," Gunnar said.

"He'd never do that."

"I own your country's path to the sea," Gunnar said. "Duke Otto knows that."

With a quick thrust, Grer pushed Ulla behind him. "Then come on," he said to Gunnar. He took a step toward the prince. "Let's have this out."

Hlafnest drew his dagger and came between the two. He pointed the dagger at Grer. "You'll speak when spoken to, smith. This matter is beyond you." Hlafnest turned to Wulf.

"This is the future of Shenandoah we're talking about," he said. "You'll understand that one day, Lord Wulf."

Gunnar shrugged. "He speaks the truth," said the prince. He looked around the room. His gaze fell on Ravenelle.

"And you, little Roman princess—of all people, you should not be part of this craziness. You and I are alike. In a few years, we'll both rule our lands. *We* could be powerful allies."

Ravenelle shook her head. Her thick black hair was held back in an ornate whalebone hair band tonight, and a few curls escaped and bounced furiously as she spoke. "We are nothing alike," she said. "I will never be your ally."

"We'll see about that," Gunnar said. The prince slowly drew his sword. It shone red in the glow from the forge fire. "Even if Ulla is ruined, there's my honor I have to defend, and the honor of Krehennest." With the tip of his sword, he gently poked Hlafnest in the back. "Stand aside, boy," he said.

Hlafnest looked back over his shoulder, startled. "But Prince Gunnar, we agreed—"

Gunnar poked him harder, hard enough to draw blood. "Get out of my way," he said.

Hlafnest slowly did so, sheathing his dagger,

Gunnar moved forward, quick as a cat, and slashed low with his sword. Wulf watched, stunned. The sword dug into the muscle of Grer's leg just below the knee.

Grer roared and reached for Gunnar's throat. But the sword had lodged in bone. Gunnar twisted it hard, mercilessly, and the big smith went down, collapsing to the side with a howl of agony. Gunnar withdrew the sword. Grer lay on the sand floor in front of him in a growing patch of blood. The smith clutched his leg, trying to stop the flow, and glared hatred up at the prince.

Gunnar smiled and drew back his sword, preparing for the kill.

Grer closed his eyes, waiting for the inevitable blow.

Wulf and Rainer struck at the same time, from two different sides. Wulf had no weapon, and Rainer hadn't had time to draw his dagger. They rammed into Gunnar at the waist.

He felt Gunnar's tabard and belt against his shoulder. There was a hard, satisfying grunt of surprise and pain from the prince.

And they were falling over and away from Grer.

Wulf looked up—straight into the pommel of Gunnar's sword, which came down to strike him between the eyes.

After that, he didn't remember anything for a while.

Brown. No, red. Red light. The forge fire. A torch on the wall.

Wulf sat up. A hand on his shoulders.

Saeunn. Wulf looked at her. The side of her face was bloody and swollen. Yet she smiled serenely. "Wulfgang, be awake," she said. She touched his face, and complete awareness flowed back into his mind. His head should have hurt, but it didn't. He pulled himself to his feet.

Ulla tended to Grer on the shop floor. Hlafnest was nowhere to be seen. Near the anvil and forge, Gunnar faced Rainer. Rainer was armed with an iron bar he'd probably picked up from one of the swages in the shop. He gripped it tight, prepared to use it on Gunnar.

But something was holding Rainer back. Then Gunnar turned toward him, and Wulf saw that the prince had hold of Ravenelle by her thick black mass of curled hair. Gunnar's sword was at her throat.

"Drop it," Gunnar said. "Drop it, boy."

"Don't do it, Stope," Ravenelle spat out. Gunnar dug the blade edge deeper into the flesh of her throat, and she gasped.

Rainer dropped the crowbar. The iron fell with a whump onto the sandy floor.

Hlafnest emerged from the shadows. He made eye

contact with Gunnar, who nodded. Hlafnest swung a hickory ax handle into Rainer's head. Rainer instantly crumpled to the floor, unconscious.

"Hold her," Gunnar said, and pushed Ravenelle to Hlafnest. Hlafnest wasted no time. He spun Ravenelle around and put the hickory piece around her waist and pulled her tightly against his body. She struggled, but he was much too large for her.

Gunnar turned back to Grer and Ulla. His sword gleamed with blood. "I'll finish this now," he said.

Wulf stood beside the forge. "Stop," he said.

Gunnar looked at Wulf. He seemed to come to a decision. "Yes," he said to himself. "That would be all right, wouldn't it?" He walked toward Wulf, his sword extended in a bent and ready hand. "I mean, *you're* the nuisance here." Now he was speaking to Wulf. "Your parents would probably thank me in their secret heart of hearts. I mean, what are you *for* after all?"

He's going to kill me, Wulf thought.

Gunnar raised his sword. Wulf took a step back. The heat of the forge fire was scorching at his back. There was nowhere to go, no way to retreat.

Something cold touched Wulf's fingers. Wulf risked a glance and saw that it was the metal handle of the charcoal shovel. This was the small scoop Grer used to feed fuel to his fire. Wulf's left hand closed around the handle. But Gunnar's sword was twice the length of the little shovel. The prince was too far away to reach, even if Wulf could manage a blow.

"Everyone will thank me one day," Gunnar said, and brought his sword down.

Wulf dipped the shovel into the coals behind him and, spinning, trying to dodge, threw a shovel of hot embers at the prince. In the final instant, Gunnar flinched back.

The sword missed Wulf by a hair's breadth. Metal

slammed into metal as the sword blade hit the edge of the forge table. Sparks flew.

And there, revealed, as if Gunnar's sword tip were pointing directly at it—

The dagger.

Wulf's shoveling had separated it from the fire, and it lay on the metal table, a few stray coals around it.

The dagger glowed red, from tang to tip.

Gunnar raised his sword again. Wulf glanced over and saw him wiping at his face with his free hand. Some of the fire coals had found their mark in his skin. But not enough. Gunnar shook his head, blinked, then snarled at Wulf.

So many times he'd faced a bigger boy in the practice yard. He had a few allies, but plenty of the first family boys and even his own cousins pummeled him whenever they could.

Do it! Useless brat. Hit him harder. Who does he think he is? He doesn't matter. Nobody will miss him. Nobody cares.

He's not even spare to the heir.

The only answer was to use what advantage you had. Even if it was slight. Even if winning was really, really going to hurt.

With his right hand, Wulf grabbed the red-hot dagger by its tang. He knew it was going to burn. He didn't know how much until his fingers touched.

A lot. Smoke rose. The flesh of his fingertips sizzled.

He gripped the dagger tightly.

Turned.

Gunnar's sword thrust was coming, straight on. Not aimed precisely, but well enough to skewer him if he didn't get out of the way. Wulf ducked down, continued his turn. The sword passed over his shoulder. His motion never ceasing, Wulf thrust the dagger upward.

Gunnar's own forward momentum carried him into it.

Through the fabric, through flesh, against the lowest of

Gunnar's ribs. Wulf held on. Glancing off. Continuing upward.

Into the heart of the Prince of Krehennest.

Gunnar grunted. His sword fell to the ground with a clang. He stumbled back.

His backward movement pulled the blade of the dagger out of his body. Wulf could not let go of it. The tang was practically welded into his own right palm in a mass of burned flesh.

For a moment, fire flickered along the blade. It was Gunnar's blood evaporating and the residue burning to a crisp.

Gunnar stared at Wulf for a moment, started to speak, but couldn't. Blood erupted from his chest. It seemed like every drop in the prince was pumping out.

Gunnar collapsed to the floor, kicked once, and died.

Wulf looked at the blade.

It wasn't glowing anymore. Now it was a dusty brown.

It also wasn't cracked. It looked like any other new-forged blade ready to take an edge and a polish.

Even though he'd done it by accident, the quench had worked. It was going to be a good blade.

He shook his hand. Nothing doing. The dagger wouldn't come loose. The tang had burned its way in. Maybe Saeunn could help him work it out without hurting himself even more in the process.

Saeunn! The others, were they all right? Were they—

A cracking sound pulled Wulf abruptly from his muddle of thoughts. He turned to see Ravenelle, grasping the hickory handle, and Saeunn with the iron bar Rainer had been using. Both girls stood over Hlafnest von Blau. He was lying on the floor, moaning and clutching his chest.

The cracking sound had been one of his ribs. Wulf knew this when Ravenelle brought the handle down again and broke another for good measure.

PART FOUR

PART FOUR

CHAPTER SEVENTEEN:
THE RIDGE

The ride up the Dragonback Ridge had been hard on the horses, even though they were small and tough ponies. The trail was steep and had lots of switchbacks. It rose for nearly a league in distance from the valley floor. Kalters, the name for this kind of pony, were thick-boned and very strong. They had a special ambling pace that other horses couldn't match.

Wulf was riding his favorite kalter, Hemdi, a black and white stallion he had taken into the country on hunting trips since he was eight years old. He fed the pony carrots at every break along the way. Hemdi huffed and puffed, but never slacked.

Wulf was gripping the reins with one hand only. On his other arm, which he held outward to make a perch, sat a screech owl. The owl was more white than brown, and her color was close to what a snow-covered branch in the winter forest might look like. She had on a small leather hood that covered her eyes. She was tied, "jessed" was the right word to use, with leather thongs to a small iron ring in the thick glove Wulf wore on his left hand. The glove was long, and stretched up to his elbow.

Riding along behind Wulf were twenty or so nobles, along with their servants, who also carried birds. Most of the birds were redtail hawks or golden eagles. The men took their birds on their arms. The women carried theirs on iron perches built into the back of their horses' saddles. The nobles were all part of the Raukenrose Castle court. They were the most powerful people in the mark.

And then there was Ravenelle. She was along because the von Kleists had invited her. There were three von Kleist siblings in the castle cohort. Ravenelle and Giesela von Kleist hated each other. Both were pretty, at least to Wulf's way of thinking, but Ravenelle was passionate, smart, and determined, while Giesela was ruthless, clever, and practical.

Giesela's older brothers Axel and Erik, the von Kleist twins, had a very different attitude toward Ravenelle. They were smitten with her, both of them. Baron Atli von Kleist, the richest of the Raukenrose aristocrats, must have seen some advantage in encouraging his sons' crush on Ravenelle—maybe because she was going to be a queen some day, even if Vall l'Obac was the mark's long-time enemy. He'd invited her to accompany his party on the hunt himself.

Ravenelle had instantly accepted. She loved hunting falcons and jumped at every chance she got. She'd once told Wulf that she was planning to add a black hawk feather splashed with blood to the Archambeault coat of arms.

There were even more servants than nobles, mostly Tier. Many of these were down on the valley floor whacking trees and branches with hickory beating sticks to flush out the game.

Meanwhile, the hunting party was climbing the Dragonback Mountains. They were heading for Ruckengrat Ridge, a line of cliffs that overlooked the Shenandoah Valley.

The view was amazing. As they made their way along the ridge, they passed an abandoned signal tower that had been used during the Little War. Below in the valley was the village of Buffalo Camp. Across the Shenandoah to the west was the looming line of Massanutten Mountain and Shwartzwald County. To the east were the rolling hills of the Piedmont Duchy.

The duke and Wulf were at the head of this long train of horses, servants, and birds. Grim was with Wulf today as attendant and bird holder. Fauns could ride horses, but Grim would rather walk a few paces behind Wulf's kalter. Beside the duke was Grim's uncle Finn, a big faun with grizzled black and gray hair, who was the hunt master. Finn rode a horse using a faun saddle with special stirrup cups. It was said (by fauns) that fauns had invented stirrups so that they could ride horses, and then it had spread to the world of men.

Another thing he wished he could ask Master Tolas about. But Tolas was gone. He'd left two months ago for Glockendorf. He'd left with only himself on a pony and leading a larger packhorse loaded with his personal collection of books and scrolls. The poor horse looked tired before it had even started on its journey.

Two months had passed, and now there was a new castle tutor. Master Mohaut, a man, was adequate, but nothing like Tolas. Wulf had jumped at the chance to skip morning classes and go hunting with his father.

Finn led along six ponies roped together, each with one or two perches mounted on the saddles. These horses carried no riders at all, only birds of prey. These were all of the raptors from the castle mews, the area where the birds were kept. There were hawks and falcons, eagles, owls, and even a vulture. Like an archer with different kinds of arrows in his quiver, Duke Otto liked to bring different kinds of birds on a hunt to handle any kind of animal, whether it was quail, rabbits, foxes, small deer—or the hardest prey of all to capture and kill, wolves.

The birds came in many sizes, from Wulf's screech owl, which might take a mouse or maybe a fat squirrel on a good day, to the huge eagles that were favorites of the duke. Wulf also loved the eagles but was a little afraid of them.

Most of all, he loved to watch them fly. Birds of prey weren't like dogs or cats. You couldn't tame them. You could spend years with a raptor, and if you did something careless, it still might reach over and tear off a piece of your cheek.

Redtail hawks could be particularly ornery that way. And an owl's beak was nothing to laugh at. That was why he was careful to hold his arm out, keeping the owl away from his face, despite the jolts and bounces of the climb to the cliffs.

The saddle perches were wound with rope so the birds could keep a grip. In the very rear of the train was a huge white horse, the biggest kalter Wulf had ever seen. On his back rode the largest of the birds of prey: a set of three bald eagles. There was one young male and two older females. They were all grown-up birds, with white heads and fierce yellow eyes.

Wulf thought they were beautiful. That didn't make them particularly good hunters, though. They were originally sea eagles, and hard to train. But when you got the right bald eagle with the right training, the bird could be devastating to prey.

In the wild, bald eagles were fishers. They lived close to water at all times. But these eagles had been captured young and specially trained to do other kinds of hunting. Once they made their kills, whatever animal it might be, they were given fish for a reward. Giving them fish was also a way to get them off a kill so the hunter could get to it.

The hunting party finally got to the top of the ridge they had been climbing and rode along the cliffs. The

Shenandoah Valley stretched below them. It was a beautiful, chilly day in Samen, the third month after Yule. Nearby was a rushing mountain stream that plunged over the cliffs to create a pretty waterfall. Wulf found a pool formed by an eddy of the stream and let Hemdi drink. He set the little owl on the front of his saddle. On the rear of the saddle was a redtail hawk on a perch.

While the horse was slurping, Wulf went upstream and filled a small bottle with water. He took this to the birds. The hawk clinging to the perch on the back of Wulf's saddle was a male named Tak. Though he was hooded, Tak felt the water trickle on his beak and opened up to drink. Wulf poured and Tak caught the water and swallowed so quickly that barely a drop spilled on the saddle leather below the perch. Then Wulf gave the little owl on his arm a drink. Her name was Nagel. She also drank with hardly a spill.

Duke Otto stopped close by and watered his large stallion.

"We'll stay here today," he said to Finn. Finn motioned to his assistant hunt masters—there were ten of them who worked for the faun—to have the other hunters spread out down Ruckengrat Ridge to the south.

"As far as you can go, as far as you can go," Duke Otto shouted to the nobles. "Wulfgang and I claim this spot for our slip."

There was some good-natured grumbling, but the others kept riding on a trail that led along the ridge. They and their horses and birds soon disappeared into the trees. Wulf waved at Ravenelle as she passed. She had her right arm extended, holding a hawk, and she looked excited.

Grim and the duke's manservant, Harihandel, took the horses to stake them out after they had drunk.

Finn meanwhile unloaded a handful of stakes as long as spears from one of the horses. Near the cliff's edge he pounded the stakes into the ground with a wooden mallet and fitted a crosspiece to them through a dovetail notch. Perches. He put the birds on them.

All of the birds still had hoods over their heads. The hoods covered their eyes. Finn gave each a mouthful of dried rabbit to chew on, except for the eagles. He gave them fish bits.

The patch of rock ran up to the edge of the cliffs. This part of the Ruckengrat was not just a straight cliff, but a slab of rock jutting out over a deep drop, a hanging overlook. Duke Otto motioned for Wulf to join him a few steps from the edge. They gazed west.

In the south of the valley, tobacco and cotton grew. Here in the upper valley were the wheat and corn that fed the people.

Duke Otto stretched out his arms and took a deep breath "What a good day for hunting," he said. "It's days like this that make all your problems go away."

"But they don't really go away," Wulf said. It had been four months since he'd killed Prince Gunnar. After a long wait for snow to clear, the prince's body had been taken back to Sandhaven. But not by Wulf, as he'd expected. As he'd *wanted*. By his brother Adelbert. Adelbert with fifty men and Marshal Koterbaum along for good measure.

"It should have been me that went to Krehennest. You know that, Father."

"Wulf, you're twelve. Adelbert wanted to go. He'll get to see his precious Chesapeake again," Duke Otto said.

"I'm sixteen, Father," Wulf replied.

The duke looked puzzled for a moment, then nodded. "Ah, right, right." Wulf knew his father would soon forget his age again. For Duke Otto, his third son would always be a certain age in his mind. The morosis had seen to that.

Before he'd killed Gunnar, Wulf would never have talked to his father this way. Since then he was beginning to feel like it was not just his right to speak his mind, but his duty.

But instead of getting mad at Wulf, the duke seemed to like it when Wulf spoke plainly.

So few people these days speak to Father like he's an adult, Wulf thought. But I can see there's still my dad under there, even if he is fading away.

"You're a strange boy, but you have a good heart." Duke Otto laughed at some private recollection. He motioned to the hunt master to bring the bird forward. The hunt master moved toward a large hawk that stood, hooded, on a staked perch. "Not that one, Finn," he called to the faun. He pointed toward another. "That one."

Wulf felt angry. He had felt angry a lot lately. "Adelbert wouldn't need to have gone to pay a blood price if you had told Gunnar he couldn't marry Ulla," Wulf said.

I wasn't going to yell at Father, Wulf thought. I promised myself not to get mad.

But his attempt to keep the anger out of his voice had made him sound cranky instead.

"Prince Gunnar is dead?" Duke Otto blinked, then shook his head, smiling sadly. "Ah, yes. Well, no one told me," said his father. "I didn't know if she liked Gunnar or not."

"*Not*," Wulf said. "Definitely not."

The relationship of Ulla and Grer was public in the castle now.

In the town, too, Wulf thought. Even though they could see one another without sneaking around, they were being very careful to keep it as proper as possible. Ulla was ready to marry the smith, but Grer had insisted they take it slow.

"That you and I should be together at all is as outrageous to my kind of folks as it is to your'n," Grer had told her. "So we have to make this strong and build it to last."

Wulf gazed down at his hand. The burn had healed over the past months and was now a chunk of reddish tissue on his palm. It didn't hurt anymore. The scar had a hollow place in its center, like a little valley cut into his hand. This formed the perfect outline of a dagger tang in his right palm. Because of it, he could hold weapons much better. His right palm dovetailed perfectly with the handle of a dagger or a sword.

But I would trade that ability in a moment for the chance to get feeling back in the palm of my hand. Wulf figured he never would.

Behind them, Finn was taking the hood off the largest of the birds.

It was a bald eagle.

"Wulfgang, Sandhaven controls our access to the sea," Duke Otto said. "They've raised their tariffs to crazy heights. It's hurting us. We have to get them lower or we'll . . . what was I going to say?"

"I don't know, Father. Maybe it was that, if the Sandhaven tariffs aren't lowered, we'll be ruined?"

"Alliance. We need one."

"I understand, Father," Wulf said. "And with a marriage alliance, we'd have a united front from the Greensmokes to the ocean. The empire would think twice before trying to move north."

"Empire?"

"The Holy Roman Empire."

Duke Otto gazed at his son thoughtfully. "How old did you say you were?"

"Sixteen," Wulf said glumly.

A big smile broke out on Duke Otto's face. "Really? My Wulf is sixteen. Did you hear that, Finn?"

The hunt master nodded. "Yes, Your Excellency."

CHAPTER EIGHTEEN:
THE FLIGHT

Then the duke turned his attention to the birds. He held out his arm, and the bald eagle leaped from its perch and, with two flaps, flew over and landed on the duke's gauntlet.

Wulf backed away, giving his father plenty of room. This eagle was a female. They were almost one third larger than the males. Duke Otto looked at the bird, then turned to Wulf. "I think it's time," he said. "I want you to slip her today, Wulfgang."

Slipping was the word for releasing the bird. To slip also meant that you were in charge of that bird during the flight. You had to watch it, follow it, and, when it struck prey, rush to the scene and help it finish off the kill.

Wulf gulped. He'd never flown a bird larger than a falcon. He'd brought his favorite of the owls in the mews, Nagel.

Finn came up beside Wulf and took Nagel from his arm.

"You can slip them both, m'lord," the hunt master said. "The owl with the eagle at the same time. We've been training them together."

Wulf was surprised. He'd read about this being done in an old hawking codex in the library, but he'd never seen it.

"What for?"

"Forests, where those sharp eagle eyes don't help so much. You need ears to hear the rustles and bustles below the branches, and that owl is the eagle's ears," Finn replied. "It was tried out west in the pine forests, and worked. So your father said he'd like to see if we could match or even outdo those western eaglers."

Finn unhooded Nagel.

With an expert flick of his wrist, he set her to flight. Nagel flew to a nearby tree limb and sat watching.

"Now let's get you ready for the big one," he said.

Finn returned and pulled off Wulf's small gauntlet, suitable for owling. He helped Wulf into the larger, thicker gauntlet that was needed for slipping an eagle.

The land dropped quickly from this ridge between the rolling mountain peaks and a wide forest below down the slopes of the Dragonbacks. There were clumps of pines and cedars with their evergreen needles, but mostly the woods were filled with bare trees with a haze of green buds.

"I have a report from a herder I know from way back. Buffalo man," Finn continued. "There's a wolf pack that has strayed from the west valley where they belong. They have been feeding on the spring buffalo calves."

"We're going to hunt wolves today," said the duke. He clapped his hands and smiled.

Wulf was excited despite himself. "I always wanted to see that."

"You are going to be *doing* it," Duke Otto said, and nodded toward the eagle. He held up his arm with the bird on it. Wulf lifted his own gauntleted arm. His father reached over and, with a turn of his wrist, set the bald eagle onto Wulf's outstretched forearm. "Don't worry. This girl is a wolf hunter."

The bird was light, as were all birds of prey. But she was close to a half stone, which was much more than a falcon or an owl. Wulf knew he should easily be able to hold her up with one arm, but he couldn't help moving his left hand under his elbow to steady himself. The eagle just *looked* heavy.

"Are you sure about this, Father?" Wulf said.

"Very sure," said the duke.

Finn turned from gazing down into the valley. "The brushbeaters have stirred something, Your Excellency," he said. "Looks to be at least a fox."

Duke Otto nodded toward Wulf. "All right then. Get ready."

"Yes, sir," Wulf replied. He turned his attention to the eagle. She eyed him with a blank, emotionless stare.

"Does she have a name?" he said to the hunt master.

Finn looked at the bird as if he were sizing her up and only now thinking of a name for her. "Blitz," he replied.

The eagle did not respond to hearing her name. Most hunting birds could not care less what humans called them.

I'm just a walking tree that gives you food, right, Blitz?

Birds were not pets. They did not love you. They did not care if you loved them. You also couldn't get them to do anything by yelling at them or being mean. They did not understand human emotions at all. Nope, what they wanted, really all they wanted, was to hunt and to get fed for doing it. As long as you remembered those simple things about hunting with birds, you could get along with them. And if you could ever teach yourself to *think* like them, you could use them in really deadly ways.

But hawk, falcon, owl, eagle, or even from time to time a vulture, the basics of falconry were the same, and those Wulf knew from years of practice.

The eagle blinked, turned her white head toward the sky. After a moment, she opened her curved, sharp beak and let out a loud cry.

Wulf got ready to make the slip. He lifted his arm and

called out, "Go, Blitz!" The bird spread her broad brown wings and instantly knew what to do. She lofted up with the movement of Wulf's lifted arm. And then the weight was gone and the eagle was in the sky. She dipped for a bit, then found what she was looking for. It was an updraft air current, and she used it to glide higher and higher.

"Look at her soar," the duke commented. "Finn and I slipped her with a vulture for a while so she could learn the tricks of saving strength and using currents. Then we trained her with the owl, your little owl, as a matter of fact."

The duke had spent more and more time at hunting and riding since his mental failing started. It was like he was going through a second childhood. He left a lot of the day-to-day business of the mark to Otto, Wulf's oldest brother.

Blitz swooped around behind Wulf, his father, and the rest of the hunting party, gathered speed, and then zoomed over their heads. Then he saw the little owl, Nagel, flying just behind the eagle, letting herself be pulled along in the wake of the eagle's passing through the air.

That's smart, Wulf thought.

There was no way the owl could keep up with the eagle on her own, but this way she let the eagle do most of the work. And it was very powerful work. He had felt the wind from the eagle's wings as she passed over his head.

And then Blitz and Nagel were soaring down the mountainside and into the valley below them. The biggest thing Wulf had seen bald eagles hunt was foxes.

"So she's really trained for wolves?" he asked.

"Aye, Finn and I think so," his father replied. "Tell him, Finn."

The faun did not look pleased that he had to speak, but he seemed to realize the duke wanted to tell his son about it himself but couldn't find the words.

"You'll remember her from when she was young, m'lord," Finn said. "We started her on foxes with a make-eagle, a training bird, but she never cared much for them foxes. So we tried the vulture and then the owl with her. She took to the owl. But when we showed her a dead wolf one day she went wild. After that, it was all wolf training for that one."

Wulf wondered how they'd done it. Probably with skin lures or carcasses pulled behind a horse. And then they would have set her on captured, live wolves when they could get their hands on one.

"And can she take down even a big one?"

"She can," the hunt master replied. "She has. Undersized so far and in a field, not a forest. But I reckon she could down a big male if the time and place were right."

Wulf and the duke watched the bird soar until she became a speck in the distance. "This is a huge slip. There must be a league of forest down there she is hunting. Aren't you afraid we'll lose her, Father?"

The truth was, he was more worried about losing the little owl. Nagel had always seemed like a good-luck charm to him. He would miss her if she disappeared into the forest. This sometimes happened even with the best-trained birds.

"She's always come back," his father replied. "And when she doesn't, she's made her kill, right, Finn?"

"That's right, Your Excellency."

"She'll be waiting for us to find her and lure her off the carcass with some fishies."

He stood silently beside his father for a while. Blitz soared one direction and then another, finding updrafts to keep her from having to flap too often, always scanning the landscape below her. The owl followed behind. If Nagel dropped too far back, the eagle slowed or doubled back to let her catch up.

Duke Otto pointed into the valley at the eagle. "She's seen something."

The eagle swooped in awesome curves back and forth—and then she came up short in one of her wide curves and suddenly headed in a straight line toward the west, away from the morning sun. She was a wheeling speck below. "Now let's find out if she can make her kill."

They watched as the bird shot across the treetops at her fastest speed, wings flapping in huge swooshes. But then, when she came over a clump of pine trees, she seemed to lose her way. She flew around in tight, overlapping circles.

"Ah, she's lost it," said the duke. He seemed very disappointed.

But Wulf was watching closely. A tiny speck rose from the trees below. It might have been a blowing leaf, but it rose up and up. It banked into a beautiful curve, and that was when he knew it was the little owl. She was practically blind in the daylight, but she still had her sensitive ears. She knew where the wolf was. And she was showing the eagle.

Something stirred in the hardwood saplings at the edge of the pines. Something was passing through the trees that was big enough to move them.

Then he saw the wolves.

There were gray-and-white splotches in the lighter gray of the bare forest below. But now that he'd picked them out, he could easily follow them.

"There!" cried Wulf. "Nagel has heard the wolves."

"Who?" said Duke Otto. "What are you talking about?"

"The owl," Wulf replied. "She hears them. Now, there it is! See the trees move?"

"Where?" The duke stared to where he was pointing. After a moment he chuckled. "Yes, yes. I see them. And so does my eagle!"

The eagle had followed the owl and spotted the wolves now. There was one that was hanging back from the pack.

This was what the eagle had been waiting for. Soon she was after it.

"A lone wolf," said the duke. "Or maybe a leader, out hunting. They will do that at times."

The eagle drew closer to the shaking below her.

The little speck that was the owl disappeared again into the foliage.

Closer—

And then, with a loud cry that even they heard at what had to be nearly a half league away, the eagle dove into the trees.

She disappeared.

The running movement stopped.

"She's got it!" Duke Otto called out.

Or it's got her, Wulf thought.

CHAPTER NINETEEN:
THE WOODS

He called himself Steel. That was his Legionnaire name, a professional name that meant he was part of the Gray Goose Legion. This was the thousand-man regiment of paid soldiers working directly for the von Krehennest family of Sandhaven. Unlike the normal levies and bands, they had professional ranks. Sergeant. Lance captain. Lance commander. Captain. They called themselves Nesties.

Many Nesties were mercenaries, men who had traveled from or been driven out of other kingdoms and principalities. Some even came from across the ocean. The one thing they had in common was that they were all very good at what they did. They were dangerous killers. They usually preferred bills and poleaxes to swords, although they were experts with swords, as well. When ordered to kill, they *never* gave quarter to an enemy until that enemy lay unmoving in a pool of his own blood.

At least, that was the idea. For Steel, the Legion was a way to get ahead for his family. He and his brother were city rats. They were the sons of a silversmith who worked in

Krehennest. They had been fairly well-to-do until a plague had taken Steel's mother and two sisters. After that his father had retreated into himself. His business fell apart. He spent his savings on wine. Soon they lived in poverty. Then the silversmith died and there was absolutely nothing left for Steel or his brother.

Except.

They did have their father's brother. He was a teamster who also supplied horses to the Nesties. He recommended Steel and his brother to the Legion's recruiter. The brothers had joined together. Since they could read and write, they'd come in as officer cadets and camp errand boys.

Over the next fifteen years, they both had done well. His brother, whose Legionnaire's name was Rask, which meant "swift" in the Tidewater dialect of Kaltish, had risen to the highest rank of all. He was the commander of the elite faction of the Legion called the Hundred. Steel had only risen to lance captain, but that was all right. Besides, he had almost saved up the fifteen hundred thalers he needed to buy his next rank. The rich officers could depend on their families for the money. For Rask and Steel, it had taken years of looting and raiding to the south to get together the silver they needed.

To go viking against the Romans was the reason the Nesties really existed. They were there to protect the sons of nobles who had to make their mark in combat. But those young men of privilege could never, ever be killed by a Roman gladius. The Nesties were there to do the dying for them.

This expedition against the Mark of Shenandoah might be enough. He had eleven hundred saved. If he could get back home with loot or, even better, with an indentured servant to sell, he might raise the four hundred extra thalers he needed to buy lance commander.

Only that wasn't going to happen.

Steel was dying. He hated the feeling. It wasn't going to be death in combat. It wasn't even a sickness he could name.

He simply felt his will to live leaking away.

It had started when the dark thing had arrived at the castle.

The thing was shaped like a man, but it had a vulture-shaped head. It smelled of death. And it was coal black from head to foot.

Instead of ordering it killed, King Siggi had welcomed it.

Only the Nesties knew, and they were sworn to follow their king's orders and to keep their king's secrets.

They'd been ordered to eat the bloody, black Roman bread.

The thing that smelled of death came into their minds.

Now they took their orders from the black thing.

For some, this had come easily. A transfer of allegiance.

Maybe it was because he had been too devoted to Siggi. Maybe it was because there was something physically different or wrong with him. When the black thing had moved in and taken control, something was snuffed out in Steel.

There was no fire inside.

His plans to make a life for himself, to marry Silke Leeuwenhoek and start a family? Gone. Instead of asking her father for her hand as they'd planned, Steel had gone out drinking that night. Alone.

Silke had been bewildered and heartbroken. She had moved on.

He didn't know how to tell her that he felt like a burned lump of charcoal inside. That he was crumbling away.

The only thing keeping him going was the harsh will of the dark thing. There was hierarchy and order. He had always liked that about the Legion, especially after the way he'd grown up on the streets. He became the bloodservant of his section commander, that commander answered to his captain, and the captain answered to Prince Trigvi. The prince belonged to the black thing.

Then the will of the black thing had suddenly disappeared. It was replaced by the mind-thought commands of Prince Trigvi alone.

He hated marching on Shenandoah. They were allies. It wasn't right. His mother had come from Shenandoah, from Kohlsted. He felt like he was marching against his own people.

Now they were going west to do *what*? To avenge Prince Gunnar, and get paid a blood price, yes. That was fair.

But once they had started out, the blood price had seemed less and less of the purpose of Prince Trigvi.

Instead of settling the blood feud, he had made it worse.

Near the border, they came upon Adelbert von Dunstig and his band. It could hardly be called a company, much less an army. Fifty men-at-arms and Adelbert had traveled east to offer terms. Gunnar was dead. Now there was a huge amount of silver and a vast eastern territory for a blood-price settlement.

Soon after Adelbert had entered Trigvi's war tent to talk with the prince, the Legion itself had been ordered to attack the men of the mark, and to leave none of them alive. Even if they'd wanted to, they couldn't have avoided killing. They were not the prince's men-at-arms anymore. They had become the prince's bloodservants.

His slaves.

The fifty men of Shenandoah hadn't stood much of a chance against a thousand. Only one man, a crazed and deadly fighter, had escaped, and it wasn't the duke's son.

Adelbert was captured. The rumor was that Trigvi had cut Adelbert's throat and sent his severed head home to King Siggi as a trophy.

It isn't supposed to be this way, Steel thought. *Shenandoah is our* ally. *They are Kaltemen. Why are we marching against her?*

He wanted to talk to his brother about this, but Rask was not along on this march.

He had left with the black thing, six months ago. Rask and the Hundred had ridden out of the Krehennest castle garrison one night. The dark thing was leading them. They had vanished in the night.

Steel felt truly alone without his brother. He wanted to be fighting Tiberians, raiding colonies, patrolling the Chesapeake. Those were the things Nesties were *supposed* to do. The things they were good at.

Instead they were well inside the Mark of Shenandoah's boundary, marching through Dornstadt Pass.

His master's will was gone. The black thing's hatred. The black thing's drive. Gone.

Now he only had Trigvi as a master. His mind-command wasn't enough after the crushing will of the black thing.

Steel thought about killing himself every day. He planned how he might do it. But the last spark inside him that hadn't been put out by the black thing and the bloody bread wouldn't *quite* let him do it.

So he'd rode onward.

Steel's entire company was passing around a case of the runs. Steel was over his, but his men were constantly ducking into the woods, or squatting down wherever they found themselves if they had to. Some had cut out the back of their trousers, their butts covered only by their tabard, so they could squat sooner. A couple were trying remedies such as eating sand from the bottom of rainwater puddles or even plugging themselves with wine corks. Steel highly doubted either was effective, but he let them go ahead, since it eased some of the boredom of the westward march.

They'd stopped for the night. Steel ordered his men to make a quick road camp with tarps, but no tents. While they were doing that, he'd told his sergeant he was going to scout for a stream for the wagon teams. The sergeant nodded glumly and started spacing his men in the driest place he could find.

Steel slipped into the woods. He rode a ways and did not find a stream. Then he rode a ways farther. He stopped his horse, and they stood still.

He was about to rein his horse back, in fact part of him thought he *was* turning the horse around, but he didn't. He lightly kicked his heels into the horse's sides and rode farther. This time he didn't stop. He rode into the night. Soon the horse began to stumble because it couldn't see. They were following no path. Steel got off and led the horse forward.

He stopped at dawn beside a stream and ate some hard bread while the horse guzzled water. Nearby was a meadow with some grass that had survived the winter. He would let the horse graze.

This was where he would die.

His true master was gone. He had nothing left inside.

Maybe this blankness inside was a sickness that only struck one in a thousand who ate the ater-cake. It didn't seem to affect the others like it did him.

That was his bad luck.

He was no longer a Nestie. He wasn't Steel anymore.

He was once again Alvis Torsson.

And Alvis Torsson was dead tired.

Alvis slept.

He dreamed of his mother. It was nothing special. She was telling him to mind his muddy boots after he'd come in from playing. He hadn't had such a dream in a long time. He couldn't really remember what she had looked like anymore.

But here she was. Telling him to wake up, company was coming!

Alvis Torsson did awake—and found himself surrounded by four bears.

They stood on two legs and carried wicked looking halberds. So not bears.

Bear men.

Steel reached for his sword. One of the bear men stepped forward. It? He? It turned its halberd sideways and slapped the flat surface down on top of Steel's head.

Darkness.

This time Steel slept a much deeper sleep with no dreams.

CHAPTER TWENTY:
THE VALLEY

"Wulfgang, remember that spot!" cried the duke.

Wulf did his best to memorize the area of the bald eagle attack, trying to picture in his mind what the landmarks around it might look like below, at eye level. He hoped Finn had also marked it, because even though he was good at tracking, Wulf didn't entirely trust himself to find the place once they rode down. He knew how easy it was to get lost and turned around in the woods, because he'd done it enough times on his own.

They moved back from the overlook and went to get their horses. Grim and Harihandel had them ready. Just before they mounted up, Wulf turned to his father. "Father, why did you send Adelbert to Sandhaven? It should have been me."

Duke Otto, who had been about to climb into his saddle, stopped. He turned to Wulf, and stared at him. After a moment, he motioned Wulf over to himself. Wulf, who was only a pace away, stepped to his father. Duke Otto pulled him into a strong embrace, hugging Wulf to his chest. To

Wulf's complete surprise, his father kissed the hair on the top of his head. When Wulf looked up, he saw tears in Duke Otto's eyes.

"Never in a thousand autumns," his father said. "They would kill you."

The Duke finished mounting his horse.

"And they won't kill Adelbert?" Wulf asked.

"Not the Siggi I know. He'll be fair."

Before Wulf could say anything else, the duke kicked his horse and they were off. Duke Otto led the way, while Wulf and Finn followed behind in file. They worked their way down a narrow trail that led them under the top of the cliff where they'd just been standing. Then they headed into the woods and left the trail. Now the duke gave way to Wulf and the hunt master, and Wulf tried to make sense of what he was seeing and tried to figure out where he was, and where the eagle and wolf might be.

The smell of early winter was in the air, and the horses' hooves crackled in the fallen leaves. There was a chilly breeze and Wulf drew his wool cloak tighter around his shoulders.

A screech came from a nearby beech tree. Wulf smiled. He recognized that voice. It was the little screech owl, Nagel.

He put out an arm, and down Nagel came to land on his glove. She then hopped from his arm and onto Wulf's shoulder. For a moment, he was going to shoo her off himself. She might take a shine to his ear and bite out a chunk. But she seemed chilly and tired after her mighty flight to lead the eagle to the wolf, and appeared mostly to need a perch that was not jostling all about, as his wrist would do.

Now to find the kill.

There's a big oak tree, but then there are *hundreds* of big oak trees in this forest, Wulf thought.

Finally, they came to a stream, and Wulf decided to assume it was the little creek he'd glimpsed from above.

But which way on the creek, up or down?

Nagel came to the rescue. She squawked and fluttered off his shoulder and landed in a tree that was clearly to the right.

I guess that's as good a clue as any, Wulf thought. Nagel was the most intelligent bird Wulf had ever hunted with by far.

He turned in the direction the owl indicated, and the three horsemen and their mounts splashed down the middle of the creek. Nagel quickly flew back down and again mounted Wulf's shoulder.

They tramped on as quickly as they could. Everybody knew the eagle might have more than she could handle in her talons.

It seemed to Wulf that they had gone way too far, but then he noticed an overhanging cliff and realized it must be a rocky area he'd seen from above. The attack had been directly across the creek from that rock.

Then they heard the cry of an eagle and knew they were in the right place. As Wulf made his way through the tangled vines that hung from the trees near the creek, he heard it again. Then they were in a clearer patch of woods, and in front of them was an explosion of hair and feathers. That must have covered an area of ten or twenty paces. And near the middle was the bald eagle.

She was sitting on what looked like a small mound of earth. Her wings were spread out to cover and hide it.

The sight caused Finn to smile for the first time all day. "She's mantling, m'lords, dropping her wings like that," he said. "That's a good sign, it is."

Wulf and his father dismounted.

"She is, by Sturmer. She's got it!" the duke said excitedly. He turned to Wulf and smiled broadly and innocently. "What a day for a hunt, isn't it? And what's your name again, sir?"

Wulf blinked. "I'm Wulfgang von Dunstig, sir," he answered. "I'm your son."

The smile on the duke's face became puzzled, but then he brightened again. "My son!" He turned to Finn. "This is *my son*. He is, isn't he?"

The hunt master didn't know how to reply. He looked to Wulf, who nodded.

"Yes, Your Excellency."

"He's a grown man?"

"And a good hunter, Your Excellency."

The duke turned back to Wulf. "I have a son," he murmured to himself, shook his head and smiled.

I want him to fade away happy like this, Wulf thought. To always see the world like it was the first time, especially at the end.

"We'd better take care of the bird, Your Excellency," Finn said as gently as his gruff voice would allow.

"Yes, yes."

Duke Otto took a spear from a holder on his horse's saddle. Wulf drew an ax from his side for his left hand—and his new dagger for his right. Grer had finished the knife two days after the fight with Gunnar.

"It's a good blade," the smith had murmured as he took it to polish and install a handle. "And had the best quenching I ever saw, too." He only smiled a little when he said it.

Wulf still had the gauntlet on his right hand, and this hid the mangled flesh of the scar, but even through the leather of the glove, the dagger fitted perfectly into the hollow between the scar tissue of his palm.

Wulf and his father walked slowly toward the eagle. This close, Wulf could see blood spatters across her white head feathers. A piece of torn flesh was in her beak.

In Duke Otto's other hand, the one that did not hold the spear, was something shiny.

A fish, Wulf realized. A trout minnow. The shine came from the scales.

Duke Otto dangled the fish by its tail. He knelt a step or two away from the bird and clucked to get the eagle's attention. He had been holding the shaft of the spear in his gloved hand, and now the duke slowly set the spear down in the leaves beside him. He put the fish on the top of his gauntlet. The eagle eyed the treat. Duke Otto raised his gloved arm, forming the familiar perch. He clucked again.

For a moment, the eagle didn't want to move. Then she pulled her wings back in and tried to fly over to land on Duke Otto's arm. This didn't work. One of her wings did not fold right. It dragged along the ground, and her try at flying turned into a clumsy hop.

The wolf sprang.

With a snarl it launched itself toward Duke Otto. Wulf's reaction was quick. The wolf was closest to his left side, so he swung the ax in that hand.

He caught the wolf in the side of the throat with the battle ax blade. The ax stuck in the animal's muscle. Wulf held on. He yanked the animal toward himself. It snarled and twisted to get at his arm.

Screeeeech!

From Wulf's shoulder, the little owl launched herself at the animal's face. She shot like a bolt across the space between. One talon caught, the other missed and sank into the animal's nose. The wolf cried out in pain, and gave its head a vicious shake. The little owl flapped away.

Wulf drew back.

—and plunged the dagger into the side of the wolf's head, putting all his weight behind the blow. The blade slid in just before the hinge in the jaw and swept upward into the wolf's brain.

The wolf yelped. Its feet kicked in spasms. And then it died. Wulf rolled it over to reveal the stomach.

A male wolf. He'd separated from the pack, and it had cost his life.

He was torn open with his guts hanging out. The eagle must have done this. There was no way he could have survived for long, even without Wulf's stabbing him. The fact that he had managed to attack one last time was amazing.

Wulf pulled out his dagger and sat back, breathing hard. The eagle had dragged itself over to his father by this time and crawled onto the duke's arm. It sat calming, crunching on the tail of the trout.

Wulf shook his head. He felt his sight swimming.

Breathe deep, he thought. Hold it for a two count like Koterbaum taught us. One. Two.

Someone was handing him something. It took Wulf a moment to realize it was Finn, giving him a pick-up piece, a reward to feed up the little owl.

Wulf sat looking at the dead wolf. His eyes were closed. His mouth was slightly open.

Wulf heard the distant sound of thunder. Was it going to rain on them going home?

This was a wild animal, and huge. He had dragged down *buffalo calves*. He might have killed his father or himself.

Still, he was beautiful.

The thundering sound grew louder.

That's horse hooves, Wulf thought. A lot of them.

Then he heard the battle cries of men.

Chapter Twenty-One:
The Owl

There was a crackling in the forest to the east of them, and a rider appeared. He held a bow with an arrow nocked and pulled back. He wore a hauberk speckled with mud. He had blonde hair, held back with a leather headband.

Like Gunnar's, Wulf thought.

The man's aim settled to a deadly stillness.

He's found his mark, Wulf thought. He drew his dagger.

The man let loose his arrow. Despite the noise, Wulf could hear the twang of the man's bowstring.

Duke Otto was just turning to look at what had caused the commotion. The arrow struck him in the side, under his arm. The eagle flapped away on its broken wing, then fell into the leaves nearby. The arrow that hit the duke sank deep, and its point came out in the middle of his chest below where his sternum would be. When it did, blood gushed out.

"Father!" Wulf cried out.

The duke tried to speak, but a bloody bubble came from his mouth.

He slowly reached out his arm toward Wulf.

The duke's lips curled into the faintest smile.

Then his torso slumped sideways, as if a string holding it up had been cut.

"Father, no!"

Wulf looked back up at the man on the horse. Now the other was aiming an arrow right at him. There was nothing Wulf could do.

A blur of motion seemed to crash into the man's face. He let out a yell of surprise and, at the same time, shot his arrow.

There was a sharp pain in Wulf's left arm. He looked down to see that the arrow had hit him in the upper arm near his shoulder. It had passed through the muscle. A deep flesh wound. Only its vanes showed on one side. On the other, the rest of the arrow hung out.

Wulf threw his dagger at the man as hard as he could.

He'd never been very good at getting a throwing knife to stick, and this time was no different. He completely missed the man. He hit his horse. The dagger pommel smashed into the horse's face below its left eye.

The horse reared, and the man came crashing off and landed with a heavy whump on the leafy forest floor. For a moment, he lay scrambling like a bug turned upside down.

With a snarl, Wulf reached down with his right hand under his arm and pulled the arrow the rest of the way through the wound in his left arm. As he pulled, he had to tear downward to get the angle. Blood gushed from a bloody hole on both sides of his arm.

Then he had the arrow in his right hand. He glanced down at it, amazed something so thin could have caused him so much pain. Its iron tip was not barbed. It was an arrow designed to pierce armor. The shaft was white birch, and it was fletched with three goose feathers, two white and one gray.

Wulf reached toward the fallen man. The man looked at Wulf.

Eyes. Light brown. Staring at him in consternation.

At the moment, he wanted nothing more than to put those eyes *out*.

"Die!"

Wulf jumped onto the man's chest. The other tried to throw Wulf off, but couldn't.

Wulf stabbed down as hard as he could with the arrow.

Instead of hitting an eye, the arrow sank through the bridge of the man's nose into the center of his face.

Squelching.

The man slumped backward, and Wulf kept his weight on the arrow.

Thud. Thud.

It was the man's feet kicking against the ground behind Wulf.

"Die, die, die!"

When he finally looked up, the clearing was filled with armed men. Finn lay dead. His still body bristled with arrows. Even the nearby bald eagle had arrows through it.

The armed men wore tabards of blue and black vertical stripes with a badge representing a gray goose in flight stitched on the center. Sandhaven.

He gazed around frantically, found his dagger lying in a muddy hoofprint, and picked it up and shoved it into its scabbard.

His father—

Wulf stumbled back to where the duke lay. His eyes were closed. Wulf bent down, put his ear to his father's mouth. Shallow breathing.

Still alive.

Putting everything he could into it, he tried to lift up his father's body. Straining, breaking into a sweat, he raised him on his own shoulder. Fresh bleeding broke out from where the arrow penetrated the duke's body.

There was no way. No way.

Then a blur of motion as something—someone—charged out of the woods toward them. Wulf turned, drawing his dagger, figuring he might have just drawn his last breath.

It was Grim. The faun sprinted up to Wulf and, without a word, took Duke Otto's body from his shoulder. Grim was huffing and puffing from his charge down the mountain, but he seemed to hold the duke without great effort.

"We run, m'lord," Grim said in his rough tenor voice.

"But—"

Thunk. Something hit his left shoulder. Pain shot through his wounded arm. He was about to stab at whatever was causing it, but there was a flutter of feathers and a faint hoot.

The owl. Nagel.

She *spoke* into his ear.

"Listen to the goat-man," she said. "Into the woods, stupid boy."

"What?"

"Run!"

Her voice sounded like a human female. He'd never heard of owl Tier. And she looked *exactly* like a screech owl.

"Follow me, Grim." He turned and plunged between two trees.

Then fell in a sprawl. Dirt in his mouth. Smell of forest floor leaves.

Something tripped me, he thought. Never mind. Get up!

He tried. His right arm collapsed and he fell again, slamming his shoulder against the ground.

Up!

A second time, this time he pushed with only his left arm. Got to his feet, stumbled forward, then got his balance.

Keep going. Got to—

No!

Behind, branches and leaves crackled. Men shouted. Mad voices. Terrified voices.

Then there was the clanging and banging of iron and steel.

Wulf stopped. He hesitated. He put his hand over the hole in the back of his arm.

Not spurting.

Sandhaven raiders. I should be there, fighting for Shenandoah. Defending—

"Father," Wulf sobbed.

The owl dug its claws deep into Wulf's shoulder. Needles into nerves. He'd thought the arrow going through his arm hurt. This was a *lot* more painful.

"Blood and bones!"

The owl took Wulf's ear in its beak and *bit through it.* Agony. It let him go. "Too many of them. Run!"

Nagel eased her talons out of Wulf's skin. Wulf's head was clear now. He wanted revenge. And if he was going to get that, he was going to have to survive.

The owl flew away. Wulf ran deeper into the forest. He glanced back to be sure Grim was following with his father. He was. His father was draped over the faun's shoulder like a bag of grain, the arrow still sticking from his father's back. A leafy stem hung on one of Grim's horns. It must have caught there during the run.

Wulf turned back and moved forward. Branches slashed against his face. His breath was coming in big sucking heaves.

Suddenly, he burst into a small clearing. There was a meadow with a creek running through it. And drinking from the creek were—

Buffalo. At the sound of Wulf's approach, they started and looked around.

From ahead of Wulf came a booming voice. "Best stop there, man of the town." Three of the buffalo Tier stepped out from the shadows of the trees. Like the fauns, they walked on two legs. The only part of their upper body that looked human was their arms, which were dark brown and hairy, except for their hands. They had the faces of small buffalos. These three carried spears with iron tips. "Them buffalo ain't like cows," the buffalo man continued. "If ye scare them bad, they'll trample ye."

Wulf stood still. He put his hands on his knees, and his chest heaved until he could get a good breath.

Grim burst into the clearing carrying the duke.

"Grim, stop," Wulf gasped. "Careful of the buffalo."

Grim obeyed immediately. He stood beside Wulf, eyeing the buffalo Tier warily.

"Tell us, man, where ye have come from in such a hasty hurry," one of the buffalo Tier said. "We might be of help to ye. Or might not."

"I'm Wulfgang von Dunstig," Wulf managed to get out, even though he was still gasping. "We were attacked. By Sandhaveners."

"*Sandhaven*, ye say?"

"That's right."

"Be strange. Sandhaveners are cheats and chiselers, but not enemies of the mark."

Wulf put a hand on his father's dangling arm. The skin was still warm. Then he realized that what he was feeling was a patch of blood soaking the sleeve of the duke's tunic.

"This is my father, your duke," Wulf said. "Those men attacked him. And they're right behind me. So if you don't believe me, you might be able to ask them yourselves."

CHAPTER TWENTY-TWO:
THE HARBINGER

Just after the melken bell rang out from Allfather Cathedral, a rider on a sweat-glazed brown stallion rode through the eastern gate of Raukenrose Township. He was wearing the silver buffalo badge of the castle garrison and would normally have been well known to the town guards. The watchmen at the gate didn't recognize him through all the caked dust on his face. His horse stood still while they questioned him. The man started to answer when the horse let out a pitiful whinny and fell down dead. It seemed as if its sinews and joints had disintegrated.

The man was knocked out cold.

Two watchmen picked the man up and poured some water on his face. Another tended to the horse. The water woke the man out of his stupor.

Closer up, they saw who it was. Captain Geizbart of the guard. Suddenly Geizbart's face twisted in fear as he gazed at the watchmen. "Are they here?"

"How long have you been riding?"

"Two days," Geizbart replied, as if this were the stupidest

question he'd ever heard, the fear on his face replaced by confusion.

"Without resting?"

"I ruined one horse, stopped to get another from an inn," he said dully. He sat up. "Let me speak!"

"Speak then."

Geizbart blinked, as if trying to remember what it was he had to stay. He squeezed his eyes together as if to force the bewilderment from his mind, and the fearful expression returned.

"They are coming," Geizbart said.

"Who?"

"Men. Thousand. More. Men."

"What men?"

"Sandhaveners."

"Did they accept the blood price for Prince Gunnar?"

It was not surprising that the watch should know about Adelbert's mission. Everyone one in town had by now heard of Gunnar's death. Most had wondered what it meant to the duke's family and to the mark.

"No," said Geizbart, shaking his head. "They're coming to attack."

"Attack the mark? But there's an alliance."

"Take me to the duke."

"He's hunting."

The officer considered. "Lord Otto, then," he said. "Take me to Lord Otto." He suddenly reached out, grabbed one of the watchmen, and shook him by the shoulders. "Right now!" he screamed in the man's face. Then he began to sob.

Ravenelle was still on the Dragonback Ridge slipping her falcon when the Sandhaven raiders came charging down the ridge and attacked her hunting party. Her cry alerted her bloodservants Donito and Raphael, who had ridden out with her. They were spread out. Donito was watering Ravenelle's kalter, and Raphael was preparing her next meal. At her call, they both came running like moths drawn to a candle flame.

It was her bloodservants who saved her. They were on a cliff with about a fifty-hand drop below them. Nearby was a trickling creek that formed a dripping waterfall, and the rock nearby it was mossy. The raiders charged the other servants, who were grouped around the raptor stands.

Ravenelle saw swords and axes rise and fall, heard yells, and then a terrible bleating like a dying lamb.

A faun, screaming, she thought. The horses thundered past where they'd slaughtered the servants. They wheeled through a clump of short cedars to make another pass. Meanwhile, archers fired on those left standing.

Beside her, Axel von Kleist roared in anger. He ran at the men, who were headed back out of the cedar stand. He tried to grab the saddle of a raider that passed near him. He got hold of it, too, Ravenelle saw, but then the raider chopped down with his saber—

Axel's hand was cut off at the wrist. He reeled back and let out a terrible scream. His brother ran toward him, and when a man on horseback came between them, Erik leaped up and managed to knock the raider out of his saddle. The startled horse jumped forward. Its hooves hit the moss by the creek, and it fell on its side. In scrambling to get up, it pushed itself closer to the cliff edge.

That horse is going over the side, Ravenelle thought numbly.

And in a moment, it did.

She turned back to see Erik on the man he'd knocked off. He was pounding on him with a rock. Baron von Kleist had run to get his sword and was drawing it from its scabbard when five saber blades struck him, almost at the same time. He fell down dead.

Who are these killers? Ravenelle thought.

How do I get out of here?

The cliff, mistress, said Raphael, her oldest bloodservant and the leader of the others. *You must climb down. Donito and I will keep the archers away long enough for you to get into the woods.*

But I'll fall. The horse—

It is not a sheer cliff. It is possible to climb down. Now hurry.

She felt a moment of resentment at being ordered around by a mere bloodservant. But this was Raphael. He had taken care of her since she was a baby. Back then, she'd called him her Bubby, and she still did sometimes when speaking only to him. He was almost entirely a part of her now.

All right.

She lay on her belly and slid her feet over the edge, moving slowly, trying to find something to balance on.

Faster, mistress. This time it was Donito who was speaking. *They are coming.*

She heard shouts of men and knew it was true.

But I have to find something or I'll fall.

And then she did find a small ledge. She let herself all the way over the cliff, clinging only with her hands to the rim. She spotted a handhold below that and grabbed it.

Her foot slipped and a small rock fell. It clattered below. Holding tight, she regained her footing. When she'd glanced down, she'd seen another small ledge. She searched frantically for another handhold so she could lower herself. Just when she thought she had to let go, she found one.

Ravenelle continued down twenty hands or more this way until she reached a spot where there were simply no footholds beneath her. A fall now would kill her, and she was panting so hard she couldn't catch her breath.

A scream, and Raphael came toppling past her. He crashed into the forest leaves below. She felt a kick in the stomach as hard as a mule. A sickly feeling washed over her, as if all strength had drained from both her muscles and her mind.

You can't die! No, Bubby! You rocked me in your arms. No . . .

Get down! Get down now, mistress!

She let go and slid down the face of the cliff. The rock scraped against her skin. Her toes caught in a crack, her hands found a knob, and she was ten hands farther down the cliff face.

Only I remain, said Donito. *Run, mistress, run!*

Another scream came from above, and she felt the life-light of Donito go dark. The sick weakness hit her again.

Arrows flew by her. The raiders were at the cliff edge. They were shooting down at her! But there wasn't anything to hold onto. She had to let go, had to—

She released her hold and let herself drop. It was nearly fifteen hands, and she hit hard, her legs crumpling under her, but she landed partly on the body of the dead horse. It broke her fall. She blinked until she was completely conscious again, then turned her head. The body of Raphael lay nearby. His eyes were open and unblinking.

An arrow thwacked into the horse next to her. The horse's still hot blood spurted onto her. She rolled away and regained her feet. The trees. Run for the trees!

They were just budding for spring and weren't very good cover, but they were all she had. She hitched up her dress and ran as fast as she could into the woods, stirring up a trail of winter brown leaves behind her. Arrows rattled through the branches. She had no idea how hard it might be for the attackers to get down from the cliff. So she had to run and keep running.

Which direction? Trees everywhere. Oak, pine, others she didn't know the names of. She was lost. She had no idea which way was home. But down seemed like a good idea. Down into the valley.

She used the red lace of her sleeve to wipe sweat from her face. It came away soaked, and she realized her hands were bleeding from the rocks.

Down. There would be water there. Maybe a chance to follow it somewhere.

Who were the raiders?

Down the hill she went, chuffing through thick layers of fallen leaves, tripping over unseen roots but always picking herself up, always moving.

She was alone. Her bloodservants were dead. She felt ripped apart on the inside as well as the out.

They were gone.

For the first time in her life, she was alone, truly, totally alone in her mind. And she hated it.

CHAPTER TWENTY-THREE:
THE SLAUGHTER

The buffalo people had a reputation for slowness and taking a long time to consider everything. But now they came to a quick decision. One nodded his big, shaggy head, motioning for Wulf and Grim to follow him. He led them away toward a path on the other side of the clearing. Before he could lead them into the woods, Wulf turned and looked across the meadow.

The other buffalo people raised their spears and walked toward the buffalo herd scattered around the grassy clearing. From somewhere deep in each of their throats came a call. Wulf couldn't make out if there were any actual words in the call, but the buffalo seemed to understand. They stopped eating or chewing on their cuds and came trotting toward the buffalo people. Within a few eyeblinks, the herd had gathered.

Then the buffalo people—there were ten or twelve of them—moved to a point behind the animals, forming a line about two arm lengths apart. When they were ready, they lowered their spears, pointing them toward the buffalo.

Then they waited. Soon there was crackling and crunching in the woods. The voices of men shouting. Still the buffalo people waited.

They stood silently. Almost peacefully.

Finally, a man came out of the woods on the opposite side of the meadow. He took a few steps, then saw the line of buffalo standing there, all of their eyes on him. He tried to turn back, but there were more men behind him, and he stumbled into them. Others emerged from the woods, some on foot, leading their horses, some on horseback, and fully visible to Wulf over the backs of the buffalo. Finally enough of the pursuers had entered the clearing for them to be crowded between the woods behind them and the wall of standing buffalo in front. Wulf could see the tops of their helmets bobbing.

The buffalo people behind the herd looked at each other. The one in the middle, taller than the rest of them, shook his spear.

They bellowed. Loud.

"Hooooooo!" It was a sound of alarm, fright, and maybe even a little panic. At the same time, the buffalo people walked forward. "Hooo, cow, hooo!"

The buffalo herd began to churn. Several animals turned toward the buffalo people. Nothing doing. Their spears were lowered. There was no way to go in that direction.

So they turned back to rejoin the herd, and those in the rear started to move forward to get away from the line of spear barbs heading for them. The bellowing of the buffalo grew loud, insistent.

Soon the pushing and ramming grew frantic. Finally, as if they'd come to a decision at once, the buffalo charged.

It wouldn't have mattered if the Sandhaveners were in front of them or not. It was the spears of the buffalo men that they knew and were afraid of.

They charged in the direction of the Sandhaveners. There

were shouts and screams. Despite the grass on the ground, a cloud of dust rose up when the turf was chuffed away. For a time, Wulf couldn't make out what was happening. Then the dust settled.

The Sandhaveners had thrown down their weapons and turned tail and *run*. Run back into the forest. Run *anywhere* to get away from the river of buffalo that was headed straight toward them like a spring flood.

Some tried to use swords or halberds against the surging animals. The pikes they couldn't get lowered in time, and the swords may have sliced into a few, but even the injured beasts were shoved forward by those from behind. The herding instinct, bred into their bones and blood, wouldn't let them stop moving. They rolled over whatever stood in their way.

They trampled over the Sandhaveners who couldn't escape in time. Men screamed as hooves crushed them, a three-hundred-stone weight digging into their stomachs.

"Hoooo, weeeee!"

The trot of the herd became a quick jog.

More screams.

The final bellow of the buffalo people seemed to shake every leaf in the forest. "Hooooo, waaaa!"

The jog became a rush. The buffalo people behind pricked at the rear of the herd with their spear tips.

The rush became a stampede.

The herd charged into the woods, some leaping over brush or fallen logs, some disappearing like a knife into flesh. Behind them, the buffalo people walked at a steady pace.

The buffalo left behind a field of trampled men. Some moaned, some twitched on the ground. When one of the buffalo people came upon one of these, they plunged their spears into the man or cut his throat.

"Come," said the buffalo man beside them. "We will go to the camp and send others. We will take the duke to a wise woman. She will know how to take care of him." He turned his sorrowful-seeming gaze to Grim.

"Do you want me to relieve your burden, brother goat? I can carry his Excellency."

"Keep your hands away, dirty coat."

The other did not smile, but there was a snort that sounded a lot like laughter. "All right, goat man," he replied. "You know that's what my mother used to call me. Little Dirty Coat. But no one else."

"What is your name?" asked Wulf.

"Likainenvuoto." The buffalo considered for a moment. "It is hard to say." He turned to Grim and snorted, then turned back to Wulf. "You may call me Dirty Coat, m'lord."

He motioned for them to follow. He broke a path through the branches and brambles and they trailed after him, moving as quickly as they could with Grim carrying the duke in his arms.

In Buffalo Camp, Wulf was met by a strange sight.

"We came on her drinking from a spring near the salt licks at Broken Cliff," said the buffalo man. "That is bad water." He thrust forward what looked like a forest witch, dark skinned. Her hair was a tangled mass, and her dress was tattered to ribbons in spots. She tried to break away from the buffalo man, but he kept one hand on her arm and pulled her up short. "We were going to kill her, but she said you would be very unhappy if we did. Will you be?"

It was Ravenelle, being held by both arms by two buffalo men.

Wulf considered for the smallest moment whether he should tease Ravenelle. But the buffalo people took things so literally he was afraid they really might stab her to death on the spot.

"She is my foster sister and my cousin."

"Ah, the terror princess of Vall l'Obac. She lives in the castle?"

"Get your hands off me," she said to the buffalo man holding her. She turned to Wulf. "Tell them to let me go, von Dunstig."

Wulf sighed. "She won't hurt us," he said. "Turn her loose, please."

Ravenelle ran at him, but tripped over her dress and fell flat on the ground in front of him. Wulf knelt and gently helped her to her feet. "You need water," he said. "Maybe something to eat."

Suddenly Ravenelle's defiance collapsed and she began to sob. Blood-red tears flowed from her eyes. Wulf pulled her close, and she hugged his neck. "My people. They died saving me."

Wulf held her. There was nothing he could say. He didn't really understand the kind of relationship she'd had with her slaves, but he knew it had been deep.

"Who were those men?"

"They were from Sandhaven."

"It's my fault," Ravenelle said with a sob in her voice. "If I hadn't let Ulla's secret slip to Prince Gunnar, none of this would have happened."

"Gunnar was an animal," Wulf said. "Nothing is your fault."

She sobbed again. His tabard cloth was soon red and smelled of blood.

Then she saw the wounded duke, and she dried her tears with the back of her dress sleeve.

"What's happened? Is he . . .?"

"He's alive, but hurt. It's pretty bad."

"I can see that, von Dunstig," she said. Her determination was back. "But what's being *done*?"

"They've sent for the wise woman."

"So you're just *waiting*?"

"I . . . I guess so."

"No, this isn't the way to do it. We will take *him* to *her*.

I've heard their shamans are all women and that they are very good healers, even though they *are* barbarians and basically animal doctors. Come on, von Dunstig, let's go find this buffalo wise woman."

The buffalo men pointed her in the right direction, and Wulf allowed her to drag him along with her. Grim followed, holding the duke as gently as he could in his arms.

CHAPTER TWENTY-FOUR:
THE VILLAGE

It was at least two watches until the buffalo-clan warriors returned from hunting and killing Sandhaveners. They brought with them as many of the horses as they could find. They also rescued several wounded of the Raukenrose gentry and servants either on horses or walking. Some were hurt. Some were obviously near the gates of Helheim and would be crossing soon.

All of them were seen to by a group of buffalo wise women. Cuts were cleaned and bound with poultices that smelled sharply of mustard and comfrey. More than one bone was set while the patient cried in agony.

Wulf's father had been taken immediately to the wigwam of the wise woman who Dirty Coat told him was the best of them all. She was also Dirty Coat's mother, he added. Her name was Puidenlehdet.

Another wise woman came and stitched up Wulf's ear. He'd forgotten. Nagel had bitten through it to get him to run.

Wulf was barred from entering the wigwam, but Ravenelle insisted she herself be allowed in, and the wise woman let her. Wulf figured there was nothing he could do but get in the way, so he went to the village's central fire pit and paced around it, waiting for word of his father. Grim brought him water in a skin canteen, and Wulf gulped it down to the last drop.

Grim also gave him a leg of smoked wild turkey. He gnawed most of the meat off it, then fed the rest to two of the castle hunting dogs that had found the camp and straggled in. Wulf recognized them from the kennels and from hunting, but couldn't remember their names.

The buffalo people had a musky odor. It wasn't a *bad* smell, necessarily, but it was strong. The closest thing Wulf could think of to it was being in a wardrobe full of coats, but that wasn't it, either, because a wardrobe was stuffy, and the buffalo people had the definite scent of the *outdoors* to them.

Grim didn't like them much. He could tell by the faun's stiff way of standing. He did not let any of them get closer than two paces if he could help it.

Buffalo Camp was a collection of wigwams, some small, some huge, made of—what else—buffalo hides. They sloped up in the center where there was a smoke hole to vent the inside fire. The camp was deep in a valley surrounded to the north, east, and south in a semicircle of the Dragonback Range. A creek burbled nearby, supplying the water. This was carried around in buckets the size of a half-barrel. The buffalo people, even the children, didn't have any trouble carrying the buckets, but Wulf tried to lift one that was filled with water and barely got it off the ground.

At one point while he was standing near the village fire pit, Wulf heard a flutter of feathers, and Nagel landed on his shoulder. She had returned from wherever she had gone during his run. The sight of a man with an owl on his shoulder very much interested several of the buffalo children nearby. They gathered around and peeked at Nagel in curiosity. The children had heads like buffalo calves, with big brown eyes and little, twitchy ears.

"They're really cute, aren't they, Grim?" Wulf said. "You have to admit it."

"Only when compared with their parents, m'lord," Grim replied.

The tall buffalo herder from the clearing was one of the last to return. He saw Wulf and strode up to him as if he were a soldier set to deliver a report. When he got to Wulf, he bent a quick knee to Wulf, then rose back up. "M'lord," he said.

Wulf was surprised, but he nodded.

It should be Father he is bending knee to, he thought.

The other stood silently, and Wulf realized the buffalo man was waiting for him to speak.

"What is your name?" Wulf asked.

"Sinisekslöödudsilm," said the buffalo man. "Your people call me Black Eye."

"I could learn to say it right."

"It is no matter."

"What happened in the woods, Black Eye?"

"The herd took many of the raiders down, and we finished the ones who were left alive. We tracked those who escaped trampling and hunted them, one by one. Many have twisted under my spear today. I believe we got them all."

"How many?"

"Fifty-two, m'lord."

"And your casualties?"

"Two hurt. No one killed."

Wulf nodded. "Good," he said. "That's great. You did well."

"Thank you, m'lord."

"Are you the *sotajohtaja* of your clan?" The term didn't exactly mean "leader," Tolas had taught Wulf. The buffalo people had different leaders for different functions. It was more like "war chief."

"The *sotajohtaja* is my cousin, Tupakkalaatu."

Wulf recognized the word. "That means 'tobacco,' doesn't it?" he said.

Black Eye tilted his head to the side. He seemed to be surprised Wulf would know this. "Yes, m'lord, it does. Tupakkalaatu fought in the Little War for your father."

"I would like to talk with him," Wulf said.

Black Eye bowed his head slightly, then pointed toward a large wigwam near the central fire pit. "He is meeting with a messenger who just came in from Bear Hall. Follow me, m'lord."

"All right." Wulf turned to Grim. "Stay near Father. The moment you hear anything from the wise woman, come and get me."

Grim nodded, and with a sidelong, distrustful glance at Black Eye, he strode away.

Nagel, who had been flitting between Wulf's shoulder and a nearby branch, flew back down and landed on Wulf's shoulder just as he was turning to follow the buffalo man. The movement startled Black Eye, and he let out a small bellow.

"This is a *person*," he said.

"Yeah, I found that out not long ago," Wulf said. "How can you tell?"

Black Eye didn't answer. "I have never heard of an owl person," he said.

"Well, the owl's with me." Wulf motioned toward the wigwam. "Let's go, Black Eye."

If Black Eye was tall, Tupakkalaatu was enormous. He was at least a hand and a half bigger than his cousin. At the moment, he was standing and talking with another buffalo man who was shorter, not much taller than Wulf, in fact. There were no chairs in the wigwam. You either stood or sat on the floor. There was a fire in the middle, kept very small, that warmed the place and provided what light there was.

Around the fire, but not too close to it, buffalo skin rugs carpeted the floor. The wood staves of the walls curved up to form a dome.

The buffalo men had been speaking in their own thick-sounding language, but switched to Kaltish when Wulf arrived.

The *sotajohtaja* turned to Wulf.

"Sinisekslöödudsilm has said that the raiding party that attacked you and your father has been trampled into the ground like bad acorns." The war leader's voice was as low as a rumble, but Wulf could understand him well enough.

"They were all men of Sandhaven?"

"So far as we can tell from the remnants of their clothing and the splinters of their shields, m'lord," Black Eye put in.

"Why did they do this?"

"We may have an answer," said the war leader. "This is Nopeaveden. He has been sent from Bear Hall to deliver a message to the clans."

Nopeaveden did not volunteer an easier way to say his name.

"What kind of message?" Wulf said.

"An invasion, m'lord," Nopeaveden answered. "Earl Keiler has word from a patrol on the northeast side of the Dragonbacks just before Dornstadt Gap. The bear people are very concerned with their territories, you know. They have taken a prisoner, a Sandhaven deserter wandering in the woods."

"My father needs to hear about this," Wulf said. "Maybe he's conscious."

The war leader shook his huge head. "The wise woman says not."

"Then my brother in Raukenrose."

"We are cut off from the town," Nopeaveden said. "When we killed the raiders, we drove as far north as we could. There are men guarding the southern entrance. Many, many men. They wore Sandhavener coats of arms. We could not fight that many, so we came back."

"This is crazy. Sandhaven is our ally."

"It is surprising to me also. We were hoping . . . well, that you might be able to explain what is happening. We were hoping that you would have commands for us to follow."

"Me?" Wulf said. The idea startled him. He didn't like it at all. "It's my father or my brother's place to command."

"You are the son of Duke Otto, m'lord. You are von Dunstig, yes?"

"Yeah, but I'm the *third* son," Wulf said. "I have nothing to do with ruling. My brothers—*they* are in line to inherit the care of the mark. I'm *sixteen*, for Sturmer's sake! The only wars I know anything about are from the sagas. I'm planning to be a border ranger if they'll have me, or a librarian!"

The buffalo man grunted. It might have been a chuckle. "Your brother Otto is cut off from us. We cannot reach him."

"Well, Adelbert then," Wulf said with exasperation.

"You have killed a man today."

"It was desperation."

Nopeaveden turned his big, brown buffalo eyes away from Wulf, as if he were avoiding looking at him. He shuffled on his feet, began to speak, then grew silent, as if he needed to say something and wasn't sure how.

"What is it?" Wulf asked. "Tell me."

"It is your brother, Lord Adelbert," said the messenger. "There is a story. It is from the deserter, and so must be checked. But he said that Lord Adelbert von Dunstig has been beheaded."

"What?"

"He was captured in a Sandhaven ambush."

"That's a lie."

"The man swears he saw it. Lord Adelbert and all his men slaughtered by the Sandhaveners."

Wulf's legs got weak, and he sank to his knees.

But Adelbert *loves* Krehennest, Wulf thought. It leads to the sea.

Adelbert.

Wulf pulled himself back to his feet and looked around for a chair to sit down in. Nothing but the rug on the floor.

Adelbert killed?

No. Murdered.

A fog seemed to form in Wulf's vision, and he thought he might collapse again.

That's the smoke in here. They keep the fires small, but that hole in the roof doesn't work nearly as well as a chimney.

He tensed his legs to remain standing. He rubbed his eyes, and his fingers came away damp.

"No. My brother wants to go to sea," Wulf said. "He is going to be a sailor."

"I'm sorry, m'lord," said Tupakkalaatu.

"You don't understand. He didn't get to *go to the sea* yet. It isn't fair if he never gets to go—"

Wulf stopped himself from saying more. He squeezed his eyes tightly shut. He didn't want to see. He didn't want to be here. Then there was a tug on his earlobe—right on his new stitches. Not incredibly painful, but firm. Another tug. Nagel had taken it in her beak.

Wulf opened his eyes. "All right, owl," he said. "Let go of me. I'm okay."

Although he knew he wasn't. Terrible things were happening, and he was obviously smack-dab in the middle of them.

"M'lord, we need to plan," Tupakkalaatu said softly. His soft boom of a voice sounded like distant thunder.

"Plan for what?"

"A march to Raukenrose. If you want to attack."

"If *I* want to attack? Did you hear anything I said?"

"We have heard . . . that the duke is not always thinking his best these days."

"My father is *fine*," Wulf said defiantly. Then he softened his tone. "Anyway, he is the duke. Not me."

"My people are sworn vassals of the von Dunstig family," Tupakkalaatu said. "Our loyalty does not end with the duke. *You* are von Dunstig."

"But—"

"We are *your* men, Lord Wulfgang. Tell us what you want us to do, and we will do it."

Adelbert had been assassinated. Otto was evidently cut off, maybe surrounded. His father might die.

It was too much. Like something out of a saga, like—

Yes, it *was*. Like *Sigurth's Saga*, as a matter of fact. Well, the details weren't exactly the same. Sigurth Hakisson wasn't the heir of the king or a duke, but only a cousin. His father Haki was the best warrior in all of Freiland.

That was why the attacking Saxehalter had locked Haki into his own mead hall along with his family, including his older sons, and burned it down. Sigurth, the fourth son, had escaped his family's fate because he was off secretly visiting a miller's daughter in the village.

Then the Saxehalter warriors had marched off to attack the king at Arnul. They didn't fear Sigurth in the slightest. He was known to be a party boy who was more interested in drinking and chasing girls than in farming or fighting.

But Sigurth fooled them all. He covered himself in ashes from the mead hall and swore an oath of revenge:

I have heard the Horn of Haki cry forth from the flames
I swear upon that mighty soul-stirrer
I will break the shields of the Saxehalter
Beat those bright knives from their hands
Dull my blade against the bones of cowards
Stuff their mouths with mead hall ash
And make their eyes a meal for ravens.

Then he led his father's surviving war band to Arnul, and

Sigurth's bright reaper dripped red with battle sweat.
He sent many a weapon-wounded warrior down Helheim's
road.
Yes, the blood swans fed well in the gore cradle that day.

But I'm *not* Sigurth, Wulf thought. Sigurth was a hero, one of the great ones. I don't want to cover myself with ashes and swear I'll get my revenge. I'm . . . a defender. I don't like to attack.

This shouldn't be happening.

What if I was more like Sigurth . . . what would Sigurth do?

Wulf knew the answer to that.

"Okay." Wulf turned to the war leader. "What I *want* is to turn the river red with the blood of Sandhaven so it fills the Chesapeake," he said. "That's what I want. But what I *need* is for somebody to help me to come up with a way to eject these invaders and bring peace back to the mark. Will you help me do that?"

To Wulf's amazement, on a signal from the war leader all three of the buffalo men sank down to their knees before him. The smoke in the hut seemed to churn around them, as if they were ghostly warriors appearing out of some kind of supernatural mist.

"We pledge to do this, Lord Wulfgang," said Tupakkalaatu. He looked at the others. "On our lives and lands."

"Aye," the other two answered softly. "We swear."

The war leader rose and turned his gaze down at Wulf. "We will also see what we can do about changing the color of the river to red, m'lord."

Chapter Twenty-Five:
The Law

Ulla von Dunstig would have to keep her promise.

That was the law.

Now that Gunnar is dead, she owes that promise to me.

Her duty is to obey. Mine is to bind her duchy to the kingdom.

Would he enjoy marrying Ulla von Dunstig? That didn't matter.

Trigvi von Krehennest always did his duty. That was who he was. His nanny swore he'd been that way from his birth twenty years ago. For better or worse he couldn't get away from feeling a sense of obligation to see things through no matter what he actually felt about them. Like now. He was doing his duty by watching something truly unpleasant that he really wished he could have avoided.

He was watching Lars Bauch, his old college tutor, have his mind torn apart.

Trigvi had taken his degree from Klugheit College at Raukenrose University, and Bauch had been his favorite tutor back in the day. Now his old teacher was on his knees and holding his head in pain.

Standing in front of the docent was the undead being named Wuten. The draugar was entirely coal black, including his hair, his eyes, and his clothes. Everything. It didn't look like skin. More like black marble. Trigvi had the feeling that if the draugar were cut open, his entire innards would be black as well.

Especially his heart, Trigvi thought.

If you could muster the courage to look at the draugar long enough—which Trigvi had done only when the draugar was paying attention to other matters—you could see that he had the head of a half-man, half-vulture. He had a curved beak. Yet he was a man in form. His manlike hair was cropped short, and Trigvi wondered for a moment how exactly the draugar cut it. Wuten was impervious to most weapons, including razors.

He must use his own knife, Trigvi thought. What else would cut through his hair?

Then there was the smell. Like a maggot-ridden corpse. Trigvi had never seen a man rot, but he had seen the rotten corpses of birds, cattle, and dogs. The same odor surrounded the draugar. It made you constantly fight the urge to puke.

Bauch was terrified. Trigvi caught only the edge of the thought. The draugar was able to direct his thoughts like a spear into the mind of anyone who was a peg down from him within the hierarchy of the Talaia faith—and that meant *everybody*.

Bauch groaned. "Please," he said. "Your orders. We obeyed. All of us."

The draugar slowly nodded. Bauch collapsed onto his stomach as if his strings had been cut. While on the ground, Bauch sobbed, either because he was relieved or was in worse agony.

Bauch had been the one who introduced Trigvi to the host. There had been only celestis, red-cake, back then. He'd played around with the substance in college. He'd been eighteen, and away from home for the first time—away from his father and brothers. Finally. He wanted to be his own man. So when Bauch secretly offered him the celestis along with a cup of blood to dip the wafer into—

"Try it, m'lord. If it doesn't leave you feeling more enlightened, more lucid, then you don't have to partake anymore, and we'll forget about it, all right?"

He'd taken the wafer, dipped it in the blood, and eaten it.

"Now I need a thimble full of your blood," Bauch said. "Don't worry. It's symbolic."

So he'd cut his palm and put in some of his own. Share and share alike. That was the Talaia way, wasn't it?

It hadn't worked out like he'd thought it would. At all. He was a bit ashamed to think that he hadn't used the mind-sharing ability given by the red-cake to pick up knowledge or learn from others, mind to mind. Mostly he and his friends had used it to play pranks on townies and tried to dominate each other for a laugh. There had even been a chart going around on who was "down" and who was "up" in the domination-submission hierarchy.

Despite what the docents had said, there was no equality. It was always one or the other for everybody.

Now the draugar was demonstrating to Trigvi the true power of the new substance called ater-cake. The docents who had joined the Adherents may have thought of themselves as a collective, a sort of big mind thinking the thoughts of a divine being, but the draugar was showing them something Trigvi had also come to experience firsthand.

What it was like to be mastered by an overpowering mind. Now the docent collective was bloodservant to Wuten.

"Up," the draugar hissed at Bauch. Bauch struggled back to his knees, his head bowed.

"Master," the docent mumbled. "I obey. We all obey. Please don't hurt us anymore, we beg—"

"The Hundred. Are they still hidden?"

"As you commanded."

"And the hammer?"

"Still not located. We've torn the library apart for clues."

Bauch began to tremble. He threw his head back and let out a scream. After what seemed a long time, although it must have been only a few eyeblinks, the scream stopped. Bauch flopped down on this belly once again.

"Find it."

"Yes," whimpered Bauch. They were within a league of the university, and so within range of the draugar's mental willpower. Trigvi could imagine all the members of the Adherents in similar positions, down on the floor praying for the pain in their heads to stop.

"I come," Wuten said.

The draugar turned to Trigvi, and the prince started back in surprise, even though he'd expected the call to attention in his mind. The mental presence of the draugar felt as if the being's death smell had gotten *inside* him. Trigvi shuddered, and once again suppressed the urge to vomit.

He had to obey. Yet didn't want to resist. This was duty. It was his responsibility to work with the draugar, as his father had commanded. He was also crown prince of Sandhaven, new heir to the kingdom.

The kingdom his father had secretly committed to serve Rome for the promise of rule of the north.

Trigvi nodded in salute and spoke softly to the dark being.

"Draugar Wuten," he said. "It sounds like your Hundred are ready in the university catacombs. My men are ready, too. It's time for Sandhaven to punish these animal lovers for what they did to my brother. When do we attack?"

"First light," the draugar replied, looking Trigvi in the eyes.

He doesn't blink, Trigvi thought. He just stares.

"And you'll be with us?"

"I go to the Hundred." The draugar turned back to the teacher still lying on the ground. He poked a toe into the docent's side. "Undress."

Trigvi watched as his old docent stripped himself naked. The draugar took Bauch's scholarly robe and put it on.

Trigvi turned away.

He did not enjoy watching Bauch suffer. But what they were doing here was not a game. He was keeping a promise he'd made to himself and to the law.

Not to his father, or even to his brother. Blood and bones, no! The law.

"I want you to make that land scream for what he did to my Gunnar," King Siggi had said to him. "You'll do that for me. Unless you don't have the guts . . . or the heart."

They should scream while paying us taxes, Trigvi had thought.

"Of course I will, Father," he'd answered.

"You don't sound very convincing."

"I will do what I say," Trigvi replied.

King Siggi had gazed at him a moment—not too differently from the draugar's stare. Then his father nodded. "Dutiful. Not much of a man, but dutiful. Your brother used to say so."

Yes, and Gunnar had always delivered the words with a sarcastic grin, Trigvi thought. Gunnar could make it sound like "dutiful" was the worst thing in the world to be, instead of the best.

"I believe in the law."

His father had smiled at that and muttered, "The law is what the law-givers say it is." He wore the same kind of sarcastic smile as Gunnar.

To cold hell with King Siggi.

To get the blood price from Shenandoah was required by law and honor. Blood spilled had to be paid for, if not in gold, then in the death and suffering of the offending family. This was the law that held kingdoms together and kept balance.

Through the flaps of the headquarters tent, Trigvi could see it was dark outside. Dawn was a quarter watch away. Soon Raukenrose would scream, just like King Siggi wanted.

Which didn't mean he always followed his father's commands. Siggi had said to him to "take care" of Adelbert von Dunstig. The fool had come with an offer to pay for Gunnar's blood with land and silver. He'd known Adelbert when he was studying at Halbinsel Academy, and Trigvi had looked up to the young lord who loved the sea.

He'd hurried and met Adelbert's company before he'd crossed the border into Sandhaven. At a nearby inn, he'd listened to the proposal Adelbert brought to pay the blood price for Gunnar. It was generous. Land, and lots of it.

His father might have taken the offer before. But now Sandhaven's duty was to Rome.

The draugar was the enforcer of this bond. He'd brought the ater-cake that allowed King Siggi to truly take control of the minds of the court and of his guard.

The price was finding the hammer. Whatever it took.

I am the one who brought the celestis to Sandhaven from the university, Trigvi thought. I am the one who started our transformation from barbarity into a civil society.

That was why he'd balanced conflicting duties and dealt with Adelbert in a civilized way.

Trigvi had slaughtered Adelbert's company of soldiers, yes. But he had Adelbert sent to be sold as an indentured on the Krehennest wharves. The gang sergeant had chained the lord and marched him back to Krehennest, where he would be sold to a ship bound for the Old Countries. Adelbert's contract, like all the indentured, called for him to serve the ship's master for twenty years. Most of those twenty years he'd spend chained below deck to a rowing bench and an oar.

You wanted the life of a sailor, Adelbert, Trigvi thought. Now you've got it.

This was fair. Adelbert von Dunstig had not killed Gunnar, so he did not have to die. Trigvi could still hardly believe the actual facts, but the youngest brother, Wulfgang von Dunstig, had done the deed. Unlike Adelbert, Wulfgang von Dunstig had to pay with his life.

"Burn the boy alive," his father had ordered. "Do it slowly in front of his father. Make him howl."

"I'll see to his execution, Father."

It wouldn't be burning. The law was very clear on what a proper blood price ought to be for a murdered heir. The killer was to be sealed in a box of stout oak with the top nailed shut. The box was to be placed in a hole twenty hands deep. The hole was to be filled with dirt and stones. After that, the dirt was to be run over with horses until it was packed tight.

Wuten took Bauch's university robe in one hand. With the other, he swung a crossbow on a strap from behind his back. He took aim at the huddled form on the ground.

"Wait," Trigvi said.

The draugar looked at him curiously. His gaze was even scarier when he wasn't giving commands.

"Killing him is a waste," Trigvi continued carefully. "Let me put a pike in his hands and send him to the lines."

Suddenly the draugar was in Trigvi's mind, probing. He was frozen in place. He felt as if a knife were scraping at his skin, flaying it off. But from the inside.

Thou ask'st that I show mercy?

Trigvi tried to bury any feeling he had for his old tutor somewhere deep. Not that the draugar couldn't get to it if he wanted. But perhaps he'd overlook it, like soldiers missed a child hidden in an attic.

The man's mind is broken. I thought at least he might serve us by stopping arrows.

A long pause. Trigvi felt like his insides were burning.

Then the draugar was out of his mind.

Wuten slung the crossbow behind his back again.

"Very well," the draugar said. "I go to release the Hundred."

Trigvi nodded. He didn't trust himself to speak without a trembling voice.

Wuten slipped out of the tent entrance without another word.

Trigvi followed behind and stood in the tent entrance, watching him go. The slightest pink shone against the black of night. Not time to attack just yet. But very soon.

Trigvi called in his guards.

"Get this man some clothes and a weapon," he told the guards. Trigvi looked down at his old docent. "Give him to Zorn's company, I think. Tell the captain to place him at the front when he attacks."

The guards dragged away Bauch. He was still whimpering.

Yes. That would do.

He would create balance. Order.

Clean up the mess others make.

The mess Gunnar made.

Gunnar was selfish. I'm a fair man. Balanced. Ulla von Dunstig will see that.

I will treat her so much better than Gunnar.

She's a duke's daughter. She'll be reasonable.

Maybe she will one day love me.

We all have our duties to perform.

I do.

So does Ulla von Dunstig.

CHAPTER TWENTY-SIX:
THE EARL

Wulf looked down at his father. His face was very pale. The duke lay on the buffalo rug pallet in the wise woman's wigwam. A small fire burned in a nearby corner.

His father seemed to be sleeping peacefully. His chest was covered with bandages. It rose and fell normally, but there was a rattle in the duke's throat. Every third or fourth breath the duke would gasp for air.

"He has wandered down the last lonely trail, but he dassn't want to go the whole way yet," the wise woman said. Her Kaltish had a full-on west-valley accent, but Wulf could understand her pretty well. He could also tell she was smiling. He'd only recently figured out that the buffalo people *could* smile. It was something you had to look carefully to see—the smallest upturn at the edges of their mouths, and their nostrils flaring out a little wider.

"She means that he almost died," Ravenelle said. "But she's pulled him back from the brink."

"This little southerner knows herbs," said the wise woman, nodding toward Ravenelle. "Said she learnt from an elf."

"Saeunn showed me a few things," Ravenelle said to Wulf.

Wulf pointed toward his father. "Will he be all right?"

"His mind is addled, Lord. That won't change."

"But the wounds," Wulf replied. "Can you maybe tell me when he'll wake up?"

The wise woman shrugged her shaggy shoulders. "He'll take a bit of broth today," she answered.

"Will he really be aware then? I mean—"

"What Wulf is asking," said Ravenelle, "is when will Duke Otto be awake enough to tell him what to do?"

The wise woman shook her head. She was *not* smiling now. "That matter's in the hands of the divine ones and the dragon. Never, maybe."

"He's got to wake up."

"No. Rest is what he's got to do. This man wakes too soon, he'll go back to sleep forever."

Wulf knelt and put a hand on his father's chest. Puidenlehdet, the wise woman, had taken him out of his bloody clothes somehow, and he was dressed in a cotton nightshirt. His bandages were made of the same material. The smell of fresh herbs from under the bandages was strong.

"You have a shadow on the heart, Lord," said the wise woman softly. She nodded toward Ravenelle. "The southern princess, she goes with *you*. To take care of *you*. Those she-men that got brought in, they can help me."

She-men meant human women. There were four lady's maids from the castle who had survived the raid. Two of the maids were wounded, but none too badly, and the wise woman had treated them.

"Okay," Wulf said. "I'll go. Soon."

"You're not doin' any good here." She looked to Ravenelle. "You find him and you some food, eh?"

Ravenelle did not seem at all irritated by the order from the wise woman. She reached down and tugged Wulf to his feet again.

"She's absolutely right," Ravenelle said. "You look famished, von Dunstig."

Wulf gazed once more at his father.

I have no idea what to do, he thought. Tell me.

Nothing.

All he had was Ravenelle. His mother, the rest of his family, and his friends were in Raukenrose.

She was in Raukenrose.

As he had during the past four watches, whenever his worries started to get to him, he called up a picture of Saeunn in his mind. He didn't know why it worked, but it did calm him. He'd used his dagger to carve her name on a small piece of wood. He took it out when no one was looking and just held it tightly until his fear and worry died down.

"What are you thinking, von Dunstig?" Ravenelle asked. "As if I didn't know. I can tell by the look on your face when you're thinking about her." She took his arm and led him out of the wigwam. Outside, she located a fire where there was a pot with stew cooking. "Let's see if they have any extra."

The buffalo people by the fire did, and soon he and Ravenelle were standing near the warmth sipping thick stew from the lips of wooden bowls.

Ravenelle smiled at the buffalo women who served up the stew and accepted it gratefully. The woman, who dwarfed Ravenelle, curtsied.

Ravenelle seems relaxed, Wulf thought. More relaxed than I think I've ever seen her. It was strange. Ravenelle was the last person he would imagine fitting in here at Buffalo Camp, and yet she did.

After they'd eaten enough to take off the edge of hunger, Ravenelle pointed toward the rising sun.

"I suppose that makes this breakfast," she said. "I kind of lost track of what bell it is." She dug out a potato from the stew with her fingers and plopped it in her mouth. "You know, von Dunstig, this may be the best breakfast I've ever eaten."

Wulf nodded. "It's good."

"That owl of yours looks hungry. Why don't you feed her a few chunks of meat?"

Wulf blinked. He'd almost forgotten that Nagel was perched on his shoulder and had been since he'd come out of the wise woman's wigwam. "Oh, right," he said. He dug a nice piece of meat from the bowl and presented it to Nagel.

"You should say thanks to Ravenelle," he said to the owl. "I would have forgotten to offer you any."

Nagel looked at him without betraying the slightest hint that she could talk. She took the meat. After downing two more chunks, she flew away and settled on a nearby birch tree's lowest branch.

As he was taking another sip, it came to him. He might not have his father for advice, but he might have one of his father's closest advisors.

"Earl Keiler," he said to himself. "Why didn't I think of that before?"

"What did you say, von Dunstig?"

He put a hand on Ravenelle's shoulder. Keiler had defeated the army of Vall l'Obac at Montserrat. He'd been the one to suggest Ravenelle be fostered at Raukenrose castle.

"We have to go to Bear Hall," he said.

"You know I used to wake up screaming about bears eating me when I was little."

"Yes."

To his surprise, Ravenelle patted his hand. "Yes," she said. "It makes sense."

"You used to get in bed with Mother and Father or you couldn't go back to sleep."

"Or with Saeunn, and have Ulla sing me a lullaby when all us girls slept in the same room."

"Yeah."

"Why'd it have to be *bears*, von Dunstig?"

"I think it's because those barbarian divine ones you don't believe in have a sense of humor."

Ravenelle nodded. "Could be," she said. "You know, in my dream . . . the place where the bears were after me was really beautiful. It was this kind of wooden hall with a bunch of lanterns on the walls stuffed with fireflies, and that was where the light came from, and there were huge tapestries with pictures of bears fishing in rivers, and roaming in forests, and standing on the tops of mountains."

"Maybe it'll be like that."

"And a door opened up and . . . they came in."

"Then the bears ate you?"

"Yep."

Saeunn heard clattering from the student armory as she made her way across the bailey on the way to class. She paused and watched the entrance for a moment.

Rainer and several other castle boys rushed out. Rainer was trying to pull a hauberk over his padded arming shirt and having a hard time with it. He saw Saeunn and ran toward her.

Saeunn felt a stab in her chest.

Then darkly fell Amberly Reizend.

The phrase from the poem, the song her star had sung to her, leaped into her mind.

The soul of an elf
Is the starlight itself

Why was she suddenly thinking of this?

Rainer ran toward her, a very serious expression on his

face, but his arms in an odd position. One of his arms was jammed up against his cheek, while the other hung down. He seemed to be stuck putting his shirt on.

He stopped abruptly in front of Saeunn.

"Rainer, what's going on?" she asked.

"Every man in the castle has been called to the town walls," he replied. "Looks like we're under attack."

"I mean with your arm."

"Oh, yeah. Can you help me with this?" He had yanked his mail shirt on hurriedly and it would not pull down all the way in the back. It was stuck at a spot he couldn't reach.

"Turn around and I'll straighten it," Saeunn said. Rainer did what she asked, and she tugged on the hauberk. "What about armor and a buckler? You don't have a sword, either."

"We're supposed to be issued what we need when we get to the township wall," Rainer replied.

"It is Sandhaven, then?"

"Yes, we think so. That's what Captain Geizbart reported."

Saeunn felt a flush of anger at the stupidity of the situation. "If they can't take the mark by forcing a marriage, they'll try to do it with swords."

"And bows and halberds and spears," Rainer said.

"I'll stay with Anya and Ulla," she said. "You'd better get going."

"Yeah." Rainer gazed at her for a moment. Then he reached down and took her hand. "Sister," he said. He kissed the top of her hand.

"Brother," she replied and pulled him into a hug.

They stayed that way for only a moment. Then Saeunn watched as Rainer made his way through the front gate and into the town.

Saeunn turned and headed into the castle to find her other sisters, the song still resonating within her.

She gave me her light
To burn out the blight,
Then darkly fell Amberly Reizend.

And again, and again the one phrase repeating . . .

Then darkly fell Amberly Reizend.

Bear Hall was the name of the main town in the Shwartzwald Forest. It was also the name of the meeting place the town was built near. It was where the bears and other Tier of Bear Valley got together for their law-speaks.

Law-speaks were meetings that dealt with everything from politics to marriages and judging personal disputes. Anyone was allowed to speak, but it was the leaders of Tier groups and clans who did most of the talking. They were part of the County Law-speak Council. The chairman of the council was the Earl of Shwartzwald, the bear man named Keiler. Wulf and Ravenelle had met him when he was in Raukenrose to speak with the duke. He was huge, shaggy, gray-haired, and scarred from the Little War. Ravenelle had been afraid of him since she was a toddler.

The road to Bear Hall left Buffalo Camp and headed west five leagues. It crossed the eastern Shenandoah Valley, then switchbacked up the side of Massanutten Mountain through a high gap and descended into Bear Valley, which was on the other side. Bear Valley was strange because it was a valley on top of a large, wide mountain. Some thought it might be the crook between the Shenandoah Dragon's side and its upper leg.

Bear Valley lived up to its name. The biggest population of bear people east of the Mississippi lived there. But there were many other Tier in the valley. Bear Hall Township was about halfway down the valley. The village was built up around the entrance to a huge cave, which was Bear Hall itself.

The road to Bear Hall was dusty. Ravenelle rode beside Wulf, while Dirty Coat and two other buffalo men were in the lead on the huge draft-size horses the buffalo people rode. Fifty buffalo people armed with spears rode behind them. The horses in front kicked up a cloud of grit that made Wulf's eyes water. He couldn't take his hand from the reins to wipe them, though. His left arm was strapped to his chest in a sling. He was glad of this, otherwise the jostling of the horse would have hurt a lot more than it did. But with his whole body bouncing up and down, it hurt enough.

Puidenlehdet had had treated the wound, and it felt much better already. She'd also told him that it would take a week to know whether or not it would have to be cut off due to the green rot, so not to worry until then. Wulf hoped the wise woman had been joking because she thought this was unlikely and not because she was trying to tell him nicely that he was going to lose the arm.

While they were climbing up Massanutten Mountain, it rained.

Dirty Coat gave Wulf and Ravenelle calf hides soaked with beeswax. They wrapped these around themselves and stayed dry, although their heads still got wet. At the top of the ridge, the rain stopped and the sun came out. Dirty Coat took away the calf-hide slickers and tied them back onto a packhorse. A light breeze kicked up.

"Great," Ravenelle said. "I'm dripping wet."

After a while, Wulf looked over at Ravenelle and was startled. The breeze had dried her hair. Normally her hair was a mass of ringlets hanging down past her shoulders, thick and shiny black, and she tied it back with a scarf hair band. She used a lot of hair clips to contain it, and had even found a way to brush it in Buffalo Camp.

It wasn't contained any more. The scarf was out, and her hair had exploded into what looked like a wild hedge bush sitting on her head. Her curls were soaring out in every direction and hung to her shoulders like a tangle of winter briars. Her black-brown eyes, crimson lips, and brown skin were startling in that fountain of black curls.

Wulf had always thought Ravenelle was pretty, but he'd never thought she was *strikingly* beautiful—until now.

She looks like a warrior queen from the sagas, Wulf thought, like Sturmhilde Ragensson from Sigurth's Saga might appear on her way to battle. A man could totally fall in love with Ravenelle. Even he could, if his heart didn't already belong to—

He tried to put *that* thought out of his mind as quickly as he could.

He forced his thoughts back to Ravenelle.

Yep, some Roman lord of the south was going to scoop Ravenelle up the moment he laid eyes on her. Or actually, she would scoop *him* up and make him prince consort, since Vall l'Obac was ruled by the eldest female of the royal family, and Ravenelle was firstborn.

"Poor Rainer," Wulf mumbled. He shook his head. "Not a chance in cold hell."

"What did you say, von Dunstig?"

"Nothing," Wulf said.

"I heard you say *something* about Stope."

"It'll just depress you. I really don't feel like talking about it."

She turned away and stared forward again. "Fine, then."

Then she was just his foster sister Ravenelle again to him. Part infuriating, part charming.

Ravenelle, for her part, was trying to think about *anything* except where they were going. They rode on the huge horses the buffalo people bred to hold up their bulk. Although the gait left her sore, Ravenelle liked the height the horse gave her.

Maybe I'll ride one of these when I'm queen. It might be

a good thing to bring some of the northern things with me when I go back. They'll think I'm half barbarian anyway.

It often worried her that she had very little idea *what* anybody would think of her in Vall l'Obac. She hadn't been there since she was a year old. And, though she was able to pick up images of Montserrat from her mother and her mother's bloodservants when the queen visited Raukenrose to see her daughter, she couldn't put them in any kind of perspective since she didn't know the city.

Messengers had been sent galloping ahead, and most of the village of bear people turned out to see Wulf and Ravenelle ride in.

Ravenelle sat as expressionless as possible, while Wulf nodded to the crowd, trying to look serious. He did wave at the cubs, though.

"How're you doing?" he asked Ravenelle out of the side of his mouth.

I'm surrounded by *bears*, she thought.

"They seem pretty well fed," she replied.

"It'll be fine."

They finished the ride through town and approached the eastern mountainside. High above on the mountain, Ravenelle could see white splashes of waterfalls through the budding trees.

Then they arrived at the yawning cave entrance. Beside this opening were two statues that were carved from gigantic oaken trunks as big around as the Olden Oak. The pole on the left was painted dark red. It was shaped in the image of the divine being Sturmer—although Sturmer had a very bearlike look to his face. On the right was a black pole. It was carved as Brenner, divine being of the fire and the wife of the Allfather. They didn't stop to look, but rode into the cavern.

The cave was not dark. Torches were set in wall holders, and they lit the path. The walls seemed to sparkle with crystals of quartz embedded in the rock.

After they'd come far enough in so that the entrance was a round circle of blue daylight behind them, the bear man who was leading them dismounted and signaled them to do the same. More bear people appeared. They took the reins of the horses to lead them down side passages.

"What are they going to do with my horse?" Ravenelle asked. She had gasped when the reins were taken from her unexpectedly, and she knew she'd let a trace of panic creep into her voice.

She couldn't help imagining that the creature was being led off to be eaten.

"They're going to the stable," said their escort. His voice was deep pitched, and his valley accent was thick as honey. "They'll be well taken care of, m'lady princess."

"Oh," Ravenelle replied. "Well, that's all right, then."

The escort indicated that they should follow him farther into the mountain. Ravenelle tried to hang back a bit. Behind her the press of the buffalo guard kept her moving forward, however.

Instead of getting darker, the way ahead got brighter. They came out into a vast room as large as the cathedral nave in Raukenrose. A huge brick chimney led up to the ceiling a hundred hands above them. The chimney vented a room-size fireplace. The burning logs were bigger around than a man. Each was at least twenty hands long. It was an even bigger fireplace than the one in the great hall in the castle.

No tapestries, though, thought Ravenelle.

On either side of the fireplace stood what looked like two trees, one a willow, the other a hickory. Their branches had a few fall leaves clinging to them, and the tips were budding out.

They have to be otherfolk, Ravenelle thought. There was no way a tree could grow here without sunlight.

The light from the fire and from many beeswax candles bathed the entire cavern in a warm glow. There were hundreds of cave formations. Stalactites, stalagmites, limestone curtains, and formations that resembled sides of bacon or frozen waterfalls. Most of the formations were white and shone as if they'd been polished. The rising sides of the cave had been cut into steps that were used as seats for the law-speak audience.

And there *was* an audience here. The steps were covered with dozens of Tier.

Bear people, raccoon people, bobcat people, beaver people, wolf and fox people, badger people, deer and buffalo people—the only type of animal person missing was the reclusive bird people who kept to themselves in the high Greensmokes. There were also humans. There were several villages of men on the north end of the valley.

The cavern was filled with the excited murmuring of the Tier when Wulf and Ravenelle entered. It seemed as if the meeting had been going on for some time. Some took advantage of the break provided by their entrance to stand up and stretch, and some ignited willow wands off candle flames to light tobacco in clay pipes and papyrus-rolled cigars.

Bear people were notorious smokers. This was not a surprise since they had built a lot of their wealth on growing tobacco. Ravenelle couldn't stand the stuff, even though she knew that the kingdom she was going to inherit one day had tobacco plantations everywhere.

Even with the fire, the air was damp.

But the cave doesn't smell like a hole in the ground, Ravenelle thought. What is that odor? She considered for a moment, then she had it.

Tobacco flower mixed with vanilla from the Spice Islands.

The fragrance must be in the candle wax, she decided. The bear people were famous for their beehives. It smelled wonderful and welcoming.

Which made Ravenelle tense up even more. Some part of her suspected it was all a trick, and the bear and other Tier would come for her with their tearing claws, biting teeth, and those beady, angry eyes from her childhood dreams.

Near the fire was a large bear man with silver hair. This was Keiler, Earl of Shwartzwald. The bear man rose from a large oaken chair and strode toward them.

He bowed to Wulf.

"Lord von Dunstig," the bear man said. "It is good to see you again."

"Earl Keiler," Wulf said. "I'm really glad to see you, too."

"I implore the divine ones for your father's return to health," the old bear man said. His voice was thin and reedy, as Ravenelle remembered, and surprisingly high-pitched for anything that big.

"Thank you, Earl," Wulf replied.

Keiler turned to Ravenelle and bowed deeply. "Princess Archambeault. It is the greatest of honors to have you in our home." He spoke as if he meant it. But then he was a practiced diplomat who could literally talk a mother into giving up her child.

"The honor is mine, Earl Keiler," Ravenelle replied quickly, in maybe too clipped a tone, she thought. She was being very careful not to say something offensive, even though the bear man standing before her had been the chief diplomat who negotiated the peace after the Little War. He was the very person who had taken Ravenelle from her mother's arms and locked her away in a dank castle in barbarian lands.

Keiler suddenly doubled over with a coughing fit. He wheezed and coughed for an uncomfortable moment, covering his mouth and nose with a silk handkerchief. The cough sounded deep and unhealthy. Then he straightened up.

"Beg pardon, m'lord, m'lady, it's the scrofula. Gotten worse lately. I'm afraid I might soon be with my dear Hilda in Helheim," he said. "But not quite yet. Come join us in the circle."

Earl Keiler wore rich clothes, and a bright red cape of fine wool that had to have come from the Old Countries. Ravenelle was envious. Her mother had never shipped her any material quite that nice.

As they walked toward the council circle, Keiler moved beside her. He bent his head toward her and spoke in a lowered voice.

"I'm afraid not everyone shares my happiness that you are here, m'lady," Keiler said. "You are Roman, and some Tier have long memories of the bad times with the colonies."

So they *do* want to eat me after all, Ravenelle thought. What would Mother do? It was hard to say. She'd only ever seen her mother in Raukenrose. What would Ulla do?

She'd go with her instinct, that's what.

"Earl Keiler, I will do all I can to help my foster family the von Dunstigs," she replied, trying to keep her voice even, but sounding, she knew, strained. "They have been nothing but kind to me."

"Well said, Princess." The bear coughed again, but this time didn't descend into a fit. "And they *are* your own blood, you know. Your great-grandmother Sybille was a von Dunstig."

"I wish I'd known her, Earl Keiler, but my mother's told me about her."

Keiler nodded. "Sybille was quite a handful, I remember. So, your being Roman, one concern we have is that you can speak mind to mind with those who are bound to you as bloodservants?"

"Yes, that is true," Ravenelle answered.

"You could show what is said in the hall to others you are bonded with?"

"Yes. If there were any within a league, Earl," she answered. She felt again the anguish of Raphael and Donito ripped from her mind and heart. That was really why she wanted to beat the Sandhaveners to a bloody pulp. She felt her eyes growing moist.

They will totally not understand blood tears, she thought. Do not cry.

She concentrated on a stalagmite long enough to get the memory of Raphael's body filled with arrows to recede.

"The raiders killed my people." She raised a clenched fist and imagined she was pounding the raiders. "I want those murderers dead, dead, dead."

Keiler cocked his head to consider her. He seemed impressed with her outburst. He turned to Wulf. "Do you vouch for Princess Ravenelle Archambeault, Lord Wulf?"

"With all my heart, Earl Keiler," Wulf answered immediately.

"All right, then," he replied. "It is my determination that she be admitted to the law-speak council. Now, let's take our places." He motioned them toward the fireplace. On either side of the fire were two half-circles of what looked like tree stumps. Ravenelle saw that that they were actually upright logs sawn into chairs. Plain wooden seats, no cushions. Barbaric. But there was so much splendor to the cave, she could see the point of not having the furniture take away from it.

There were all sorts of Tier in the council semicircle. Some of the Tier were more manlike than others. The badger person looked very like a stocky man, but with brushed-back hair with a gray-white stripe down the middle. His ears were small and folded like his namesake animal. Otherwise, he was human in appearance. Well, until he raised a hand and revealed long claws for nails.

Bear people and buffalo people were some of the strangest appearing of the Tier, since their heads were very much like the animal's, and their lower bodies were more manlike. The antelope and horse clans of Tier were different. They had manlike upper torsos. There were no fauns here except Grim. He had ridden behind them and was now seated somewhere in the law-speak audience. Fauns were goat people. There were no centaurs, horse people, but there was a deer person in the council circle. She was a doe, and wore a green silk blouse that Ravenelle thought was gorgeous, and a veil tied around her head with a scarf. Only the male deer people had antlers. The buffalo war chief Tupakkalaatu had ridden with them. Keiler bowed in his direction and motioned for him to take his place in the council circle. From the casual way they acted, the two seemed to know each other well.

Keiler indicated two empty side-by-side stump seats saved for Ravenelle and Wulf. They sat down. Keiler went to his own seat, which was not a stump made into a seat like the others, but a padded chair with massive carvings on the legs and arms. He remained standing in front of it.

Keiler then held up a large staff with a bear's head carved on the top. He banged the staff against the floor three times. There must have been a hollow space underneath the rocky floor, Ravenelle thought, because the bangs of the staff sounded like a kettle drum being pounded.

"I call this law-speak back into session." Keiler turned to Wulf and bowed. "We have with us Lord Wulfgang von Dunstig, son of Otto von Dunstig, our duke and liege lord. We meet in dire circumstances. It is right that we ask Lord Wulfgang what action he wishes us to take."

Ravenelle glanced at Wulf. He looked shocked. All the color had gone out of his face—what color there was to begin with—and he looked like he was going to faint.

She poked him in the shoulder and whispered, "Stand up, von Dunstig."

Wulf stood. He took a moment, and spoke in a quavering

voice. "I'm here to find out what you are planning, Earl. I want to help."

He sounds like he's been called on by Master Tolas and hasn't done his reading for class, Ravenelle thought. Not that Wulf ever skipped his reading.

Earl Keiler didn't speak for a moment. He turned his great bear head and considered Wulf.

"Look . . . I mean to say . . . I'm the *third* son of my father." Wulf shrugged, as if that explained everything he was trying to say, but when no one spoke, he continued. "The truth is, I wasn't trained to *lead* a battle, if that's what we're going to do, I mean, *have* a battle. I'm trained to fight, and I will, but I just don't have the background to give someone like *you* orders, Earl Keiler. I mean, Father says you were his right hand in the Little War."

"Well . . . that was long ago . . ." Although it was hard for her to read bear people's expressions, from the tone of his voice Keiler seemed surprised at Wulf's reluctance, and a little worried. "Let us . . . sit down and discuss what's to be done."

Wulf sat, and Ravenelle put a hand on his arm. "Relax, von Dunstig," she whispered to him. "Stop whining."

"I am *not* whining," Wulf whispered back.

"Nobody here cares that you're the third son," she said. "You stand for our family."

Wulf turned to her. He smiled. "*Our* family. I'm going to remember you said that, Ravenelle. And never let you forget it, either." He took a deep breath. "Earl Keiler?"

"Yes, m'lord?"

Wulf stood back up. "The princess reminded me of something important—that I'm a von Dunstig." Wulf turned and addressed the rest of the half-circle. "We will take back Raukenrose and kick out these invaders. At least, that is what I plan to do, with the help of the divine beings. I ask your aid in doing this."

Wulf remained standing, obviously trying to figure out what to say next. Ravenelle quickly reached a hand up, grabbed a bunch of cloth from the back of his tabard, and pulled him back down into his seat. She leaned over and whispered. "That's more like it, von Dunstig."

Keiler's expression was unreadable, but Ravenelle could hear the relief in his voice.

"The people are with you, m'lord," he said. Though he spoke quietly, his deep voice echoed in the silent cavern. "We are vassals to your family, and we are yours to the death."

CHAPTER TWENTY-SEVEN:
THE WALL

The Sandhaveners threw another set of siege ladders against the wall, and a line of men began climbing up. Some tried to do it quickly and uncovered; some tried to climb with one hand, holding shields over their heads.

Stones and arrows smashed down. When a man got to the top, he was met with poleaxes and spears. A sword point could normally not puncture plate mail, but a poleaxe thrust with enough power could get through. Sometimes it didn't even take that. A push from a spear could knock an attacker off balance and send him flailing off the wall.

After one ladder had been cleared of attackers, Rainer helped four other townsmen topple it. Even from this distance Rainer could hear cries and groans of pain when the ladder fell onto those below.

There was no time to wait. Rainer ran down the wall hoarding to the next ladder and helped pitch it off as well. An arrow from below sunk into the wood near his head, but Rainer ignored it and pushed as hard as he ever had pushed to get the ladder off the wall of Raukenrose.

The attack had come from the northeast. The Sandhaveners had encircled the town, but their main force of what was supposed to be three or four thousand men according to some estimates was concentrated north and east. At least, that was the way it appeared.

Rainer knew there might be a nasty surprise coming, maybe an attack from the south, or even somehow up from the river and out of the west. Or it could be something else.

Otto has a lot on his mind, Rainer thought. But there's nobody who can handle it better.

In a way, he was glad the duke himself was cut off while out hunting. Rainer hoped he, Wulf, and Ravenelle were all right. But the duke in the confused state his mind had fallen into lately was a terrible bet to lead a defense of the town. His son Otto most definitely *was* the right man.

Otto was brave, but not reckless. He liked to think things through. Rainer had seen him scratching out pro and con lists on wax tablets when he had a decision to make. He might not be as smart as Wulf or Adelbert, true, but he was steady and nobody's fool.

Because most attacks in the history of the mark had come from the south, the north wall was not as well tended as the south. Fortunately, the town had advance warning of the attack. Lord Otto had taken command of the township forces, which mainly consisted of the castle garrison and the town sheriffs, plus any other able-bodied man or woman who could lend a hand.

There was not any walkway hoarding on the north wall, so the first task was to take what there was out of storage and install it. They had robbed the south wall of its hoarding planks to finish the task. It was a gamble. The attackers might circle around the town and try to force the south gate, and then the hoarding would have to be put back in place.

But the attack was from the northeast. There were some sections still putting up hoarding even then, but most of the walkways had been finished. Archers were peering over the top of the wall. Otto had taken a position at the northeast corner bastion and sent his captains to direct the defense from other bastions along the northern and east walls, and in the barbican tower at the eastern gate.

Rainer was near Otto's position. He'd sought out his foster brother as soon as he'd received standard plate armor as well as a battle-ax and buckler from the north township armory. The men had helped one another buckle on the plate before reporting for duty. But to Rainer's disappointment, Otto had immediately made him a runner. When the ladders had been thrown against the wall, Rainer had been returning from delivering messages far down the eastern wall. Things were quiet there, and he had nothing to report to Otto from his southernmost commander, so Rainer had thrown himself into helping the defenders get rid of the siege ladders.

After the Sandhaveners were blocked from overrunning the wall in that spot, Rainer headed for the bastion where Otto and his command group were stationed.

"All quiet to the far south," he reported to the duke's son. "But there was some fighting just down from here, and we threw off three ladders and killed or wounded . . ." Rainer rapidly did the calculation in his head. "About twenty or thirty men."

Otto turned his grave face toward Rainer. "We?" he asked.

"I helped as best I could."

"Be careful," his foster brother said. "You have a lot of fighting spirit, brother, but remember, your first duty is to deliver my orders."

"Yes, m'lord," Rainer answered. "Has the commander any further orders?"

"Not at the moment, but stay near," Otto answered. "I have a feeling Siggi or Trigvi or whoever is out there is about to pitch everything he's got at us."

"Yes, m'lord."

Arrows were flying overhead in clouds. The Sandhavener archers seemed to be shooting in union, so Rainer risked a glimpse through the bastion loopholes between volleys.

There were a lot of Sandhaveners on the mud-flat plain to the northeast. There was no way he had enough time to count them, but he was sure it was thousands, and not hundreds. This was going to be a very long day.

An arrow flew past Rainer's cheek, and the fletching cut a thin line into his skin as it passed. Rainer ducked down, but it was too late. Some archer had made a perfect shot through the loophole and almost killed his man. So much for the theory that he could look out between volleys.

Rainer mouthed a quick thanks to God.

The Sandhaveners had hurried to make their attack, and they hadn't built any stone slinging equipment or shielded siege towers. For the moment, they would have to depend on exposed ladders. The east gate was also vulnerable. It was made of great oak slats banded together with iron. Though the wood had been doused repeatedly with water in the past few hours, the gate might be forced or burned if fire could be applied long enough. But Otto had concentrated his defenders there, and archers were perched in every window of the guard tower, with a dozen human and bear-man longbow archers on the roof.

Rainer was good with a bow, but the longbowmen were true masters. The best longbows were made from the Osage orange tree, and bow staves made from the tree were a well-known export product of the mark. A longbow stave was a hand taller than the man who used it.

The bow wood came from a triangular stave slice made from the sapwood under the bark inward to the dense heart of the tree called latewood. The sapwood was wonderfully bendable, but the heartwood was strong. It held the shape that the bow would return to after the bowman took his shot. Bowstrings were made of carefully worked hemp. Faun-grown hemp was considered the best.

A bow was useless without the man who could handle it. A longbowman had to pull the string back to his ear. It was almost impossible for a normally muscled man. Rainer had enough work pulling a regular bow's string back and getting a shot on target. Good bowmen, even amateurs, practiced every day and shot hundreds of arrows in a week. Their arms were bare so they could easily put on armguards. Even from here Rainer could see the beefed-up muscles the longbowmen developed in order to shoot their weapons.

For the bear men a longbow was the same as a regular bow. They still had to repetitively practice, but a normal bear man was already strong enough to shoot a longbow.

Thousands of arrows in barrels had been stacked in the rooms on the three floors of the barbican. The archers shooting from windows helped themselves to more when they ran out. Many of the arrows had a brand near the fletching, a pickax, showing that it had been made by bowyers in Kohlsted. Those made in Raukenrose had the sign of the Raukenrose bowyer guild, a tree shape that represented the Olden Oak.

Rainer's father owned stock in a large shop where dozens of men and women made arrow after arrow. He'd visited one day with his father when he was on summer vacation. The place smelled like boiling glue. Inside were rows of craftsmen and women. Some turned the shafts on treadle lathes. Some dressed the goose feather fletches. All of the arrows were fletched with goose-feathers imported from Sandhaven and the Chesapeake Bay, where millions of geese spent their winters. The feathers came in huge burlap bags labeled as left wing and right wing, because all the fletching on an arrow should be from the same side wing.

Other craftsmen made the hardwood hickory nocks with small saws and files. A row of smiths turned out triangle-shaped barbed arrows for hunting and for maximum flesh wounds in battle, and the narrower bladelike bodkins for piercing armor. Then there were the assemblers, mostly women, who glued all the pieces together and set the finished arrows to dry on huge racks.

The town's fauns ran barrels of arrows to the archers. The fauns were as surefooted as mountain goats and streaked up and down inclines and stairways.

Arrows were made from Shenandoah birch or from a type of cedar wood brought in from the far west. Rainer liked birch arrows the best because you could straighten them with your hand just before you shot them. But when the idea was to get off ten shots for every twenty breaths, cedar was best.

Now we're trying to kill the men who sold us the fletching, Rainer thought. And the Sandhaveners were shooting at the defenders of Raukenrose with bows made by Raukenrose bowyers from Shenandoah Osage orange trees.

"They've got fire!" a lookout yelled. Rainer glanced out and saw a line of arrows being lit by a man with a torch passing down a row of archers with drawn bows. Moments later a rain of arrows with burning ends wrapped in tow cloth soaked in birch pitch and lashed on with hemp cord flew over the wall.

Many landed in the streets of the town behind the wall. Rainer looked back and didn't see anyone hurt. People had found cover or gone back into the town. He saw a row of arrows that had buried their tips in the cross timber of a building. It looked like a shop with a couple of stories of family rooms over it. They were catching the building on fire.

Eight people carrying a ladder together, men and women, ran up and were followed by other people bringing rope-handled wooden buckets sloshing with water. Others were doing the same thing where other flaming arrows hit.

Rainer turned back to see what was going on in the bastion.

"Curse the Sandhaveners!" Otto yelled. "If they burn the town, they get nothing." He motioned his couriers to gather round. "Tell the captains to send every bowman they have to the wall. Drive those fire archers out of range. Go, go, go!"

Rainer spent the next watch running the hoarding, delivering Otto's orders. Some townsmen had by now been hit, and they'd bled on the hoarding. Twice he almost slipped on blood-slick boards and tumbled off. If he hadn't been wearing his hobnail boots, he probably would have. He nearly pushed a man off himself. The fellow had come away from the wall, dropped his pants, and was pissing off the edge of the walkway.

Archers on the wall had a lot better view of what they were shooting at than the enemy below did. Even though most of the militia archers were townsmen with a bow, a lot of them were very good shots. Plenty of townsmen added to the family cook pot by going hunting every few days for quail and turkey, deer and squirrels, in Bear Valley up on Massanutten Mountain or in the forests of the Dragonback Mountains nearest town. There were also hunting clubs that rented property from landholders, including the duke.

The practice was paying off. Their steady rain of arrows was driving the Sandhavener fire archers back. Shooting a flaming arrow was not easy even for someone trained to do it. You couldn't pull the arrow as far back as you could with a regular shot so your range was less. Also, the operation took at least two people, because someone besides the archer had to set fire to the wrapped tow cloth on the end of the arrow while the bowman held his draw.

Finally the steady shooting from the walls made the Sandhaveners pull back out of range for fire arrows, and they switched back to normal arrows with deadly tips—but no flame.

CHAPTER TWENTY-EIGHT:
THE BLACK BOLT

When Rainer got back to Otto's command bastion, he could see the mood had gotten better. Then hundreds of Sandhaveners with siege ladders ran forward together.

Otto sent Rainer for a count of ladders, and he spotted twenty of them along the eastern wall, then doubled back and counted five on the north wall. The hoarding was filled with shouting, frantic men. But they were still working well together. Some teams were dumping stones handed up from the street below down on the ladders. Archers were firing into the sides of the Sandhaveners climbing up, and other groups on the wall were trying to lever the ladders away with pieces of timber shoved between the wall and the top rungs.

The Sandhaveners were just as determined. Once you started up a ladder there was a man behind you and you couldn't go back down. Some had made it up and had swarmed over and onto the walk, fighting to clear a way for those coming behind them. Rainer's way was blocked several times by hard fighting. Men of the guard and militia were being wounded and killed. Once a huge Sandhavener slashed at a man who was directly in front of Rainer. Rainer saw the militia man's helm fly off and then saw the sword bite into the side of the man's skull. The man clattered to the hoarding.

The attacker, who was well armored, stared down for a moment at what he'd done, and Rainer took the chance to charge over the dead man and swing a vicious blow with his ax into the side of the Sandhavener's knee between the greave on his shin and the cuisse on his thigh. The man roared with pain. He struck a hard blow with his sword, but Rainer's helmet and partially raised buckler deflected it, and the blade skittered away. Rainer's ears rang from the blow, and for a moment he saw black spots.

He shook it off, and charged forward into the man, shoving with his buckler. The Sandhavener's sliced knee collapsed, and Rainer's push sent him tumbling off the walk to fall twenty hands to the paving stones below. Rainer looked over the edge and saw the man lying in a tangle, his helmet off and his sword several paces from his body.

It appeared the man was dead, but then Rainer saw the warrior move an arm.

That is one tough guy, Rainer thought.

He was considering whether he should find a way down to finish the guy off when a gang of children emerged from an alleyway with wooden stakes, followed by a pack of mongrel dogs. They gathered around the big man and began to stab him without mercy between his armor. The dogs barked with excitement.

"Tretz receive his soul," Rainer said, then turned his gaze from the spectacle.

A defender had jammed a spear pole between the wall and the ladder and three men were pulling on the makeshift lever to get the ladder off rim of the wall. Rainer jumped up and grabbed the shaft over the back of the man in front of him. He heard shouting from the ladder on the wall.

Sandhaveners were climbing up, though he couldn't see them from where he was.

"All together now!" someone grunted, and the four defenders gave it everything they had and managed to flip the ladder off the wall. The men who had been climbing up yelled in fear and frustration as they fell backward with it.

Rainer raised a fist in victory to the three men he'd helped, then charged past, working his way against archers and sword and spearmen as he headed back to report north wall ladder numbers to Otto.

He had to stop and catch his breath, and it was then that he saw Otto and his personal guard fighting two Sandhaveners who had gained the eastern hoarding where that wall cornered with the north. From where he stood, Rainer had a perfect view of the fight. The Sandhaveners fought savagely, but they were being hit from both sides and it wasn't long before someone ran up with a halberd, got the point in, and stabbed one man deep in the side. The attacker wore a hauberk, but it parted at such a sharp blow from the razor-sharp blade. The man collapsed.

The other attacker fought on. Otto himself charged the man. He fended off a blow and quickly made a counter, slicing his sword across the man's neck. His opponent fell against Otto, and Otto shoved him off the hoarding.

Otto stalked back to his bastion.

Better get over there and report, Rainer thought.

It took him a moment to work his way around a series of defenders. Then just before he got to the command bastion, he caught a whiff of . . . something horrible.

The death smell. There was plenty of the sharp tang of spilled blood, and smoke from the township fire that had been put out, but there shouldn't have been the odor of flesh rotting. It was too soon.

He gazed down into the town below and . . . there! A bit of black, half hidden in a doorway.

It was the draugar. He knew it. He had seemed to Rainer a creature of the night, of a near dream state. What was he doing out in full daylight?

Whatever it was couldn't be good. Rainer charged toward Otto's perch to tell him what he'd seen. But he had to wait a moment when he arrived because Otto was shouting orders to two couriers. After a moment the men took off, one shouldering past Rainer, to deliver their messages.

Otto turned to Rainer. His face was sooty, and there was a smear of blood on one cheek, but he was smiling.

"We took those Sandhaveners *out*, brother!" he said.

"Yeah, you did," Rainer replied.

Both of them were yelling because you had to in order to be heard above the din. In addition to men yelling, there were trumpets blowing command blasts and drums beating constantly.

"I think that was their worst. We got through it," Otto said. "Looks like they really were mostly here at the northeast. Everything's quiet to the south."

"So we held them off?"

"I think they've spent themselves for today," Otto said. He smiled grimly. "They'll have to settle for a siege. We'll win a siege. Last year I beat it into the town council's heads to be sure the township had good grain stockpiles."

"And they listened?"

"I made sure each one got a warehouse in his district, and the funds to stock it."

Otto was good at politics. He had a lot of patience, and knew how to make deals.

"We have wells so we won't die of thirst. We still control the riverfront. We can stand them off for a long, long time."

Rainer nodded, then remembered. "M'lord, I saw something. Something bad, I think."

"What is it?"

But then another courier ran up with urgent news, and

Otto held up a hand to tell Rainer to wait while the man delivered his report.

Rainer looked back down into the town. Where was that doorway?

Then there it was again. The draugar held a crossbow.

At that moment, Otto turned back to Rainer.

"What was it you wanted to tell—"

An arrow suddenly caught his foster brother in the shoulder.

No, not an arrow. A bolt. A crossbow bolt.

A fleck of blood spattered across Rainer's face. Blood welled from Otto where the bolt had penetrated the breastplate metal. Otto reached up and grabbed the shaft. It wasn't in deep and, with a cry of satisfaction laced with pain, he worked it out.

The bolt was a short piece of iron. Its tip came out bloody.

"That one came from the town," he said to Rainer. "Why did it come from—"

He opened his mouth to say more, but instead of words, a red blood bubble emerged. Otto looked at the bolt, still in his hands.

A lumpy black pitch coated the upper portion of the crossbow bolt's shaft.

Then Otto began to shake violently. His face was an expression of complete shock. He dropped the bolt. He opened his mouth to scream but could make only a gagging sound.

Purple-black bile flowed out, drizzling down his chin.

He raised a hand to his mouth, covering it, trying to stop the bile. Rainer rushed forward, but he was too late.

Otto collapsed, and Rainer knelt at his side.

The bile cleared for a moment, and Otto drew in air noisily. He breathed in and out in gasps, then something seemed to seize up in his throat. He grabbed Rainer's arm.

"We were ready," Otto croaked with what was left of his breath.

Then Otto began to convulse. Rainer tried to hold him, but it did no good. His legs twitched and his boot heels bounced up and down on the stones. Then Otto's shaking stopped and he stared blankly ahead, his eyes fixed.

No.

We need him to not be dead, Rainer thought.

"Otto! Come on Otto!"

But he was gone.

Others had seen what had happened and were shouting, kneeling down to try to revive their leader, pushing past Rainer and, not meaning to, shoving him out of the way. Rainer let them. He was numb.

Otto was dead.

Obviously it had been caused by some kind of poison that the draugar had tipped the arrow with. Even in battle, people did not die that fast from an arrow wound to the shoulder.

"Tretz receive his soul," Rainer whispered. "Hold my brother in God's light."

Rainer crawled over to the edge of the bastion and looked down into the town.

He saw the draugar. It was standing with the crossbow slung at its side, gazing up to see what it had done. From an alley near the draugar a stream of men burst forth. They were not blackened creatures, but were real flesh-and-blood men wearing tabards with the gray goose volant in front of blue and black vertical stripes—the crest of Sandhaven. They carried drawn swords, and they charged into the townpeople below. They began swinging, hewing, cleaving.

Sandhaveners, Rainer thought. Inside the township.

More and more emerged from the alley. They didn't yell. They didn't sing. They were completely silent, as if this were another day at a job they knew well.

They moved down the wall in both directions.

They're going to charge up the ramps, Rainer thought. Nobody is expecting an attack from the rear. We'll be slaughtered.

He shouted a warning and ran toward the nearest hoarding ramp to try and stop them. Others had seen and fighting had begun at the top of the ramp. It wasn't enough. The Sandhaveners cut the defenders down and broke through.

We've been betrayed, Rainer thought. Somehow we've been tricked.

Curse them to cold hell!

Rainer charged toward a Sandhavener. But the man lowered his buckler and met Rainer's charge dead on. As Rainer was bringing his ax around to hit the man in the head, the Sandhavener twisted his shield and shoved again. Rainer went flying over the edge of the walk. He fell twenty hands to the ground below.

He landed stunned, the wind knocked out of him. His years of training kicked in and he moved even before he was back to full mental awareness. His buckler arm along with the buckler was twisted under his torso. He rolled over and pulled it free. The arm wasn't broken. He looked around carefully for his ax, but didn't see it.

Then a body fell in front of him. It was a guardsman, his throat cut. He hadn't even had a chance to draw his sword. Rainer stumbled over to the body, his head clearing further, and pulled the sword from the man's scabbard. The man wouldn't need it anymore.

Armed, he turned to see . . . Sandhaven soldiers. Everywhere. They wore armor and carried bright swords. These were no recruits from the farms and fields. They were professionals, dozens of them. They were inside the town.

They saw Rainer too, and a couple broke away from the mass streaming toward the wall gangways to take care of him.

There is no way to fight all of them, not now, Rainer thought. They'll just slaughter me like a pig.

Otto is dead.

My brother.

Rainer felt another wave of emotion rising, but he beat it down.

He would deal with it later.

The best option was to run and live to fight later.

But the two Sandhaveners were after him. One was very fast, faster than he was, and he caught up with Rainer and shoved him to the ground. Rainer fell into a pile of horse manure. He managed to hold onto his sword.

But then the Sandhavener stepped onto his arm with one boot and with the other kicked the sword away. Rainer rolled, his back to the manure, and yanked his arm free. The two Sandhaveners were standing over him, their own swords drawn back, ready to cut him to pieces.

The one who had kicked away the sword was huge and lean. One glance at him told Rainer this would be a hard man to beat even in the best of circumstances. The man shook his head, as if it were a shame to kill Rainer while he was down, but that did not stop the sword from beginning its thrust into Rainer's throat.

And then a very strange thing happened. The sword stopped in mid-swing. The man held up. For a moment his arm hung there, trembling. Then he withdrew the sword, stepped back, and sheathed it.

"What is it, Captain Rask?" the other soldier asked the man.

"New orders, curse it to cold hell," he said. "He wants us on the wall."

The other looked at him curiously. "Well, I didn't hear any—"

Then that man's expression froze as if he were a dog that had caught the scent of a deer.

"Oh," he said. "Right, Captain, sir. But what about this one?" He pointed his sword at Rainer.

"This one?" The other, Rask, took a step forward and swiftly kicked Rainer in the head. The other was about to kick him, too, but saw he was standing in fresh manure and backed away, trying to scrape a sticky piece off his foot.

For Rainer, all was a blur of pain and confusion. He thought he heard someone say "Let's go." But where was he supposed to go?

To the castle. He had to get to the castle. Warn them. Protect them.

He made it to his knees before the dizziness was too much for him and he collapsed back onto the cobblestones. Then, after letting the buzzing in his head settle a moment, he tried to get up again, and could this time.

The sword. He needed a weapon.

He found it. It had skittered halfway under a wagon. Bending down to get it almost sent him tumbling again, but he steadied himself with a hand against the wagon's side. He grabbed the sword. It wouldn't move. It had jammed under the iron-hooped wheel of the wagon. He pulled harder—and the blade broke. It broke a few fingers from the hilt. There was no way he could use it now.

He looked at the broken sword stupidly for a moment. Then he threw it aside.

Where was he going again?

To tell the family that Otto was dead. To tell the duchess. Ulla.

Anya.

This was going to be the worst thing he'd ever had to do in his life.

He said a quick prayer. "Tretz, please let them have closed the gate."

Rainer felt a twinge of guilt, since this was more of a wish than a prayer. But his father, his real father, had told him it was never a mistake to pray.

"God answers prayer," he could hear Lug Stope saying. "But God also helps those who help themselves, son, and don't you forget it."

Rainer looked around and figured out where he was, then made his way at a jog down Market Street toward Raukenrose Castle.

He was too late.

CHAPTER TWENTY-NINE:
THE LAW-SPEAK

Not all Tier were known, as Wulf's discovery of Nagel's nature had shown. Most of the known talking animals in Shenandoah had, over centuries, organized themselves into families, clans, counties, and principalities, depending on how they dealt with territory. Some were attached to a certain area, but others could be found most anywhere. Some usually worked at particular trades. Fauns were in service to humans and, sometimes, bear people. Raccoons were tinkerers and armorer's assistants. They were also well known as fishers who sold barrels of live trout up and down the river. Beaver people made the flat boats they floated on.

The roaming Tier usually belonged to families and clans that looked out for one another.

The bear people of Shwartzwald County were the most powerful of the Tier. They were on a level with humans in wealth and they were well armed.

Though Tier were often treated as second-class citizens by men—even in the mark—most of the Tier didn't think of themselves that way at all. They figured that working as hard for a living as men and fighting for the duke when he went to war made them men's equal.

The otherfolk were very different from the Tier. Most of them were secretive. Their essences—their "dasein," as Tolas called it—were usually tied to complicated natural objects like groves of trees and waterfalls. Some couldn't go far away from these places without getting sick or even dying.

Nobody knew where the Tier and otherfolk originally came from. Most, including Tier themselves, just thought that they had always been there. The Tretzians had the idea that the Tier and otherfolk had come into being when Tretz had risen from the dead, and that they were spirits of the damned he'd brought back with him from the coldest depths of Helheim. These souls couldn't take human form again, so they found bodies that *would* work. They slipped into the most complicated animals or objects, which were all that could hold them, and transformed them into half men and half animal, tree, or other natural thing.

Wulf thought this explanation was pretty far-fetched. Wulf had asked Rainer what he thought. Rainer had shrugged and said he figured that believing Tretz made the Tier was as easy as believing Sturmer made the thunder with a big hammer pounding on the mountains, so why not?

Elves and gnomes were different. The gnomes considered themselves human. They had a system of lore that claimed they had once been man sized but had bred themselves small so they could become the servants of dragons. Gnomes claimed that there were *still* cousins of theirs inside the dragons. Dwarves.

Elves claimed to be connected to the stars in the night sky in some way. Like the gnomes, the elves had a special purpose. Saeunn had never been able to explain what it was to Wulf. Or hadn't wanted to.

After Wulf and Ravenelle settled into their council seats in Bear Hall, the Tier began to speak. This was not the court.

Earl Keiler was not the King of the Tier. More like the leader everybody could settle on.

Wulf had read about meetings like this in the sagas but had never seen one. Nobody had privilege of place. No one was considered better than anyone else.

It was an idea that hadn't even *occurred* to Wulf until Tolas had brought it up once during a tutoring session.

"That would be total chaos," Wulf said. "People can't *decide* to rule themselves. They could do . . . anything."

"Is that so?" Tolas said. "Is that what happens in the sagas?"

"The law-speaks mostly decide on something everybody can agree on, I guess. But those are just—"

"Stories?"

"Yes, Master Tolas. I mean, I *like* stories, but they aren't *truly* real, most of them."

At that, Tolas had smiled in his sardonic way. "It would appear that I have taught you very little at all, von Dunstig," he said. "Now I want you to write me a five-hand scroll on the benefits of rule by an aristocracy. By tomorrow, please."

"But nobody else has that assignment," he'd exclaimed. "It's not fair!"

"Fair? What does 'fair' have to do with anything," Tolas answered, unmoved.

"And if I *do* finish the assignment, then that *proves* my natural superiority," Wulf said with a wicked smile.

"Hope springs eternal in the dim light of morning, von Dunstig," answered Tolas. "I'll expect to hear you declaim your argumentation before the Elder Bell rings imbiss."

He'd gone with an argument against chaos, the war of all against all. You needed a king or strong ruler to make and enforce the law or everybody would suffer.

But by the time he'd considered all the counter arguments—which he knew Tolas would expect from him—he hadn't been so sure at all.

✤ ✤ ✤

"We have been gathering information," said Earl Keiler. "Master Roland Washbear, third cousin to Baron Fisher of Flussufer, will give a report."

A raccoon man stood up to speak.

"We think that the Sandhavener force is a vanguard," he said. His voice sounded like a child whining, but Wulf knew this was just the way raccoon people spoke. "It is commanded by Trigvi von Krehennest. We believe King Siggi is waiting to see how the new crown prince handles the assignment. If he takes Raukenrose, then Siggi will send in the full might of the Sandhaven army. But if we deny the Sandhaveners a hold, Siggi will not have a base in the mark. He will have to launch attacks from Potomak."

"Not likely," said a beaver man. "The Skraelings will revolt if he fills up the garrison there. It's a very tricky situation. The Powhatans are practically at war with the Tidewater as it is. I'm in Potomak once a month on trade, and you hear things . . . "

"Potomak has talked about seccession for over two hundred years and nothing has ever come of it," said Keiler.

"We've only started to watch them," Washbear continued. "They're clustered to the northeast. Yes, the township has fallen, but most of the troops are camping near their supply wagons outside the walls. We have a count of five thousand, more or less, with three thousand line units and the rest support. But I want to point out again that these are estimates, not established facts."

Keiler turned and spoke to Wulf. "Thoughts, Lord Wulf?"

For a moment he panicked.

Why is Keiler asking me? *What does it matter what I think?*

But from the earl's expectant tone of voice, it was obvious he was trying to pull Wulf into the discussion.

Wulf cleared his throat. "I don't know," he said, then

remembered Ravenelle's advice. Well, they were practically orders. "I mean . . . we don't know enough. Master Koterbaum would say we need to know their dispositions, where the fighting men actually are, and how they're equipped and organized. We don't know any of that stuff, do we?"

"Do we have time to find out before an attack?" Keiler asked Washbear.

"Give me a couple of days and yes, we can," Washbear answered.

"So the matter before us is—"

"Just a cursed eyeblink," said a high, grating voice. "There is something more to talk about."

Wulf located the voice's origin. It was a thin-faced little fox man. He'd only met a few of his kind. They stood only a hand or so taller than the gnomes.

"Baron Smallwolf," Keiler said. "Please tell us what you mean."

"What I mean," said Smallwolf, "is why fight at all? Tier for the Tier!"

There was a murmur from the crowd that let Wulf know some agreed with him.

Quite a few.

CHAPTER THIRTY:
THE DISPUTE

"The Tier were here before men," said Smallwolf. "The valley belongs to us, not to them."

He's got the history wrong, Wulf thought. Half the Tier clans migrated to the Shenandoah Valley after Duke Tjark opened it up.

Maybe this was politics, and he ought to smile and listen to the fox man rant on.

"Men are a cursed lot, hated by the divine ones if you ask me, and they bring evil with them," Smallwolf continued. "They believe the land belongs to *this* man or *that* man. We Smallwolf spit on that. All the land is sacred."

What a load of crap, Wulf thought. Anybody who'd heard or read the sagas, especially *Tjark's* and *Ake's* sagas, should know that the Tier had been constantly at *war* before Duke Tjark came along, and not just war among different animal people, but among their own kind, too. There had been fifty different bear kingdoms, and all of them fought each other.

"Actually," Wulf said, speaking up loud enough to be

heard. "Tjark's Saga does say there were people in the valley when—"

But Smallwolf either wasn't paying attention or didn't want to hear. "I say let the men fight. Let them slaughter each other. Then this will be Tier land again. To cold hell with them, to cold hell with men—" Smallwolf glared at Wulf. "Down with men!"

A few in the shadowy audience of the law-speak shouted in agreement. Others—more, he thought—growled their disapproval.

"Thank you, Baron Smallwolf." Lord Keiler gave the fox man a small bow of the head. "As always, powerful words to think on."

Wulf started to say something, but Keiler glanced at him and shook his head slightly.

Wulf could imagine what Master Tolas would have replied to Smallwolf.

He'd cut him to pieces with logic and examples, Wulf thought. Of course, it would be hard to make Smallwolf look like more of a complete idiot than he already did.

But Tolas was a teacher and a scholar. I'm . . . curse it to cold hell, I have to say *something*.

He turned to Smallwolf. "Baron Smallwolf, we were attacked. *We*. And if there's one thing I know, it's that the von Krehennests *hate* Tier. Every Tier in the Tidewater is either dead, in a work camp, or indentured. They'll do the same here if they can."

Analyze it. Think. Like Tolas taught you. Like Koterbaum would expect of a thoughtful warrior.

"Look, there *is* the option of retreat into Bear Valley. That has always been the plan for the last defense of Shenandoah," Wulf said. "You can see on any map that the valley is a natural fortress. It is a valley carved *into* a mountain. There is only one easy entrance, and that's to the north. The sides are shaped almost like a bowl they're so regular."

"What Lord Wulf says is true," Keiler said. "This is the last refuge. It is also the heart of Tier country, where more of us live in peace than anyplace else that is known."

"We could bottle up the southern entrance to the valley and hold out here a *very* long time," Wulf continued.

"We might gather force here and wait to assault Raukenrose until every possible fighter has joined us," put in Count Davos Bara, the wolf person leader. "But the Sandhaveners will not sit still waiting for us to march out to face them. They'll reinforce. They could bring thousands more in from the east. They have them."

"Meanwhile the Romans will easily see the weakness on their northern march," said Washbear. "We don't have a great deal of information from the south yet, but it's logical that they would try to take advantage. The Empire wants the north. They wish to spread Talaia and the iron hand of Rome to every corner of the world, if they can." He nodded toward Ravenelle. "Pardon my bluntness, Princess," he said to her.

Ravenelle looked like she was about to snap a reply, but checked herself. Wulf squeezed her hand, trying to reassure her.

"Look, for the moment it doesn't matter what the Romans might or might not do," he said. "The Sandhaveners *have* invaded. They would like nothing more than to bottle us up in Bear Valley. It may be a fortress with only one gate, but that means there's only one way *out* for an attacking force, too. They can keep us contained with a small force and choose when they want to attack."

"He has a point," Earl Keiler said. "Furthermore, a decisive victory by either us *or them* would make the Romans think twice before moving north. Sandhaven may not fear Shenandoah, but only fools ignore the Roman Empire. So they will probably realize that they have to take control of the mark as quickly as possible, and take the fight to us sooner rather than later."

"So we have to take the fight to *them*," Wulf said. "We have to take back Raukenrose and the northeast. We *have to* fight."

"For humans," sneered Smallwolf.

"For everyone," Wulf said. "Sandhaveners might want to rule humans here. But they want to *eradicate* the Tier. We can't let that happen."

Now there were more shouts from the unseen gallery, and enough were things like "the boy's right" and "down with Sandhaven" to cheer Wulf up a little after Smallwolf's depressing outburst.

Smallwolf glowered even more hate at Wulf. Keiler, on the other hand, had his headed cocked to one side, as if considering Wulf in a new way.

"Thank you, Lord Wulf," Keiler finally said. "You sound like you know what you're talking about when it comes to Sandhaven. Some of us have relatives there. We hear the terrible stories."

The bear man stood up, straightening his cape as he did so. His voice rose in timbre.

"We will fight. The men of Shenandoah let bears be bears! They let Tier be Tier. Men may be evil in other places, but there is no better place than this valley. No sweeter land than these fields and mountains."

The speech was too much, and Keiler spasmed into another coughing fit from his scrofula. Everybody waited patiently for him to get it under control. This time his handkerchief came away with a smear of blood.

Keiler straightened back up and raised an arm toward the roof of the cavern high above them.

"We will fight." He paused for a moment and let a hush settle over the inside of the circle, then finished in a long growl, a bear-whisper, that reverberated through the cave. "The dragon roars beneath our feet. We will be the dragon's teeth and fire. This is our home, and we have to defend it."

Several of the Tier called out their approval of this. Although most Tier spoke Kaltish, their emotional cries came from the animal part of themselves. Some squawked, some screeched, some growled—and the beaver people uncurled their tails from beneath their butts and beat them against the ground.

The gnarled wooden columns Wulf had noticed beside the fireplace seemed to do more than that. They blurred and *dissolved*. In their place stood beautiful, tall, and brown men and women. The tree people *were* here.

"These are good words you speak, Keiler, but they are not needed for the Lindenfolk. We did not come to discuss running away," one of the brown women said.

The fox man, Baron Smallwolf, waved a hand dismissively. "Your kind *can't* run away. You're too slow. But what can you do if it comes to a real fight? You can't keep those mannish forms for long. And then they'll chop you down."

"This is Lady Meiner Fruling," said Earl Keiler to the fox man. "Please be careful how you address her."

The tree woman raised a branchy hand in acknowledgment. She turned to the fox man.

Lady Fruling turned to the fox man. Wulf expected to see a look of scorn on her face, but instead she seemed saddened, as if the little fox man had disappointed her with his implied insult. "We guard the woodlands," she said. "We have always guarded the woodlands."

Then, almost as quickly as they appeared, they changed back into trees that, if you looked carefully, had knotholes and burls that appeared almost, but not quite, like faces.

"We need more than the Tier," said Earl Keiler. "The gnomes train. They fight as units. The Greensmoke centaurs are the finest archers in all of Freiland. There are also the Gray Elves, if we can find them, or they us. Maybe even the Smoke Elves would help."

"The Smoke Elves cannot come. Eounnbard is cut off from us by Vall l'Obac." This time it was a man, a man of the southern valley by his accent, who spoke.

"We are *not* at war with Vall l'Obac," Earl Keiler replied, looking pointedly at Ravenelle.

"Maybe we should be," said a woman's low clear alto.

Heads turned toward the voice.

It was the tree woman, Lady Fruling, who had changed from a tree to a humanlike form again.

"What do you mean, Lady Fruling?" asked Earl Keiler. He sounded confused.

He didn't expect this interruption, Wulf thought. Even canny old Earl Keiler can be surprised.

"We have heard whispers across the Dragonback in the eastern woods," she said, "that a new Roman mold has come to the Tidewater, coughed up through a smoking mountain by the dragon of Tiber. The Talaia priests have murdered the Tiber dragon, and they have used this black mold to gain power over House Krehennest. The Tidewater may be allied with Rome. Or, even worse, they may be enslaved to the bishops of Rome."

"We Romans are not *enslaved*," said Ravenelle indignantly. "The bishops and the Pope are *spiritual* leaders, and that's all."

Wulf winced. He'd thought it was probably better if she didn't speak in a meeting like this.

"What we have is *order*," she said. "Each of us has a certain nature. Some are born to think, some are born to rule, some are born to work."

I've heard *that* before, Wulf thought, from Ravenelle's Talaia priest, Father Calceatus.

"We care for our bloodservants as we would children. They would be lost without us, and we would be lost without them, like a soul without a body."

"We?" asked Fruling.

"The gentry, I mean." Ravenelle was trying her best to sound reasonable, but Wulf knew that to any Kalte man or beast it sounded *very* condescending. "We have *servants*. Slaves are made to work with whips and chains. That's how you Kalte treat your indentures. I've seen it in the fields around Raukenrose. Our bloodservants labor out of duty. They are happiest when they are working in the fields. They even sing while they work, you know. I'm told it's very beautiful, even though I haven't had a chance to . . . "

Ravenelle's voice trailed away. There was complete silence in the cavern. She looked around. All eyes were on her, and the Tier did not look happy at all.

She's about to see her bear nightmares come true, Wulf thought. Then he realized that they *might* actually harm her, they looked so angry. Many Tier were bloodservants in the southern colonies.

"What Lady Ravenelle means to say," Wulf piped up, "is that most of the south is not looking for war with the north."

"This new Host is a terrible thing," Ravenelle put in, her voice trembling now. "It goes against all balance and order. It has to be stopped." She reached inside the bosom of her dress and pulled up a little packet tied on a string around her neck. She held it up. "I got this from Prince Gunnar," she said. "It is ater-cake."

"Why do you carry it?" asked Fruling in alarm.

"The real truth?" Ravenelle said.

Uh-oh. Wulf realized he was holding his breath. When Ravenelle told the "real truth," there was no telling what she might say.

"Yes, please," Fruling replied in her honeyed voice. But Wulf was sure he heard a trace of acid in it as well. She seemed a being you crossed at your peril.

"To protect myself," Ravenelle said. "I found out the hard way. I can be mentally dominated by someone taking ater-cake. I plan to never let that happen again."

"So this packet contains the ater-cake?"

"Yes."

"And if you partake of it, your . . . ability to control others is stronger?"

"Very much stronger."

Fruling nodded. "Interesting indeed." She turned to Keiler. "Earl Keiler, we may have a use for this . . . girl."

Keiler nodded. "I see what you mean, Lady Fruling."

"What are you talking about?" Ravenelle said. Her voice was trembling now.

"Several nights ago bear and tree people caught something very interesting wandering through the eastern woods. We have had it delivered here."

"What is it?" Wulf asked.

"It is a man, m'lord. He claims to have deserted the Sandhaven army. If he is one of your . . . type, Lady Ravenelle . . . you might be able to discover what he knows."

"I could try it," Ravenelle said. She looked around at the staring Tier. Wulf could see her shudder.

"If Ravenelle says she is on the side of the mark, you can believe her," Wulf said. He stood up and put a hand on Ravenelle's shoulder. "I stake my life on it." He paused, and gazed around the circle. He tried to make his own expression as hard as theirs. Finally, he spoke. "And I promise you that I will fight to the death anyone who lays a hand on her."

From the back of the room came a clear voice that echoed through Bear Hall. Wulf recognized it immediately.

"Let's hope it doesn't come to that, Lord Wulf."

The eyes of all the Tier and otherfolk turned toward the sound. Next they heard the clip clop of horse hooves. And then from the entranceway, a male centaur emerged. Wulf had never seen a centaur before, and at the moment he thought it—he—was the most noble-looking person he'd ever laid eyes on.

But the voice had not come from the centaur.

Riding on the centaur was a gnome. He looked almost like a doll on that creature's broad back. It was the gnome, however, and not the centaur who had spoken with his big, bell-loud voice.

"Master Tolas!" Wulf and Ravenelle shouted together.

Chapter Thirty-One:
The Revelation

"Is that your friend Ahorn?" Wulf asked Tolas. After Earl Keiler had greeted him and admitted him to the council, Tolas had dismounted. He smiled broadly and came over to Wulf and Ravenelle.

"Yes, he is," Tolas answered. "And it is very good to see you both."

Ravenelle knelt down and hugged the gnome tightly. He seemed surprised. So was Wulf.

"I'm so glad you're here, Master Tolas," she said.

"My dear little princess," Tolas said.

She finally let him go and quickly wiped away a couple of blood tears. No one but Wulf and Tolas seemed to notice the color.

A bobcat man moved, and Tolas sat next to Wulf on the other side from Ravenelle.

The stump left Tolas sitting very low in relation to the rest of the council. Earl Keiler motioned to the side and a woman brought Tolas a velvet cushion to give him more height. Tolas climbed down from the chair, and she placed the cushion on his seat.

Wulf wasn't paying attention to what Tolas did next. His eyes were on the woman.

Her hair was red and there were freckles sprayed across her face. Her eyes were startlingly green. She was very much human.

And she was lovely to look at.

She caught him staring at her and gave him a small smile. Then she went back to a desk in the chimney shadow by the fire. Her position in the shadows was probably why he hadn't noticed her before. Now he couldn't help looking at her. There was a scroll and a goose-feather pen on the desk. She took up the pen and seemed to be making a record of the meeting.

Wulf was distracted from staring at her by the restless movement of the centaur Tolas had ridden in on. Ahorn had joined the Law-speak Circle and was looking around eagerly for something—what, Wulf could not figure out.

"Ahorn's looking for a buffalo woman he says he's in love with." Tolas raised up, then settled himself better on his new cushion.

"Your wise woman Puidenlehdet is not here," said Tupakkalaatu from across the circle. "She would be, but she tends Duke Otto's wounds at Buffalo Camp."

"I hear you," the centaur nodded gravely. "I have medicinal herbs I gathered for her. They are for treating deep wounds. She will need them, I think."

"That be as it may," Tupakkalaatu replied. "We know ye would have come through the gates of Gulch to see her."

"Gulch is their version of cold hell," Tolas said to Wulf. "I hope that you have been keeping up with your lore since my departure?"

"I haven't slacked too much, master," Wulf said. "But I've been . . . busy." Wulf sighed and smiled. "Master Tolas, it's really good to see you."

Tolas reached over and gave Wulf's shoulder a squeeze.

"You can make up your deficiencies, which I am sure have grown as wide as a canyon, with some late-night study after this business with the Sandhaveners is taken care of."

"I would like that," Wulf said.

Earl Keiler cleared his throat. "Master Tolas," he said, "since you have brought Ahorn—or, it seems, Ahorn has brought you—we are eager to hear a report of your travels."

Tolas turned from Wulf and nodded. "I have news, Earl Keiler," he said. "I do, indeed." His hand strayed to the plain brown robe he wore. He patted it, found the lump he was looking for, and pulled his pipe and tobacco pouch from a previously unseen pocket. "Pardon me. I can go without sleep, but I find long periods without a good pipe smoke extremely trying." Tolas packed his pipe with tobacco.

"Somebody get him a light," Earl Keiler said.

The gnome shook his head. "No need," he said. Tolas took a thin leather sheath from an inner pocket of his brown robe. He pulled a punk stick from the sheath. It had a hot coal on the end. Tolas blew on this coal a couple of times to get it smoking, then dipped the burning coal into his pipe bowl and used it to light the new tobacco. Then he put the stick carefully back into the sheath.

Tolas took two pulls on his pipe. He blew out a cloud of smoke that drifted upward into the darkness of the ceiling vault. The gnome sat back contentedly.

"Much better," Tolas said. He glanced over at Ahorn the centaur. Ahorn was trotting around and searching behind chairs and people's backs. "Lord Ahorn, she truly is *not here*," Keiler said. "You do seem a fool in love."

"I am who I am," Ahorn said dejectedly.

"Then you most definitely should keep looking for her, my friend. But there's much more light over by the fireplace. Why don't you look there?"

Ahorn laughed. "That is ridiculous, Albrec." He looked

serious again. "Maybe I will take a stretch of the legs to Buffalo Camp after the law-speak, though."

Tolas took another puff on his pipe and addressed the council semicircle. "I had worries that something like this was brewing," he said. "I was greatly alarmed in Wintervoll when Grand Docent Lars Bauch told me that I was being dismissed from the Raukenrose University faculty. I knew Bauch, and I knew he was hiding a secret. I tried to find out what was really going on, but I was prevented from entering the library after my robes were taken."

"Did you find out what the secret was?" Earl Keiler asked.

"No," Tolas said. "I knew that Bauch's group had been arguing that the Talaia celestis could be put to good use to create a rational society. I believed they were up to something to further their cause."

"Getting involved with red-cake? Are they crazy?"

"No, just academics," Tolas said. "They were the pawn of greater powers. I'm very concerned about who or what those powers might be."

"You are a university man. Why not take part in their revolt?"

"Because I know we'd be living in a slaughterhouse if they were in charge."

Keiler nodded agreement. "So you went to the centaurs?"

"First I went south, to my people. I felt I could make them understand the danger I felt. Then I rode to the centaurs. Since I'm of a certain size, I was able to use the mark's message express service."

"You rode the mail service relay ponies?"

"In a way. I mailed myself to Barangath in the Greensmokes," Tolas said with only a trace of a smile, and took another puff from his pipe. "I found my good friend Ahorn and managed to convince him of the danger."

"There are five hundred centaur archers and warriors a

day behind me," Ahorn put in. "We had already foreseen much and were preparing to leave when Albrec arrived."

Ahorn spread his arms as he continued speaking. "The stars are singing of horrors. The dragon sleeps restlessly and sends troubled dreams." Ahorn clenched his palms into fists. "We have foreseen war. But more than this war."

"War with whom then, Lord Ahorn?" said Keiler in a frustrated tone. "You create more questions than you answer."

"Men will fight. They always have. But there is evil rising, a war of darkness against life that will soon overtake us, men and Tier."

"And you will fight?"

"We will," answered Ahorn. "But the Dragon Hammer must return. Along with the silver buffalo, it is the symbol of Shenandoah. Yet the hammer is much more.

"It is lost," said Keiler. "For two hundred years."

"We may have a way to find it," Tolas said. The gnome took another puff on his pipe, and let his words sink in.

There was a long silence in the cavern.

Earl Smallwolf was the first to speak. "The Dragon Hammer is a total myth," he proclaimed in his high voice. "Everybody knows that."

"The Dragon Hammer is supposed to be magical, right?" said the wolf man leader in the circle. "What does that mean, though? Will it turn the Sandhaveners to birds or something?"

"Turn them into birds?" said Tolas. "Really? Count Bara, is it?"

The wolf man nodded.

"No, m'lord, I think that it is a relic that's beyond magic. It may be beyond time itself. I doubt it will turn anyone into a bird."

"What's it good for then?"

"*Tjark's Saga* describes it as the root of all dasein."

"Dasein? What in cold hell is that?"

"Magic," Wulf said, speaking up. "Well, magic is the effect. Dasein is the thing in itself."

"It is a universal essence that can be instilled with purpose by the mind of people or the will of the divine," Tolas replied. "In the saga, Duke Tjark used the hammer to make the were-beasts vulnerable to ordinary weapons."

"I know the saga more or less, at least I used to . . . So that destroyed this 'dasein'?" Count Bara asked.

"No. Dasein cannot be created or destroyed. I think what the hammer does is to wipe away purpose. It blanks the dasein back to its original form."

"Sounds powerful," Keiler put in. "But that doesn't tell us how to use it."

"The saga just says Tjark used the Dragon Hammer 'mightily' against the were-beasts," Wulf put in. "*Inulfsson's Saga* says they melted into puddles of guts and blood. Inulfsson was writing a hundred years later, though."

"Werewolves! What a load of manure," said the wolf man who had spoken before.

"Were-creatures are hybrid Tier. They certainly exist."

"Unnatural git. We wolves don't allow it for good reason. And that one should watch where he puts his staff." The wolf man pointed to Ahorn, the centaur. "Horses and buffalos should not mix."

"The laws of interbreeding are something we disagree on, Count Bara. None of which matters at all in the present circumstance. I really don't think we ought to get into such things in this council or this law-speak," Keiler said. He sounded very uncomfortable with the topic. "The Sandhaveners aren't werewolves or were-anything."

"No, but four months ago, Lord Wulfgang von Dunstig and his foster brother Rainer Stope saw one of the draug in Raukenrose," Tolas said.

There was a murmur in both the council and the

gathered law-speak audience.

"Let me get this straight, Master Gnome. The draug are elves that have gone over to evil?" said Washbear.

"Yes," answered Tolas. "Some authorities even claim that they created the celestis for their own purpose."

"Kalte propaganda," Ravenelle whispered to Wulf.

"There is more evidence," Tolas went on. "The university docent led by Lars Bauch and his Adherents group at the university have adopted Talaian ways. Prince Gunnar of Sandhaven was using a powerful new type of celestis. Princess Ravenelle here can confirm this."

Ravenelle stiffened. Wulf felt sorry for her. She was frightened enough, and now she was going to have an intimate detail of her life exposed.

"Yes. The ater-cake," Ravenelle replied. She sighed and help up her necklace. "It is this that I showed the law-speak in my amulet. It's for dominations. Gunnar nearly turned me into his own bloodservant then and there. If I hadn't had more experience than he did, he probably would have been able to."

"This all paints a picture," Tolas said. He took his pipe out of his mouth, looked over the end, then carefully broke off a fingerwidth length of the clay stem. Wulf had seen Tolas go through a complete stem in a day doing this. He was sure the gnome had a stash of new clay stems hidden in a robe pocket.

"You think something more than Sandhaven has come to Raukenrose, Master Tolas?" Keiler said.

"I do."

"Do you really suppose the empire is behind it?" Keiler asked. "We beat them before, after all."

Tolas smiled. "That you did, Earl Keiler, but what you beat was a small Roman colony." He nodded toward Ravenelle. "No disrespect intended, Princess. Just stating facts." He turned back to Keiler. "My Lord Earl, Duke Otto and you proved quite good at warfare, but you weren't fighting the entire Holy Roman Empire."

"Aye—and don't I know it. But now we might be?"

Smallwolf cackled in laughter. "None of this matters," he said. "Arrows and steel will either save us or doom us. If you know where this hammer thing is to be found, Tolas, then tell us. Otherwise why don't you go back down south where your kind belong?"

"My *kind*, Sir Fox?"

"Dragon-turds, some call you."

"We gnomes call ourselves that sometimes," Tolas said. "When we're feeling ornery."

"Your kind may. But as for us, we're *smallwolf*. Nobody calls us 'fox' any more."

"Fox is a good name with a lot of history."

"It's meant to call us sneaky and no good," Smallwolf said. "It's used to hold my people down, and we won't stand for that no more." The fox man moved to the edge of his seat and stabbed a pointing finger toward Tolas. "Say it again and you'll be hearing from my sword."

"Interesting theory," Tolas said, laughter in his voice. "Maybe we can wish away all kinds of things just by changing the names and threatening those who keep using the old words. Let's begin by calling 'evil' 'good' and go from there."

Smallwolf looked as if he was about to come over and get into a fight with Tolas. Master Tolas, for his part, seemed defiant and ready to return blow for blow.

Keiler beat his staff against the floor again, and it boomed through the Bear Hall. The old bear man turned a serious gaze to Tolas. "Master Gnome, if you know anything about the location of the Dragon Hammer, now would be the time to inform this law-speak."

Tolas turned his unflinching gaze from Smallwolf and nodded to Keiler. "It happens that I do," he said. He took a long draw on his pipe and seemed to relax back into his calm self once again. "There was once an iron box in my hometown of Glockendorf. Very small, actually. Not much larger than my two outstretched palms." Tolas held his pipe in his mouth and held his palms together to illustrate. "But this box has a very clever locking mechanism designed by Dondras Gerrisen, a legendary locksmith of my people.

"I could tell you a great deal about Gerrisen, but I will spare the law-speak a history lesson—although I think some of you might greatly profit from such a remedial course." Tolas looked at Smallwolf when he said this.

"In any case, the box is extremely strong and is considered impossible to open without its key. Gerrisen designed the interior in such a way that any attempt to force the box open either by force or lock picking would destroy the contents instantly."

"And what *is* inside this box?" asked Earl Keiler.

"A very small scroll that tells where the Dragon Hammer is. There is also a small cache of spirit of niter that will flash flame that scroll to unreadable ash if the box is opened improperly."

"Excuse me," said Washbear, who was a raccoon man and was said to be a master spy. "Before you said 'there *was* an iron box' in Glockendorf. Where is that box *now*?"

Tolas reached under his wool frock with both hands and worked something out of an inner pocket. He drew it forth.

It was just as Tolas had described it—a small box, unadorned, with a keyhole on what looked like a button that could be pressed.

"Here is Dondras Gerrisen's box," Tolas said. "When he made it, he wanted the key hidden where it couldn't be easily got at. So he sent it to the centaurs."

"For two hundred years, my forbearers and myself have been the keeper of the key," Ahorn said.

"Well, do you have it, Lord Ahorn?" Earl Keiler said. He was almost shouting.

"No need," said Tolas. He smiled. "Ahorn and I, of course, checked to be sure the mechanism worked before I brought the information here. Wouldn't do if the scroll were already burned up." Tolas pressed the button on the front of the box, and its lid sprang open.

Wulf looked down. Inside was a scroll, just as Tolas had said, about as long and as big around as his little finger.

"Wow," Wulf said. He looked at Tolas. "Have you read this?"

"Yes," Tolas said. "But I thought you should be the first to receive it."

"Me? What about Earl Keiler? Or Tupakkalaatu there?"

"No," Tolas said. "They are vassals. So am I. His Excellency Duke Otto is apparently badly wounded. Lord Otto, the duchess, and Raukenrose are cut off from us. For better or worse, you are the only von Dunstig available. You must, therefore, receive the information."

"Are you sure?" Wulf looked around the council. "Earl Keiler?"

"Without objections, that is the will of the law-speak. Take it, Lord Wulf."

"Do what he says, von Dunstig," whispered Ravenelle, on his other side. "You can show them that you're the middle ground, the one everybody can trust."

Wulf let this sink in for a moment. Tolas put the box in front of him, and Wulf took out the scroll. It wasn't bound by anything, so he held it with one hand and unrolled it with the other.

There were letters on there, Kaltish letters. Their shape was old-fashioned, but Wulf had read so many old scrolls and codexes that there was no problem making them out.

He read the scroll.

Then he let it drop to his lap. It immediately scrolled itself back up, not by magic but because it had sat in that shape for so many decades.

Wulf shook his head. Then he chuckled. "Blood and bones," he said.

"What is it?" Ravenelle asked, poking him in the arm. "Does it say where the thing is?"

Wulf nodded. "Yeah. It says exactly where to find it, and I'm pretty sure it's still there, since it's somewhere that hasn't been moved or even much looked at for over a hundred years. Too bad, though."

"What's the problem, von Dunstig?"

Wulf took a long, deep breath then replied. "The problem is that it's in Raukenrose."

"Pity," Earl Keiler said. "We might have used that. We can't even get word to those in the township."

Suddenly a raspy voice spoke next to Wulf's ear. It was Nagel, and she definitely wasn't talking in a whisper this time. She wanted everyone in the Law-speak Circle to hear her. He hadn't realized she could speak so *loudly*.

"Hey, boy lord, I hope you realize that you could send *me*."

CHAPTER THIRTY-TWO:
THE NIGHT FLIGHT

"Lord Wulf, allow me to present my daughter," said Earl Keiler. He motioned to the redheaded woman with freckles to step forward. "This is Ursel."

She was about Wulf and Ravenelle's age. She wore a green dress with red trim and was a hand shorter than Wulf. Her red hair was drawn back with a green scarf. Her hair was nearly as curly as Ravenelle's.

She made a curtsy. "M'lord," she said.

Wulf bowed to her. "A pleasure, Lady Ursel," he said.

"It's Ursel, m'lord. Only Ursel."

"All right," he replied. "As you say, mistress."

She shrugged "It's just that I'm a foundling," she said. "We bears are very particular about our titles."

"You really don't look like a bear."

"Ursel is my *adopted* daughter," Earl Keiler said with a chuckle. "She is as much one of the clan as any of my people, though, and I'll tear apart anyone who says different." Earl Keiler's tone softened. "She is family. I have settled a grand dowry on her."

Keiler fell into a fury of doubled-over coughing, and everyone waited as politely as they could while he dealt with it and stood back straight.

Wulf tried to take up where he'd left off. "Pleased to meet you, Mistress Ursel Keiler." He turned to Ravenelle. "This is Princess Ravenelle Archambeault," he said. "My cousin."

"Princess." Ursel Keiler curtsied very deeply this time, and Ravenelle looked pleased.

"Your father must think very highly of you to bring you to law-speak," Ravenelle said.

For a moment Ursel seemed tongue-tied when confronted with a princess, but then she recovered and answered Ravenelle in a firm voice. She had a heavy Shwartzwald County accent. "I try to be of service to Papa. He says I'm good at keeping up with details."

"She's the lady of Bear Hall and my best self now that Hilda is dead and the boys are grown. Ursel keeps the books. She never misses anything," Earl Keiler said. "And she never forgets. So don't slight her. She's a bear in that way. She knows how to strike back."

"I'll try to avoid that," Wulf replied with an uneasy smile.

Ursel turned her gaze to him. "Papa exaggerates," she said.

Ursel smoothed the fabric of her dress, rumpled from the curtsey. When she bent an arm to straighten her sleeve, Wulf saw that she had *very* defined muscles.

Archer's muscles, Wulf thought.

It took years of practice to get them. This meant she was probably also a crack shot.

Ursel saw where he was looking and smiled shyly. Her green eyes sparkled with amusement. She finished tugging down the other sleeve, and Wulf found he could not take his eyes from her.

He didn't until Ravenelle kicked him in the shin to get his attention.

"Let's get out of here, von Dunstig," she said in a low voice. "Bear Hall still gives me the creeps."

Nagel didn't know if she even *was* a person. There were Tier who looked much more like animals than humans. The beaver people and, especially, the mice people were like that.

But they all had some distinguishing feature that marked them as people and not just animals. She didn't. She looked just like any screech owl. She had been raised by owls. Not owl people. Owls.

When the falconers took her as a fledgling, she'd been wild beyond imagining. She was completely unaware she had the ability to talk. She had discovered that she was far smarter than her siblings. But she didn't feel better than them. Her parents knew things that she did not. They knew how to locate a mouse by sound alone, and how to find the best currents for soaring. She had tried hard to learn. But she had seen early on that the intense love she felt for them was not returned. They fed her. They taught her. But they would never love her. They didn't understand what it meant.

So she had come to live in the mews. It was there, with fauns and men speaking around her, she had first understood language. It had taken her many months, but finally she'd learned how to make the whistling air that passed through her beak when she exhaled into understandable Kaltish words.

It excited her when one day she discovered that she could easily understand what the fauns and men wanted her to do. Hunting came naturally to her. They had tried her as a "make owl," and she knew she'd done amazing work. The eagles were easy to anticipate and to lead. She might be able to talk like a human, but she could definitely also think like a raptor.

She had felt that she was waiting for something. The love

she'd felt for her parents she'd buried so deep she hardly knew it existed any longer. But then the boy had come, and everything had changed.

He was her boy. Hers. And she was his. It wasn't mating. She didn't want that. She wanted another kind of love, the fierce love she'd once felt and had seemed to lose. She wanted to be able to devote herself to a being who was capable of appreciating her, who maybe one day might come to love her.

It was a harsh love. A fierce bloody love. Often it came across as dislike, but she didn't mean it that way.

Now she had something to do. She had information to deliver that might make a real difference in a world she'd always thought she was too little to affect.

Flying to the castle was familiar to her. She'd sometimes been released in nearby fields and expected to return to the mews herself, so she had flown there several times. Nagel never forgot a landscape.

She came in at night.

When she landed in the castle mews, she was in for a shock. They were empty. Most of the birds had been taken out on the hunting trip to the Dragonback Mountains. The birds that stayed had not been fed or watered. Most were dead. Those that were alive were famished and thirsty.

Here she could do more. She did not have hands, but she was clever with her beak, and she worked the mews doors open. The survivors could get out. Not that they would thank her. Raptors didn't feel gratitude.

She took a moment to get back her sense of direction, then headed for the castle itself. She was almost stabbed by a guard. He saw her, reached up with the tip of his poleax. The ax tip cut across her belly.

But it was only a small wound. Her strength returned. She waited, sitting quietly on a gargoyle above the main door until a Sandhavener opened it from the inside. She ducked through the small opening, feeling more like prey than hunter at the moment.

Now she could make her way inside the castle.

She doubled back several times to avoid notice. But by listening and following a guard on watch, she discovered where the bedchambers were.

The heir was not present. She had expected not to find him. But neither were any of the others Wulf had told her to look for. The older sister. The elf woman. The warrior boy who was Wulf's friend. Even the mother.

In the end, Nagel had to deliver her message to the little sister. The one named Anya.

After considering, Nagel realized that this was not a terrible plan in any case.

Anya was a little girl, but not too young to understand. She would maybe be unguarded. Even if Nagel could find him, approaching the eldest boy seemed out of the question. He would just shoo her away or, worse, he or one of his men would cut her out of the air with a sword for bothering him. Even if she had found the sister, the mother, or the elf, they were *old*. She would have to take a lot of time convincing them she could be trusted.

And even though she was Tier, they were not used to Tier who looked *exactly* like the animals they were paired with.

No, the little girl was the one who would listen to a talking owl who only had a little time to deliver her message.

Anya was a human. She could then get the other humans to believe her.

So it would be Anya von Dunstig.

The only problem was, she'd never seen Anya.

Then she heard someone call out Anya's name, and saw the little blonde-haired girl slip into her room. This had to be Anya. She looked very much like a young Wulf.

She had to approach and not be seen by anyone else. This was dangerous.

Nagel loved living, but she wasn't afraid of dying if she had to.

But first she had a message to deliver.

Chapter Thirty-Three:
The Archer

They stayed at Shwartzwald House. The earl's residence was a huge wooden structure on the edge of Bear Hall township. There were lots of rooms, and Wulf and Ravenelle both got their own bedchambers.

After Wulf settled in, he met Ursel Keiler again. She knocked and entered with another bear woman to bring Wulf new clothes. They also brought a hauberk—a chainmail shirt—and a small set of armor. This included a cuirass breast and back plate, cuisses for the thighs and greaves for the shins, sets of bracers for arm covering, and a helmet with a grima noseguard. The set was light. It all fit into a flannel bag that could be tied onto a packhorse.

When he'd looked over the armor, Ursel gave him a swordsman's cape. It was bright red with yellow piping and was marked with the symbol of Shwartzwald County, the Dragon Hammer. This was embroidered in orange and darker red tessellations across the cape. It was held in place by a clasp and by a padded leather poulon that belted across his shoulder.

"The cape belonged to my brother when he was a cub," Ursel said. She sent the bear woman out, and she returned with a sword. "This is my father's short sword. He wanted you to have it. He used it in the Little War." The bear woman left, and returned with a buckler.

"Your brother's when he was a cub?" Wulf asked. He set the buckler aside, but drew the sword out of its scabbard. The scabbard itself had leather loops to attach it either to a belt or to a strap over the back.

He gave the sword a twirl to feel its weight. Perfect. He thought about how much Rainer would have liked the feel of it.

Then he slid it back into its scabbard.

"Tell you father thank you," Wulf said. "This is a fine sword."

"I will," Ursel said. "I hope you use it well. May I ask what your plan of attack is?"

"I thought I'd look to your father for that."

"He does know a thing or two about fighting," Ursel replied. She smiled slyly. "And I know a thing or two about sneaking up on your quarry."

Wulf arched an eyebrow. "That's very intriguing, Mistress Ursel. What do you suggest?" He pointed to a nearby chair and nodded for her sit down.

"They'll expect us to come in from the southwest," Ursel replied. She gathered her skirt and lowered herself in the chair. "But we don't have to. Not at all. We can go east a league or more south of the city. Come up the Valley Road and attack from the *east*. That will also be good for a dawn attack. The sun would be at our back."

"Sounds interesting."

"We have many traders here and friends along the way who know the roads well. There are lesser known paths. Shortcuts through the forest. And we *own* the forests."

"The otherfolk do, you mean."

"Yes."

"You know them well, don't you?"

"I spend a lot of time in the woods."

"So we should circle to the south of the town, come in from the east," Wulf said. "Anything else?"

"I believe Father was thinking of some kind of diversion."

Wulf nodded. He sat down across from her. "You and Earl Keiler seem to have thought this sort of thing out pretty well."

"It's . . . well, since my mother died and the scrofula has gotten so bad, he and I spend a lot of time talking about the old days. Fighting with the duke. All the plans they considered. It was very close, you know. We could have lost the Little War."

"Yeah," Wulf said. "I got a lot of history lessons from Master Tolas. *A lot.*"

"Maybe he was preparing you."

"For what? Otto is going to be the next duke."

"You might be of use to the mark in all kinds of ways."

"I guess."

She rose from the chair. "Take it from me," she said. "Things hardly ever turn out the way we think they will. But that doesn't mean they can't turn out happy in the end."

Wulf rose, facing Ursel. They were very close, and he reached over and took her hands. "Thank you for the sword."

They stood together for a moment wordlessly. Her hands were warm. Her freckled face seemed flush, and she wore the slight smile, almost teasing, that Wulf was coming to see was her normal expression. Finally she sighed, and spoke. "I'll leave you to your dressing. Good night, Lord Wulf."

"Good night, Mistress Ursel."

With a quick curtsey, Ursel and her bear-woman maid left his room.

It was good to get out of his old clothes. He'd been in them for three days. He'd fought in them. One arm and the chest of his shirt had been soaked with his own blood and Ravenelle's tears. He'd also been spattered with other people's blood, both from his father and from the man he'd killed. He'd run through briar-filled woods. He'd ridden through dust and rain.

The clean clothes were Ursel's. They were men's clothes she used for travel in the woods. They were tight for Wulf and too short in the sleeves and ankles, but he only needed to wear them long enough to have his other clothes washed.

After Ursel left, Grim brought in hot water in a basin and Wulf gave himself as much of a bath as he could. He didn't really need to shave yet, but he gave his face a scrape with a razor to clear away the fuzz.

Then he put on Ursel's clothes. They smelled of lavender. He imagined her skin probably had the same faint odor. For a moment he imagined what it would be like to take her in his arms.

But thoughts of Saeunn blotted out the daydream. He felt guilty having thought too much about Ursel when Saeunn was in danger.

His own clothes came back one bell later with the grime gone and most of the blood scrubbed away. His boots were clean and polished.

Although she'd said she wouldn't be back, Ursel looked in one more time.

The bed looked inviting. The heat from the fire is his room was making him sleepy.

"You'll let me know if there is anything else you need?" she said.

"Yes, I will," Wulf replied. "I wish we'd met under better circumstances."

"Me too, Lord Wulf," she said.

She smiled at him and brushed red hair from her face. Those green eyes. That milky skin.

She curtsied, then turned and left.

Wulf looked at Grim, who had been watching.

"What?" he asked the faun.

"Nothing, m'lord."

"Tell me what you think."

Grim considered a moment. "Could do worse, m'lord."

"How do you even know? She's not a faun."

"A faun could do worse, m'lord," Grim said.

For a moment, Wulf felt a tinge of jealousy—but then thought about how stupid that was. So what if Grim was attracted to the foundling girl?

She was showing every sign that she liked him, Wulf. He wasn't used to this kind of attention. The castle girls never gave it to him. If they drooled over a von Dunstig, it was Adelbert, who was very handsome and romantically in love with the ocean.

She barely knows me, Wulf thought. I'm just a von Dunstig to her.

I'd love to see her shoot that bow.

He thought about Ursel as he settled down in the first comfortable bed he'd seen in two days. He imagined her nocking an arrow, drawing her bow, then sending the arrow into a target.

Then he imagined her doing it naked. Would she have freckles *everywhere*?

Grim dropped a piece of wood onto the fire. The sudden crackle and flying sparks brought Wulf back to the present. He thought about his father's injuries, he thought about Raukenrose and his family, probably under siege in the castle.

Poor Anya. She must be so afraid.

But *she* will be looking after her, Wulf thought. She'll keep Anya safe.

She is there.

And it was Saeunn Amberstone's face he saw as he drifted to sleep.

✣ ✣ ✣

The next morning, Grim brought him coffee. He told Wulf that Albrec Tolas had asked him to smoke with him on the porch of the huge log house.

Wulf took the coffee, wrapped his new cape around his shoulders, and went out. Tolas was standing on a bench and leaning over the porch railing. His pipe was in his mouth, and he was sending clouds of smoke into the cold morning air.

The gnome motioned Wulf over.

"Glockendorf perique," he said, indicating the tobacco in the pipe. "Odor of my youth."

"I suppose I might take up a pipe one day," Wulf said.

"Don't," said Tolas. "It causes dampness in the lungs when they overcompensate for the heat. Look at what's happened to Keiler with his scrofula. The fellow was a constant pipe smoker when I was his aide de camp. Although how he ever stood the orinoco, I can't explain."

"Do you think Earl Keiler is dying?"

"Unquestionably," Tolas said. "Scrofula is a terrible disease. You drown in your own bodily humors."

"Yuck," Wulf replied. "All right, you've convinced me to never draw a breath of tobacco smoke."

"Too bad." Tolas smiled. "It can be very calming."

"But you said—"

"It's time you started thinking for yourself a bit more," Tolas said. "I can't do all of it for you."

"I *can* think for myself, Master Tolas," Wulf said, feeling a bit of resentment rising inside himself.

Tolas looked at Wulf as if considering whether he'd failed at his job or not.

"All right, if we accept that, then I would say you ought to be thinking practically right now, for instance."

"What do you mean? Tell me, and I'll do it."

"I mean the stick you carved with Lady Saeunn's name on it. I saw it before you tucked it beneath your belt"

"What about it?"

Tolas took a long drag on his pipe and waited a moment before he puffed it out.

"You understand that to tempt Lady Saeunn to love you is dangerous for her," Tolas finally said.

"I don't think we have to worry about me tempting her."

"Be that as it may, you cannot marry her."

"I know that, Master Tolas. I know it very well."

Tolas took another long drag.

"Someone like Ursel Keiler, on the other hand . . ." He turned to Wulf again with a smile. "I do not believe you understand how rich she is going to be when she is married."

"Keiler said he was giving her a fat dowry."

"Fat, as in his holdings in the entire western Shwartzwald. It is a fortune to rival that of a princess."

"Good for her."

"She likes you, von Dunstig, and you are attracted to her. Don't deny it. I have not spent fifteen years as a teacher of boys not to see as much."

"She's very pretty . . . and very nice."

"She's a hunter, an expert archer. She's trained in medicine. She knows how to handle bear people when they're angry—something that is difficult to do and extremely useful for a son of the ruling family in Shenandoah to have at his disposal."

Wulf shrugged. "What do you want me to say, Tolas?"

"I want you to consider Ursel Keiler as a woman. It would be a match that is extraordinarily good for the stability of the mark."

He hadn't thought of it that way. And he really didn't like it.

Why can't I just be a ranger, Wulf thought. Patrol the border. Go home at nights to my cabin and read a saga or two.

"Remain in the present, von Dunstig," Tolas said. He was

speaking almost . . . gently, Wulf thought. "Let the future and the past take care of themselves."

"Okay, then. Here's my answer: I wish I could, Master Tolas. Ursel's incredible. To think she's a foundling . . ."

Tolas shook his head. There was the slightest of smiles on his face. "I wonder about that," he said.

"What do you mean?"

"Nothing I wish to discuss at present," the gnome said. "See here, von Dunstig, what I'm telling you is that frankly you must consider someone, anyone, besides Saeunn Amberstone. That way lies heartbreak for you. And for her, too. You must not force her to chose between you and her own immortality."

"Are you actually giving me advice in love, Master Tolas?"

"It seems somebody has to point out facts that are as plain as the nose on your face," the gnome replied.

"Well thanks." He touched his nose to be sure it was still there.

From the stables, which were a separate building, a bear man brought out a smallish brown draft horse. It was saddled and looked prepared for a trip.

"Horse is ready, Master Tolas," called the bear man. "Sure you don't want a pack animal as well?"

Tolas chuckled. "I'll be fine, Master Groom. Are my things in the saddlebags?"

"Yes, sir. That all you're taking?"

"Yes. I'll be there directly. Let me finish this pipe, if you don't mind."

"Not at all, sir. I'll just give her a treat before she's off." The bear man pulled an apple from a pouch at his side and fed it to the horse.

"Where are you going, Master Tolas?" Wulf asked.

"South," Tolas replied.

"You mean you're leaving Bear Hall *now*?" Wulf felt betrayed. Then he thought about how immature that was.

But there was an empty feeling that settled in his stomach. "Do you really have to? I could use . . . well, I would really like for you to be around."

"Nonsense," Tolas replied. "Your most immediate need is to discover how to be your own man." He looked toward the town. "The gnomes are heading north on the Valley Road. I'll meet them and fall in. I'm assigned to a pike unit."

"Are you the captain?"

"Hardly," Tolas answered. "I'm a foot soldier. But that's the way it should be. I haven't been able to drill with the brigade for years."

"You could get killed," Wulf said.

"Von Dunstig," the gnome answered, "it is very probable that we will all get killed."

"I think it would be a big loss to the mark if you in particular die," Wulf said. "That's what I mean."

"I am flattered you think so, von Dunstig," Tolas replied. "But you certainly don't have enough experience to be making such judgments, especially regarding myself." He pulled on his pipe. "We gnomes are fierce, you know, and deadly when we fight in an organized fashion. If we can just make it to Raukenrose in time, I think we're likely to surprise you."

"I will never underestimate a gnome again," Wulf said.

"A worthy sentiment," Tolas said. "Probably more honored in the breaking than in the keeping with you, von Dunstig."

"Master Tolas, this is . . . I'm really worried . . . you're right about me. I don't know what I'm doing. I've . . . I've killed two men in the last four months. I'm not even sure how I did it."

"Hardly surprising. They put a sword in your hand at six and Elgar Koterbaum trained you for ten years in the art of fighting. You were bound to be capable of it."

"But I killed grown men."

"Have you checked yourself lately, von Dunstig? You've filled out." Tolas looked down at his pipe and saw the bowl was done. He knocked the ashes out over the railing.

"I never wanted to be a warrior."

"If only we lived in the world where Wulf von Dunstig and Albrec Tolas were left alone to be scholars and adventurers who never had to make any hard choices." Tolas dipped his pipe into his tobacco pouch and scooped more tobacco into his pipe bowl. "The question is how do we do what our conscience tells us is right." Tolas tamped the tobacco down with his thumb. "You'll find your answer in time," he said. "Now I have to go."

He hopped down from the bench he'd been standing on and walked to the porch steps. Wulf trailed behind him. The groom held the horse by the bridle as Tolas took hold of a stirrup and scrambled up on the horse as if he were climbing a mountain.

"Good-bye, von Dunstig," he said when he was comfortable in the saddle. "Wait for the centaur archers to arrive, then make your decision on what to do. Listen to Keiler, but think for yourself. And I'll see you in Raukenrose."

"See you there, Master Tolas."

The bear-man groom stepped away. Tolas bent down to speak in the horse's ears. "After we get outside the village, we'll find out what you can really do, girl," he said. He shook the reins, and the horse started moving. Tolas passed between the buildings of Bear Hall. Wulf could hear the horse hooves clopping long after he lost sight of the gnome.

Wulf finished his coffee. He stood on the porch listening. From far away, he heard Tolas shout "Hyah!" and the whinny of a horse.

"Must have cleared the village, m'lord," the groom called to him from the yard. He also had been listening. "She's light on her legs, that one, but he's nothing but a feather to her. Now he can really let her run."

Chapter Thirty-Four:
The Hostage

The town fell, but the castle held. Four days had passed. Some of the guard and militia managed to break through the soldiers who had been hidden within the town and attacked them from behind. Many of the town's fighting men were caught between the Sandhaveners who had overrun the walls and the Nesties who had appeared inside the township. They were cut to pieces. Those who surrendered were herded into makeshift cells in the catacombs of Raukenrose University. Those badly wounded were killed. The rest were put to work. Prisoner details cleared the dead.

Duchess Malwin had kept the castle gates open as long as possible to allow people from the town to flee inside. Now there were nearly a thousand people crammed into the keep. Each ate away at the castle's precious stored food. Duke Otto had prepared for a siege, but had never expected a refugee crisis like this one.

Some crumbled inside after just a few days. Giesela von Kleist, a castle girl who had always been lively and popular, if a bit vicious, wandered around like a ghost. She might appear anywhere in the castle looking frightened and bewildered. When people asked her what she was doing or where she was going, she tried to answer but usually burst into tears.

Saeunn weathered being shut in better than most. She had her star to remind her of the world outside. She also had something important to do. She had made it her job to take care of Anya von Dunstig. The little girl was doing well. She was even enjoying the big crowd of children who had suddenly appeared.

Anya knew all three of her brothers were missing, and that her father, Rainer, and Ravenelle were missing, too. Saeunn understood that deep down Anya was terrified that something very bad had happened to them. She did her best to keep Anya and her new friends distracted. She led games of tag and hoop toss, put on puppet shows for them, and even tried to teach them the elven rainwater dance.

After three days, the food was already running low. Everyone in the castle could hear the shouts of the guard as they patrolled the battlements and fired down on the forces outside. Then, on the fourth day, a messenger from the guard came running to find Duchess Malwin.

When the messenger arrived, the duchess was in the game room with Saeunn, Anya, and Ulla. The older girls were teaching her to play Hang the Fool.

"Your Excellency," the messenger said to the duchess, "there is something outside that Captain Morast thinks you should see."

The duchess looked up, irritated at being interrupted when she was concentrating so hard on playing her hand. "Why don't you just tell me? What is it?" she said.

The messenger hesitated.

Saeunn knew Duchess Malwin had no patience for this kind of behavior. Rules and manners were supposed to make communication easier. But the man's troubled look put Saeunn on alert. He had come with bad news.

"Tell me!" said the duchess.

The messenger bowed stiffly. "Your Excellency, there's a truce delegation from the Sandhaveners at the front gate."

"Another one? Just tell Morast to say no," she replied with a shrug.

"Yes, Your Excellency," said the messenger. "But it's Prince Trigvi . . . and he's got Lord Otto with them."

The duchess gasped. Saeunn felt her own heartbeat pick up.

"What do you mean?"

"Nothing, Your Excellency, except that they are both there."

"Is Morast sure it's Otto?"

"He says to tell you he'd swear by it, Your Excellency."

"All right, then." Duchess Malwin rose. "Ulla, you come with me. Saeunn, please stay here with Anya."

"No!" Anya cried. She tossed aside her cards. "I want to see Otto! I want to see Otto!" she said, tugging on one of Saeunn's sleeves.

"Saeunn, keep her here," the duchess said.

"I will, Lady Malwin," Saeunn replied. She bent down and put an arm around Anya. "Come here, Evinthir, and we will go see that new set of puppies under the kitchen stairs."

"Moli, yay!" said Anya. "Moli" was the name of the mother dog. She led the way. Duchess Malwin and Ulla followed the messenger to the barbican, a guard tower that projected out from the wall near the castle gate.

They had gotten halfway to the puppies when Anya suddenly pulled away from Saeunn and slipped into the empty butcher's stall on the west side of the castle bailey. Saeunn followed her inside at a run, but then she discovered a hole in the back of the stall that was big enough for a child but too big for her. She could hear Anya making her way behind the bailey shops.

"Anya, come back here," she called. "This isn't funny."

How had the little girl kept the discovery of this escape route from her? Anya usually told Saeunn all her secrets.

She obviously counted on my believing that, Saeunn thought. *She had to recover the child.*

Anya emerged near the gate on the northern wall.

"Anya, come here right now!" Saeunn shouted.

"I have to see Otto!"

Before Anya could get to the girl, she bounded up the spiral stairs that led to the barbican where her mother and Ulla had gone. Saeunn followed after. She caught up with Anya on the stairs, but Anya let out a wail when Saeunn picked her up and started back down. She struggled in Saeunn's arms. From above, a guard's voice called down.

"The duchess said to let her up."

"Are you sure?"

"She said if the little one wants to that bad it must mean something, so to come on up with her."

Saeunn shook her head. She did not like this at all. But she set Anya down and, holding tight to her wrist, guided her back up the stairs to the barbican balcony.

Before the balcony, there was an observation room with arrow slits. This room had a door that led to the balcony. The balcony had a small protective wall, a balustrade, around it. From the balcony you had a full view of the area in front of the gate. But the balustrade was the only protection from arrows shot from below.

Duchess Malwin and Ulla were standing in the protected observation room, gazing through an arrow slit at something below. Both of them were very quiet.

"Mother, Mother!" said Anya. But when the duchess turned to her daughter, tears were flowing and there was a disturbed look in her eyes. Anya stopped short. "What is it?"

Duchess Malwin didn't answer, but turned back to what she had been viewing. Saeunn scooped Anya up again and, mostly to keep the girl from throwing another fit, she cautiously held her to an arrow slit.

Below, a group of stern-looking soldiers had formed a line on the far side of the dry ditch that the castle drawbridge would cover when lowered. In front of them were two men. Saeunn didn't recognize one of them, but the other was—

"Otto!" Anya said.

"Hush," said Saeunn. "That man is speaking."

The man identified himself as Prince Trigvi von Krehennest of Sandhaven, in command of the forces that had taken Raukenrose township.

"Duchess, we truly wish to have an audience with Duke Otto to discuss the situation. Would you go and get him? Or is he on his death bed, as we've heard?"

So they don't know he's missing, Saeunn thought.

"I am the duke's ears and his voice. Say what you want to me."

"Otto looks really tired," Anya whispered. "He's just staring at the gate."

Saeunn looked down at Otto. It was true. He was not responding to the sound of his mother's voice. Then suddenly he jerked his head upward and stared with wide eyes at the barbican. Anya gasped. Otto's face appeared expressionless.

"Duchess, I would like to see you. Your son would like to see you. I give you my word that you will not be harmed if you step out on the balcony."

"Pardon us if we don't trust your word, Prince Trigvi."

There was silence for a moment. Then Otto cried out in a shrill voice, "Mother, please! Go out on the balcony."

This was too much for Duchess Malwin. She did as she was told. The guards stepped aside, and she walked through the door that led to the balcony. With a whimper of worry, Ulla followed after her mother.

Then Anya did it again. She twisted out of Saeunn's arms and ran after her mother, with Saeunn close behind. On the balcony, she clung to her mother's dress.

"I'm so sorry, Duchess Malwin," said Saeunn. "She's being difficult. I'll take her back inside." Malwin put an arm down and drew Anya close. "Let her stay," she said in a voice close to tears. "You stay, too. I think we are safe."

Saeunn wasn't so sure, but she went to stand beside the duchess. Anya slipped her hand into Saeunn's. "I can't see over the balustrade," she whispered. "Pick me up, Saeunn."

"They might shoot you with an arrow, Evinthir," Saeunn told her.

"I want to see my brother."

Saeunn lifted Anya up and held her on her hip.

"Thank you, Duchess," Trigvi shouted up. "Now I can hear you better. You were muffled before."

Duchess Malwin moved to the edge of the balcony and gazed down at Otto.

"What have you done to him?" she called out.

"He's been well treated," replied Trigvi. "But we've had to confine him for his own good. He was trying to harm himself, you see. We can't have that."

Otto nodded, as if in agreement. "Yes," he cried out. "I'm feeling better now, Mother."

"Duchess, we know your people are starving," said Trigvi. "You have to let us in so we can feed them. It's the merciful thing to do."

"No," said Malwin. "We will hold the castle."

"You have to realize that's not possible."

Anya was tugging on the top of Saeunn's sleeve, and when that didn't work she tugged on Saeunn's hair. "What is it, Evinthir?"

"I see Rainer," Anya whispered in her ear.

"You . . . what? Where?"

"Look over there on the top of the wainwright's house. The one with the red roof." Anya raised her hand and tentatively pointed. Saeunn looked in that direction, found the one building in sight with a red roof . . . Anya was right. There was Rainer. He was waving his arms frantically.

She reached up and cradled Anya's pointing finger. She gently pulled down Anya's hand.

"Yes, Evinthir," she whispered back. "I see him, too."

Was there any way to let Rainer know he had gotten her attention?

In the end, she just waved back with the arm that wasn't holding Anya. There was no way anyone on the ground could tell what she was waving at. At least she hoped not.

Rainer had seen her, because he began making another signal. He crossed his arms over his head again and again.

Trigvi was finishing up a reply to the duchess. "The main reason you must open the gate, Duchess, is because if you don't, I will kill your son right here, before your eyes."

Trigvi stepped back from Otto. His bowmen sighted in on their real target.

Otto called out once again. "Open the gate, Mother. Let me in. They're going to kill me. Please, let me in."

Anya gasped. She squeezed Saeunn's neck tightly.

On the red-roofed building, Rainer was signaling wildly, crossing his arms. Even at this distance Saeunn could see he was shaking his head vigorously.

"He doesn't want us to open the gate," Anya whispered.

"Duchess," she said, tugging on Lady Malwin's dress sleeve. "I am being signaled that we must not open the gate."

"Signaled?"

"A man on the roof yonder." Saeunn nodded in Rainer's direction, but did not point. "I think it is Rainer Stope."

The bowmen held their stances. Trigvi looked up at

Duchess Malwin. "Truly, I plead with you, Duchess. Don't let Lord Otto be slaughtered here like an animal."

"I believe Rainer knows something we don't," Saeunn continued.

"Rainer?" She gazed frantically around, but was too agitated to spot Rainer. "I don't see him."

"But I do, Duchess."

"I don't know, Saeunn. I don't know. Maybe we should—"

As if in anticipation of Duchess Malwin's wavering, Otto shouted again. "Please, Mother! Open the gate! I am your son. Please save me. I'm begging you!"

Duchess Malwin stumbled backward. She was shaking, and Saeunn could see her foster mother was undone. But she caught herself and hurried back to the balustrade.

"All right!" she called out. "We'll open it. We'll open the gate, just don't kill my boy!"

Prince Trigvi's expression softened. "Of course not, my lady." He motioned for the bowmen to lower their bows. He bowed deeply to the duchess.

Rainer was still frantically signaling for them not to do it.

Duchess Malwin called into the observation room. "Open the gates, Captain Morast," she said. "That's an order. Open the gates and let them through."

"But Your Excellency . . ."

"Do it now."

CHAPTER THIRTY-FIVE:
THE DEAD

Saeunn looked at Ulla, who was shaking her head.

"This doesn't feel right, Saeunn. Something's terribly wrong with Otto."

"Yes."

"Can we stop them?"

"I don't think so."

Ulla nodded. "Maybe I can talk some sense into her."

She rushed past Saeunn to go after her mother. Saeunn followed, still carrying Anya in her arms.

Duchess Malwin was standing directly in front of the gate when Saeunn walked out of the tower's spiral staircase.

"Castle guards, lay down your weapons," the duchess called out. "No one is to make the slightest resistance. I want no excuse for a slaughter." She turned to Captain Morast, who was standing near. "Morast, see to it."

Morast nodded that he would. When he called out the order to disarm, there was a sob in his voice. Saeunn retreated across the bailey with Anya. They crouched under the overhanging roof of the castle stables. Across the way, she saw Ulla hurry to Grer's side outside the smith's shop.

Duchess Malwin stood alone as the gate rose and the drawbridge was cranked down. When it was all the way down, the Sandhaveners charged in. They wasted no time. With swords, spears, and halberds they prodded the men toward the center of the bailey, rounding them up like sheep.

"Hands on your head!" shouted one of the Sandhaveners. He was very tall and seemed to be the captain. The guard slowly obeyed, and the Sandhaveners prodded those that didn't with points of weapons until they did.

"On your knees," the Sandhavener captain yelled. "And keep those hands over your heads!"

Some of the guard submitted. The rest were beaten to their knees by soldiers who waded in among them.

"All right, Nesties, bind those hands behind them and throw them on the ground," the man called out. The men with weapons moved in. Each had several ropes dangling from their belts.

The Nestie soldiers were disciplined. They did as their captain ordered with little fuss.

If men resisted, they were beaten. There were a few guards and soldiers who were Tier, and they were hit and kicked even harder.

After the castle warriors were secure, the Sandhaven captain whistled and motioned for the prince to come in. He strode forward. Otto walked beside him. His legs moved woodenly. His toes dragged with every step.

Then something horrible entered the bailey. It walked several paces behind Otto.

The horrible thing was a coal black creature with a vulture's head and the form of a man. On its body, bizarrely, hung the tattered gold and gray robes of a Raukenrose University docent. The thing's coal black clothing shone through the tattered robe as it moved.

I know what that is!

Saeunn let out a shriek before she could cover her mouth.

"Saeunn?" asked Anya. "What's wrong? What is it?"

"Evil, little one. Look away."

It was a draugar.

The draug were elves. Or they *had* been elves. They had begun as elder elves who had awakened into being in the time before both men and Tier. Only a handful of stars twinkled in the sky then. The dragons were embryos just beginning to take their forms.

The draug had *given up* their stars. They had been seduced by the evil one, the void, Ubel. Ubel hated the dragons. He would later hate men and Tier and everything that came from the dragons. The draug did, too. The draug gave up their stars. They filled the place where their starlight soul used to be with Ubel's bitter malice. While their stars fell from the sky, they survived. It was an eternal life in death. They were chained to Ubel's will.

She wasn't sure which of the draug this one was. There had once been four. One was no more. Now there were three.

> *Graus's dread, fallen joy*
> *Geizul's whip, broken pride*
> *Trester's lust, twisted love*
> *Wuten's rage, rancid revenge*

The draugar Trester was gone, but the other three lived on, if you could call that living.

Saeunn watched in horror as the draugar stepped forward. It was walking carefully. And for each step it made, Prince Otto made one, too. Their walks were an exact match.

Otto shambled up to Duchess Malwin. He jerked to a stop directly in front of her.

"Mother," he said. Saeunn saw the draugar mouthe the same words. "You should have known."

Duchess Malwin was trembling. Saeunn knew she wanted to grab Otto and hug him. Something held her back.

"Known what, my dearest?" the duchess asked in a small voice.

"You should have known . . . that I was already dead, Mother."

And with those words, the animation went out of Otto's body. He collapsed in a heap at the duchess's feet.

She screamed. Then she knelt to hold Otto's body.

"Cold, so cold."

Saeunn held Anya tightly. The little girl buried her face in Saeunn's dress. She was shaking. But she wasn't crying.

"I knew it," Anya said. "I knew he was dead. Poor mother."

Saeunn shifted her gaze back to the draugar as if pulled by a force she could not control.

He was looking straight at her. Saeunn gasped.

The draugar mouthed a word. She couldn't hear it, but she knew what it had said.

"Elf."

Its death smell filled the bailey. She heard somebody gag and vomit.

The smell was a sign. Rancid revenge.

This was the draugar called Wuten.

Saeunn was so intent on the draugar that at first she did not hear Anya whispering in her ear. It wasn't until Wuten looked away from her that she was finally able to listen to Anya.

"What is it, little Evinthir? What did you say?"

"I can't tell Otto now. I promised to, but he's dead and I can't tell him."

"I'm sorry, little Evinthir," she answered. "Otto knows you love him. That isn't Otto over there. He's somewhere else. The real Otto loves you."

"I know *that*," Anya said. "It's something else that I promised."

"I don't understand, dearest."

"I can't tell Otto what the owl said."

"What the owl . . . what do you mean, Evinthir?"

"I promised the owl I would tell Otto something, but now I can't."

Saeunn gazed down at Anya. Anya was looking up at her. Her eyes were clear, and her jaw was set.

"The owl told me where the hammer is."

"What hammer?"

"The dragon one. The Dragon Hammer. She said to tell Otto where it was. I promised I would, but now I can't."

Saeunn tried to make Anya's words make sense. She grasped at the only part she understood.

"You can tell me," Saeunn said. "Where is the Dragon Hammer, Evinthir?"

Anya told her.

PART FIVE

PART FIVE

CHAPTER THIRTY-SIX:
THE DUEL

"Anya is not imagining things," Saeunn said.

"But the child's had a terrible shock," Grer Smead replied. He worked the bellows and fired his forge as he spoke. "How can you be sure?"

"I know her. This is real. Tell him, Ulla."

"Saeunn is very good at figuring out lies, dear," Ulla said to Grer. "I never could get away with telling her one."

"But if Lady Anya believes what she's saying, it isn't a lie to her."

"Not this," Saeunn said. "I know when Anya is telling a story. This isn't made up."

Grer nodded gravely. He took an iron stirring from a swage block and spread the coals in the forge furnace. "We must go and get it."

"How?" Ulla said. "The gate is guarded day and night."

"Rainer is out there," Saeunn said. "We could signal him."

"What is he going to do, m'lady?" Grer asked. "That's the sort of thing that's going to take special tools to remove it."

"*You* could do it," Ulla said. "But *don't.*" She stepped up next to Grer and held on to his arm as if he might be yanked away from her at any moment.

"Aye, I could," he said. He sighed. "And you know I have to."

Ulla shook her head in frustration, but didn't contradict him.

"We'll have to get you out," said Saeunn.

"I suppose you have a plan, Lady Saeunn?"

Ulla squeezed Grer's arm. "Saeunn always has a plan. She's very devious. And her plans usually work."

Ulla and Saeunn had been allowed the freedom of the bailey. The castle was filled with Sandhaveners, and there was no way past the gate. And unlike the poor men-at-arms, who were chained below in the castle dungeon, Grer was permitted to work and move freely in the keep.

Saeunn was beginning to understand Prince Trigvi. He believed in justice and law. But the just thing turned out to be whatever Trigvi wanted. Grer's minor freedom was an example. It was supposed to be a balanced punishment. Grer would be forced to work like a dog. Every limping step Grer took would be a reminder that Gunnar had crippled the smith for life. Saeunn had seen Trigvi smiling serenely while he ordered Grer to fetch water and haul wood for him.

Saeunn thought Trigvi looked ridiculous.

The prince had completely misunderstood Grer. The smith only cared if somebody thought he was slacking at his job. Nobody, even Trigvi, could accuse Grer of that. He worked like a madman keeping the castle fires supplied with wood and water in the central basins. He also handled endless requests for horseshoeing and armor repairs from the Sandhaveners.

Trigvi looked on Ulla with a mix of revulsion and lust. He had announced that he would marry her in time. But first she must learn her place as his queen. He'd made her a housemaid. Her job was to draw water from the castle basins and sweep the halls after his men.

What alarmed Saeunn was that he was also paying attention to Anya. Trigvi had said to Ulla that he might take her sister as a second wife as soon as Anya was of age in the old tradition. That was three years away.

Ulla and Saeunn had been prepared with an excuse if they were stopped when coming to the smithy. None of the guards seemed to care. As long as the girls did not make for the gate, they were ignored.

Saeunn was not bothered by the way she had been treated. The lewd comments she'd received from the Nesties were laughable. She knew they were too disciplined to go against orders and try to take her against her will. She feared for the women of the township, though. The Sandhaven common soldiers she'd seen at the castle were much less disciplined.

Mainly she tried to avoid getting anywhere near the draugar. She could feel the pull of his empty soul. Being near him was like standing in a high place and thinking about jumping. Daylight and clouds never harmed her connection to her star, but being near the draugar made her feel weak, sick and out of touch. She also had the sneaking suspicion that the draugar had some special plan for her. She dreaded finding out what that might be.

He was many thousands of years old. The elder elves hadn't even been shaped like people at first. They had been forces of nature. The four draug were powers of the north, south, east, and west of the world. They had been sent from the never and forever to soothe the dragons' dreams. They'd done their duty for eons. Then Ubel, the void that existed in the tiny spaces between the dragons, had talked the elder elves into giving up their stars and following him.

He had promised them freedom, then made them slaves.

Wuten was trying to find the Dragon Hammer. He was

questioning everyone in the castle, one by one, but men first. It would be only a matter of time until he got to her— and to Anya. They had to do something before that time came.

This was the reason for the meeting in Grer's shop.

"I do have a plan," said Saeunn. "I went to visit my horse friend Slep in the stables to see how she was doing. Not well. The place is packed with Sandhavener horses. The stable boys are mucking out the manure constantly. So far they've been piling it in a wagon outside the stalls. They've been terrified to take it down to the river and dump it."

"Aye, they should be. If you get on the wrong side of those Nesties, they'll throw you in the dungeon with the castle men-at-arms. It happened to my apprentice, Luki."

"A strong man could pull that manure wagon," Saeunn said. "He could tell the gate guards he was going to dump it. It's a job that *has* to get done."

Grer was silent for a moment. Then he let out a quiet, "Aye."

"But why wouldn't one of the Nesties do it?" Ulla put in.

"They don't know where to take it. Those Nesties are hard, but they're by-the-rules sort of men. They wouldn't like the idea of dumping it outside the gate. They'll want it properly taken care of."

"You are willing to gamble my fiancé's life on them having proper manners?" Ulla replied.

"They'll turn him back if they don't want him to do it."

"Or throw him in the dungeon if they're in a bad mood," Ulla said. "I'm not sure if I like this idea, Saeunn."

"He has to try," Saeunn said. "The evil thing is on the trail. If he gets it . . . I think this land will die."

Grer nodded. "She's right, Ulla. That thing . . . what do you call it?"

"A draugar. I do not like to say his name. We elves are ashamed of the draug. They are our own kind gone bad."

"It's evil, that's plain enough," Grer continued. "It's been going into the dungeons, you know, asking its questions. You can hear the men scream. Grown men and soldiers."

"It senses that the hammer is close."

Grer sighed. "I must do what I can," Grer said. "I'll need tools."

"You can hide them in the manure."

Grer nodded. "Right then. When should I do it?"

"At imbiss bell the stable hands change shifts. That would be the time."

Ulla breathed in quickly. "So soon?"

"The sooner the better," Grer said. "I want to get this over with before I realize I'm staking my life on what a talking owl said to an eight-year-old girl."

Captain Rask strode determinedly past the picket and headed for the cane patch in the bend of the river. This was where his brother had told him the fight was going to take place.

No. Not a true fight. A duel. Blood and bones!

Of all things, his kid brother had gotten himself into a stupid duel.

What was his fool of a brother thinking? Alvis had been acting strangely for the past year. He'd wanted to talk to Alvis about it, but suddenly he was deployed to Raukenrose with Prince Gunnar. He'd stayed hidden for months in the university library's catacombs, a weapon to be used at the perfect moment.

All the boring time there he had worried about Alvis.

Harrald, Rask's birth name, and Alvis Torsson were soldiers, and good ones. They were professionals in a land of amateurs. They were part of the elite Sandhaven palace guard, the Nesties. When he and his brother had become Twenty commanders, they'd taken on new names, warrior names. Nesties had done this since the distant past.

Alvis called himself Steel. Harrald had chosen Rask, the Sandhaven word for swiftness.

Now Lance Captain Steel had sent Captain Rask a message asking him to be his second.

In a cursed duel.

Alvis—Steel—was going to fight over something that could have been handled a dozen better ways, all without risking his life.

The story Steel had peddled was that Steel and his lance commander had argued about the division of loot during the sack of the town. Steel wanted more than the traditional third for his men. The lance commander refused and called him a son of a slut for asking.

That was when Steel had challenged the man to a duel. For insulting their mother. It was as if they were city boys again fighting in back alleys.

Steel *knew* that Rask absolutely hated duels. Even though dueling between Sandhavener officers went on in the shadows, even among the Nesties, Rask believed duels were a waste of time. Rask knew because he'd been in two duels. In one, he was a principal. In the other, he was a second. Both times he had killed a man he would rather not have killed. He hated spilling the blood of his brothers in arms, and hated more the idiotic feuds that flamed up to cause it.

How could Steel let himself get sucked in over such a petty matter?

Division of loot? A trivial insult?

It was like fighting over the biggest piece of goose at Yuletide. On the Chesapeake, there were thousands of geese to go around at Yule. Millions of them returned every year to the bay. Every man could have a whole goose. Why argue over who got the biggest leg?

There were plenty of riches in Raukenrose.

Why fight over some meaningless percentage when you could loot the entire town?

Rask reached the edge of the river cane. There was supposed to be a trail here that led to a secluded clearing by the water. This had become the place for duels. Rask had heard about it even where he served in the castle. He was the commander of the garrison, the leader of the mysterious all-black being's personal Hundred.

Rask's Hundred was the elite of the elite. That was why it had been his Hundred that had been smuggled into the township months before the invasion. They had erupted and taken the town militia from behind, like a dagger stabbed into the back of an enemy.

The river clearing was used mainly because it was easy to chuck the body of the loser in and let it float away. Practical. But he was going to see if he could stop this duel before it got started. Rask had gotten more prestige than he'd ever imagined possible. His Hundred had killed Lord Otto von Dunstig. And his Hundred had taken and held Raukenrose castle.

He was sure he could browbeat Steel's commander into backing down. If he could do that, then he knew he would be able to talk some sense into his brother. Rask rehearsed in his mind what he would say to them both.

But when he broke into the clearing, Captain Steel was nowhere in sight. Instead, there were twelve gigantic men with the heads of buffalo staring down at him—and Rask was a very tall man. Twelve buffalo men and one regular human. The man seemed very young. But he looked as stoic and determined as the buffalo men.

"Cold hell," Rask said, reaching for his sword.

He never got a chance to use it.

"All right, pull," said the young man.

It was then that the net sprang under his feet. It wrapped him in rope netting and catapulted Rask up into a nearby willow tree. His hands were pinned tight and his sword remained in its scabbard.

Rask began to scream for help, even though he knew he was too far away from the pickets to be heard.

"Dunk him," said the young man.

One of the buffalo men walked over and swung him and the net away from the tree trunk. Another unhitched the rope and let Rask drop into the water.

They kept him down a long time. When they brought him up, he was too busy coughing out water to make a sound or call for help again. He was still coughing when they took him out of the net, laid him on the ground, and bound his wrists so tightly he couldn't feel them. They mercifully waited until he'd got his breath back before stuffing a cloth into his mouth so deeply that there was no way he could spit it out.

"Time to go," the young man said. He kicked Rask in the stomach. Rask doubled over. A buffalo men picked Rask up and slung him over his shoulder. The buffalo man's hairy head smelled like the creature had washed it in rancid milk.

Rask concentrated and forced himself not to gag. If he did, he might very well suffocate in his own vomit.

A few paces down the river was a beached canoe. The buffalo man dumped Rask into it. Then he and another took seats in the aft, with the young man in the fore. They pushed off and paddled upriver.

Rask had no idea why he was still alive. He also did not know that his brother had tricked him into this, which he had. He would never have suspected that Captain Steel, Alvis Torsson, had deserted and been picked up by the cursed talking animals of this cursed valley.

"Be still," the young man said to him. "We're doing you a good turn, even though you probably will never know it."

CHAPTER THIRTY-SEVEN:
THE NETTLES

His wrists ached. They'd marched him very fast after the capture with his hands tied behind his back. The spear butts of the buffalo men prodded him forward, and when it wasn't that it was the bear-man claws digging into his shoulder blades, turning him to the right or left. He cried out, but that didn't stop them.

He knew they were bear *people* and not bears, but what did that mean? They still had claws and big teeth. Now he was not only surrounded by Tier, he was in their power. They'd marched him without letup, and when he'd given out, they'd picked him up like a sack of grain and carried him.

Now here he was and something had just happened to him, something terrible, but he couldn't remember *what*.

He had strange memories of eating bloody flesh. Of a cut made across his own arm and his blood draining. That was the most terrifying thing of all. Had they killed him? Was he a ghost? Where was Helheim?

You are not a ghost, man from the east.

The voice came from everywhere around him. It was a

female voice, but deeper, somehow more velvety than any he'd ever heard.

That's the voice I imagine a spider having, he thought. A black widow spider.

Ravenelle stood in a dark, flat landscape. It wasn't perfectly level but was more like the floor of one of the great deserts she'd heard existed in the west of the world. There were no stars. What light there was came from the horizon. It looked like early dawn, but Ravenelle knew that in this place there would be no sunrise. Yet the light was enough to see by.

The captain lay several paces away.

He was pulling himself up from the ground. He struggled to a knee. His hands were not tied here, but he rubbed one of his wrists where the rope had cut into it in the real world. Then he saw her. He quickly reached back down to the ground nearby and picked up a large rock. He weighed it in his hand, tossed it away, and picked up another rock, slightly bigger.

He charged at her. He held the rock high, ready to bash her head in when he reached her.

He was the type that fear made brave.

Should have guessed it, Ravenelle thought. A captain, a man of war. He'd have learned to turn his fear into something useful.

Ravenelle looked quickly about.

Stinging nettles, Ravenelle thought, and these were duskies, the nastiest kind of all. She had been to this dream desert. This was where new bloodservants were brought to be punished.

She reached for a handful of leaves and was rewarded with a burning pain in her right palm. She bit her lip and managed not to shriek with the agony she felt.

Then she felt something smack into the small of her back. Hurt shot through her from the blow, more intense and sudden than the nettles' stinging resin.

She turned and saw that the man was only a few steps away. He'd thrown the rock at her and hit her with it, hard. He had another stone in his hand.

Should have expected him to figure out what to do here to survive, Ravenelle thought.

Then he attacked her. Before he could bash her with the other rock, she turned and thrust the stinging nettles into his face.

He dropped the rock and screamed in pain, as she'd known he would. He clawed at his face for a moment, then fell to the desert floor, holding his face and weeping.

She sat down beside him in the patch of duskies.

All right, she thought to the other bloodservant who had been hiding nearby. *You can come out now.*

I have something to tell you.
Shut up.
Your brother is here.
You lie. He raised the stone, stepped closer.
But I'm not lying. Tell him.
Harrald?

His brother had not been present before. He was sure of it. But there he was standing less than a ten-pace away. Alvis walked toward Rask, stepping through the nettles. But he wore heavy boots here, and the nettles didn't seem to affect him.

Alvis? What are you . . . this is a trick.
It's me, Harrald. I left the Legion. The talking animals found me. I was dying from the ater. They brought me to her.

Rask looked at his attacker, the smallish woman who had conquered him with leaves.

She was a Roman, obviously. Ebony-brown skin. A cascade of curly black hair. She seemed so frail. Clearly that was not the case.

She saved me.

This doesn't make any sense.

Harrald, listen to her. She can save you from that thing. It's burning out your mind like it was burning out mine. She gave me back myself.

Rask sat up. His eyes were watering, and his face felt like he'd been attacked by an entire beehive. But the pain was starting to go away.

He had no idea where he was. If this wasn't Helheim or a land of ghosts, what was it? Then he saw the stone he'd dropped. He reached over and picked it up. The nettle trick wouldn't work again. If the dark woman tried to hurt him again, he would bash her. But for the moment he had to figure out where he was—and how to get away. So he would keep his brother, or whoever this was, talking.

So what? I'd just be a slave to her instead of it. No thanks.

It's not like that. She's not like that.

What is she like?

Good.

But you're still her slave.

It's not like that. She's . . . I'm part of something. It's better than before. I was dying.

The small, dark woman spoke. *I'll take care of him. Always. I promise. But first you have to do what we want.*

We?

Me.

How can I know you'll keep your promise?

You know the draugar.

Yes.

Do you enjoy hurting children?

No.

Then what do you have to lose?

He sat for a while, considering. Alvis started to say something, but Rask motioned him to silence. Finally, Rask dropped the stone.

All right. What do you want me to do?

For the first time, the dark woman smiled. And she was not so frightening to look at anymore, despite her wild hair. She was actually quite pretty.

First, answer all my questions, said the woman. *Then we'll send you back.*

No! The thing. He will know what's happened. He'll strip it out of my mind.

She held out a handful of the nettles.

No, she said. *After we've finished, you'll eat these and forget.*

Ravenelle shook her head. She was back in the clearing near the army camp. The Sandhaven captain lay unconscious on the grass beside her. "Better take him to the wise woman to tend to his wrists," Ravenelle said to the bear-man guards. She smiled wickedly. "Then get him back to Raukenrose. Tonight if possible."

After that, she sent for Wulf and Keiler. Alvis Torsson, her new bloodservant, brought her a cup of tea. He'd also found a buffalo skin, and she sat on this and waited.

She had learned a great deal. Some was useful. Some was terrible news.

Otto was dead.

Wulf arrived first. He put a hand on her shoulder. When she looked up, he must have seen the red tears glistening in her eyes.

"What is it?" Wulf asked.

She shook her head sadly.

"I'm sorry," she told him. "Wulf, I'm so sorry."

Then the blood tears flowed.

Chapter Thirty-Eight:
The Plan

Nine days, Wulf thought. It had been only nine days. It seemed like a lifetime ago that he'd left Raukenrose on the hunting trip with his father. Nine days ago he'd wanted no part in ruling the mark. He'd wished the dragon-trance would go away forever. He'd wanted to leave it all to Otto and Adelbert, to Ulla and Anya, and go to the university. Go to the ranger border patrol. Or work in a library. Get out of the castle for a long, long time.

Well, he was out of the castle, all right.

He was the rallying point for the mark's army. He no longer felt like running from the responsibility. He didn't feel lost anymore, or unable to figure out what was required of him.

He had a place. He knew where he belonged. It wasn't about ruling or status. It wasn't about whether or not you felt up to the job.

It was what it was. He had Keiler, who had forgotten more about war than most warriors had learned.

He had troops. More coming in almost every hour.

He was part of the plan, and the plan partly belonged to him, and partly to a thousand others.

Wulf was all right with that.

Now finally they were making definite plans to go back. In force.

Taking Raukenrose township should be impossible without a large army. Raukenrose was a town surrounded by a wall. Sieges took huge resources and many, many troops.

Everyone at the war council meeting knew this, and it hung over them like a dismal cloud during their planning.

They had met in Earl Keiler's private chambers. There were several chairs, but most of those present, including Wulf, were pacing back and forth or leaned over a central table with a map of Raukenrose and its surrounding area laid out on top.

A fire burned in a large fireplace and the centaur Ahorn was warming himself there. Across the room and as far away from the fire as possible was the Lindenfolk leader, Lady Meinir Fruling.

In addition to Wulf and Earl Keiler, there was Count Davos Bara, the wolf-man leader, Tupakkalaatu of the buffalo people, Bamber Esserholz, who was a beaver-people leader—as well as, Wulf had been told, a legendary riverboat trader—and the raccoon-man head of Keiler's intelligence, Roland Washbear.

Baron Smallwolf, the fox man, had declined to attend but had sent a representative fox whose name was Aldrich.

Washbear laid out the facts while some smoked pipes and others sipped mugs of Keiler's mead.

According to Washbear, the biggest advantage they had was that the Sandhaveners had not moved into the town proper yet. Most of the troops were camped outside the northern, southern, and eastern gates, with some also clumped along the eastern bank of the Shenandoah River, which lay on the townships' western side. Inside the town, it seemed that some kind of furious search was going on, and there were only a few hundred troops allowed in at a time.

Otherwise, why the Sandhaveners were keeping the bulk of their troops outside the walls was not known.

"But we believe it's because they are looking for the Dragon Hammer," said Earl Keiler. "They need the place clear for search parties. They need to roust the populace little by little, not all at once. To comb through the place."

"How do they know it's even there?" asked Wulf.

"We believe the draugar you fought might be drawn to it, though we aren't sure if that is possible."

"Nobody really understands the draug," Wulf said. "Not even the lore masters."

"Or they hope to find someone who knows where the thing is and torture it out of them," said Count Bara, the leader of the wolf men. He blew out a stream of cloud smoke for emphasis.

"In any case, we must take advantage of the situation," Keiler continued. "We need to attack at a weak point."

"The only weak point I can see is one of the gates," Wulf said. "And the Sandhaveners will have reinforced themselves there."

"Yes, but although there are a lot of them, Raukenrose is a fairly big place. They can't be everywhere."

"So we need to find the least guarded gate," Wulf said.

"That is exactly what we've been doing," Washbear replied. "We've used the otherfolk, particularly the trees. They have an extensive network, rapid communication, and are excellent spies."

"What do they say?" Wulf asked.

"That the Sandhaveners least fear an attack from the east. They assume we are gathering somewhere to the south or perhaps Bear Valley. They do not have a spy network, and we have been deliberately misleading what cavalry reconnaissance they send out."

"What about Kohlsted, though?" Wulf asked. "It's the second biggest town in the mark after Raukenrose."

"Yes, this is why they've also reinforced the north gate. Those additional troops have had to be taken from somewhere else, and where they've come from is the eastern gate, where they believe they are least vulnerable. The eastern forces that remain are camped on a meadow and wheat fields there between the town and a small rise called Bone Hill. The road then leads into the forest and across a creek."

"Leach Creek," Wulf said. "I know it. And that flat area in front of the eastern gate is called Raukenrose Meadow, even though it isn't really a meadow anymore. Mostly wheat and barley fields."

Earl Keiler nodded. "The area to the south of Dornstadt Road, the road heading east, is hilly, the forest dense. The best place to emerge is from just north of the road."

"Alerdalan Woods."

"Yes," said Washbear, consulting his map. "We have a strong network of otherfolk settled there as well." He looked toward Fruling, who was seated nearby sipping a glass of water.

"The Lindenfolk will make the path easier," Fruling said. "You may depend on it."

Keiler turned toward Esserholz. "Do you have the diversion ready?"

"Planned out," said Esserholz. "Whether it'll work or not is anyone's guess."

"Well, be ready with it."

"Yes, m'lord."

Keiler turned his gaze to Wulf. "The idea, Lord Wulf, is to lure a number of the Sandhavener troops away when we attack. We'll then have a smaller, more confused force to deal with. We will kill a great many of them before the soldiers we trick come back, and then we can take on that force." Keiler coughed into a blood-spattered handkerchief, then continued. "At least that's the plan. I *don't* expect it to go that way. We've planned for several other possibilities."

"Like what?" asked Wulf.

"What if the gate force is *reinforced* instead of being weakened? We may have to withdraw then, lead them after us into the woods where the otherfolk will harry them. That way we can live to fight another day."

"Retreat," Wulf said.

"We have to avoid being completely destroyed as a fighting force," Keiler said. "Sometimes there is no other way."

Wulf nodded. "What else?"

"We wonder what will happen if the draugar you have reported personally generals the battle," said Washbear in a low voice, as if merely bringing up the creature's name might draw its attention. "We must be ready to face magic."

"How do we do that?"

"It will be difficult," Keiler conceded. "Our best hope would be to isolate that danger, whatever form it may take, and throw everything we have against it."

"*If* you know where to find him," Wulf said. "*If* he stays there."

"There are unpredictable drawbacks to this plan," Washbear said. "We simply do not know what we're dealing with when it comes to this menace. But thanks to Princess Ravenelle, we now know *much* more."

"There isn't a whole lot in the lore about Draugar Wuten," Wulf said. "What there is, Ahorn and his people know. They're as good as any scholar at the university, Tolas has always said."

"Thank you, m'lord. And yes, Tolas is right," said Ahorn from across the hall. He was standing near the fire, warming his human torso. He turned and walked back toward them, speaking as he clopped over the flagstone floor. "Since my people have arrived at Bear Hall, we have been practicing our archery. There is a certain sort of arrow that is reported in some ancient texts to be useful against the draug, perhaps fatal."

"We have to use it, then!"

"Alas, we cannot," replied the centaur. "We do not have it. It is made of dragon amber. It is known to my people as the Sageata Aur, the Amber Arrow. It is said to reside in the Most Westerly West. Where that might be is up for dispute among the scholars."

"Is there anything else that might work against a draugar?" asked Esserholz, the beaver man.

Keiler hesitated, then seemed to come to a decision and answered. "We believe Princess Ravenelle may be a weapon we can use against him."

"What do you mean?"

"We decided we must use her presence here to our advantage. We kidnapped and provided her with a Sandhavener captain to dominate using her Roman ways," Keiler said. "Not just any captain, either, but the leader of the personal company of the draugar. He has been sent back to Raukenrose, his mind wiped of any knowledge of his own domination."

"Under the proper circumstance," Washbear said, "this man might be used as a dagger in the back of the draugar or Prince Trigvi."

"She must be protected at all costs, then," said Count Bara. "I will provide her with a personal guard."

Keiler nodded. "Thank you, Count Bara. That would be welcome."

"And when do we attack?" asked Aldrich, the fox man. "My people are getting restless with nothing to do but chase rabbits in the forest."

Keiler nodded gravely. "We must gather more forces and wait as long as we can for—"

"—the gnomes?" said Aldrich. He sniffed contemptuously. "A false hope. They won't come. That gussied-up charlatan stole a horse and ran away, never to be seen again, I'll wager. The mud rats only care for themselves. You'll see. They won't come." His voice was filled with doubt.

And maybe something more sinister, Wulf thought. Something dangerously close to treason.

"I gave Master Tolas that horse," growled Keiler in a low voice. "I'll thank you to keep your conspiracies to yourself, Manly Aldrich."

The fox man crinkled his nose and sniffed loudly. He didn't answer.

"We postpone as long as we can for the gnomes," Keiler said. "They will be a huge boost to our chance of victory."

Aldrich pretended to stifle a scornful laugh.

"How long are we to give them, m'lord," asked Count Bara.

"Two more days."

"Is that wise? Master Washbear has pointed out that our advantage is that they have remained in their encampment. What if they move inside the town walls?"

"It is a chance I believe we must take," Keiler replied. "Lord Wulf?"

"You seem very sure of this, Earl Keiler," Wulf said, trying to keep the doubt he felt from his voice.

"That is because I have seen gnomes make war."

"Then I agree. Two days."

Keiler nodded. "Very well. We'll begin the march in two days and attack at dawn the following morning. The sun will be at our backs," he said. "That will make only eleven days from the fall of the township. I know it seems both a long time—and also too short a time, in its way—to hold off. Yet I still hope to catch the Sandhaveners by surprise and kill a great many before they know what hit them." Keiler had a coughing spasm, then tried to continue as if nothing had happened, although Wulf could see he was trembling. "We will use both centaur and fox-man, er, smallwolf, archers on our right and left flanks. This will be more than harassment. Our middle may remain weaker than their force, even if it is smaller. But if they push us back, they'll be walking into crossfire."

"At least that is the plan," Ahorn said. "We have come with a great many arrows, and are preparing more."

"And we smallwolf have our crossbows," said Aldrich.

"Then, by the will and might of the Allfather," Keiler said, "we will destroy the invaders."

And if we don't? Rather than voicing his doubt, Wulf only thought it.

There are so many of them. We gain more every day, but we are still so few. And we cannot wait any longer.

He thought of Anya. His family.

Saeunn.

Whatever the tactics and strategy, his goal was always the same.

Rescue his friends and family.

Or die trying.

But there was something he had to do first. He hadn't believed it when the feeling had returned, but now he was certain.

The dragon was calling him once again.

CHAPTER THIRTY-NINE:
THE GRAY ELF

It was late afternoon of the next day when Wulf finished the travel from Bear Hall and climbed the eastern side of the valley to Raven Rock. It had been a good ride through the Shwartzwald Forest. The day before, the war council had made its plan. He'd felt at ease. Ready.

Now, suddenly, he did not.

A lot depended on what would happen over the next few days.

Otto was dead.

Ravenelle had used the new celestis to delve into the mind of the brother of the Sandhaven deserter. There wasn't any doubt about it.

And the deserter himself had brought news of Adelbert's death.

Two brothers in a week. It was almost overwhelming. Would have been, but he needed to keep going.

They knew much more about what the Sandhaveners were doing in Raukenrose.

The deserter had been a Sandhavener officer. He'd felt betrayed by his king into mental slavery. Something had gone wrong when he'd been issued the new black-colored celestis, the ater-cake. His mind had been nearly burned to a crisp by the draugar.

But he hadn't died. Instead, Ravenelle had saved him. Whatever she'd done, the Sandhavener was now completely devoted to her.

And found out his captain was the leader of the elite force from the Nesties, the Hundred.

The mission had been to capture or kill the Hundred captain. They had captured him. And released him to go back to the castle.

Otto was dead.

Adelbert, too.

And I am in a murderous frame of mind, Wulf thought.

I don't care about recapturing the town. I don't care about an old relic.

I want to kill Sandhaveners. Personally.

He knew he needed perspective. Knowing was a lot different than *getting* though.

The dragon never showed you things *you* wanted to see. It showed you what it wanted you to know.

He had to try.

He had to stop his bloody circle of thoughts.

He had to get over it.

Because he was never going to be able to *actually* kill Sandhaveners until he did.

Which set him to thinking about killing them all over again.

Raven Rock overlooked both Bear Valley and Raukenrose. It was supposed to be a place where a portion of the land-dragon surfaced. It would be a good place to come if the dragon was calling.

Suddenly, though, the dragon wasn't calling. The feeling had grown weaker, at least. Had he been imagining it before? No. There had been no doubt. Until now.

The rocky overlook marked the northern end of Bear Valley. Below him, the "army" of Shenandoah was camping. Tomorrow they would finish the march on Raukenrose and then attack the following dawn.

At least, that was the plan.

Raven Rock was shale. It was made of huge slabs jutting along a ridge at a steep angle. The path to the overlook led between these jutting slabs. Buzzards nested along the way, and Wulf was careful to avoid them. Buzzards could make a brutal assault when they thought their hatchlings were threatened.

At the end was the highest slab stabbing up into the sky. The path wound along behind this, ending where the rock slope began. A hundred paces up the angled rock was the summit, Raven Rock, with a view of Bear Valley to the west and the Shenandoah Valley and Raukenrose to the east. The slab was just level enough to climb up the rock without having to crawl on hands and knees.

Wulf used a trick that Rainer had taught him while they were rock climbing steep slopes in the mountains outside Kohlsted. The method was to keep your weight over your feet. But to do that you had to lean back, way back. This felt *very* wrong and possibly fatal. Nagel soon had enough and flew off to find a perch at the base of the rock.

But the technique worked.

When Wulf got to the top, the rock flattened. The summit was a spot where three people could stand if they crowded close. Wulf was alone.

The late afternoon sky was blue with fluffy white clouds. There was a light breeze and it was warm enough that he'd left his new cape at the base of the rock with Grim.

Raven Rock was supposed to be connected to the sleeping dragon below.

But it wasn't working. He touched the rock. He lay down on the rock. He tried to use his dagger to make a connection—the dagger Grer Smead had made him to replace the other that got stuck in the Olden Oak. No good. Nothing.

I'm fooling myself. The dragon calls you, you don't call it.

Twilight came, and a sliver of moon rose. It was getting colder. He regretted that he'd left his cape below with Grim.

Otto. Adelbert. Kill the cursed scum. Kill them.

And the thoughts started over again.

He was also getting a very sore butt. The top of the rock was flat, but that didn't mean it was smooth. There wasn't anywhere to sit that wasn't on some bump or another.

"You have good reason to want them all dead."

"I know. But I can't let it control me. Besides, it's my fault. I started it all by stabbing Gunnar."

"Oh, I doubt that *you* were the first cause of anything."

Wulf snapped back to attention. Had he dozed off? Had he been dreaming?

An elf was sitting across from him.

The elf had the elegant elven face that seemed forever young. Even in the twilight, Wulf could see that his hair was gray. His eyes were the same light gray as his hair.

He wore a cloak of buffalo fur loosely around his shoulders, but it had either been bleached or it was from a rare white buffalo. His other clothing, pants and a simple shirt, was gray wool. His boots were black, the only dark color on him.

"Hello," the elf said.

Wulf called out in alarm. But there was no answer from below.

"They won't be able to hear you. Don't be upset. We don't mean any harm. We won't be long."

"What are you doing here?"

"Passing through. We try to come by this place when we're nearby."

"Who is 'we'?"

"My company."

He motioned down the rock slope at nothing. But then shapes seemed to grow out of the Raven Rock surface. They took the shape of cloaked figures. Then they sat back down and they were just rocky shapes once more.

"The Gray Company. I'm called Eifer. I think you must be Wulfgang."

"How did you know that?"

"The dragon dreams. You are someone who shares them. So am I."

Wulf hesitated. But what was the use of lying?

"All right, yes. My name is Wulf."

"And since nobody but a von Dunstig male would do that around here, you must either be the duke or one of his sons. You are not the oldest. Otto is in his late twenties, and you are clearly younger. I have met Adelbert—"

Wulf cut in. "You've met my brother? When? Where?"

"It was on a ship in the Chesapeake. A story for another time."

"I want to hear it."

"He may tell you himself."

"He's dead."

Eifer reached up and touched his own forehead with his fingertips. Then he touched his heart. He gazed into his own palm for a moment. He seemed not so much sad as puzzled. "I am very sorry to hear that," he finally said. "Adelbert was a good man." The elf looked back at Wulf. "You aren't Adelbert or the duke. That's why I know you're Wulfgang."

"You know me, but I've never heard of you."

"We are passing through. Headed for my kin in Eounnbard."

"The Smoke Elves?"

"Yes."

"Why are you here?"

"This rock? The same reason as you, Wulf. It's a gate into the dragon's dreams."

"The dragon isn't showing me any dreams. I've been here all day."

Eifer ran a hand over his smooth chin. "I wouldn't be so sure," he said. He gazed at Wulf for a moment. "There are all kinds of dreams." He seemed to be considering something.

"What?" said Wulf.

"My company can't go into battle with you tomorrow," the elf said. "I wish we could, but we are genuinely needed in the south."

"I don't expect you to join us."

"I can give you something, though. I will."

He took a pendant on a metal chain from around his neck. The chain looked like steel. The pendant was a stone. It was brownish-black, flecked with white bits. It was small enough to fit into the elf's palm.

"What is it?"

"A piece of a fallen star, Wulf."

"It's some kind of magical talisman or something?"

"No. It isn't magic. Not in the way you mean. It is just a piece of star."

"That sounds pretty useless."

"You might be surprised. It's a star stone. A meteorite. Will you take it?"

"Why?"

"Why not, Wulfgang?"

Wulf took the stone on the chain in his palm. He ran his finger over its pitted surface.

"I guess it can't hurt," he said.

"Lean forward a bit." Wulf did. The elf took the chain back from him and draped the necklace over Wulf's head. The star stone rested on Wulf's chest.

Wulf looked down at the stone, then past it to the moon-traced bumps of Raven Rock.

The stone in his hand changed. Its surface cleared. He could look *through* the stone at the rock below him.

It was as if Raven Rock was the surface of a clear lake. If he held his vision one way, he could see the rock bumps and cracks like still waves on a still lake. Now he concentrated on looking below the surface, and the waves disappeared. The layers stripped themselves away, pulling back and disappearing.

He was seeing *inside* the Earth. Deeper and deeper. And it was—

Dragons. Thousands and thousands of them. Dragons were wound about one another, clamped tightly together. And even though he saw heads and tails and bodies, it was hard to tell where one stopped and another began.

"There must be . . . there are so many of them."

"Some little, some big," said Eifer.

The dragons seemed chaotic, all twisted together in many sorts of ways. But there were patterns within the confusion that seemed to almost come together in Wulf's mind, and then everything seemed chaos again, a compressed, round clump of dragons.

"The whole world is a clutch of dragons," said Eifer. "It's an egg filled with young dragons waiting to be born."

"Blood and bones, what did this thing do to me?"

"I told you. The stone can help you see clearly," the elf said. "We have to go."

Wulf sat clutching the star stone, trying to understand what he'd just experienced. He risked a glance down through the stone again, but the rock was just a rock now.

"Weren't you here to . . . commune with the dragon?"

Eifer laughed. "Have you ever heard the saying 'the souls of men are the souls of dragons'?"

"It's from a really old skald song."

Eifer nodded. "Your brother said you had the makings of a lore master."

"I guess," Wulf answered. He fingered Eifer's stone. "What is this?"

"It's someone," Eifer said. "Someone I once loved."

"You were a star?"

Eifer stood up. "I am a star," he said. "She gave hers up, and it fell."

"What was her name?"

"Brenunn Temeldar," said the elf.

Wulf looked hard at Eifer. "That's the name of the Pillar of the South in the old cosmos tales."

"It is."

"*This* is Brenunn Temeldar?"

"Yes," said the elf. He offered a hand to Wulf. "Now I have to go. And you should get some sleep."

"I'm still waiting for the dragon," Wulf said. But he gave the elf his hand and stood up beside him.

Eifer laughed. "I have a prediction, Wulfgang," he said. "I foretell that waiting for the dragon will be the story of your life."

The elf motioned, and the Gray Company rose like a ghostly mist from Raven Rock.

"Go with God and the divine ones," Eifer said.

He turned and walked easily down down the Raven Rock slope. The Gray Company silently followed.

Wulf stood a while longer. Nothing. Finally, he made his way back down the rock. He was careful of his steps in the darkness.

When he got to the bottom, Grim was waiting with a cup of coffee and a blanket.

PART SIX

CHAPTER FORTY:
THE RIVERBANK

It was only a matter of time until someone searched the bakery. Rainer was armed with an old war ax. He'd found it in the back room of the bakery. It had probably belonged to the baker's dead husband. It had a wide blade on one side, a hooked blade on the other, and a protruding pointed top that looked dangerous. The brand on the shaft said it was made in Raukenrose, but he didn't recognize the smith mark.

What was he going to do?

Should he try to sneak into the castle? Should he try to free the garrison troops? Pretty much impossible. It was even more unlikely he would be able to rescue one of the girls or the duchess. They would be guarded.

Should he try to escape the town and find Wulf and Ravenelle? That was something he was pretty sure he could pull off. But then he would picture Anya having to live in the castle with that *thing*, and he found he couldn't go. So he decided to wait. It was his best quality as a fighter, he believed. He would wait for whoever he was fighting to make a mistake and jump on it.

So he found a hiding place where he could watch the castle gate.

The mistake came in the afternoon of the next day. A stable manure wagon came across the guarded castle drawbridge and over the dry moat. One man was pulling it. The other, in breastplate armor and helm, was walking along beside and not helping at all. His hand was on his sword hilt.

The man pulling the wagon was Grer Smead.

Taking the ax with him, Rainer moved from his hiding place and darted to another inset door across the street. Some people had returned to their streets and stalls. They were trying to get back to normal lives.

Rainer walked behind Grer and the soldier. He was careful to keep someone between them at all times. The war ax was a problem. People turned and stared. But when they saw Rainer's tabard with the buffalo argent, stained though it was, they nodded and made no sound to give Rainer away. Whatever he was up to, they approved of. The soldier walking with Grer noticed nothing. He was well ahead of Rainer and had his back to him.

Rainer followed them down one street and onto another, wider dirty path. This was a road that led down to the Shenandoah River.

Grer's going to dump the horse manure in the river, Rainer thought.

But why was *Grer* doing it? Why not one of the stable hands? That had to mean something. Rainer looked for a way to the help the smith—whatever Grer was up to.

Grer Smead was glad he had switched from the first plan, which was to hide his tool bag under the horse manure in the cart. The bag was heavy. In the bag was a bolt-cutting saw, a hammer, chisel, pry bar and lever extension rod, tongs, and wrenches of several sizes. The two big Sandhavener gate guards were suspicious the moment he limped up to the castle entrance pushing the manure cart in front him and asked permission to dump it outside.

"Where do you think you're going, cripple?"

"To dump this in the river," Grer replied, trying to keep his voice low and unchallenging. "Same as always, sir."

He kept his eyes down far enough to appear submissive. He tried to stoop as much as he could, but Grer was a large man. He was bigger than both of the guards. With his smith's muscles he could probably crush either one in a wrestling match. But their swords could kill or maim him much more quickly. He'd learned that from the sword cut to his leg.

"Who said you could take that out?"

"Stable master's orders."

"Why's it have to go now?"

"We've got double the horses in the stables, Sergeant. Yours and ours. If we don't muck it out, we'll soon be swimming in the stuff. Your horses'll start to sicken."

The sergeant nodded. "That's true," he said, "but let's make sure that *is* what you're up to, boy." He turned to the guard beside him. "Poke around in there."

The other stepped back from the cart, considered its contents. "With what, Sergeant?"

"What do you think? With your sword."

"Are you having me on, Sarge?"

"Do as you're told, Trottel."

"All right, Sarge," he replied dejectedly. He reluctantly drew his sword and leaned over the low boards that held the manure in at the sides. After a moment, he began to poke around.

"More," said the sergeant, who was enjoying the performance. "Dig it in there, same as you were talking about doing with the scullery girl."

Trottel gave the sergeant an exasperated look, then walked around the cart and poked his sword around in the manure.

If there had been somebody hiding, Grer thought, that would've gotten him out, or killed him. And the sword probably would've struck my mallet or something else, too.

"All right, that's enough," the sergeant said.

Trottel pulled his sword out. He looked around for somewhere to clean it. Seeing nothing else, he stepped over and wiped both sides of it on Grer's back. This left two brown stripes on his fustian cloth shirt.

The guard went back to stand by the sergeant, a grin on his face.

"Very funny," said the sergeant. "Now you go with him to . . . where are you going, boy?"

"Down to the river, Sergeant. That's where we always dump it."

"Go with him down to the river, then. Make sure he does what he says he'll do."

That wiped the smile off Trottel's face. "Yes, sir," he answered dolefully.

Grer got a good grip on the two wooden handles that protruded from the cart. He pushed. The cart slowly rolled forward.

This has got to be a cursed hard task for a real stable boy, Grer thought. *It's making me strain.*

He pushed again.

"Stop!" said the sergeant. He walked up to Grer and the guard. "I'll just have a look under that wagon."

The sergeant bent down to do this when a scream came from the bailey behind him. He stood up, spun around to look, and so did Grer.

There was Saeunn, tussling with another of the Hundred. "Get your hands off me, get your dirty hands *off*!" she yelled.

"Messer!" the sergeant called out.

"I never, Sarge!" said the man. "I swear I never! Stupid elf!"

Saeunn slapped him, then charged into him with her

shoulder. He was so big, she merely bounced off, but then she crawled forward on the stones and tried to yank the man's legs out from under him. He danced away.

"Come on, boy," the soldier named Trottel said. "Let's get this over with."

Grer followed Trottel under the gate and out of the castle.

He trundled the cart on streets he knew led to the river, trying to figure out what to do. Once he had to stop and maneuver the cart around a dead dog lying in the middle of the cobblestone street. Its stomach was slit open, with its guts wound out.

"If I caught the one who did that I'd let him have . . . I wouldn't do that to a dog, not ever," Trottel said, shaking his head. Then he smiled at Grer. "To a man? Now, that's a different story."

He had to get away from the guard. But with his limp, there was no way he could run fast enough.

I'll just have to kill him, Grer thought. The pitchfork. That's my best chance.

He would not have bet on himself to succeed. Trottel, like all of the Hundred occupying the castle, was a trained man-at-arms.

When they got to the water, Grer wasn't sure where the dumping spot was, since he'd never actually done this before. He picked out what looked like a cow path to the riverbank. It was just wide enough to roll the cart down. A weaker man would have lost control, and the cart would have rolled into the river, but Grer kept it slow and steady until he was on a small stretch of sand next to the water. Trottel was right behind him.

Grer reached for the pitchfork. When he did, he heard the guard's sword slipping out of its scabbard. He turned to see Trottel point the blade at him.

"Just to be sure," Trottel said. "Those forks are mighty wicked looking."

Great. So much for his only plan.

Grer shrugged and started pitching manure from the wagon, desperately trying to think of something else he might try.

From the top of the bank above them there was a creaking sound. Both he and the guard looked up. A wagon's wheels were poking over the edge. The wagon was too wide for the path, and the axle straddled the pathway. The wagon stayed there for a moment, then it moved forward again a hand's breadth, then another. Grer and Trottel watched half mesmerized.

The wagon trundled over the high bank. It rolled down, straddling the path for a moment. Then the wheels caught on scraggly river vegetation and it flipped, coming end-over-end right at them.

Grer and the guard both dove out of the way. The wagon slammed into the manure cart. It splintered down the middle, and stinking manure flew in every direction.

Grer looked up from where he was lying to see the guard stand up, his sword drawn, his eyes wide and wild, looking up the bank path.

Which is why Trottel didn't see the war ax swinging toward him from behind. When the ax chopped into the flesh of Trottel's neck, it was a complete surprise. The blade sank until Trottel's spine stopped it, then whoever was wielding it twisted it out, drew it back and punched its pointed top into the guard's back for good measure.

Trottel fell forward, the ax protruding from his back, his head lolling unnaturally to one side.

"Koterbaum was right. I guess these things really do punch through plate armor," Rainer Stope said. He looked at Grer. "You okay?"

Grer nodded and reached for the pitchfork. "Help me look in the splinters yonder for my tools. I hid them under the stable cart."

"Tools for what?"

"Taking a clapper off a bell," Grer said.

"Why would you want to do that?"

Using the pitchfork rammed downward for support, Greg pulled himself to his feet. He looked across the guard's body at Rainer. "Because that particular clapper is the hammer everybody's been looking for," he said.

CHAPTER FORTY-ONE:
THE CHARGE

Ursel came to find Wulf just after sunset the day before the attack on Raukenrose. She stopped him outside the buffalo hide he and Grim were using for a makeshift tent.

"Lord Wulf."

"Mistress Ursel."

She was wearing a green velvet cape clasped below her throat. Underneath she had on a blouse and britches stuffed into boots. He'd never seen a woman dress so mannish. Yet this seemed natural for her. The red light of day's end caught her red hair and made it luminous. Her green eyes sparkled in the fading light from the west.

"You've spent a lot of time with my father."

"I've been learning," Wulf replied. "Earl Keiler knows what he's doing."

Ursel stepped closer.

"I wanted to ask you for something, Lord Wulf ... a favor."

"Of course," he replied.

She reached up to her hair where she wore a pale red scarf. She untied it in the back and pulled it out. Her red curls cascaded about her face.

"I've heard some men like to carry a token into battle. From a woman."

"Yes."

"It would be an honor . . . I would like . . . would you take this from me . . . to remember that I wish you well, m'lord?"

"Thank you, Ursel. This means a lot to me."

He reached out, and she put the scarf into his hand, brushing her own against his as she did so.

"Ursel, please call me Wulf. Or even von Dunstig, like Ravenelle does. But I don't feel much like a lord of the battle. I feel kind of lost, to tell the truth."

"Why is that m'lord . . . I mean, Wulf?"

"Because I don't have very much idea what I'm doing."

"You're leading."

"What does that even mean? I'm out of my depth here. Your father is the one who is holding things together and giving us a chance."

She stepped closer and almost without thinking he reached out and took her hands in his.

"Listen, Wulf," she said. "When I look at you I see someone who doesn't give up. You killed the man who hurt your father."

"I got lucky."

"You made your luck, just like you're doing here."

Wulf shuddered. He'd just remembered what Ravenelle had told him about Otto. His oldest brother was dead. And Adelbert dead, too.

He was heir.

He didn't like it one bit.

"If I matter in the big picture, that means my brother *doesn't*. I *hate* that. I don't want it."

"You'll always matter to me, Wulf," Ursel said. She leaned her head slightly back. Her full lips were partly open, waiting.

She wants to be kissed, he thought. A beautiful, fascinating girl wants me to kiss her and fall in love with her.

"I can't." He stepped back from her, and let go of her hands. "Ursel, I'm being stupid, I know. You're amazing. You're a dream come true. If things were any other way, I'm sure I would fall hard for you. But you've got to be somebody else's dream."

Ursel looked up, hurt written across her face.

"I'm only good enough for a commoner, that's what you mean," she said defiantly. She shook her head, and her lovely red curls flounced.

As quickly as her anger flared, it subsided. "No, no. I know you're not like that. I've been watching you with the people." Her voice was calm. And sad. "It's just that I . . . Wulf, please. Why can't it be?"

"Because I'm in love with someone else," Wulf said. "I don't even know if she loves me or ever will. I hope she *doesn't* because it can never work. But none of that matters. It's her. It's always been her."

"Lady Saeunn? I've seen your stick with the runes on it."

"Yes. Saeunn."

"I understand. She'll stay beautiful forever. I'll get old. I'll turn into an old crone wandering in the woods one day."

"I doubt that."

"*You* don't get to say what will happen to me."

"No," Wulf said. "I don't. But can I please keep your scarf? It's . . . to know you care about me . . . even though I missed out on something great. It will mean a lot to me."

Ursel finally smiled. "Of course you can, m'lord." She used the scarf, still in her hand, to pull him toward her again. He stumbled forward, and when he did, she kissed him on the lips. Full and deep. Her lips were soft and warm, and he let her. Finally, she pulled away.

"Remember *that*," she said.

She turned and walked away from him, leaving her scarf dangling in his hands.

✤ ✤ ✤

Regensday dawn. Twelve days had passed. Twelve days away from Raukenrose. From her.

How could it be so few? How could he have waited so long?

There were practical answers to both questions, whether he liked them or not.

Wulf stood at the edge of Alerdalan Woods looking at a row of Sandhavener army tents. He smelled fire smoke and the stink of a nearby gully the Sandhaveners were using for a latrine.

Please Sturmer, Tretz, dragon, God, whoever or whatever is listening, please don't let me be a coward.

They'd picked this spot *because* of the latrine. It was formed by a small creek that only flowed during rainy weather. It came out of the woods. It must have run more steadily in past times, because the wash of the creek flowing down toward the Shenandoah had made a notch in the forest the size of a large field. It was full of good bottomland soil. At the moment a cover crop of clover grew on it. Spring planting would begin in a few weeks.

So it was flat, not wooded. It was clear of tents. Nobody wanted to camp too close to the latrines.

They'd done almost exactly what Ursel had suggested before.

Circle to the south, approach from the east.

They'd come down from Massanutten Mountain in darkness. They'd crossed the Shenandoah at Fishbridge Ford at midnight. They'd taken Ford Road east until it intersected the Great Valley Road. Earl Keiler had sent out forward skirmishers, but they had not run across any Sandhavener pickets or guard stations. It was just as Washbear's reports had said. The Sandhaveners were staying close to Raukenrose.

At Fishbridge Ford, a group of fifty beaver people led by Bamber Esserholz had split off. It was a small force, but they were all that could be spared.

They were the diversion.

The idea was to fake an attack by river first. This would attract the Sandhavener's attention, and at least confuse them. The main force would then attack from the east. The beavers were prepared. They had managed to collect a hundred boats, dinghies, skiffs, and barges at the ford. These they had tied together bow to stern in trains, and placed burlap bags filled with dirt and straw inside them. The bags were shaped to look like people, at least from a distance. They'd cut poles to look like spears and pikes.

The fake flotilla should reach the Raukenrose riverfront very soon. They had timed it to arrive at sunrise over the Dragonback Mountains. This would also put the sun at the back of the main force when they came out of the woods.

The troops were both Tier and human, and all from Bear Valley and the upper Shenandoah. There were surprisingly well armed. It turned out that there was an amazing amount of weapons left over from the Little War. There were swords and halberds taken down from attics. Almost everyone in the entire valley supplemented whatever else he did with hunting, and was skillful with a bow. There were shields and mail shirts. Almost everyone had found an old helmet that either he or a relative had worn in the battles of twelve years ago. There were spears, shields, and maces. There were even quite a few horses equipped with armor, tarnished with age but still strong and serviceable.

For such a peaceful place, we have some very warlike citizens.

Maybe having everyone and his brother (and his sister) capable of being armed on not much notice was one of the *reasons* Shenandoah had stayed such a peaceful place, Wulf considered. When you have a neighbor with a halberd over the fireplace and a sword in the attic, maybe your first thought was how to solve a problem while *avoiding* getting into a fight.

At the intersection of Ford Road with the Great Valley Road, they'd taken to the Alerdalan Woods and moved northeast, skirting the eastern side of the township. Footmen, horsemen and even supply wagons had moved silently through the forest. The tree people had made clear paths. The paths were so obvious that, even though the moon had set, the band of nearly two thousand was able to move through the forest with barely a sound.

Then they'd wheeled to the west toward the town. They'd reached the edge of the Alerdalan Woods just before dawn. There they waited.

Please don't let me be a coward.

How could he be worried about this? He'd fought. He'd killed.

Those had been forced on him in the heat of the moment. He could work himself up, but part of him knew he didn't have to be here.

He had chosen this.

I chose this, Wulf thought. I'm finally *doing something.*

Or about to, at least.

Wulf sat on the black and white draft horse the buffalo people had given him to ride to Bear Hall. He'd been told that this horse had been the favorite horse of Tupakkalaatu, the buffalo-man war chief. Tupakkalaatu was sitting on a mare he claimed to like just as well.

He patted the horse's neck. "Won't be long now, boy," he whispered to it. The horse snorted and shook its head. It sensed the anticipation around it and was ready to go.

Nagel soared down from a nearby tree. She flew over the heads of several bear men with upraised pikes, and landed neatly on Wulf's shoulder.

"Smell blood," she said in his ear. "Like it."

"That's funny," he said in a low voice, "All I can smell is horse manure."

The tents nearby were a quarter league from the town wall. There were an awful lot of them. He hoped Washbear had not underestimated how many enemies they faced.

He warned you not to take what he said as established fact, Wulf reminded himself. Please, please keep me from running, divine ones. I don't have to fight like a madman. I just have to fight. You can help me do that, can't you? Gods, God, Tretz, anyone listening?

Earl Keiler moved up beside Wulf. He rode a horse even bigger than Wulf's. The bear people bought their horses from buffalo-people breeders. Behind the earl were five bear men, two wolf men, and two humans. These were Bear Valley people Keiler knew well and trusted. He'd picked them to run orders. The bear men and humans rode large horses. The two wolf men rode purebred hunters, smaller than the draft horses. They were all black horses with gray dapples. These were the horses of wolf people. They used them for woodland hunting.

There were clouds to the south. Otherwise, the sky was clear. The last of the starlight was being washed away by the coming dawn.

"Today is the day we take back Raukenrose, Lord Wulf," the earl said to Wulf.

Suddenly there was a murmur and stir among the outer ring of Sandhaven troops. Men ran from their breakfast to snatch weapons from tents and arms stands.

"Do you think they've seen us?" Wulf asked. He heard a nervous quiver in his voice.

Please let me fight well.

"The skirmishers say no," Keiler replied. "I believe the Sandhaveners have seen our riverboats. We may have fooled them. Be that as it may, they're distracted. Now's the time. M'lord?"

"What? I mean . . ."

"He wants you to order the attack, daft man," Nagel whispered in his ear. It was the first time she'd called him "man."

What was he supposed to say? How did you start a war?

"All right. Begin the attack, Earl Keiler," Wulf said. "If that's what you meant."

"I did." Earl Keiler gave a set of rapid-fire orders to his couriers.

The air inside Alerdalan Wood was still. No leaf trembled. The woods itself seemed to hold its breath.

Earl Keiler drew his long sword and raised it high. Wulf did the same with his bear-man's short sword. It was the size of a regular sword for him.

Keiler nodded to a man who had a horn strung at his side.

"Three blasts, Ernst," Keiler said.

The man raised the horn to his lips.

"Bwaa, bwaa, bwaa!"

The horn sounded. Three long notes.

"Charge!" roared Earl Keiler. Then the earl immediately doubled over in his saddle, wracked with coughing. His horse went nowhere. Wulf stayed with Keiler for a moment. All around them, the woods were erupting.

Time to go.

He kicked his horse into a trot. There was no room for a canter, much less a gallop. As he moved forward, Wulf began to cry out. He had no control of it. It was an eerie sound made up anger, fear . . . and pure hatred.

He hated the invaders in front of him. He wanted to kill them.

He wanted to make them shriek and bleed and die.

Screaming at the top of his lungs and holding his sword ready to draw blood, Wulf made for the Sandhavener tents.

CHAPTER FORTY-TWO:
THE BATTLE

The front line was made up of about a hundred mounted troops. Behind them came the foot soldiers.

The horsemen lowered their swords, pikes, and halberds.

When the leading horses crashed into the tents, it was not at great speed. But the jolt of the horses clustered together was massive.

The river distraction seemed to have worked. The Sandhaveners were mostly facing *away* from the charging horses and were overrun from behind. Many were frantically trying to get into armor to join the charge northwest toward the river.

Several of the horsemen had moved ahead of Wulf. They rode down men who did not realize what hit them.

Wulf headed for a group of Sandhaveners standing in front of a tent. But then a big horse cut in front of him and slowed him down. He tried to ride around it to the left, but another moved to block his way. It was two of the bear-man guards. Wulf wheeled around. There were five of them. He was surrounded.

"Blood and bones, get out of the way!" he shouted. But they would not.

When he got to the outskirts of the Sandhaven tents, the enemy had already been cut down or trampled.

They aren't going to let me fight! Those fools aren't going to let me fight!

A man crawled out of a nearby tent and charged at them with a sword. One of the bear men neatly shoved Wulf's horse to the side. Then the bear man met the Sandhavener. The soldier was frantically trying to draw his sword from a scabbard. He never had a chance. The bear man swung his own sword in a brutal arc. It sheared through the side of the man's neck above his leather armor. Blood and gore spouted out like a geyser.

Wulf felt weak. His head swam and his guts felt loose.

Suddenly in front of Wulf, a man arose from the dust. He'd been trampled and, swaying on injured legs, he pulled himself up. He positioned himself to take a swing at Wulf. The man looked big, even if he was wobbly.

This is it, Wulf thought.

Please, please, let me—

Wulf lowered his sword, raised his buckler, and prepared to go at him. But before he could do it, two bear-man guards charged past him. They stabbed the man from either side with the razor-sharp points of halberds.

They weren't going to let him fight.

"Nagel, do you see this?" he screamed. The owl squawked her anger back at him. She wanted to be in the fight, too.

"Curse it to cold hell, you *will* let me!" he shouted. It had no effect. There were shouts, screams of rage and pain, the clang of steel, the clatter of blades hitting wooden shields, and the pounding of horse hoofs on the soft ground.

The smell of human feces from the latrine had been replaced. Now the air was filled with the tangy odor of fresh blood.

I was going to do it! I was!

They weren't going to let him. He felt irritated by it, even though he ought to have known.

He could get away with not pushing himself further. He was in the battle. Nobody would call him a coward now.

Why not leave it at this? He'd shown he was ready and willing. He'd charged with all the others.

He could barely see flashing swords and raised bucklers through the surrounding horses of his guards.

Why not ride back to the woods and get out of this craziness? People were getting their heads split, their arms lopped. Arrows were starting to fall.

He glimpsed a human, a woodsman in green, stagger back toward the woods with a battleax in his back. He collapsed onto the dusty ground near the latrines.

He saw another man walking slowly away, holding onto the wrist of an arm where there used to be a hand.

People were dying in a whirlwind of blades and arrows. It would be all right. He could back up. Watch how the situation developed.

Nobody would blame him.

It made sense, didn't it?

No. It did not.

Because the dragon would know.

The land would know.

He turned his horse and started back toward the edge of the forest.

"Boy, what are you doing—" squawked Nagel.

"Shut up," Wulf said.

"Boy, you must try to fight, you must—"

"Shut *up*, I said," Wulf yelled at Nagel.

Nagel reluctantly did what he asked, but he was afraid she might bite him on the ear out of sheer malice.

Have to convince them I've retreated. One or two more eyeblinks, and—

Wulf yanked on the reins and swung his horse around. A less spirited horse would have thrown him at that moment. A less skilled horseman would have fallen off. But his black and white neatly made the turn and Wulf stayed on.

Wulf kicked his mount in the flanks, and the horse seemed to almost heave a sigh of relief. It broke into a trot back toward the battle. Wulf spurred the horse into a full-on gallop. He would only need to keep the gallop going until he could get away from the guards and—

Wulf burst through the ring of startled bear-man guards. He charged back toward the fight. He saw that there was no way he was going to get the horse through the line, though. The foot soldiers were jammed too tightly together. If he wanted to fight, it would have to be on foot.

Hardly missing a beat, Wulf swung himself down from the horse. He squeezed his sword hilt into the scar on his right hand.

Then he ran for the lines. He shoved his way between men, moved forward.

Finally he was facing Sandhaven shields. He'd reached what there was of a front line.

Wulf raised his sword.

Once again, he began to scream.

CHAPTER FORTY-THREE:
THE BUTTRESS

The Nestie's tabard with its gray goose on blue and black was a little large for Rainer and blood-soaked in the back. He belted it on anyway. Grer looked like what he was, a common smith with a bag of tools. If they ran into any Sandhaven soldiers, Rainer planned to walk fast and pretend he was carrying out an order.

This was maybe not the best of plans, but it was all Rainer could think of.

I'm wearing their cursed badge now, he thought. I'm officially a spy.

He could be burned, crucified, or beheaded. Maybe he'd get lucky and it would be a clean hanging. Were there rules for executing a spy?

Wulf would know, Rainer thought. He felt loneliness and misery try to settle into his mind. As he had done many times before in the past days, he shoved them away.

"I'll ask him when I see him," he muttered.

"Do what?" said Grer. He was walking alongside Rainer as fast as his limp would let him.

"Nothing," Rainer replied. "We've only got a couple of blocks left."

"I always get lost in town. You'd think I wouldn't since I've lived here all my life."

"I could find my way through Raukenrose in the moonless dark," Rainer said.

"And you have," chuckled Grer.

They were about to get to Allfather Square. Rainer put a hand in front of Grer to hold him back. They both carefully peeped around the wall of the alley.

The square was full of soldiers. Sandhaveners. Several details of five or six men carrying buckets were in line to get water at the fountain.

Across the square, a group of guards stood at attention near the entrance to the cathedral. Rainer counted eight.

"Curse it to cold hell," Grer said. "How are we going to get past *that*?"

Rainer considered. "We don't. We circle around and come out on the side of the cathedral."

"But there're no doors on the side," grumbled Grer. "You come in through the front."

"Yeah, I know," Rainer said.

Whack, whack, whack.

Metal on wood. A huge splintering, cracking sound drowned out everything else for a moment.

What was that? Then he saw.

A detail of soldiers was cutting down the Olden Oak. They had almost finished. It was already leaning. One side was notched so the tree would fall along the north side of the square, parallel to the cathedral. The upper notch was well into the heartwood.

The tree shuddered. It swayed.

Hundreds of years growing, to die like this.

He wondered if they would cut out Wulf's dagger. Maybe someone already had.

Curse them.

He and Grer backed into the alley again and worked their way around to the other side of the square. From the side streets Rainer watched the belltower of the cathedral come in and out of view above the roofs of the buildings.

They came out near the east wall of the cathedral. The wall was rimmed at the ground by an evergreen hedge. There were two flying buttresses on this side bracing the main structure. Rainer and Grer were across a cobblestone street from the front spanner.

Rainer examined the buttress, and then the wall. He turned to Grer and smiled.

"They didn't do it," he said. "I mean, why would they?"

"Do what?"

"Tuck mortar in the joints," Rainer replied. "The masons did it on the castle wall. That's why it's smooth."

"All right," Grer said. "Are we going to try to pull the thing down with our bare hands?"

"It means that I can climb it," Rainer said.

"Up there?"

"The bell's not coming down to us."

Rainer squirmed out of his hauberk. He'd been wearing the mail shirt for days. He instantly felt much lighter. Then he took off the padded arming shirt underneath.

Now he was wearing a fustian shirt and a pair of britches stuffed into his boots.

He thought for a minute. They were heavy, with the hobnails hammered through the soles.

"Switch boots with me," he said to Grer.

Grer's feet were bigger than Rainer's, but the shoes were made of soft leather. Rainer used the straps to pull it tight enough to fit him. The toe was nearly a finger length too long for him, though. After fiddling around a moment, Rainer saw how to fix the problem. He curled the boot toe over itself so it fit under the front bootstrap. When he was done, his toes pressed up against the front of the boot.

He could climb in these.

He wouldn't be needing the battle-ax anymore, so he hid it in the alley. Grer secured Rainer's dagger in its scabbard with two leather ties he pulled from his tool bag.

"Good rule. Always carry a piece string," the smith said.

Rainer then ran the belt through the frog loop in the knife's scabbard and put the belt back on, the knife turned behind him.

"I'm ready," Rainer said. "Let's walk to the cathedral wall. Slow and easy."

They would be exposed for a few eyeblinks. It was a moment of danger. If enough of the soldiers saw them, they would be dead. The front staircase of the cathedral spread out to either side of the main building, however. If they got to the wall without being noticed, the staircase would hide them from the soldiers in the square.

Whack, whack, whack.

These must be the final blows to the Olden Oak. Rainer risked a glimpse around the corner.

A huge creaking sound filled the air. Then the crackle of splintering.

For a moment all eyes in the square were turned away from them. They must be on the Olden Oak.

"Let's go," Rainer said, pulling Grer along with him.

They walked quickly across the street from the base of the buttress to the cathedral wall that formed the belltower. Grer tried not to show his limp. For a moment, Rainer got a glimpse of the square. Soldiers everywhere. But they were still looking away.

The upper branches of the Olden Oak fell into view, crashing into the flagstones of the square. There were only green buds, no leaves yet. The bare branches clattered against one another. Then he and Grer were hidden behind the back of the cathedral staircase.

Curse them. The oak had fallen. But he was here, and had a job to do.

An overwhelming urge hit Rainer. He pulled down his trousers in the front.

"What are you doing?" Grer asked him.

"I've got to take a piss."

"Against the *cathedral*?"

"It'll be okay with your divine beings, I think," Rainer said.

Rainer did his business quickly. Then he pulled up his pants, tied the waist string, and buckled his belt.

"Ready," he said.

He squeezed behind the shrub. It was too close to the wall. This might be a problem. There was no way Grer would be able to hide behind it.

Grer would have to figure that out.

Rainer jumped up to get a grip on the wall . . . and fell off.

"Don't worry. Getting started is always the hardest part," he mumbled.

He tried again. He didn't leap so high this time. His feet found a crack, and the fingers of his left hand slid into enough of a crevice between stones to gain a hold.

I know how to do this.

He turned his knuckle bone to jam his finger into the crack. He moved his feet up. He twisted his finger again to release the jam and pull it out. He reached for another hold.

Rainer worked his way upward. He had to go fast, but he had to be careful. But this was not a sheer-faced cliff. It was a lot like climbing up and down the tower wall to his bedchamber. He could do that in the dark.

Soon he'd covered twenty hands or more.

This put him above the protruding cathedral stairs. He

could see the soldiers in the square. Which meant if they looked up they could see him.

Don't look up. Keep filling your buckets and talking. Nothing to see here.

Upward he climbed.

Chapter Forty-Four:
The Killers

Wulf held the bear short sword in front of himself. He looked for a spot to thrust in past a shield and cut into flesh and bone. For what seemed like a long time he just stood there. His own soldiers were beside him. The enemy was in front of him. And he couldn't do a thing.

There was a solid wall of three shields in front of him. The soldiers beside him—he thought one was a bear and the other a wolf man—were hacking and poking at the shields with halberds. These splintered the wood but weren't having any other effect. They kept the Sandhaveners out of the reach of Wulf's sword.

Suddenly the fighters on either side pushed away. The Sandhaven shield wall parted.

Wulf charged through.

He took only a few steps. He found himself face-to-face with a man about his own height and size.

The other wore a helmet and a hauberk with a sleeveless tabard over it. On it was the gray goose on a russet field, the badge of a regular soldier. The man had a sword raised to strike. He chopped the sword down straight from a raised position and Wulf instinctively raised his buckler to stop it. He'd practiced this a thousand times in the castle yard.

And he knew an easy countermove.

With a backhand motion, he brought the edge of the buckler toward the face of the Sandhavener. The man turned away in time to take it on the side of his helmet. He staggered back from the impact. Even while Wulf was moving his buckler he felt the wise woman's catgut stitches on his left arm breaking. The wound opened enough to make him grit his teeth at the sharp pain. He couldn't think about that now.

Wulf stepped into his own buckler blow and got inside the man's sword swing.

Another situation he knew from practice.

If your opponent didn't have room to pull back for a thrust, it didn't matter how sharp his sword was, he couldn't hit you with it.

For a moment, Wulf and the man stared at each other. Sweat was dripping down the man's face. He blinked to clear it from his eyes. He opened them up again, very wide.

He's terrified, Wulf thought.

Of *me*.

Wulf had already pulled back his sword above his left shoulder as he moved in. With a grunt, he arched it down into the man's neck. The blade sank in where the neck met the collarbone, just above the mail. Even in the din of the battle, Wulf heard the skin and muscles part with a meaty squelch.

He didn't wait. He twisted and pulled the sword away. He took another swing at the man's exposed legs. He was wearing leather wrappings on his calves, but no greaves. Wulf's sword sliced in below the left knee in his calf muscle. It cut through the wrapping, and the blood swelled from under the leather.

The man collapsed. After he hit the ground, he had

enough room to bring his sword up. He attempted a weak thrust at Wulf. Wulf knocked the sword aside with his gauntleted left hand. He pointed his own sword down and plunged it into the man's chest.

Because he hadn't drawn back, the tip didn't penetrate the mail. It didn't matter. With his weight on the sword, Wulf held the man down. A gush of blood pumped from the wound in the man's neck. Wulf had hit the artery. The man shuddered, bled out, and died. The look of wide-eyed terror was still on his face when the light went out of his eyes.

"Aaaar!"

Wulf looked up to a see a huge Sandhavener barreling toward him. The man had a spear in his hands held at waist height. Wulf raised his buckler, knowing the little shield would be useless against that much momentum. There was no way to get his sword up in time.

But the two fights going on to either side of Wulf crunched back together. He was pushed back behind the bear man and the wolf man. The man with the spear turned his charge. He looked for another target and pushed his spear past the soldier the wolf man was fighting and into wolf man's gut. Wulf watch in horror as it came out the wolf man's back.

The wolf man gave out a howl of pain and stumbled to a knee. His opponent was thrown off balance and stumbled forward. Wulf was about to move to attack him but was shoved away again. Men moved in to take the fallen wolf man's place. Soon Wulf couldn't see the wolf man, the Sandhavener, or the spearman anymore.

He was behind the front line, and took a moment to catch his breath.

I killed a man, Wulf thought.

A frightened man who didn't have much training, yes.

But he was trying to kill me.

And I killed him instead.

He'd killed three men now. That was a lot for a potential librarian. Maybe even for an apprentice ranger.

"Killing is joy," said a voice in his ear. "Now you know."

Nagel, who had been missing in the woods, had found him and landed without his being aware of it.

Others were shoving up behind him. He bounced down the front line, moving mostly to his left. Here and there he saw a place to get a sword thrust through, and he did it.

The second time, he connected with flesh. But he was instantly knocked back. If it hadn't been for the scar on Wulf's hand, he'd have lost his grip on the sword.

He bounced farther, looking for a place to strike. Then he came to what seemed like the end of the battle line. He stumbled into the clear.

Here was something Koterbaum had taught him about. A flanking move.

Could he work his way around the side of the line and attack? He looked for an exposed Sandhavener. He was so intent on finding his man, he almost didn't hear the shout.

"Get down, get down, you cursed fool!"

Wulf spun around. A group of fox men were about a dozen paces away. It wasn't a clump; it was an organized group. There were two straight lines of about twenty. What were they doing? Then Wulf saw the wooden and metal weapons in the hands of the front line.

Crossbows.

The flanking attack *had* begun. He was standing in front of it.

Wulf dove for the ground.

Grer tried to stand casually by the cathedral wall. He did not let himself look up. He figured he'd know if Rainer fell. Rainer would crash into the street below and break into a thousand pieces. If that was what you did. More likely he'd just turn to pulp inside.

Grer tried to think of other things. Ulla. The two swords he'd been working on before the invasion. He'd planned to give them to Wulf and Rainer as presents before they took rooms at the university next year.

Ulla.

It had been a bright day, but the sky had gotten cloudy. Rain was on the way. Another thing to worry about.

Suddenly a soldier rounded the staircase and came walking down the street toward Grer. Grer panicked for a moment. Then he remembered what Rainer had done here. He turned to the wall, jacked down his pants with a thumb and pretended to be taking a piss.

"Cold hell, man," the soldier said as he passed Grer. He stopped walking. "It's a cathedral. Show some respect."

Grer sighed, hitched up his pants, and turned around.

"When you've got to go, you've got to go," he said with a shrug.

The soldier considered. "I guess." He started to walk away when something seemed to occur to him. "Supposed to be a cathouse around here somewhere. Next to their own cursed cathedral, believe it or not. You know where I can find the place? It's called the Red Door."

Had he seen any red doors on the way here? If he had he couldn't remember. Where would a cathouse be, anyway? The only ones he'd heard of were on the waterfront.

"Nah," Grer said. "But they got plenty down by the river."

"Yeah, I know about those, but so does everybody else in the stinking camp. There's *lines*, even for the ugly girls."

"Sorry about that."

The soldier rubbed his chin, looked around. "Well, there's got to be a few red doors around here. Think I'll knock on every one of them until I find what I'm looking for. Even if it ain't a cathouse, if you know what I mean." He winked and walked away, finally turning down a side street. His footsteps faded.

Grer realized he'd been holding his breath. He let it slowly escape through his lips in a sigh.

"Hey you!" A hard tap on his shoulder. "You!"

Grer turned to face another soldier. This one looked much rougher than the one before. His face was pockmarked. There was a scar running from an eye across his nose to his lip.

Grer didn't take time to think. He lunged forward and head-butted the man. The soldier staggered back, but Grer grabbed his tabard and pulled the man toward himself. He butted him and again and again, each time pulling him back.

Each time the man looked like he was going to make a sound, Grer head-butted him again.

After the fifth time, Grer raised his hands up and put them on either side of the man's head. He twisted. Hard.

Many years of pounding with a heavy hammer and lifting glowing steel with tongs went into the twist. There was some resistance, and then the man's neck popped. The soldier slumped to the ground.

Grer felt numb. He noticed something.

Those are fine boots he's wearing. They look just right for me, too.

His own toes were crumpled up inside Rainer's too-small hobnails.

Grer quickly tugged the boots off the dead man. He kicked Rainer's off and pulled the others on. As he'd suspected, they were just the right size. Supple.

Good boots.

Now what was he going to do with the body?

He reached down and grabbed the man by the tabard and pulled him up. The man probably had a dead weight of fifteen stone, but Grer raised him easily. He held the man with one arm below the other's limp arm. He let the body slump against his. That was it. He could appear to be helping a drunken buddy.

Right. That wasn't going to fool anybody. The soldier's head hung at a *very* unnatural angle, for one thing.

He looked around, but all he could see was the line of shrubbery next to the wall. As Rainer had found out, there was not room enough to slide the body between the branches or stash it next to the cathedral.

Grer looked with worry at the back of the cathedral stairs. There were no more soldiers coming . . . but he did see something. There, near the bottom of the back wall.

A grate?

He threw the body over his shoulder and walked toward it. Yes. It was an iron grating set in the cobblestones. He looked down into it. There was a long drop. It led into the drainage system under Allfather Square.

He set the man down and took hold of the grate. Yanked. Nothing.

It was firmly set. He tried again. The grate didn't budge.

Grer stood back, then slapped a hand to his forehead.

Blood and bones! What am I thinking? I have tools.

He trotted back to get a pry bar from his bag. He worked it in between the grate and the cobblestones around it, using the leverage to push the grate back and forth. It moved. It loosened. He grabbed hold of it and pulled again. This time the grate came up.

The drain hole wasn't very wide, but it would do.

He picked up the dead man by his two bare ankles. Straining, but not pushed to the limit, Grer dangled him headfirst over the drain opening. Grer worked the body through the opening. The shoulders were a bit tricky. After that it was easy. When the dead man was in to his knees, Grer dropped him.

In an eyeblink, there was a splash below. Grer wasted no time. He put away his pry bar and replaced the grate on the drain hole.

He walked back over to the cathedral wall and dared a glance up.

Rainer was a speck, far, far above.

The sky was even darker. A wind had whipped up. It blew against the shrubs, and they scratched against the sandstone of the cathedral walls.

"Storm's coming," Grer said to himself. "Hurry up, Rainer Stope."

CHAPTER FORTY-FIVE:
THE FOX

A swarm of bolts shot over Wulf's head. They thudded into the sides of the Sandhaveners he'd been about to try to cut down with a sword. The bolts were a lot more effective than he would have been. Their bodkin heads easily penetrated armor, even plate. A whole line of men seemed to shudder. They fell down in a staggered way, some clutching at the bolt in their side or arm or leg, and some slumping instantly, already dead.

Then the crossbowmen started to reload. The shortbow archers stepped forward. They sent another deadly cloud of arrows over Wulf's head and into the Sandhaveners. These archers reached behind them to where they'd poked arrows into the ground headfirst, plucked one out, and shot again. They'd gotten off eight arrows before the fox crossbowmen were ready again. They stepped between the archers and fired their quarrels.

Wulf rolled out of their way. He stood up and looked wildly around, trying to find a way to get back in the fight, but a voice growled beside him. This time it wasn't Nagel.

"Stupid man, what the cold hell are you doing?"

It was Smallwolf.

"You've bloodied your sword, boy," Smallwolf yelled in his ear. "Now let the Tier do their job."

The fox-man archers swarmed around them. Smallwolf whistled loudly. He cupped his hands around his muzzle and shouted, "He's over here!"

The bear-man guards came bustling up. They'd found their escaped charge. Two stationed themselves on either side of him.

The other bear men moved between Wulf and the fighting and raised shields—just in time. A flight of arrows came over the front line from Sandhavener archers. They were returning fire. The arrows thwacked into their shields, some poking through. In front of them, several of the arrows caught fox men. Some fell with shafts coming out of their fur. Some screamed and tried to moved forward before they stumbled and died.

Keeping their shields up, the bear men slowly walked Wulf backward. He tried to resist, but they forced Wulf to go with them.

They walked down a small depression. Bodies lay all about. Some looked untouched. Some had their insides hanging out, and crows were beginning to feast. Most of the dead had not thoughtfully fallen on their fronts. They were facing up or on their sides with all the gore exposed and looks of agony on their faces.

Flies buzzed. Wulf looked down to see a group of them gathered around the open, glassy eye of a dead Sandhavener. Were the flies drinking the liquid of his tears?

Then the eye *blinked*.

Wulf realized with a shudder that the man was not dead, but only terribly wounded. One of the bear-man guards also noticed, and called for a pair of buffalo-man stretcher-bearers to come and take up the man and let him die in the shade.

They came out of the body-filled depression and walked up a small rise. It was about three hundred paces from the edge of the woods. This was where Keiler had located his watch station. Tier came running or galloping in with reports. Keiler was busy sending out orders.

The sun was fully up in the sky. The clouds in the south looked threatening. A storm was coming.

Wulf stood and watched Keiler for a while. His vision was foggy and he realized he was incredibly thirsty. He'd seen carts to their south. These had big kegs of water tied to them. Runners were carrying canteens back and forth from the fight.

"To lose a battle because of thirst is about the stupidest mistake you can make," Koterbaum had once said.

Wulf told his bear guards he was going to get a drink and would be back soon. The leader grunted assent but detailed two bear men to accompany Wulf. The rest of them were intent on watching the progress of the battle, since the hillock gave them a view of the left side of the battle line.

Wulf walked off the hillock toward the water carts. They were a hundred paces away, near a small stand of three cedar trees. The trees had grown up around a big rock that was too large to move, so the farmer had ploughed around it. Two lines of flattened clover marked the path the wagons had taken from the woods.

Wulf found a cart with a tapped keg. He searched around for a cup or a container to drink from. He couldn't find one, so he leaned down and put his mouth under the keg spout and pulled up on the wood slide. He let the water stream out into his mouth. He took swallow after swallow, trying to gulp everything that came in.

The bear men saw another wagon with a tapped keg sitting on top of several others. A mixture of wounded was lined up there. The bear men didn't have cups, either, and this keg was at a better height for them to drink under. They got in line.

Wulf drank deeply. Then he took a palm-full of water in his right hand. It formed a small, longish lake in the scar. Wulf smiled grimly and sipped the water from his hand.

As he stood up, an arrow hit the side of the wagon where he'd just been stooping. Wulf dropped the water. He reached for his sword in its scabbard.

Where had the arrow come from?

He spun to look behind him and saw an archer standing only a few paces away. The archer was standing in firing stance and had nocked another arrow. He was drawing back the string and sighting along its length.

The archer was Smallwolf.

Where had the fox man come from?

He must have followed me all the way from that line, Wulf thought.

He obviously meant to kill Wulf.

Wulf leaped to his right, but Smallwolf expertly followed and lead him. The arrow struck him in the middle of his back, and Wulf felt the thump. But there was no stabbing pain. He'd swung the buckler onto his back, and it had caught the arrow.

"Curse you to cold hell," Smallwolf said. "What does it take to kill you, boy?"

Where were the bear men? Wulf glanced around frantically. The wagon was blocking the bear men from seeing him. It was just himself and Smallwolf.

Wulf turned back around. Smallwolf nocked yet another arrow. Wulf thought about pulling his buckler around, but there was no way he could do it in time.

"I'm not your enemy!" Wulf called out.

"You're a man," Smallwolf called back.

There was the whisper of an arrow in flight. Wulf thought for an eyeblink that Smallwolf had released. But the fox man's fingers on the bowstring went slack. The nock slipped. The string hit the arrow, but on the side, spinning it a few paces away before it fell harmless to the ground.

Smallwolf let out a curse and stumbled forward.

There was an arrow in his back.

It had stuck in the fox man's leather armor.

Smallwolf dropped the bow and sat down. His black nose twitched. He looked like he was sniffing the air. Then blood erupted from his nostrils.

The arrow had gone through the leather and pierced the fox man. Smallwolf slumped to the side, and blood flowed from his mouth down his furry neck and from the wound.

His eyes remained fixed on Wulf. Wulf thought the fox man was still glaring at him with hatred. He waited. When Smallwolf didn't move, he realized the fox man was dead.

Wulf looked toward the woods where the arrow must have come from. It was at least a hundred paces distant. A near impossible shot. Who was back there?

The baggage train was hidden among the trees.

He saw someone on the edge of the woods holding a bow. He couldn't make out the face. Then there was a gust of wind. A red cape swirled around the form.

Ursel.

She let fly another arrow, and this one missed the fox man by a hand's breadth. It buried itself in the ground. That didn't matter. The first had found its mark. Smallwolf was already dead.

That was the most spectacular shot I've ever seen, Wulf thought. Keiler had claimed his adopted daughter was an amazing huntress. He had spoken the truth.

Wulf walked over to the dead fox man. He looked down at him for a moment, then put a toe under his body and kicked him onto his stomach. He stepped on Smallwolf's back and pulled out the arrow. It was a bodkin. No wonder it had punched through the leather. Ursel had not only made the shot, she'd picked the right arrow for the job.

He held the arrow up and waved it back to her.

The bear men charged up, but saw that they were too late to do any good. They growled anyway—at nothing.

Wulf looked down at Smallwolf. Was the fox-man leader one of many? Was it his own hatred that had made him try to kill Wulf? Wulf hoped it was only him. But there had been a lot of voices calling out their agreement with Smallwolf at the law-speak.

Wulf climbed back up the hill. He still had the bolt in his hand. He saw Keiler talking with one of his runners, and waited for the earl to finish. Then he walked up to the bear man.

"Your daughter just saved my life," he said.

He showed Keiler the arrow. When he saw the blood on it, the bear man's graying muzzle broke into a smile. He flashed sharp teeth.

"How far?" Keiler asked.

"At least a hundred paces."

"Ursel's had a bow in her hands since she could walk," Keiler said. "Who did she kill?"

"Smallwolf," Wulf replied. "He was trying to shoot me."

"The idiot," Keiler grunted. He nodded toward the arrow. "Save that. Maybe it will keep you warm at night when you realize she's not in your bed and you could have had her."

Wulf was silent for a moment.

Keiler's not wrong, he thought.

"I will," Wulf finally said. "And I'll never forget."

He'd had it easy so far, even though he hadn't known it. The last section of the belltower was impossible. Rainer was beneath an overhang. The cupola was on a platform that gracefully flared out so that anyone climbing it would have to hang upside down.

Charge it. Go at it with complete commitment. Forget about falling.

I can do this—

But wouldn't it disappoint the cold hell out of Wulf if I *did* peel?

He'll know this wasn't that hard of a climb. At least until the end. He won't say anything bad while they're burning me at the funeral. He'll think I made a stupid move, though.

What would Wulf do here?

He'd brood for a while.

He'd think about all the ancient words of the skalds, then pull some quote from a saga out of nowhere. Not because he was trying to impress anybody, but because he knew the cursed things like he knew how to breathe.

And this would be his way of thinking things through.

Wulf would think this through.

Then so will I.

Rainer took a long breath.

There was no way to muscle this whole way. You had to rest or you would peel. You had to find an eyeblink here, an eyeblink there, when the strain was off one set of muscles or another.

First, he needed to rest.

Rainer changed his grip to rest one arm, then the next. His muscles hurt less.

Now or never.

It began to rain.

"No," Rainer said to the sky. Then he shouted, "No!"

The sky responded with a roll of thunder. Wind whipped droplets in Rainer's face. Soon his clothes were soaked. Grer's boots were wet. His hands were slick with water.

Now it *couldn't* be a matter of just holding on tight. It was impossible to hold tight to wet stones. He would use jams or he would fall.

The rain showed no sign of letting up. It was time to go.

Carefully, joint by joint, Rainer worked his way across the bottom of the cupola. He had to let each set of muscles relax slightly, one set at a time, or all of his muscles would freeze, lose tension, and he would fall. But he could do it. He knew how to do it now.

The flare of the belltower cupola began to shield him from the worst of the rain. The wind still sprayed him with droplets, but he wasn't being hit from above.

Then he was out from under the balcony's shelter. Rain pelted him again.

This was the final move. He had to get over the balustrade. He found a grip, and it was a good one, but the angle was wrong and his feet came loose from below. For a moment he was hanging by one hand from the cupola siding. The rain was like a river pouring down.

Then he swung his other hand around and pushed his fist into a keyhole shape cut through the balustrade stones. He twisted it sideways. Jammed.

He had his grip.

He hung, jammed in, swinging back and forth until his feet came up against something to push against, and he was back on the tower. Hand over hand, he pulled himself up the siding. It proved to be a parapet wall with designs cut through the rock.

He rolled off the top of the balustrade and onto the top floor of the belltower.

Under the cupola roof was the Elder Bell. Ropes dangled from the bell wheel down through a hole in the center of the platform.

He caught a glimpse of the clapper sticking out a fingerbreadth below the bell. It seemed to have a flat head from what he could see. It *could* be some kind of hammer.

The Elder Bell moved.

The Elder Bell began to ring.

Someone was yanking on the bell rope. It was attached to a big wheel that was itself attached to a yoke that held the bell. The rope got yanked. The big wheel spun. The bell rang.

Rainer covered his ears. The sound rattled his teeth. It hurt.

What time was it? It was too early for Nickerchen bell, wasn't it? What was the ringing about?

Rainer pulled himself up to look over the cupola wall.

Below in the courtyard the soldiers were gathering in front of the fallen Olden Oak. There were shouts of command.

It was an alarm bell.

The bell kept ringing. The troops double-timed it out of the square. They ran toward the eastern gate.

"Tretz, let this be what I think it is," Rainer prayed. "Let this be the counterattack."

CHAPTER FORTY-SIX:
THE CRUX

Max Jager heard the distant clanging of the cathedral bell for the first time in his life.

Was it already Nickerchen bell? It seemed like he'd been fighting forever.

He'd heard bells before—his home village had one in its chapel tower—but nothing so deep and *powerful* as this. It carried over even the clash and clamor of battle. He guessed it was the Elder Bell, something he'd known about all his young life but never heard before.

Jager was nineteen years old. He was a rarity among the Tier, a bobcat man. Brullen, his small village of hunters and trappers, was in a cove far in the south of Bear Valley. There Jager had been an assistant to his uncle, who was a tanner of hides.

Jager was tall for a bobcat, but barely the height of a short human. Despite his small form, the fifteen bear men in his company respected him because they'd grown up near the back-valley bobcat village where Jager was born and knew that Jager was smart and a ferocious fighter. When the call had come to gather at Bear Hall, they had elected him their leader despite his age and followed him up the valley.

These fifteen had gathered in their cousins from elsewhere in Bear Valley. A band of misfit otter, beaver, and raccoon men had thrown in with the group as they made their way toward Bear Hall.

Before Jager knew it, he was leading a group of over seventy. Soon everyone was calling him "captain." The company was calling itself the "Raufers," which was valley slang for "brawlers." They'd even provided him with something he'd only dreamed of ever owning, a horse.

Jager didn't care what they called him or each other. He just wanted to fight.

Once at the Bear Hall gathering ground—a muddy, trampled barley field outside the village—the earl had assigned a squad of squabbling buffalo men to the Raufers, as well. The group of twenty had been fighting with each other and with their leaders, and nobody had known what to do with them.

Now these Tier men he'd barely had time to meet, much less learn their names, were fighting for their lives outside the gates of Raukenrose, a town Jager had never visited.

He'd been fighting for what seemed like hours. He was not built to be part of the shield wall, but he'd used his size to his advantage, like he'd always had to do. He'd climbed up the backs of buffalo and bear men and stabbed down into the scrum of Sandhaveners, drawing blood again and again. He'd worked his way between legs and under shields to cut into Sandhavener shins and groins.

Jager growled in rage when the Raufers were pushed back toward the forest edge. He ran up and down the line of men, sometimes pouncing on shoulders, sometimes scrambling under legs.

If we have to move back, Jager thought, I'll damned sure keep us from breaking.

"Push, boys, push!" Jager screamed. He'd seen when he'd joined the front lines that his awareness narrowed like a steep walled canyon to just those fighting directly near him.

There wasn't any use shouting out general orders. There was only one command that counted.

"Stand with your left man! Stand with your right!" he shouted.

He'd thought about ordering a step-by-step retreat, but had seen a band of bear men break after trying that. He'd lengthened and thinned the Raufer line far more than he'd wanted to filling up the hole the retreaters had left. Had to be done.

"Cut 'em down, boys," Jager screamed. "Make 'em pay!"

More of his men fell. Some could be pulled away, and he ordered it done, but most would have to lie where they'd gone down, usually wallowing in their own blood.

We're *not* gonna break like those cursed buffalo, Jager thought.

But things were looking bad.

He had a squad of bear-man longbowmen that he'd kept pouring arrows into the Sandhavener second and third ranks. They were also a reserve.

He climbed on the shoulder of Odis Knudsson, the bear man's chief archer. Knudsson was Jager's best friend from Brullen. He was about to order them to lay down bows and take up spears, when he caught a movement to the rear.

It was a clump of twenty or so of the buffalo men he'd been assigned. They were headed toward the forest.

No you don't!

"Hold the cursed line, Odis," he growled. "Move your boys forward if you have to. I'm takin' after them quitters."

Knudsson nodded, too intent on nocking another arrow to make a reply. Jager pounced from his shoulder and took off after the buffalo men. He was very fast when he wanted to be, and he soon caught up with them.

No time for yelling and screaming. Jager took out his sword—which would have been little more than a long knife to a bear man—and stabbed one of the buffalo men in the butt. This brought forth a scream and curses, as Jager had intended it to, and the whole group turned to look.

Jager bounded in front of them.

"Turn around, boys!" he shouted. "Turn around and fight! There's men that need you back there."

For several of the group, this was enough. They did what Jager ordered. But there was a knot of ten or so buffalo men who did not obey. One of them huffed loudly.

"You get out of the way, little cat."

Snot streamed from the buffalo man's nostrils.

Scared out of his mind, Jager thought.

He shook a halberd at Jager.

"I'll trample you myself," the buffalo man shouted. He stepped forward, trying to move around Jager.

Mistake.

With a quick movement, Jager spun and stroked his sword across the back of the buffalo man's heel. He'd skinned enough hides to know exactly what was there.

The sword sliced through the rear tendon in the buffalo man's lower leg.

Jager cut the other tendon for good measure. The Tier fell, howling in pain and amazement.

"You stinking bobcat!" yelled a buffalo man behind Jager. "I'll cut you down!"

He charged at Jager, and Jager dodged again. He repeated the exact same procedure. Another buffalo man went down screaming and clutching at his ruined legs.

Jager raised his sword. He gazed up at the remaining buffalo men. "Get back in there and fight!" he yelled. "Get back, or I promise you, by Sturmer, I'll do the same to you!"

Eyeblink.

Jager shook his sword.

Eyeblink.

The remaining buffalo men turned and headed back to the fight. Jager wasted no time. He raced in front of them and led them like a spear into the Sandhaven lines. Jager reached around a shield and stabbed up through a Sandhavener's chin. Jager twisted his sword and yanked it out as the man fell dead.

In a moment, the buffalo men were past the spot where Jager stood over the dead Sandhavener. They were fighting more furiously than ever.

He headed back to his bear man archers.

"Down bows and up spears!" he yelled to the bowmen. While they were doing this, he climbed back up onto Knudsson's shoulder.

"Want me to bring 'em up behind those cowards, keep 'em at it?"

"Nah, those others will hold," Jager said. "They got something to prove." Jager balanced with his feet on Knudsson's broad shoulders and stretched up as far as he could to get a look at the fight. He was mindful that he was making himself a target for Sandhaven archers, but he needed to glimpse what was going on.

He saw what seemed like a roiling sea of fighting, screaming, bleeding men and Tier. But behind them he made out a column of Sandhaveners marching up in rows of four. He couldn't see how many there were. He wasn't high enough. But he knew there were plenty of them. They were headed at an angle to the company's left. It was where the line was thinnest.

This looked dangerous. The approaching Sandhaveners needed to be bloodied as quickly as possible or they might punch through.

"Got to take 'em left," he said to Knudsson. "Take 'em in hard." Jager jumped from Knudsson's shoulders. "Follow me, boys!" he shouted.

Once again, Jager charged.

They were losing.

The flank attack with archers worked for a while. Centaur and fox-man bowmen on one side, bear-man longbowmen on the other. The Sandhaven dead and wounded piled up.

But there were always more of them. And reinforcements were charging out of the town. Two thousand warriors of the mark, most of the Bear Valley recruits. Five thousand Sandhaveners.

Numbers began to matter.

It took a while, but the Sandhaveners finally got organized behind a wall of shields. They moved forward together and started to push back the attackers. The Alerdalan Wood got closer and closer when Wulf glanced over his shoulder. Keiler had abandoned the rise where they'd been watching the battle. Now they were getting backed up against the tree line.

It was a fighting retreat, but it was a retreat.

Earl Keiler moved his horse up beside Wulf. "I wish we had reserves, but we don't. Now would be the time to throw them in."

The earl sounded almost apologetic.

"It's not over yet," Wulf replied.

Keiler started to answer, but began to cough, and the fit lasted a long time. The scrofula was getting worse. Blood spattered from his mouth and dripped down the hair of his chin. He finally straightened. "We'll have to make a stand against the woods," the earl said. "If they push us into the trees, they can hunt us down one by one."

Keiler led a group of leaders he'd picked back toward the woods at a trot. Wulf followed. When they got there, the earl spread out these troops along the edge of the woods. "You have to stop them. You have to turn our own if they break, boys!" he shouted.

They waited for the battle to come to them.

They didn't have long to wait.

The Sandhaveners were attacking in tight boxes of eight or ten men, each two men deep. They were taking no prisoners. They were slaughtering any Tier or men they caught.

And pushing the rest back. Farther back.

"It's going to get desperate pretty soon, Lord Wulf," the old bear shouted at him.

"Seems so," Wulf shouted back.

"We *cannot* be pushed into the woods."

"I know." Wulf smiled. "Are you going to let me fight?"

"Draw your sword."

Wulf pulled the bear sword from its scabbard and got ready.

The front line got closer and closer. Troops were shouting. They cried in pain as they were stabbed or slashed, going down.

Something dripped on Wulf's nose. Was his head bleeding? Another splash. More and more.

The rain was here. Thunder rumbled. The rain grew heavier.

"Curse it all!" Wulf shouted.

Nagel, on his shoulder, shook out her wings.

I'm not going to die wet and beaten. I'm not going to run through the forest being hunted.

A cluster of Sandhaveners broke through the lines. They headed toward Wulf and Keiler.

He pointed his sword at the advancing soldiers. He kicked his horse into movement and charged forward to meet the oncoming men.

The rain did not let up. For a moment Wulf thought it might hide his approach.

But the Sandhaveners saw him and were ready.

This is it, Wulf thought.

He saw her face.

Blonde hair. Blue eyes. Willowy. Skinny.

Beautiful to him because of who she was.

Saeunn.

It wouldn't be a bad thought to go out on.

When Wulf was twenty paces from their line, the Sandhaveners seemed to cringe back.

They look *terrified*.

Did I do that?

But then, an eyeblink before he reached them, a cloud of arrows flew over his head and into the enemy. Many fell. An eyeblink later Wulf trampled through the rest with his horse. Another cloud of arrows flew over his head. More Sandhaveners fell.

Then he heard a roar of wild joy coming from the crusty, ancient Earl Keiler.

"The gnomes are here! The gnomes! By Sturmer, now we'll see some fighting!"

Chapter Forty-Seven:
The Victory

Grer was standing in the rain on the spot where he'd killed the man when the bell cord dropped and hit him on top of his head. He looked up and saw Rainer's face barely poking out from the belfry cupola. Rainer had thrown down the cut end of the bell rope. It was a three-twist hemp rope, and the end was already starting to fray. Grer tied his tool bag to it. He gave the rope a tug.

Seemed tight.

Grer pulled himself up the rope with his hands until he was above the shrubbery. Then he put his feet against the cathedral and began walking his way up. Twice the sandstone grit rolled under the soles of his new boots and his feet slid off. He slammed into the side of the cathedral. Even with his forge-made muscles, climbing up the belltower was one of the hardest things he'd ever done.

When he pulled himself over the balustrade and into the belfry, he was breathing in gasps. His arms felt as if they'd been beaten like a rug.

"How was it down there?" Rainer asked.

"Nothing I couldn't handle. Pull up the tools!"

Rainer nodded. He began to quickly lift the bag of tools toward them. "So, how are we going to do this?"

"Rainer, have you even looked to see if it's in there?"

Rainer shook head. "No. I mean, what if it's not?"

"Okay. I'm going to need you to tilt the bell so I can get to it," Grer said. "Grab that bell wheel and turn the yoke. It's yon iron wheel you cut the rope from."

Rainer turned it. Nothing happened.

"Put your back into it, man," Grer said.

Rainer strained harder and slowly spun the bell wheel, which turned the yoke the bell was attached to. The bell gave a low clanking sound as the clapper came to rest against the inside of the bell.

Grer pulled the wheel-lock lever. The stopper clicked into place.

"All right, I think you can let go now," he said to Rainer.

The Elder Bell was on its side.

Grer had a look.

What a beautiful piece of iron, Grer thought.

The clapper was attached to a staple. The staple bar was likely held in by a cotter pin, and that would be the first thing to remove if he was going to take the bell apart.

The interior was different from the outside. It was polished, and it seemed to shine from its own light. The clapper—

"How do you like that?" Grer said.

"What?" asked Rainer, his voice trembling.

"Well," said Grer, "looks like somebody put a hammer in this bell."

The gnomes charged out of the woods almost as fast as their arrows flew. There were hundreds. They moved like a living carpet, low to the ground. It was a carpet that bristled with sharp and pointy weapons.

Some rode kalter ponies, but most were on foot. They moved at the pace of a fast-walking man. They didn't speed up and they didn't slow down—even when they hit the Sandhavener lines.

The Sandhaven soldiers were taken by surprise. They didn't lower their shields, and the gnomes swept under them, stabbing at the joints between greaves and cuirasses. Slicing upward to cut the arteries that led from groins to legs.

Men fell screaming, clutching at their private parts. And when they did, more gnomes were on them, stabbing, hacking, and killing. Some they ganged up on and drowned in rain puddles.

The gnome forces did not stop coming out of the woods for a long time.

There must be thousands of them, Wulf thought. Had the whole village of Glockendorf been converted to soldiers?

Looking closer, Wulf saw that this was maybe true. The gnome women fought alongside their men.

The rain slackened.

The clumps of Sandhaveners that had been pushing ahead broke first. These men rushed into the ranks of their advancing countrymen. Panic started to spread back through the ranks.

Wulf could see it happening. The shields falling out of place as this man or another turned to run. The line was unable to join back together, leaving big gaps that the mark's forces charged into and split apart like a wedge.

The gnomes kept marching. They were like a living organism, like a deadly ant swarm. They were so small it didn't seem they could do much good. They couldn't individually. But when they fought together, they were unstoppable. They overtook the enemy who had broken and fled and hunted each down individually. Men collapsed into the mud and died.

Behind the gnomes came the human and Tier forces of

the mark. They marched forward raggedly, but holding together. It was enough.

We are winning, Wulf thought. We have to. If we don't, we'll be dead.

We're going to break their bones, cut their throats and make them bleed.

We're going to take back Raukenrose.

Raukenrose. My family.

Saeunn.

Wulf spurred his horse. He had his sword out, ready.

He was scared. He was repulsed by the death and the waste of people's lives.

But charging into danger, not away from it? That was a good thing.

Fighting like a madman when the stakes were life and death? It felt right.

Blood and bones, he thought. I expected that. But I didn't expect to *like* war.

I do.

Jager had never believed that all was lost. But there was no denying the treeline was getting closer and his men were getting tired. He done a lot to keep them going. Making sure water was brought up. Getting a whole rank of buffalo men—ones that hadn't cut and run, but had fought like furies—to send up a huge chorus of bellows for encouragement. And killing more humans than he'd ever *seen* in his life before this day.

At the moment, he was dealing with a Sandhavener officer. The Sandhavener was double Jager's size. The fight was brutal. Jager parried a blow with a buckler he'd picked up moments ago from *another* man he'd killed. Then Jager struck with his feline speed and ripped out the Sandhavener's left groin. When the man fell, Jager leaped on top of him and put a sword through the gap in the man's helmet. He pushed through until he struck the metal on the helmet's back side.

Something as small as Jager and almost as quick ran up to his right. Jager glanced over. It was a gnome. Another was on his left. The two pushed past in an organized unit, flowing around him like a stream around a rock, and were soon cutting into the Sandhaveners in front of him.

Jager stood up and worked his way over to Knudsson. The bear man was fighting nearby, but Jager pulled him back from the line.

"Them gnomes move like a bloody wind from Helheim," Knudsson said. "Almost pity the Haveners."

"Yep," Jager said. "Give me a boost."

He climbed back up and balanced on the bear man's shoulders. Over the heads of the soldiers in front of him, Jager saw—

By Sturmer, if that ain't the town wall, Jager thought. We're no more than fifty paces from it.

Then something more disturbing. A fully armored Sandhavener on a horse also in plate was pushing through the line directly in front of him and Knudsson.

"Trouble on the way," Jager said.

"Wish I had my bow and a bodkin-headed shaft," Knudsson said. "I'd take 'im down at this range even through steel."

The horseman headed straight for them. Jager considered. The armor was slowing the horse. There was an exposed spot on the breast above either leg.

"Think you can handle the animal?" he asked the bear man.

"Reckon so."

Knudsson readied his spear. Just before the horseman reached them, he kicked in his heels and speeded the horse. He lowered his weapon, a halberd.

Knudsson ducked and thrust his spear at the horse. Jager

pounced. The halberd passed between them without striking.

Jager crashed into the horseman. The man was driven back in his saddle, but did not fall. He did drop his halberd. But this also freed up his fist. He smashed a steel-reinforced glove into Jager's face. The man's knuckles partly caught the side of Jager's helm, but the rest of his fist connected with Jager's cheek, smashing it into the bobcat man's teeth. Blood filled Jager's mouth.

Jager drew back his sword, but the man reached for him with his other hand and grabbed him around the neck. He started to choke Jager, shaking him back and forth. Jager gagged on his own blood. He felt his windpipe closing down. He reached for his neck with his free hand and tried to pry away the choke hold. No good.

Then the man let out a cry of surprise and lurched sideways, taking Jager with him. Knudsson had brought the horse down. Jager twisted as he fell and the man's hand came loose from Jager's neck. But the Sandhavener was quick, too. He landed with crushing weight on top of Jager. The bobcat man howled in pain. He still had hold of his sword somehow, and he desperately tried to position it to stab into the man's side. Made the thrust.

And it glanced off armor.

The man sat up. Now he got two hands around Jager's neck. He squeezed. Jager struggled furiously, but the world started to go dark.

Suddenly, the squeezing lessened. Jager looked up at something strange. A long tongue seemed to have stuck out from the Sandhavener's mouth. A pointed tongue. Then Jager realized it was the tip of a dagger. Someone had run the man's head through from the rear. Which was no mean feat, because the man wore a full helmet with a grima noseguard.

The tongue slid back in, the dagger was withdrawn. The Sandhavener fell to the side. Jager looked up to see a human, a young man. He wore a green and blue jerkin over a gray linen shirt. Jager recognized him immediately. He'd seen him while the human had passed among the troops at Bear Hall.

It was Lord Wulf von Dunstig.

The nobleman looked down at his knife.

"Good steel my smith forged," he said. "Right through the back of the helm."

Lord Wulf sheathed the dagger. On his other side was a sword, also hanging in a scabbard.

Funny the nobleman had used the dagger instead of the sword, Jager thought. He must think it the better weapon.

The lord reached out a hand to help Jager up. Jager took it.

Knudsson was nearby working his spear out of the horse. It had gone in deep. Lord Wulf's own horse was standing patiently to the rear of them toward the woods.

Jager stood beside his lord. He came about to the height of Lord Wulf's navel.

They gazed toward the fighting several paces in front of them.

"We're winning," the young lord said.

"That we are, m'lord," Jager replied. "Thanks to them gnomes."

"And to you for holding on so long, Captain."

"My boys fought hard," Jager replied. "And we're still fighting."

Lord Wulf nodded.

Knudsson gave a loud grunt and pulled his spear completely free of the horse. It was still alive and faintly struggling. The bear man put a boot on the horse's neck. This was hard for the bear man. He had been a stable hand in Brullen, and practically worshipped the horses he cared for there. He killed the horse with a quick thrust through the eye, looking away at the last moment so he didn't have to see the horse's death throes.

"Our left flank has reached the wall," Lord Wulf said. He pointed to a spot Jager wasn't tall enough to see. "I want to cut off that gate." He pointed to their right. Jager could see the eastern guardhouse standing tall above the heads of the fighting men.

"We have to keep them from escaping through the gate. Herd them together."

Jager considered. "Yep, m'lord. It'll take some doing, but we can." He turned to Knudsson. "Let's wheel 'em left, Odis. Push for the wall on the right."

Knudsson nodded. "All right, Captain," he said. "We'll make it so they don't have nowheres to go."

"You stay here and just watch us do it, m'lord," Jager said. "You should tend to your horse there."

Lord Wulf shook his head. "My horse can take care of itself," he said. He shot Jager a savage smile and pointed toward the fighting with his sword. "*That's* where I belong. And that's where I'm going." In that moment Jager believed he would follow this boy lord anywhere, even into the pit of Helheim. "Now let's finish this, Captain."

Jager nodded, and Lord Wulf charged toward the fight.

Jager raised his own sword and followed his liege lord back into the scrum of battle.

CHAPTER FORTY-EIGHT:
THE SORROW

"I need Ravenelle."

I never thought I'd hear myself say it, Wulf thought, she's been so prickly for so long. But I've got to find her before we go in.

Now it was not bear men who were hemming him in. There was a new set of guards in tow. They were four centaurs armed with deadly looking longbows. Wulf rode back to the supply wagons, looking for Ravenelle. Instead he saw Ursel nursing a beaver man's shoulder wound.

She motioned for him to stay on his horse. "We'll talk later, m'lord," she said. "I'm a bit busy right now."

"I understand," said Wulf. "Have you seen the princess?"

"She was with the ambulances when I last saw her. The body carts."

"She's not—"

"No, she's alive. She was helping sort out the living."

Wulf breathed a sigh of relief. He had to ask several of the teamsters, but he finally got pointed in the right direction. He rode to the north.

He came to the train of ambulance wagons and rode along it. There were a lot of dead Tier. Flies were already settling on the bodies in a cloud, and the smell, like raw meat in a butcher shop, was very strong.

He found Ravenelle about halfway down the line of wagons. She was walking beside one of the wagons with bodies in it as it moved along at a slow pace. A horse, the one Ravenelle had ridden to Bear Hall, was tied to the rear of the wagon and was plodding behind.

Ravenelle saw Wulf and his bear men, and motioned to the driver to hold up.

Wulf was about to speak sharply to her about going off by herself when she might be needed very soon inside the township. But he saw sadness on her face. He climbed down from his horse and stood beside her. The centaurs kept back, but scanned the nearby country. Their bows were strung. Archers didn't string their bows unless they thought they might use them. Carrying them around strung tight at all times ruined the bow wood.

"I'm coming back to town," she said. "I was about to leave, it's only . . . I didn't want him to be alone."

Ravenelle put her hand on one of the bodies placed near the edge of the wagon. Wulf was confused for a moment, but then he saw the wispy beard and the small horns sticking out from curly brown hair.

It was Grim.

"Oh, no," Wulf said. "He was . . . I thought he'd be safe with the wagons. I ordered him to stay back, but . . . How?"

"Some Sandhavener men on horses circled and got into the supply train," Ravenelle replied. "We fought them off, but . . . I'm sorry, von Dunstig, I really am."

Wulf put his hands on the faun's shoulders and gazed at his still face. There was a piece of burlap cloth covering his goatlike lower parts. Wulf lifted it up briefly and saw a terrible wound to the groin where the leg met the hip. The brown hair of his rump and leg was matted with still-wet blood.

"He died fighting for us. He and Ursel Keiler with some of the buffalo-man teamsters," Ravenelle went on. "He saved my life. Others, too." She looked down at the faun, shook her head. "A lot of people."

Wulf glanced at Ravenelle. A blood red tear rolled down her cheek. There were red trails that others had left on her skin.

He drew back from Grim and put a hand around her shoulder. After a moment, the buffalo driver shook his reins. The wagon with Grim and the other faun dead trundled on toward the tobacco fields north of town. There the dead fauns would be placed on pyres set up in a cleared spot ringed with huge stone pillars. Wulf had seen it before, but only from a distance. This was the sacred place where fauns burned their dead.

Wulf thought about offering a prayer to Ostern, the female divine being the fauns most revered, but found he couldn't do that. Grim had been quiet and not very expressive, but he had never once failed or abandoned Wulf. The prayer should be authentic. Wulf wasn't sure who he believed in anymore.

The divine beings, maybe? Should he pray to Tretz? He would feel stupid doing that after so many years thinking it was nonsense.

So he ended up bowing his head as he held on to Ravenelle and speaking to no god or divinity in particular, but to all of them. He used a form he'd heard before at the funerals of veterans.

"Let us be worthy of Grim's sacrifice," he said. Those words, too, sounded hollow, and he felt his own tears welling, choking off any words that didn't seem real.

Finally Ravenelle spoke. "Go on, von Dunstig. It isn't stupid."

He stood silent a moment longer, watching the wagon go.

This reminded him of something in *Tjark's Saga*, when Hefni, the old duke's son, fell in the fight to win the valley. "Let Shenandoah hold him in her arms," Wulf said. He paused a moment then spoke the rest of the stanza. "To live again in the Never and Forever."

"You are such a barbarian," Ravenelle said, but she was crying again, and she buried her head against his right shoulder and stained yet another spot on his tabard red with her tears.

They rode back to the eastern gate of Raukenrose as fast as they could. When they got there, Earl Keiler was off his horse, standing near the eastern-gate entrance. A Sandhavener with a truce flag was speaking to the earl. Suddenly Ravenelle stiffened on her horse beside him and pulled up. Wulf did, too.

"That's one of Rask's Hundred," she said. "I can feel his mind."

"Can you get in?"

"He's one of mine now. Do you want me to?"

Wulf considered. "No, not yet. But can you find out if he's telling the truth without his knowing it?"

"Not usually." Ravenelle paused for a moment, concentrating on the man. She nodded. "He's weak. His thoughts are leaking," she said. There was a wisp of a wicked smile on her face. "Yes, he won't know I'm listening in."

Wulf handed the reins to one of the guards and got down from his horse. He and Ravenelle walked over to hear what was being said between the earl and the soldier.

"—in Allfather Square." There was the drawn out "a" in "Allfather" marking the man's accent as coming from the Chesapeake Tidewater.

Earl Keiler glanced over to Wulf.

"Messenger from Trigvi," he said. "He wants to meet us. Discuss terms."

It's the end of a fight. You've got your opponent beaten and desperate. That hadn't happened to him very often in the ring. But it happened to Rainer all the time.

What would Rainer do?

"Finish it off. Don't mess around," Rainer would say. "If you waste time ragging them, they might try something that works."

Wulf shrugged.

"The terms are simple. Unconditional surrender," he said.

The soldier made a grimacing expression that might have been meant as a smile. "I hope we can come to a more honorable arrangement," he said.

"No," Wulf said. "Tell him. And tell the other."

"What 'other' are you talking about?" said the soldier.

"The draugar," Wulf said. "Wuten."

The other paused, as if searching for words. His face grew pale.

Scared to death.

"Unconditional surrender," Wulf said. "Tell Wuten. He's the real commander here. Tell him I'll meet him in Allfather Square."

The other stepped back, made a slight bow. "Prince Trigvi will be there," he said.

"Prince Trigvi can go to cold hell," Wulf said. "It's the draugar who needs to be at the square." Wulf pointed toward the gate entrance. "Please get out of my sight."

He looked over to Ravenelle, and the two watched as the man went through the gate back into the town.

"Is he going to do it?" Wulf asked her.

"He'll do it," she said, "but he's absolutely terrified. And not of you."

Wulf breathed out the tension he'd been holding in. "I'm terrified too," he said. "But I'm getting used to it."

Once again, Keiler went into a coughing fit. This time it

did not go away. After being doubled over, he sank to his knees.

From somewhere nearby, Ursel ran from the crowd of soldiers. She knelt next to Keiler and put an arm around his neck to comfort him.

He said something to her, and Ursel motioned Wulf to come over. He knelt down beside her. There was a pool of blood the earl had coughed up on the ground below him.

"Has he ever been like this?" Wulf asked Ursel.

"Not for months," Ursel said. "He was getting better, but the strain of the past few days has done this, I'm sure."

"Will he get better?"

"It will take weeks."

"We don't have weeks," Wulf said. "We have one watch, at most."

Keiler gestured for Wulf to come closer.

"You'll have to go without me," Keiler whispered.

"I need you, Earl," Wulf stammered.

"No," Keiler coughed again. More blood poured from his mouth.

"His lungs are bleeding," Ursel said. "He will drown in his own blood if he doesn't rest."

Keiler reached over and grabbed Wulf's arm. He pulled Wulf even closer. "You can do this," he whispered. "But take Tolas."

PART SEVEN

PART SEVEN

Chapter Forty-Nine:
The Temptation

Saeunn had been afraid when the draugar sent for her.

This was it. He'd tortured the castle guard. He seemed sure that someone in the castle knew where the Dragon Hammer was hidden.

Now it was her turn. And she *did* know.

Two of the Hundred brought her to the highest spot in the castle, the crow's nest lookout that topped the tower that Saeunn's quarters were in.

They shoved her onto the flat stone roof. There was no stone balustrade, no railing of any kind here.

Wuten stood near the edge. His vulturelike head turned this way and that, like a carrion eater looking for dead things to feed on. He was gazing out on the town below.

She smelled his stench, but it was a little less here with the wind whipping some of it away.

Saeunn moved away from the draugar to the opposite side of the lookout. She gazed out. There were fires in the distance, and smoke rising beyond the walls.

The Hundred guards withdrew. By now everyone could

tell that the draugar had Romanlike mental control over the soldiers who occupied the castle. They were a company of slaves.

"Come here, little elf, I will show thee." He beckoned Saeunn to him. There was no point resisting. He could drag her if he wished. She stepped over and stopped, a pace away from him.

"What do you want?" she asked.

"To watch the ruin of the dragons," Wuten replied with a shrug. He turned from the scene beyond the balcony and looked at Saeunn with his round, black eyes. "The prince has lost."

What prince? Saeunn felt a sudden joy in her heart. Trigvi has lost? Nobody in the castle knew what was happening outside. A band of the Hundred had marched out earlier and not returned.

"Good," she said.

"The town lies burned. Looted. Made use of."

"They'll rebuild."

"No, this charade must end," Wuten said. "The heir will give me the relic."

"Who?"

"The boy. The new heir."

"Adelbert?"

"Thou know'st he is dead."

Wulf, Saeunn thought. He's talking about Wulf then.

The rush of relief and happiness inside her was almost too much to contain. But she would not show anything to this monster.

Did Wulf have the Dragon Hammer?

"He knows where," Wuten said, as if he'd read her mind. "Thou hast a choice."

"What choice?"

"Give thyself for the heir that he might live."

"Me? What do you want me to do?"

The draugar stepped close to her. It was all Saeunn could do to stand where she was and not run away. But she couldn't stop herself from trembling.

"Thou art young. But thy dasein is strong," he said. "Thou can'st grow into great power."

"I don't understand what you mean."

Wuten did not answer her, but continued. "I will soon have the relic. The relic is beyond age. Beyond the master's control."

"Are you talking about Ubel?" Saeunn asked.

Wuten hissed. "*Do not say his name!* He is drawn by it."

"What do you care? Like you said, he's your master."

Wuten's hand shot out. He grabbed Saeunn by an arm and yanked her toward him. His curved beak was a finger's breadth from her eyes before he stopped. The smell of death was almost unbearable this close.

"Not forever, little elf," he rasped. "With the relic, the three will rise. The master gorges on the Tiberian dragon. He is prideful in his strength. He does not suspect."

"You are a fool, then," Saeunn said. "He knows."

"I tell thee he does not."

"What do you want from me?"

Wuten grabbed Saeunn's wrist with his other hand. His taloned nails dug into her skin.

"Yoke thy dasein to mine. We shall be the strongest of the three."

He pulled her hand up, forced her palm open with a sharp poke of his thumb.

"Rule with me."

Then he lowered the tip of his beak onto her palm.

Saeunn tried to pull away, but his hold was like iron on her wrist.

With a small flick of his head, Wuten laid her skin open. A line of red blood welled up.

He let go of her hair, keeping hold of her wrist, and

reached for something he wore on his belt. It was a small pouch. From inside it, he took something, something small. She couldn't see what it was.

Then he opened his own palm under her sliced one and slowly turned it over. The pooled blood dripped into his open hand—and onto the black wafer that lay in his palm. The wafer thirstily absorbed her blood. After a moment, Wuten let her go and Saeunn pulled away quickly, nursing her hand against her breast.

She watched in horror as the draugar's beak opened, and Wuten ate the blood-soaked wafer.

She saw him swallow. For a moment, he stood still, as if savoring the taste.

Then he held up his empty left palm facing himself. With the tip of his beak, he pierced his own flesh. Black ichor welled up. It flowed more like fatty oil than blood.

With his right hand he took another wafer from the pouch. He placed it in the liquid gore of his hand. "See the ater-cake's power," he said. He showed her how the wafer drank up the offering.

Again, he moved with lightning speed and grabbed her. This time he held her by the hair at the back of her neck. He pulled her close, and forced her to look down.

The gore-soaked wafer was in his hand. It was sopping with the draugar's black, oozing blood.

"Take, sister," he said. "Eat. Join with me."

"No," Saeunn whimpered.

"Die, little elf, and live through me."

"Never."

"If thou do'st not, I will flay the skin from the heir. Slowly," he said. "He will beg for death. I will give his sisters away for the use of the soldiers."

"You would do that anyway."

"No. Between us will be a dasein ring, an unbreakable bond. Choose me, and they will live."

My star . . .

He pushed his hand near her mouth. If she wanted, she could reach the ater-cake with her tongue. Saeunn gazed down at the wafer. If she ate it, Anya and Ulla would be saved. Wulf would live.

Where are you, my star?

For her, it would all be over. All the striving and fighting and heartbreak.

Or would it?

My star? My own?

Wuten plotted rebellion against Ubel, the originator of all evil. Did this mean there was a part of the ancient elf still inside the draugar? Was that part of himself living on in agony and screaming to escape?

I don't want to find out.

"No!" she cried, and pulled back from him with all her strength.

"Then suffer," Wuten told her. "And die." He closed his hand over the ater-cake and, with a vicious yank on her hair, drew her away from himself, his claws still holding to her hair.

He's going to kill me now, Saeunn thought. He can't let me live knowing about his plan to rebel.

It was then that her star finally answered.

You have escaped the shadow, my child, my own. Now the way is clear for us.

What do you mean, my star?

Before her star answered the draugar twisted her by her hair and made her look out at the town.

"We go."

"Go where?" she whispered.

The draugar didn't answer. "Thou wilt calm the young one."

Anya.

"What will you do to her?"

"The heir will tell, or his sister will die," Wuten said.

"No," said Duchess Malwin. "She can't!" She rushed forward and threw her arms around her daughter, tugging her away from the draugar.

Captain Rask stepped up and took the duchess firmly by one arm and Anya by another. He pulled the duchess away from her daughter. Then he flung the duchess backward to land at Ulla's feet.

Ulla pointed at the draugar with two fingers of her left hand. Saeunn knew in Ulla's creed this meant a curse was being cast.

"I curse you to the eternal night beyond Helheim," Ulla said to the draugar. "No eyes. No lips to speak. No ears. No nose. No feeling, but for nothingness. Nothing, nothing, nothing! You are nothing!"

The draugar considered her for a moment. He turned to another of the Hundred. "Hit her," he said. The man walked over and backhanded Ulla to the ground. Blood dripped from her nose and lip, and there was a red smear under the skin of her cheek that would soon be a purpled bruise.

"Take them to the barbican," said the draugar, indicating the duchess and Ulla with a sweeping gesture. "Make them watch us leave."

Rask pointed to two soldiers. They hurried forward and grabbed the two women. They took the duchess by the arm and Ulla by the neck. They bent her head and shoulders down, forcing her to stumble forward.

Rask brought Anya over to Saeunn. "Take her," he ordered.

Saeunn opened up her arms and Anya ran into them, burying her face in Saeunn's dress.

"Leave twenty," the draugar said to Rask. "The rest will march with me. Bring horses." The draugar paused and considered. "And what is left of the dead lord's body."

"Your will." Rask bowed and turned to shout orders.

He'd strapped a bundle wrapped in dirty muslin to the back of a black horse.

Otto's body. Dragged from some dank place it had been dumped.

The draugar motioned to the captain of the Hundred to take Anya. She tried kicking and screaming, but there was no use. The man seemed to be nothing but muscle.

Wuten mounted a horse, a black stallion without a trace of white on him. It was a living horse. But it seemed used to the draugar and didn't bolt. Saeunn was lifted to her own horse. Anya was placed in front of her on the saddle. They passed out the gate and beside the jutting barbican. Saeunn risked a look up.

There were the duchess and Ulla leaning over the balustrade. They watched Anya go.

Broken, Saeunn thought. All hope gone.

Anya waved feebly to her mother and sister. After a moment, the duchess waved back.

The draugar fell in next to them. He leaned over toward Anya. "Allfather Cathedral, little one?" the draugar said to Anya. "Like thee told me."

Anya began to cry.

"You don't have to be sorry for anything, Anya," Saeunn said to her foster sister. She half expected the draugar to order her muzzled, but he said nothing. He kicked his horse and rode ahead once again.

He doesn't know. That's why he's keeping us alive. He may not even know where to look.

Anya spoke without looking back at her. "Saeunn, I didn't say where. He couldn't get me to say. But he hurt me and I said Wulf knows. I'm so sorry."

"It's all right, Evinthir," Saeunn said.

"But Saeunn," Anya cried, "that was worse than to tell. He's going to hurt Wulf."

"No."

"He killed Otto."

"Wulf figures things out. He is . . . more dangerous."

"I shouldn't have told. Oh, Saeunn, I *told*!"

"Evinthir, you are the bravest little girl I have ever met. Be brave a little longer. I will protect you. I will do whatever it takes."

I'll eat the ater if I have to, Saeunn thought. I'll do whatever it takes.

She felt Anya relax and lean back against her. And then she knew what her star had meant. She knew what she was going to do. The way was clear.

CHAPTER FIFTY:
THE SQUARE

The stench of death filled Allfather Square. Wulf rode in from the east on his Bear Valley draft horse. Ravenelle was with him. So was Tolas. The gnome rode on the back of the centaur Ahorn.

Tupakkalaatu of the buffalo people also rode beside Wulf. The fox-man archers had volunteered to come, but Wulf had forbidden it. He wanted to find out whether or not Smallwolf was a lone traitor or part of a conspiracy, and not by getting an arrow in his back. Instead, bear longbowmen fanned out in the buildings that overlooked the east side of the square. Centaurs found spots at ground level where they could provide cover fire if things went wrong.

Ravenelle rode behind Wulf on her black horse. He'd told her to stay hidden behind the front line as much as possible. He didn't want the Sandhaveners to see right away that there was a Roman in the ranks of the mark.

Hooves clopped against cobblestone. Horse tack squeaked and clanked. Even though it had rained, the square smelled unclean.

The day was still overcast, and there was a pall over the sun. A breeze left over from the storm rattled the branches of the—

Wulf gasped. A new shudder of sadness went through him.

The Olden Oak was lying on its side. It had been chopped down.

It had fallen to the north along the front of Allfather Cathedral. Its fall had split the stone basin of Regen's Fountain. Now the water trickled out of its spout and pooled on the ground until it ran down a nearby grated storm drain.

Wulf got down from his horse, and a soldier took its reins. He went to the Olden Oak and ran a hand gently along the place where the ax had chopped it. It still smelled of fresh green wood.

He shook his head in disbelief and disgust at the men who would do this. There, a few hands from the fatal cut, his old dagger was still plunged in. Its pommel seemed different—

What the cold hell?

It appeared that a clump of green leaves had grown out of the dagger's hilt. Wulf ran his thumb across them. They were real.

Tolas, riding Ahorn, moved forward to stand beside him, as well as Tupakkalaatu the buffalo chieftain and a bear-man guard of four armed with halberds, swords, and daggers, and looking very dangerous.

"It isn't surprising they felled the tree," Tolas said quietly. "It stood for the mark and the von Dunstigs. But it is a terrible shame."

"Yes," Wulf said.

He had been mad enough to kill Sandhaveners before. Now he felt like marching on Krehennest itself and turning King Siggi's city to rubble.

It's just a tree, Wulf thought. Just a tree.

Wulf turned away and walked back to join the others on the eastern side of the square. They were waiting for nickerchen bell to ring.

It didn't ring. He could see from the shadows that it was past time for that.

Had the Dragon Hammer been found? Did the draugar have it?

Then from the southwest, which was the direction of the castle, the Sandhaveners came. They rode Sandhavener mounts. These were at least three hands shorter than the big Bear Valley draft horses. Wulf had never met Trigvi von Krehennest, but there was no mistaking his resemblance to Gunnar. Beside him, wearing black mail under a black cloak, was the source of the smell of death.

It was the draugar he and Rainer had fought in this very square. He had a name now. Wuten.

Trigvi dismounted from his horse first. Wuten raised a black-gloved hand and the men-at-arms behind him stopped. Some were mounted and some were on foot. The draugar got down from his horse. Instead of the russet gray, the guards wore blue and black stripes under the Sandhaven badge on their tabards. They were Nesties. They were the Hundred. They fanned out and lined the southern side of the square.

The draugar made no visible signal, but there must have been a mental command. As one, the Nestie guard drew their swords and held them diagonally across their chests. Wulf noticed that a couple of the guards were left-handed. These held their swords straight up from the waist.

They've practiced this, Wulf thought. A lot.

The draugar motioned again with his hand. Several guards turned to the side to create an opening in the ranks.

Three Nesties stepped through it. They carried a body wrapped in dirty white linen.

Wulf sucked in a breath. This was going to be something bad. His heart began to race.

"Show him," said the draugar. There was the same harsh hiss to his words. They didn't sound human. They must have formed in a dry, bare place inside him. It was like a bone flute was speaking.

The guards placed the body on the ground and took hold of the gravecloth. They lifted upward together. The linen unrolled. Wulf's stomach knotted. Finally, they yanked the linen away. There was a body. It lay on its side. The skin was ghostly pale. It was covered with a dark stain beneath the skin along the middle of the back where the blood had pooled.

The face was split with what looked like black-rimmed cracks. But Wulf could not mistake who it was.

Otto.

Ravenelle's information was correct. Otto was dead.

There were several gasps and cries from those behind Wulf. People had recognized his brother.

Prince Trigvi spoke for the first time. "He was shot in the back. I won't say he was running away, but that *is* where we found the arrow that killed him."

Trigvi stepped forward. He looked directly at Wulf. "This was not an execution," he continued. "Otto fell in battle. His death does not satisfy the blood price for Gunnar von Krehennest." Trigvi put a hand to his chin as if he were considering and making some judgment. "The death of Adelbert von Dunstig does satisfy part of it, however."

"You killed my brother, you Sandhavener scum," Wulf said.

Trigvi looked appalled and embarrassed, as if Wulf had made some terrible breach in protocol.

"I'm done with this stupidity, Trigvi," Wulf said. "I'm here to accept your unconditional surrender."

Trigvi smiled. "Oh, I don't think we'll be doing that," he said.

"Your forces are beaten," Wulf said. "We have nearly two thousand prisoners, including all of the Nesties who aren't part of this group. You're finished here, Trigvi. Lay down your sword or I'll bring the rest of my warriors into the town and have them kill you all. That's the blood price *I* demand, you filthy piece of crap, and it isn't up for negotiation."

"Is it not?" said the draugar in his low, rasping voice. "Here are my terms. Thou hast this one to do with as you wish." He pointed a gloved finger at Trigvi, who bristled but said nothing.

"The terms are unconditional surrender, Wuten of the Draug. That includes you."

The draugar fixed his attention on Wulf. "They said thou wert a scholar," he said. "Thou know'st my name."

"I know you. I will never deal with the likes of you."

Wuten stood still. He made no motion, but the line of guards parted farther. Through the larger opening stepped Captain Rask. Rask had a drawn dagger in one hand. The other mailed arm draped across the shoulders of a girl-child. He urged her forward.

It was Anya.

Chapter Fifty-One:
The Standoff

Anya wore her favorite blue-gray dress, and her blonde hair was drawn back with a ribbon. She was wearing the tense smile that Wulf knew meant she was trying not to act afraid.

Rask brought Anya to stand near Wuten.

Another Nestie stepped through. He pushed a blonde woman ahead of him. She stumbled momentarily before gracefully catching herself.

"Saeunn," Wulf said.

She looked up. He caught her gaze. For a moment Allfather Square and the past few days disappeared. He saw only her. Her face was smudged, her hair hadn't been brushed, and her white dress was stained with dirt.

She was as beautiful as ever.

Yet instead of the playful half-smile she usually wore, her expression was sad and her eyes were wistful.

Everything inside him screamed that he should run to her, but he held himself back.

He wanted to kill the man who was touching her. He wanted to kill every Sandhavener who had set foot in the mark.

Maybe he would order their deaths after all.

"Time for revenge later, boy," the draugar said. "Now we trade. The little one for the hammer. Thou know'st where it lies."

"If I did, I'd be pounding you to dust right now," Wulf said. Without turning, he called out. "Archers! Take aim!"

He knew from the rustle behind him that more than bear men and centaurs had obeyed his order.

The draugar hissed. He waved a hand toward Anya, and Rask raised his dagger to the girl's throat. He pushed the edge of the blade against the skin. Anya gasped. She started to struggle, but Rask held her tightly with his other hand.

"Tell them to lower their weapons," the draugar said. "Now."

Wulf shook his head. "Let the girls go."

"Not yet."

Wulf cocked his head over his shoulder. "Lower your bows!" he shouted.

"Sensible boy," said Wuten. "Give the hammer to me, and they"—He nodded toward the girls.—"shalt live."

"If you get the hammer, you'll kill the dragon." Wulf shook his head in defiance. "I can't let that happen."

Wuten turned to Rask. "Kill her," he ordered.

Wulf saw Rask's muscles tense as if to obey the command. There was the slightest tremor in the hand holding the dagger across Anya's throat. But the hand and the dagger did not move.

It took the draugar a moment to realize that his order was not being carried out. "Kill her!" Wuten shouted at Rask.

Sweat beads rolled out from underneath the metal of Rask's helmet and ran down his face. But still he did not move.

Wuten scanned the square as if he were a dog sniffing for a scent. Then he found it and gazed at someone behind Wulf. Wulf didn't have to turn to know it was Ravenelle.

"Roman," said the draugar. "What dost thou?"

"Let her go!" Ravenelle shouted.

"Wuten, do something," another voice shouted. It was Trigvi. Several of the soldiers behind him had lowered their swords to point at the *prince*.

Trigvi danced away from them. "Something has taken them over!"

Wuten didn't even glance at the prince.

"Ater-cake? Where come'st thou by it?" the draugar asked Ravenelle, but then shrugged. "No matter. I will break thee."

For a moment, there was silence in the square. Wulf figured there was a terrible struggle going on between Wuten and Ravenelle. The men moving toward Trigvi ceased their advance, but kept their swords pointed toward him.

Suddenly, Wuten's legs seemed to give way. He fell to his knees on the stones of the square. He shouted with pain and clutched his head.

Rask slowly took the blade away from Anya's neck. He still kept his grip on the girl.

Wuten rose back to his feet.

"Thou hast skill, dark princess. But I have power. How long can'st thou hold?" He drew the Iberian falcata with the curved blade from a scabbard on his waist. "No matter. I will kill the girl myself."

Wuten waved a hand in Ravenelle's direction, and she screamed in pain.

The Nesties regained control of their swords and pointed them away from Trigvi. Yet Rask did not move to kill Anya.

Ravenelle is still holding on to him, Wulf thought.

Wuten turned toward Anya. His arms were open as if he meant to hug her, but the sword was in his hand. He took a step toward Anya.

"Come, child."

There was no way for Wulf to get across the square in time. The draugar reached Anya and yanked her away from Rask.

He raised his curved sword.

"Wait!" Wulf shouted.

Wuten paused.

"The Dragon Hammer is in the cathedral," Wulf said. "In the bell. Inside the Elder Bell."

"How came thee by this?" Wuten rasped.

Tolas spoke for the first time. "My people hid it there," he called out. "Two hundred years ago. It's true. The hammer is in the Elder Bell! Now let the child go."

The draugar seemed to consider for a moment. Then he nodded. "Thou speak'th the truth, then boy," he said.

"Let me go," Anya whimpered. "Please let me go."

Wuten turned up his beaked face toward the sky. He let out an unearthly screech. It was like a thousand fingernails being dragged across slate.

He raised the curved sword. He brought it down.

The arc would have put it deep into Anya's chest, but a mailed arm swung in an intersecting arc. It knocked the falcata to the side. Then another hand grasped the draugar's wrist.

It was Rask.

Rask, under Ravenelle's control, tried to take the sword away from the draugar. The dark being let go of Anya in the struggle for possession of the falcata.

"Run, Anya!"

The little girl turned to go, but she seemed confused which direction to turn. She stumbled back a few steps. She seemed mesmerized in a state of terror as she watched the struggle between Rask and the draugar.

Wulf ran toward her. But he had the whole square to cross.

The draugar was fast, but so was Rask. The two grappled, each seeking a hold with one hand, each with one hand on the draugar's hook-shaped sword hilt.

Rask was the first to get a hand on the draugar's neck. He

squeezed. If it had been a normal man even one-handed the powerful Rask would have choked him to death. But Wuten did not breathe.

Slowly Rask turned the draugar's own sword toward the being's chest.

Almost there.

Then the draugar jerked its head, and its curved beak found Rask's face. It raked across Rask's forehead until it caught in an eye socket.

Rask screamed as his eyeball was shredded.

In agony, Rask lost his grip on both throat and knife. The draugar jerked away. With a counterstrike, he swung the falcata across Rask's face, laying open his cheek and slicing through the other eye. The captain cried out and stumbled back, his hands over the bleeding remains of his eyes.

"Archers, stand ready!" Wulf shouted as he ran.

The draugar stalked toward Anya.

"Nesties!" screamed Trigvi. "Attack!"

CHAPTER FIFTY-TWO:
THE SACRIFICE

Darkly fell Amberly Reizend.

The line from the poem echoed through her mind.

She had spent days barely speaking with her star. She had been terrified the draugar would somehow pick up on it and overhear.

My star, my own! How I have missed you.

And I have missed you, my child, my own, the star replied. *It is time to act.*

But—

You wish to save the girl?

I do!

You have seen the choice in your moon-vision.

But not him! *No, my star, my own! No! Never him!*

You must. He cannot be killed otherwise.

No.

This is why there are elves, my child, my own. The dragons must hatch. The draug must fall.

My star—

But her star was silent.

The draugar would kill Anya. He would kill Wulf. He would kill everyone.

He would kill Anya.

Evinthir.

"Darkly fell Amberly Reizend." It came out as a near-whisper. Her voice wavered, more breath than speech. But she said it. She meant it.

A star, a soul, could be given away.

Wuten was an elf with no star. Empty. A vacuum where his soul should be.

She could fill that void.

"Karltundelkan nalith Ebereth Serian!" she shouted.

Wuten held up his sword strike.

He turned toward Saeunn as if drawn by a lodestone.

"Elf girl, what do'st thou?"

Saeunn walked toward him.

"Run, Evinthir!" she shouted. "Run to Wulf!"

Anya turned and ran.

The draugar let her go. He was transfixed, looking at Saeunn.

"Karltundelkan nalith Ebereth Serian!"

The draugar lowered his sword. "Stop!"

"Then darkly fell Amberly Reizend."

"No!"

He held the falcata up as if it could ward her away. Saeunn drew closer.

"Karltundelkan nalith Ebereth Serian." The words were Saelith, the elvish tongue. "Then darkly fell Amberly Reizend."

"Stop it," he said. He sucked in a ragged, rasping breath, then breathed out noisily.

"Karltundelkan nalith Ebereth Serian."

She felt it then. Separation from her star.

My child, my own!

My star, my own!

Saeunn gasped at the pain.

My star, my own, let go, let go!

My child. Oh, my child. Good-bye.

She looked at Wuten now and saw him as he was. Not the black vulture shell he lived in, but the elf he once had been. He was still there, trapped inside the draugar's form.

He was ancient. His face was a ruin of wrinkles. Dried up. His eyes were sticky with fluid. The maw of his open mouth was covered with a spider web of dried mucus, as if a terrible scream were frozen there.

The one that I love is dying.

Saeunn's vision was darkening, closing into a tunnel.

My child!

Her world was fading. The light was failing. Her memory was drying and crumbling.

I can't remember why I'm doing this, but I have to.

"Evinthir!" she shouted.

She let go.

And her star found him, the elf inside Wuten. A place to hold. Memories to set in motion.

She clutched the draugar with talons of light.

The life began to trickle back into Abenweth Grevenstran, Pillar of the North. The scream frozen on his mouth became a real scream, the anguished cry of a living being. His eyes moistened, focused. They were green. Sea green. The lines on his face shrank. The furrows of his skin filled. Blood began to flow. Color returned to his features.

"No." He began to sob. "I won't! I will not!"

Saeunn Amberstone's soulless body collapsed onto the stones of Allfather Square.

Why am I falling?

So darkly.

Abenweth Grevenstran whimpered. He was alive. He hated it.

✥ ✥ ✥

The draugar screamed in pain.

Only it wasn't the draugar at all.

It was a pale skinned elf with pure white hair and sea-green eyes. Wuten—now the elf—dug his fingers into the skin, seemingly trying to rip it away from his face.

The black was disappearing from his clothing. It leeched away to reveal him wearing a white cloak, lined with white fur.

He was definitely an elf. He was tall and thin with a gaunt face. It was a face that he was trying to rip away.

Wulf met Anya at the center of the square. He picked her up, turned around, and ran back the way he'd come. He found Albrec Tolas.

"Get her out of here, Tolas!" he said.

"Of course," said the gnome. "Hello, my dear girl."

Anya stared at Tolas for a moment. Then they hugged. Since they were both the same height, it was hard to tell who pulled whom into it.

Wulf spun around, facing back to the square.

"Archers," he shouted. "Fire!"

CHAPTER FIFTY-THREE:
THE REVENGE

Arrows were flying. Men dropped as they were struck. The Hundred charged.

Things became bloody fast.

After the sides met, the centaurs threw their bows down and pulled swords. They had no armor besides a leather jerkin here and there and leather guards on their arms. Still they attacked.

Men and bears roared and grunted as they swung their weapons. Centaurs cried out, and when they were in pain, screamed like horses. Gnomes hacked at legs and tendons. Some were sliced by downward swinging swords. Others got stomped to death by the heavy boots of the Nesties.

Wulf headed for the elder elf.

He had forgotten that the bear men were guarding him, but they came to his rescue twice as Sandhaveners tried to intersect and cut him down.

"Let me though, curse you to cold hell," he yelled at his guards.

Those beside him fell back. Two bear men pushed ahead.

One was slain with a sword through the neck. This left the other bear man facing an unarmed opponent. He brought a halberd down into the man's skull.

Wulf ran past them.

The elf was pulling himself back to his feet. His face was scratched and bleeding.

Almost there.

There was a shout of anger. Wulf turned almost too late to see Trigvi. The prince lunged at him with a sword.

"M'lord!"

One of the archers leaped between them. Trigvi's sword sank into the shank where man shape turned into horse shape. Blood poured, and the centaur collapsed. It slid off the end of Trigvi's sword.

Trigvi looked up triumphant.

Wulf lunged. The tip of his sword punched into Trigvi's chest. The mail hauberk stopped the blade from cutting deeper, but Wulf felt something give.

He pulled back. Trigvi tried to raise his own sword, but Wulf plunged an elbow against the inside of Trigvi's arm, and the sword flew from his grip. It clattered on the stones.

Prince Trigvi took a staggering step back. He raised a hand to feel whatever was causing the pain in his chest. He couldn't catch his breath. Wulf's stab had broken something.

Wulf drew back the bear-man sword with two hands. He hacked into the prince's neck with a sweep. The blade sank in until it was stopped in the space between two vertebrae. Wulf twisted it to pull it free.

Trigvi's head flopped to one side. A look of amazement stayed on the head's face. But Trigvi von Krehennest was dead before he hit the ground.

Wulf's spun around to find the elder elf.

The elf was headed toward the cathedral.

But then there was a flash as something brown and white crashed into the elf.

Nagel. The elf swatted, but missed. Nagel banked and flew at him again. This time the elf caught her with a mailed fist. The owl squawked in pain, and went tumbling to the cobblestones. She lay motionless.

"You," Wulf shouted to the elf. "Turn around!"

The elf turned. He stood gazing at Wulf for an eyeblink. Then he pulled the curved sword from a scabbard. The sword was no longer black. It shone like bright, sharp steel.

Wulf raised his own sword to ready and moved in.

The elf screamed and charged. He swung his sword in a wicked downward arc at Wulf's head. Wulf grabbed his sword by the tip and by the end and swung up into an overhead block.

The two swords connected and rang like an angry bell.

The elf pulled back and swung at Wulf's side. Wulf smashed the blade down.

But the elf had lifetimes of experience. He recovered with lightning speed. He lunged and Wulf barely danced back in time. The elf had stepped in with the lunge. He swung the falcata's hilt to the side and smashed the metal guard into Wulf's head.

Agony. Wulf reeled away. He tried to stay on his feet.

The elf made a backhand slash at Wulf's neck. Wulf reached for the blade by instinct and caught it in the palm of his gauntlet, barely stopping it in time.

But this left his side open, and the elf punched viciously into Wulf's kidney. Wulf yelled in pain. He let go of the elf's sword and staggered back.

He stumbled into the tree trunk.

His head ached, and his side throbbed with pain. His sword felt as heavy as lead.

This is it, Wulf thought. All I've got left.

The elf seemed to sense his weakness. His sea-green eyes danced.

Then something glinted on Wulf's chest. The elf looked down, and so did Wulf.

The elf was staring at the star stone.

"Brenunn Temeldar?" said the elf. "Sister?"

Wulf lifted his sword up. It felt like he was trying to move it through honey. The elf slapped it out of the way.

"Where come'st thou this?" said the elf.

"Rot in cold hell," Wulf replied.

The elf frowned. He looked into Wulf's eyes once again. Then he drew back the curved sword to make the kill.

A shadow passed over Wulf's shoulder. Boots crashed into the ancient elf's chest.

The elf's sword flew away, and it landed in a heap on the cobblestones.

Someone had jump from the tree trunk.

Whoever it was landed on his feet.

The elf scrambled upright. The two stood facing one another.

Instead of a weapon, the man had what looked like a lump of iron just out of the forge. It was brown-black. It had the shape of an ax or a hammer, but it wasn't either one.

"Who art thou?" the elf said.

The man turned partially toward Wulf, and he could make out his face.

"Nobody," said Rainer Stope.

Rainer swung the hammer from his shoulder as he might a sledge, arching down, aimed to crash into the skull of the elder elf.

The elf skittered out of the way, and the hammer slammed into the cobblestones, throwing stone chips in every direction.

Before Rainer could raise it again, the elf rushed him. His long fingers whipped around Rainer's neck.

Have to help, Wulf thought.

His right hand closed around the handle of his old dagger.

He yanked on it.

It wouldn't budge.

Rainer moved his arms inside the elf's grip. He tried to push upward and break the grasp, but the draugar brought a vicious knee into Rainer's crotch. Rainer doubled over with the pain, and the draugar pushed him farther down by the shoulders. Rainer's head slammed into the elf's knee.

Rainer collapsed to the ground.

The elf kicked Rainer in the ribs. Rainer groaned. He kicked Rainer again.

Wulf dove for the Dragon Hammer.

CHAPTER FIFTY-FOUR:
THE DRAGON HAMMER

Wulf rolled over on his back, clutching the hammer. The sky above flared red and burned. He twisted his head and saw the stark black outline of the cathedral belltower against the burning sky. Streamers of fire whirled everywhere. Instead of the sun, there was a ragged hole in the sky like a hole in glass that a pebble has broken through. From this hole, more fire streamed, purple mixed with black.

The purple and black fire churned and swirled. It seemed to gather near the belltower, to spin around the belfry like a whirlwind. Faster and faster. Until the purple and black flames—

Came together.

Took shape.

It was a dragon. A winged dragon. Reptilian. It was perched at the very top of the belltower. Then it spread wings, huge wings that sparkled with a golden color. It pushed off and *flew*.

Movement like a soaring raptor, around the belltower once, twice. Then it turned its head toward the square below and toward Wulf. It changed course.

It was coming toward Wulf. Too fast to scramble away. Too fast to move at all.

Closer.

It swooped directly toward him.

He saw the dragon eyes, enormous. A man could step through the pupil slit as if it were a door.

Then he felt it.

The dragon *saw* him.

Closer.

It's coming for me, Wulf thought.

The dragon opened its mouth. It whipped its head back, opened its maw.

Flame shot forth. A ball of liquid fire headed straight for Wulf.

The flame struck Wulf. Pain. Understanding. Transformation.

His mind burned away.

He was in the dragon.

He *was* the dragon.

Yet he was himself. He was Wulf.

This is what you were made for, he thought. *For whatever reason or chance, this is the purpose of hearing the dragon-call. This is what the call, the trance, the visions were preparing you for.*

Then a deeper, echoing voice within him spoke.

You have traveled through me. Now I travel through you.

No, it wasn't a voice. He didn't hear words, not really. It was understanding. A piece of understanding placed in his mind. There had been a dragon-shaped emptiness inside him before. Now it was filled with burning dragon essence.

Flowing through him

Into the Dragon Hammer.

What is it? What is the hammer for? *What does it* do?

Nothing.

Everything.

The hammer was a chip of the Never and Forever. A not-thing from before the beginning of all beginnings.

What is it for? How did it come to be here?

The answer came as understanding.

The hammer had the power of making and unmaking of all things.

When the time comes . . .

It is—

It will give us—

Flight.

Into the sky. Out of the world.

To the Never and Forever from which all souls spring.

Then Wulf was back in Allfather Square, the Dragon Hammer in his hands.

More understanding. Not words. Sudden, total comprehension of what he had to do.

Now is the time. While the emptiness of Ubel is dispelled and Abenweth Grevenstran is within creation once more. Now is the time to unmake the fallen Pillar of the North.

Wulf stood.

The smell brought Rainer back to consciousness. The maggoty death smell.

He looked up.

The elder elf stood over him.

Or was it the draugar?

The elf's face began to extend. The beak was coming back. Tendrils of blackness spread like a night-crawling vine under the pale skin. The elf's eyes were still green, but while Rainer looked, they clouded over, as if black shells were growing thickly over their surface.

"Rendrener drenlevantenteos!" the draugar shouted. "Die, star, die—"

The words twisted into a cry of pain. The cry of pain became a scream of agony.

Black fluid ooze seeped from the draugar's mouth. Then the ooze turned from black to red, and it was blood that ran down one side of his chin. The coal blackness of the face disappeared.

The draugar was the elf again.

The elf pitched forward, facefirst. He landed on the cobblestones in front of Rainer.

Rainer looked up. Wulf stood over the elf with open palms, the deep scar on his right hand glowing an angry red.

Rainer looked down.

The Dragon Hammer was lodged into the elf's back. The elf's hauberk had parted. Blood was matting the links. It looked like the ax's dull "blade" had punched through and pierced the ancient elf's heart.

"Wuten, Rage of the North," Wulf shouted. "Be unmade."

The elder elf threw back his head as if to roar anger at the sky. No sound emerged from his throat.

"Abenweth Grevenstran, Pillar of the North!" shouted Wulf. "Be unmade!"

And it was so. The elder elf began to disintegrate.

Like a statue of gray ash crumbling away, Rainer thought.

Then the ash making up the remains of the elder elf collapsed. The grains that had formed him sparked like fireflies, flaming in all directions, then dying to nothing.

Gone.

The Dragon Hammer fell to the flagstones of Allfather Square with a dull thump.

"Merciful Tretz," Rainer murmured. He took a deep breath, then let it out slowly. Finally, he looked up at Wulf.

"How did you do that?" he asked.

Wulf shook his head. "It wasn't me. The hammer did it."

"Blood and bones," Rainer said. "What does that even *mean*?"

"How the cold hell do I know, Rainer? It was like in the

trance. Only the dragon was in *me* instead of me being in *it*."

"So is the black thing gone? Do you at least know *that* for sure?"

Wulf nodded. "Gone. Like he never was in the first place. Gone for good. Gone forever."

For a moment they both were still and silent. They gazed at the hammer.

It still looked like a lump of misshapen iron to Rainer. Almost natural. But also almost, but not quite, like it was forged by human hands to use as a tool.

Rainer's body began to ache like it had taken a beating. He groaned softly.

"Give me a hand up?" he asked Wulf. His friend helped Rainer get to his feet.

They looked down at the hammer again. Rainer felt his strength returning. But the aching didn't fade.

After a moment, Wulf bent down and picked it up. He looked it over.

"Don't ask," he said to Rainer. "I have no idea what it really is."

There was a soft whirring sound, and something landed on Wulf's shoulder.

Rainer stepped back.

It was a small owl. It gazed at him fiercely.

He was about to knock it away, but Wulf stopped him.

"No," Wulf said. "She's with me."

Rainer looked around the square. The Sandhaveners had stopped fighting. In fact, they stood motionless. Some got ruthlessly chopped down in that pose. But then the mark forces, man and Tier alike, understood that the Hundred wasn't fighting anymore. The soldiers weren't moving at all.

"Ravenelle's gotten hold of them," Wulf said to Rainer. "Her captain must still be alive."

All he really understood in Wulf's words was a simple fact he'd been hoping to hear for days.

"Ravenelle's here?"

"Yep."

"Well, that's good," Rainer said.

He was about to ask for more details, but the words died in his throat.

Wulf was gazing in horror at something he saw across the square.

"Saeunn," his friend whispered.

CHAPTER FIFTY-FIVE:
THE FALLEN STAR

Wulf knelt beside Saeunn's body, afraid to touch her. He still had the Dragon Hammer handle in one hand. He rested its head against the cobblestones.

Saeunn lay limp. Her eyes were open. They were unfocused and fixed on nothing. He took her hand in his and lifted it. Cold.

He sat for a long moment, trying to feel anything but numb inside. There were footsteps, small and quick. Anya was beside him, Tolas walking up.

"Saeunn?" she said.

Wulf shook his head.

He reached over to push Saeunn's eyelids down.

When he did, the star stone on the chain around his neck brushed against Saeunn's neck.

She blinked.

"Saeunn?" Wulf said. "Saeunn, can you hear me!"

"Gone." Her voice was flat.

Wulf didn't understand. He gazed around the square. It was strewn with bodies. Dead Tier, dead men. Although it was still early spring, what flies there were had found them. Crows were cackling, waiting for the pesky living to get out of their way so that they could begin the feast.

"Yeah, it turned into a fight," Wulf said.

Saeunn sat up. Wulf tried to help her, but she did it quickly and firmly. She looked around. Deliberately. First one way and then the other.

"Wuten?"

"He's dead, Saeunn."

"Yes," she said. "The star died."

"Saeunn, are you going to be okay?"

She looked at Wulf, her face expressionless. "Saeunn Amberstone is not here. Only her memories."

"Her . . . what?"

"Saeunn is not alive," she said. She paused for a moment, a look of concentration on her face. "Not here," she repeated.

"Who *are* you?"

"No one. Not a person."

"But Wulf is talking to you," Anya put in. "You're talking back. You have to be Saeunn."

Saeunn turned toward Anya, but there was not the warmth, the love, in her expression that Anya expected.

Wulf spun around. "Tolas!" he said. There were tears in his voice. "Tell me what to do."

The gnome shook his head. "I do not know, Lord Wulf. This is far beyond me. I'm very sorry."

Wulf looked to Rainer, standing nearby. Rainer wiped away tears.

Wulf turned back to Saeunn. Anya was trying to draw Saeunn out. "Saeunn, it's me, Evinthir. Say it, Saeunn! Say my name. Don't try to fool me. It isn't funny. Say it the way you do."

Saeunn was silent.

The little girl burst into tears.

Wulf pulled Anya toward him, hugged her with one arm.

"I know it's Saeunn," Anya said, and pushed her face into Wulf's tabard.

Saeunn sat expressionless.

"I do not think I will live much longer," she said. She paused, then spoke again. "I do not understand why I am alive at all."

"So she isn't really here?" whispered Anya. "We didn't save her."

"I don't know what happened," Wulf said.

"She gave away her star."

"What? How?" Wulf asked his sister.

"She made him take it," Anya replied. "The thing."

"How do you know that, Anya?" Anya usually didn't make things up to fool herself, but in this situation, maybe. Wulf didn't blame her.

"She told me what she was going to do," Anya said. "While we were riding on the horse. It was like she was practicing it in her mind."

"She . . . are you sure, Anya?"

"She told me," Anya said. "She was going to give away her star."

"Elves think that a star is their soul," Wulf said. "It's the way they say that someone died."

"Yes, I know *that*," Anya replied, reproof in her voice. "But a star can bring an elf back to life. Saeunn told me. That was how she made the bad thing be an elf again," Anya said. "She did it so you could kill it."

"Blood and bones," Rainer murmured. "Saeunn saved us all."

Wulf was kneeling at Anya's eye level. He turned Anya toward himself so he could look her directly in the eyes.

"Tell me what she said. Everything you can remember."

"I did," Anya said. "I think she needs a new star."

Right. The most impossible thing to get in all of creation.

Then he realized he had one. Or what used to be. Was there life left in a fallen star?

Wulf took the steel chain from around his neck. He took the stone in his hand and cradled it in his scarred palm.

Please, he thought. Let there be some of you still here, star of Brenunn Temeldar.

He leaned over and gently put the chain and stone pendant over Saeunn's head. He pressed the stone pendant to her breast.

Saeunn gasped. Her hands flew up and grabbed Wulf's.

The movement startled Nagel. The owl flew from Wulf's shoulder and found a perch on a nearby windowsill.

Saeunn's eyes focused. She looked around wildly.

"Saeunn?"

"Where am I?"

"Raukenrose."

"I don't know any—"

Then the bewilderment seemed to leave her.

"Oh."

Saeunn's eyes focused on the Dragon Hammer in Wulf's grip.

"What is this?"

"The Dragon Hammer. We found it. Well, Rainer did."

She reached over and took hold of the handle of the Dragon Hammer with both hands. She sat there for a moment, holding on, a look of intense concentration on her face.

Then she breathed out a sigh. She looked into Wulf's eyes and smiled.

"We're both here," she said. "Saeunn Eberethen and Brenunn Temeldar."

"Saeunn?" said Anya in a small voice.

"Yes, Evinthir, it's me."

"Oh, Saeunn!" The little girl threw her arms around the elf.

Finally, Anya let her go. She stood back, smiling, wiping away her tears.

Saeunn breathed deeply. Then she moved as if she wanted to get up, and Wulf offered his hand. She took it. Saeunn stood.

She looked at Wulf's eyes. "It's me," she said.

"I thought I'd lost you," he said.

"You did," Saeunn said. "But I'm back. I don't know for how long, so I'd better—"

Then she kissed him.

EPILOGUE

EPILOGUE

CHAPTER FIFTY-SIX:
THE QUEST

Otto's body rested on a pyre in the death ship. It wasn't an actual ship. The shape of an old-style longboat had been formed on the ground with rocks. Within the ship's outline, there was a wooden platform over a pile of dried birch. Sprinkled with the birch was mistletoe and magnolia leaves.

Otto had not married, but there was a woman he'd been seeing for the past year. They had kept it secret because she was a von Blau and the von Blaus and von Dunstigs were not supposed to get along. But Ulla knew about it, and invited her to the funeral.

After a prophet of the divines said the final blessing, Wulf's mother took the lit torch to start the fire that would burn Otto's body to ashes and carry his soul to Helheim.

The traditional site for human pyres was on Ship Hill, which was to the east of town on a rise that overlooked both the castle and the river. The Sandhaveners had camped here and torn up many of the rune-stone markers that were usually left inside a burial-ship after the funeral.

Rainer and Ravenelle came but didn't join in the ceremony. Both their traditions believed in burial.

Saeunn was here.

He was glad. Wulf felt as if someone had ripped a part of his body away as the flames grew higher and higher. She reached for his hand partway through the burning, and he held hers while the pyre burned.

Otto had always been there. The eldest. The heir. The one who had to be grown up even when he was a kid. Wulf felt guilty sometimes that he'd had a much less stressful childhood than his brother because, well, nobody expected much of Wulf. And because of that, Wulf had found his own way and done his own thing much more than Otto ever had or ever could.

They trailed back to the castle, escorted by a guard of over five hundred.

Along the way, they passed by a hickory tree with two men hanging by their necks from the branches. One had his stomach cut open.

They wore Sandhaven badges. There was revenge killing going on in Raukenrose. Sandhaveners who went away from their prison camp were taking their lives in their hands.

Anya hadn't needed to see that. But the little girl had seen so many terrible things in the past few days, he didn't think one more horror piled on the others would do more damage. Still, it wasn't good.

Wulf ordered the bodies cut down and given a proper funeral burning.

The Sandhaveners had not left yet. Wulf was going to send them back east with no weapons whatsoever. He was going to have a thousand mark soldiers march behind them to the border to make sure they went away.

Unconditional surrender.

But to do that he had to have the weapons confiscated, which took time.

And so long as the Sandhaveners were still here, there was the chance for more fighting, but the balance had shifted dramatically. More and more bands of levies from throughout the mark were flowing into Raukenrose, and now the number of armed and dangerous people in Raukenrose outnumbered the Sandhavener invasion force by ten to one.

Of course Sandhaven had a much larger army it could gather back home. Now that Wulf had killed not one but *two* of King Siggi's five sons, he thought that this might not be the last the mark saw of von Krehennests seeking revenge.

But Saeunn was here. She held his hand.

That was Wulf's definition of victory.

In a side chamber off the castle great hall, the Dragon Hammer lay on the long dining table. It was the same table made of fir planks that Duke Otto had planned to use for Ulla's wedding feast.

That seemed so long ago to Wulf, but it had only been four months and a few weeks.

Duke Otto had been returned to the castle, but was still bedridden.

Wulf hoped his father would get better. But the wise woman had told him there was nothing anybody could do for the illness in the duke's mind.

The duchess left his side only to eat and visit with her daughters. She had no interest in running the mark.

So Wulf was in charge.

Wulf had called a council to discuss what to do with the hammer now that it was found. Tolas was there. So was Earl Keiler. He was in an invalid's reclining chair, covered by blankets. Ursel was was present to tend him.

Ulla was there, and Wulf had asked Saeunn to come.

Tolas had Wulf and Ursel hold each end of the hammer laid out along the table. Wulf held the head. Ursel held the end of the hammer. There was a sword from the armory lying next to it.

Tolas climbed up on a chair facing the hammer. He picked up the sword, raised it over his head, and, before anyone could even shout in surprise, brought its blade down hard against the Dragon Hammer.

The blade broke. Its point went skittering along the planks of the table.

"The hammer is impervious to steel," Tolas said. "No alchemic agent has any effect. Fire and cold do not even cause it to measurably expand or contract. It does not seem to be a thing of this world. Yet it has weight and volume. The weight varies, by the way."

"What do you mean?" asked Wulf.

"Sometimes it weighs more than other times," Tolas said. "I've verified that. But there's no rhyme or reason to it that I can tell."

"What about the lore?" Wulf asked. He let go of his side of the hammer. As he straightened up, he caught Ursel's green-eyed gaze as she pushed back a lock of red hair. She was as beautiful as ever.

He wondered if she was jealous of Saeunn. Probably not. Ursel seemed to have moved on.

Tolas set the lower part of the broken sword down next to the broken blade.

"You know the lore."

"Last night I found another reference in Harraldsson the Younger," Wulf said. "That last strange saga of his, *The World Dragon*."

"Yes," Tolas said, with a nod toward Wulf. "'When the Hammer returns, the King of Dragons will rise.'"

"Pretty obscure, I guess. And it may not even be talking about the Dragon Hammer."

"The passage has usually been interpreted to mean the end of time," Tolas replied.

"So the hammer is basically useless except to end the world?"

"No one is sure what Harraldsson meant." Tolas shrugged. "He obviously wrote it before the Dragon Hammer of Shenandoah was used in the fight to rid the valley of were-beasts. Was it a prophecy? We don't know. Anyway, that is the lore of men. Saeunn's folk know other things perhaps. But I'm not sure the evil one himself knows what its true purpose is. That is probably why he's afraid of it."

"Doesn't the dragon know what it's for? It *gave* the hammer to us."

"Dragon lore. The emperor of disciplines." Tolas smiled wryly. He had been a docent in the subject, after all. Wulf planned to restore him to that position if he had to march an army to the university and make them take Tolas back. "We live on the dragons. Saeunn's folk sing to them. None of us really understands them. What some think is that the dragons don't really 'know' anything. They are unborn. Asleep. Dreaming."

"Dreaming what?" Wulf asked.

Tolas held out a hand, gestured airily around himself. "What do you think?" he said.

Wulf considered.

"Us? The world?" Wulf replied.

"Maybe."

"All of this is a dream?"

"If it is, then it's our job to make sure it doesn't become a nightmare," Tolas replied.

Ulla sighed. "That's *quite* fascinating," she said with a trace of sarcasm in her voice. "But can we talk about what to do *right now*?" Ulla was sitting in a cushioned chair. She was embroidering. She'd shown her work to Wulf earlier. It was a field of daylilies for Anya's wall. Anya loved daylilies.

"Can't we just hide the hammer again?" Ulla continued. "That *did* work for two hundred years."

Tolas shook his head. "I don't believe so, m'lady," he answered. "The Elder Bell is special. It is a sort of shield. There are no other adequate hiding places, I'm afraid."

Wulf had thought the same thing as Ulla. It *had* seemed too simple. "And they'll be looking for that, I suppose," he said.

"Okay, I guess so," Ulla replied and went back to her work. "But can we keep the discussion a bit more down to earth?"

"Most sensible, m'lady," Tolas said. He made a small bow in her direction. Tolas had tutored Ulla for many years, and she was a favorite of his.

"We can defend it," Wulf said. "Shenandoah Valley is a fort. A double-walled valley. And there's Bear Valley on top of Massanutten. We're a natural stronghold."

"Which is perhaps why the Dragon Hammer appeared here," Tolas said.

"What do you think, Earl?" Wulf asked.

Keiler drew himself up in his slanted invalid's chair. Ursel immediately moved to help him. "We can hold out for a long time. But if the might of Rome is thrown against the mark, they'll overrun us," Keiler said.

"The Kaltish kingdoms will help us," Wulf answered.

"They might," said Keiler. The bear man gripped his blankets, fighting off the urge to cough. Finally he appeared to overcome it. His grip relaxed, and he continued. "*If* they can stop fighting idiotic blood feuds. *If* they understand that if the mark falls, they'll be destroyed, too." Keiler shook his shaggy head. "No, we can't count on them. Your father and I started fighting the Little War thinking help was coming any moment. It took us a while to figure out that nobody was going to help and we were going to be made into slaves if we lost. That's when we found the will to win."

"What if we *use* it, then?" Saeunn said. She'd been standing near the table, her hand on her chin, considering the Dragon Hammer.

"To end the world?" Wulf asked.

"To hatch a dragon," Saeunn replied.

"What do you mean, Lady Saeunn?" asked Tolas.

"There is one place we know where a living dragon rises to the surface."

"Amberstone Valley," Tolas said.

"If the Dragon Hammer can be brought there, it may . . . fulfill its purpose—and help us to defeat the enemy once and for all."

"Lady Saeunn, Amberstone Valley is six hundred leagues from here," Keiler said. "And you know that it's a hazardous journey because you've made it yourself. Between here and your valley are the Wild Kingdoms, the Mississippi River and the Highbreit Mountains."

"That's true," Saeunn said. "When I came east, we kept to the Elf Road. It's the only way across, and even that is dangerous."

"It's one thing for a small band of travelers to cross without drawing attention," said Keiler. "I doubt even a small army could cross unchallenged. It would be one battle after another."

"Then you may have to send a small band of travelers," Saeunn softly replied.

"With a relic the entire Roman Empire is looking for?" Keiler said. This time he couldn't control his cough, and Ursel held a handkerchief to his muzzle until he finished.

They waited for the earl's scrofula to settle.

"We may not have a choice," said Tolas. "Rome knows that the draugar Wuten is dead. Our waiting to be attacked is not a good plan."

"What do you say, Wulf?" Keiler asked.

Why did they keep looking to him for things like this?

Did they think the dragon was constantly telling him what to do? Being the new heir was one decision after another that he didn't feel qualified to make.

"I'm going."

"Wulf, I don't know," Saeunn said softly.

"Saeunn *has* to go, so I'm going." He spoke firmly. Finally he'd found a decision he didn't have to second-guess. "We don't know how long the star stone will keep her alive. I will not lose her again."

Tolas shook his head. "You have other duties, Lord Wulf. Duties to the mark."

"Mother won't do them, but . . ." He turned to Ulla. "Ulla could—"

"No!" his sister said. "I'm not the heir."

"You'd make a better one than me," Wulf said. "I'll appoint you Duchess Regent."

Ulla laughed. "And what about Grer? How do you think the first families would react to having Earl Grer Smead as their better? Or Ulla Smead, for that matter?"

"He already *is* better than the lot of them." Wulf replied. "Ulla, I'm serious. You should rule the mark."

"That's just like a boy," Ulla said. Her face, which she kept so lily white, blushed. Ulla was getting upset.

"What do you mean?"

"You want to go questing when things get tough. Grow up, Wulf."

"I'm trying to do the right thing."

She glared at him. "You can't get out of it," she said "The dragon's called you. The dragon *didn't* call Otto. I know he never talked about it to you, but he told me. He was always worried. 'Why don't I hear the dragon-call, Ulla?' Adelbert could have cared less, but it never happened to him either."

"What about you?"

"Nothing," Ulla said. "Not a whisper."

"You are perfect to be regent," Wulf said. "The dragon-visions aren't important."

"Listen to yourself!" Ulla said. "They're the *only* thing that's important. It's why there *is* a Mark of Shenandoah." She smiled sweetly at Wulf, but he knew his sister, and she was deadly serious. "No. You are heir, Wulfgang. Deal with it."

But he *was* dealing with it. He hoped Ulla would see that.

"That's why I'm going," Wulf said. "I may be heir to the mark, but because of that I'm also heir to the Dragon Hammer. This is my responsibility."

"And it's not just so you don't have to be away from your girlfriend?" Ulla said. He wasn't going to let her bait him. Besides, what she said was true.

"Yeah. That, too."

CHAPTER FIFTY-SEVEN:
THE REQUEST

Rainer found Ravenelle in the Chapel of the Dark Angel. Her new bloodservants stood outside the door. For a moment Alvis and Harrald Torsson moved to block his way.

Harrald Torsson was blind. Yet he still looked deadly.

"Really, guys?" Rainer said. "Can you ask her if I can come in?"

They didn't reply, but after a moment's pause they stepped aside. Rainer shook his head and walked through the chapel door.

Rainer was back to training, but he was sorely missing Marshal Elgar Koterbaum. He hadn't realized how much he really liked the master at arms, despite Koterbaum's tendency to suck up to the gentry.

And even if he did almost get me killed, Rainer thought.

To die from a cowardly sneak attack, as the reports said. It had been a bad way to go for the gallant Koterbaum.

In the mornings, Rainer had started working with the town guard. They'd put him to work teaching townie boys how to fight with weapons. He was learning a few things about fighting on the streets in return. There were boys lining up to take his classes, and even a few girls. Rainer didn't care. It was first come, first served for him. Everyone needed to be ready when trouble came the next time.

He expected that would be soon.

Maybe learning from the townies was enough to make up for the school lessons he was missing. He had plenty of time to catch up. Raukenrose University, which he'd planned to attend next year, was a mess. Two-thirds of the faculty were dead, their brains burned out. The whole town was going to be many months recovering. Some things might never be the same.

Father Calceatus was at the altar. Ravenelle had taken communion, and the priest was leaving to clean the blood cup. He nodded curtly to Rainer as he passed him.

"Come in," Ravenelle said.

Rainer walked the rest of the way down the aisle. He stood with Ravenelle before the altar. He looked up at the image of the Dark Angel. She was naked, of course. Her wings were unfurled, and her arms were spread wide in welcoming. Yet there was something menacing in her gaze.

"She looks kind of like you," Rainer said.

"I doubt that," said Ravenelle. She gestured around herself. "I wanted you to see this place, Stope. This is where the heart of the Talaia happens. Even if there isn't a blood ceremony, I always feel peaceful in here. Does it seem even a little bit peaceful to you?"

Rainer looked again at the Dark Angel. She seemed to be smiling at him like he might make a tasty morsel.

"Yeah, I guess so," he said.

"Oh, don't lie to me, Stope. I can always tell. That's how I beat you at Hang the Fool."

"Oh yeah? How can you tell?"

"Your earlobes get red," Ravenelle said. "Or even redder than they already are."

Rainer self-consciously tugged on an earlobe. "Feels normal to me." But it was a bit warmer than he had expected.

"Let's sit down."

"Where?"

"Up on the altar, in the cathedra chairs."

"Isn't that . . . I don't know . . ."

"Sacrilegious? They're just chairs, Stope. They only have to be empty during communion."

They climbed the two slate steps to the altar. The altar platform was made of one large piece of black marble. Rainer could imagine how much it had cost to bring here. They sat down in the altar chairs. These were upholstered with red velvet and much more comfortable than they looked. Now Rainer was even closer to the Dark Angel. He felt like she was glaring down at him, but when he glanced up, she still had the same placid expression.

"So how's your romance?" Rainer asked. She'd left a scroll rolled up on the front pew. Rainer knew this was where she usually came to read.

"That's *The Red Rose Dies*. It's been there since . . . well, I haven't read one for a while," Ravenelle said. "I feel like I've been living one, you know. I'm not so sure how I like to be inside the story instead of outside and able to walk away whenever I want."

"You *have* to walk away," Rainer said. "You're going in a month. Your prison term with us barbarians is over."

"True. Even though I haven't heard a word from mother in weeks. The mail service man told me it's gotten really hard to get messages across the southern border." Ravenelle cupped her hands together. She looked like she wanted to say more, but instead she reached up and smoothed back her hair. A dozen black curls had come loose, as usual, and she managed to stuff a couple under a hair pin.

"You're holding something back," Rainer said.

"What makes you say that, Stope?"

"When you get nervous, you play with your hair." Rainer smiled.

Ravenelle pulled her hands down to her lap. "I guess we know each other pretty well," she said.

"Yeah."

"You're right. I have a favor to ask you."

"Okay."

Ravenelle nodded. "I'm very worried you'll say 'no' when you hear what it is."

"Just tell me, Ravenelle."

Ravenelle caught herself trying to smooth her hair again, stopped herself and clasped her hands together. "Okay, what I was saying about messages not getting across the southern border? It's really a huge worry to me. You know I've been waiting for years and years for the day I can go home, and now I don't hear anything?" She bit her lower lip. "I think nobody's coming for me, Stope."

Rainer leaned forward. He spread his hands. "They'll come. They always have."

The month that Ravenelle's mother spent at Raukenrose Castle every year always meant huge trouble for everyone. The place was full of bloodservants, and you couldn't say anything because *everything* they heard would instantly get back to the queen.

Rainer was used to nobles putting on airs and trying to boss him around, but Ravenelle's mother was in a class by herself. He always tried to make himself scarce for as long as he could during her visits.

"I know she'll send someone. She always said she would. It's just . . . what if she doesn't?"

"You'll be all right either way. The duchess loves you, even if she doesn't quite understand you."

"You think so?"

"You know she does."

"But I could never be *her* child. You're all such pale faced barbarians," she said. "Look at Ulla and Anya's silky hair and mine, it's just . . ."

"Like wool from a black sheep?" Rainer volunteered.

"Yeah, thanks, Stope." She frowned. He had meant it as a compliment, but he'd clearly missed the mark.

"I like your hair," Rainer added.

In fact, he thought her hair was beautiful. He thought she was the loveliest creature he'd ever seen. But what was the use?

Get it out for once, coward, Rainer told himself. She's leaving anyway. She's leaving, and I don't like it.

"Look, Ravenelle, I want to say something."

"You?"

"Yeah, me." He swallowed. "I think you're . . . amazing. More than anyone. Always have been pretty much in love with you. So there it is."

Ravenelle leaned back against the chair.

"You shouldn't talk that way to a princess," she whispered, almost to herself.

"Yeah," Rainer said. "Right."

"Stope . . . I . . ."

"Don't say anything. I mean, forget it."

There wasn't anything else to say about it. So he stood there. Finally he spoke. "Ravenelle, ask me whatever it is you want."

"Okay," she said. She reached up to smooth her hair again.

He could feel the breath catch in his throat.

Tretz, when she does that . . .

"I want you to take me home," she said in a quiet voice.

Home? That was leagues and leagues away. And Kalte men weren't exactly welcome down there. At all.

"To Montserrat?"

Ravenelle nodded. Then she sighed and put her hands back in her lap.

"Take me home, Stope," she whispered. "Please."

CHAPTER FIFTY-EIGHT:
THE AMBUSH

Cavalry approaching.

When the fox-man pickets came galloping in reporting a band of at least a hundred warriors on horses, Captain Max Jager at first didn't believe them.

Earl Keiler had ordered the northern and eastern approaches garrisoned immediately. If there were reinforcements on the way from Krehennest, he wanted plenty of warning.

Jager's Raufers had been given the job.

Then more reports came in to Jager, and he was forced to conclude there was a Sandhaven troop that had crossed the border and was riding west through Piedmont Duchy.

The Raufers' job was to hold Dornstadt Pass. His garrison was important enough that it had nearly a hundred troops. But Jager knew he had the high ground. The road went through several sloping hills that were perfect for archers. Horsemen would not get off the road here. The woods were dense and cut through with stream gullies. It would be a hard passage for a horse.

No, they'd come through the pass. He had ridden east several times and had already picked out what he considered the perfect spot for an ambush. There were four bands of archers in his company, including one made up of bear-man longbowmen—eighty archers in all. And out here on the border an archer did double duty as a hand-to-hand fighter once the fight was going strong.

So, although Jager was understandably worried about taking on a force four times his size, he believed his chances to send them packing back to Sandhaven were good. At least he would bloody them terribly. He'd already sent riders west to alert the other forts and village garrisons along the Plank road. If they got through him, a large force of the mark would be gathering, waiting to take the enemy on.

He trusted his scouts, so he believed he was facing no more than five companies of horsemen. Whether it was the leading edge of a larger army marching west he'd worry about later.

One problem at a time, thought Jager.

It was two months since the Battle of Raukenrose Meadow—which was what the counterattack was starting to be called. Jager was still nineteen years old.

Despite his small form, the Tier he'd grown up with in his small village respected him. He'd gained the respect of the other troops in the company in the meadow outside Raukenrose by rallying his wavering company. He'd cut through the heel tendons of two frightened but dangerous buffalo men who had ignored his calls to stop and tried to bully their way past him to the rear. He'd left them wallowing on the ground, lamed for life.

That had set an example for everyone else.

You could either fight the Sandhaveners or face your insane bobcat-man captain, who was willing to saw through your legs if you decided to run.

Then, when they saw him fighting like mad alongside

them, ordering water and arrows brought up, and intelligently directing them toward a weak spot in the Sandhavener line, their fear turned into respect.

After he'd seen to his wounded from the battle, he even sent a wise woman to stitch the stragglers' tendons together. They might walk again, but their running days were over. He had, amazingly, ordered them back to duty in his company, giving them a chance to redeem themselves. He knew one of them hated him and might very well put a spear in his captain's back if he got the chance. But Arkakeveri, the other, was happy for the chance.

It looked like he would get that chance today.

Jager watched as a dust cloud to the east announced that the cavalry troop was coming. The archers had already strung their bows. Jager, who was an expert bowman himself, checked his arrows. Most of his archers had done as he had and stuck five or six arrows in the ground in front of them so that they could shoot and then nock and let go another arrow quickly.

Then the Sandhaveners came into view, and Jager knew there would be no killing today. The front two riders carried large white flags. They seem to expect the pass would be guarded, so they stopped the horses behind them and waited.

Jager also waited a moment, worried this might be some kind of trick. But they had their swords and sabers sheathed and their shields slung around the backs of their horses, or on pack horses. This was not a group ready to fight.

"All right, curse it all to cold hell, I'm going down to see what those crab eaters want," Jager told his bear-man second in command, Knudsson. "I want Spindler's band to go with me. The rest are to stay put and be ready."

Jager made his way out of cover and down the hill to the road. Ten buffalo men armed with wicked-looking spears went with him.

He strode up to one of the men bearing a white flag,

looked up at the man on his horse, who stared down at Jager, an expression of amazement on his face.

"What's the matter? You never seen a Tier before?" Jager said to him. "Who's in charge?"

"I am," said the man. He had evidently decided he had better speak to this rather terrifying-looking half-cat, half-man. He gave the reins to the man beside him and got down from his horse.

The man cautiously approached Jager. The buffalo men, who were led by a bear-man sergeant, lowered their spears in the ready position. Jager signaled for them to stand down.

"Now tell me what you want and be quick about it," Jager said.

The man's expression saddened, and he shook his head. He seemed to Jager to be a man in mourning, but Jager knew he was not the best at reading the expressions of men.

"We want refuge," the man said. "I've got five hundred in my band, and another five hundred are following us."

"Refuge?" Jager said. "From what?"

"Romans and their blood cake," the man said. "Piedmont and Vall l'Obac have taken Krehennest. The Romans have control of the whole of the Chesapeake."

"You mean to tell me that Sandhaven has fallen to the Empire?"

"With barely a whimper. King Siggi was one of those dirty blood eaters," the man said. "They took us completely by surprise, and the home guard didn't stand a chance."

"That who you are?"

"No. They were killed to a man," the other said. "We're two battalions of Nestie cavalry. We had to fight our way out of the city." The man sighed. "Sir, we have nowhere else to go. We have come begging for you to take us in."

"You people just invaded our land and killed our heir."

"I am aware of that," the man said. "At least of Trigvi's army coming to get the blood price."

"So why in the name of the dragon would we let you through this pass?"

"I and all my men are prepared to swear allegiance to Duke Otto and the Mark of Shenandoah if you will take us in. The Romans moved fast. They'd been building up in Ore and planning this for a long time, looks like. We're cut off to the north, and they're behind us. They are going to be here at the border soon. Don't know if they'll stop."

"We'll stop them," Jager said. "Don't you worry about that."

The other said nothing, but acknowledged Jager's defiance with a bow of his head.

"Now, as for you," Jager continued. "I'm going to have my men collect your swords and weapons. You can keep your shields."

"But without our weapons, we won't be any good to you."

"I may or may not give them back to you. I'll send for orders on that. But I'll have your swords or you'll not get through the pass alive."

The man nodded agreement. "All right," he said. "We will do it. I wish to thank you—"

"Don't thank me yet. I may get orders to hang the lot of you, but until then . . ."

Jager took a good look at the horse troop gathered up behind the man in two columns. The horses were sweat-stained, and their riders looked hollow eyed and completely spent. Many were wounded and bloodstained.

"Until I get orders, we'll let you camp outside the fort and we'll get you some grub. We're stocked with plenty of provisions, and we can share without too much trouble."

"I thank you, sir . . . cat."

"I ain't 'sir' anybody. And I'm bobcat. There ain't no cat people," Jager replied. "And if what you say about the Romans is true, we'll be ready for them. No matter how many of them there are, only a certain number of men can go through this pass at one time."

"I promise you on my family's honor that I'm speaking the truth," the man replied. "I'm Lord Ekhard von Gurster of Tar."

"I don't know your family, so that don't mean a thing to me," Jager said. "All I know is that you are rotten Sandhaven scum fit for the vultures. But I'm taking your warning serious, and if it turns out to be right, then you'll have my respect for that at least. Until then, drop your weapons and I'll have my troops collect them."

The other bowed and turned back to his men to give them the order. Jager called up the hill for Knudsson to send down a detail to collect the swords.

Blood and bones, Jager thought. Sandhaveners come begging. He never would have thought to see it. What was more disturbing was what had brought them.

Jager had paid attention to his lessons from the village schoolmaster. That was another reason he'd been elected captain. He was the only one of the volunteers who could read. Those lessons told him that the empire had been kept to the lower Chesapeake and the southern mountains for three hundred years. Before that, through war after war, the Kalte had been pushed north, but the Romans had been stopped in Sandhaven and Shenandoah.

Now, if what von Gurster said checked out, Shenandoah would be two-thirds surrounded by Roman slave-driving colonials. It didn't take a genius to figure out what land the Romans would try to eat next.

He'd thought when the border was secure again, he would be able to go back to Bear Valley and take up where he'd left off three months ago when the call had come to assemble at Bear Hall. He'd been apprenticing with his uncle to learn the tanner trade.

Looks like it's going to be a while before I scrape hides and lime the vats in Uncle Gus's shop again, Jager thought. A long while.

Which wasn't necessarily a bad thing. Jager had wondered how he was going to go back to taking orders from his tyrant of an uncle after being in command of a hundred troops. Maybe he wouldn't need to find that out.

If there was a long and bloody war coming, the mark was going to need him and his company. Their duty as vassal levies was for a year or, if there was a war, for the duration of the fighting.

We may be in it for the long haul, Jager thought. And despite the fear in the gut he felt at the thought of a Roman phalanx headed straight for him, he knew he wouldn't run, and neither would his troops.

They'd proved that in the meadow outside Raukenrose. He would stand, and he would fight. For the mark. For his duke. And for the boy who was now heir.

He had saved Jager's life. That was no small thing. And he had also led the troops into battle and to victory.

I trust him, Jager thought. Lord Wulf will see us through.

CHAPTER FIFTY-NINE:
THE TREE

Come to the tree.

The dragon was calling again. It was the old familiar feeling. His skeleton seemed to shake inside him. The thoughts in his head echoed back and forth until he could barely think straight. Everywhere he looked, he saw people and things as unchained from time—young, old, middle-aged, bones and dust. It only happened for an instant, then they were themselves again. But he couldn't predict when a vision would hit him.

So he went to the tree with Rainer beside him. This time it was in broad daylight. He took a couple of guards along—more to gently brush away people wanting to pull him aside for a talk on this or that than because there was any danger.

The Olden Oak still lay on its side, stretched across the square. He hadn't had the heart to order it removed.

We're here, Wulf thought. I'm answering the call. What am I supposed to do?

He went to the Olden Oak and touched it, trying to make

the same kind of connection he had before. It was no use. He could feel the tree was no longer part of the land-dragon.

The crystalized rock was still there. He put his hand on it. Nothing.

What did the dragon want him to do?

Maybe there was nothing *to* do but put up with the call. He walked from the rock back to the Olden Oak trunk and leaned against it. The bark was starting to peel off and crumble away.

Rainer went to the dagger, still lodged in the wood. The leaves growing from the pommel had turned into a wooden stem. There were even more leaves curling out now.

Just then the Elder Bell in the cathedral rang imbiss bell. It had only a regular clapper now.

Rainer carefully ran his hand along the growth from the dagger, and Wulf came over to look at it, too.

"The townies call this the Allfather's blessing. Sent to tell us all will be well. That's why nobody's messing with it."

Rainer gently stroked another leaf.

Wulf shrugged. "Maybe a little branch worked its way into the cork under the leather and came out the end like that."

Rainer looked around where the dagger entered the tree. "Yeah, maybe," he said.

Suddenly Wulf's body shook. A trembling shockwave ran through him from head to toe. He felt like he was under a mighty waterfall. Power rolled through him.

He leaned against the tree, gasping.

He was having a dragon-vision. It was the dagger. He was seeing it throughout time.

He looked down at the dagger hilt. It was still a dagger, but now *more* branches had erupted.

Then that vision wavered and he saw the forge fire and heard the beating of Grer's hammer as he worked the steel in the dagger.

Then he saw the Olden Oak in his mind's eye. Growing tall and strong.

No. It was a new tree. A new oak.

Then he saw . . . what was it? The land shaking. The ground under the tree buckling up, and the tree thrown aside.

Something rising from the ground. Rising and rising.

It was a dragon being born.

Just as quickly as the vision came, it disappeared, and Wulf was staring at the curious dagger again.

He smiled.

"I know what to do now," he said to Rainer.

He reached for the dagger. He curled his fingers around the hilt and pulled it from the wood. It came out like he was pulling a knife from butter.

"Blood and bones," Rainer said. "You did it. You got it out."

Wulf walked the dagger over to the green crystal rock in the center of the square.

"Watch this," he said to Rainer, and thrust the dagger's blade against the stone.

It slid in. Up to the hilt, past the hilt. So did his hands.

In so far that only the stem and the leaves that grew from the pommel were showing.

He let go of the dagger and withdrew his hand from inside the stone where the dagger, the root, had sunk.

"Now grow," he told it.

Then the dragon-call faded from his mind like a bell at the end of its final peal.

✢ END ✢